Eye of The
Redeemer

A NOVEL

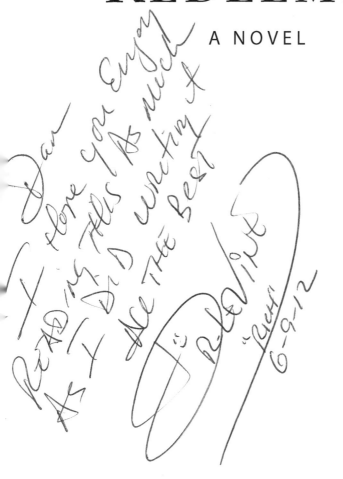

Richard I. Levine

ISBN: 1466482036
ISBN 13: 9781466482036

There are so many people that have come into my life through the years that have played important roles and have influenced me in ways one could never imagine. Sadly, some have left way too soon. I think of them often. When you recognize the good in me, I hope you can see that which I have borrowed from you. Special thanks to my parents who are part of the greatest generation, to my wife who challenges me to be the best that I can be, and to my children who challenge me to be better than that.

"Now when these things begin to take place, stand up and raise your heads, because your redemption is drawing near."

(Luke 21:28)

In the physical manifestation of our own reality,
can we ever truly achieve redemption?
And if so,
are we then in fact our own redeemer?

Department Of The Navy
Office Of The Chief Of Naval Medical Operations
2000 Navy Pentagon
Washington, D.C. 20350-2000

In Reply Refer To
1650
Appeal Req Med-B3/Rej675
5 December 1975

From: Office of the Chief of Naval Medical Operations
To: Raymond Silver

Subj: Appeal Of Medical Denial/Enlistment 17 June 1975

Ref:
(a) Letter of Appeal
(b) Supporting letter from personal physician
(c) Medical records
(d) Radiographs (x-rays)
(e) Supporting letter from radiologist (private practice)

Dear Mr. Silver:

In review of the above stated references (a) through (e) and in accordance with Naval regulations pertaining to physical qualifications, along with reports and recommendations made by examining doctors of Naval medical staff, this office is unable to grant your appeal for enlistment into the United States Navy.

This letter serves as official and final notification that your application for enlistment is denied.

B.A. SAMPSON, CDR

1

Sitting in his workshop, Ray leaned back into the well-worn and somewhat off- balanced chair as he slowly lifted his right foot to rest on the edge of his desk. Made of unfinished three-quarter-inch plywood sheets and supported by angled lengths of 2 x 4s, he was proud of his handiwork. It was an "L"-shaped desk that he had carefully designed (on the back of a napkin), measured (with a bent retractable tape measure), and cut to fit into the southwest corner of the small area he called his "workshop". Although the only kind of work he did there was either internet searches or settling in with a good sea adventure novel, he did build his desk as well as an attached workbench—with the aid of a power saw, hammer, and plenty of bandages. Ray was the first to admit that he was not a natural handyman type of guy, but he did reluctantly take on "real man" tasks either out of necessity or the occasional need to successfully complete a project just to boost his ego. Having completed this little project—without help—he proudly called the small extended area of the one car-garage his workshop.

The desk sat snug to the wall and just underneath the bay window of the detached garage of a 1940s Craftsman-style house that looked out at the passing ships on Puget Sound. One year after moving in, he still looked up from his "work" every time a passing vessel sounded its horn. On the wall to the left of the window he had mounted two small analog clocks that ticked off the seconds in unison—unless one started to lose battery power. Somehow he never heard the cadence of tick...tick... tick...when the clocks were in lockstep. But when one battery prematurely lost some juice, the tick tick...tick tick...tick tick... grated on him like nails on a chalkboard. He could not regain his concentration until he surrendered his resistance to search for a new "AA" battery and painstakingly manipulated the clocks into sync once more. He thought about changing both clock batteries at the same time on the slight chance they would lose power simultaneously—thereby always keeping cadence—but it was a passing thought at best.

The clock on the left was set to West Coast time while the clock on the right was set three hours ahead.

The wall to the right of the window was lined with 12 x 12 squares of corkboard. An 8 x 10 black and white photo of an old Navy ship was pinned to the center of the tiles. On either side of the picture; a few small maps stuck with a dozen or so colored pins and official-looking Navy department letters— some yellowed with age—pinned one on top of the other. A handwritten list of names, some of them matched to cities, others crossed off in red pencil and still more followed by a question mark, was tacked to the upper left hand corner. In the other corner of the homemade bulletin board, exposed by a small incandescent lamp, there was a faded, dog-eared, half-folded telegram, whose only visible words were "It is with deep regret..."

Ray glanced at the five smaller pictures of Navy men neatly placed in a row along the bottom of the tiles. The photos of his grandfather, dad, and Uncle Jim were—like the folded telegram—yellowed with age. The colors on his brother's picture were also starting to lose a little bit of that sharpness. He closed his eyes and tried to recall what little features he could of the gaunt, unshaven face he had seen through the dim of the smoke and the bar girls that night inside Felipe's and wondered if it could have been Frank. Again he looked at his brother's picture, and again he closed his eyes and tried to find the resemblance. He was tired. He couldn't be sure. The picture, a third reprint, was starting to show its age. The guy in the bar had looked much older, but then again, Frank too would be much older now.

The newest addition to Ray's picture collection was of his son, Jimmy. He was both proud and envious of the double gold braid that adorned the lower sleeves of his son's dress blue uniform. He was equally impressed with his boundless energy. In the five years since completing undergraduate and Navy ROTC, and in the nine months since his graduation from law school, Lieutenant Junior Grade Jimmy Silver had been busy nonstop. He was just as busy now, working for the Judge Advocate General. Ray thought about how his son's time was being spent sorting through cases not worthy of a made-for-television crime drama. Still, all of his hard work and aggressiveness at the JAG offices in Bethesda pleased his superiors. With an ability to quickly resolve "major" cases such as petty theft, misappropriation of equipment, drunken brawls, and stolen care packages, Jimmy had easily garnered a quick promotion from Ensign along with a requested transfer to the USS Enterprise as it headed back to the 5th Fleet in the Persian Gulf.

Ray had one other photo. This one of his daughter, Casey, in her camouflage fatigues. Above one breast pocket was a small patch with black embroidered lettering spelling out the name "SILVER". Above the other breast pocket, "U.S. NAVY". Her lieutenant bars were pinned to the tip of her right collar, and the left one carried the caduceus. This picture, he kept in front of him. It sat in a small frame next to the computer monitor on his "custom-made" desk.

As much as he tried not to think about the possibility of either of his children being in harm's way, his father's words still came back to haunt him:

"There's gonna be a big demand for nurses in the Gulf region now that this war is underway."

"She'll be fine, Pop. She's a newly commissioned officer fresh out of school. It'll be quite a while before she'd be sent anywhere near the Gulf. And I'll bet this thing'll be over as quick as Desert Storm was."

"From your lips to God's ears... God forbid, Raymond, I'm not worried about Jimmy. He's not gonna be in harm's way, if ya know what I mean, but if anything happens to that little girl, if she's flyin' in to a hot LZ on an evac and they take fire and somethin' happens to her, God forbid, Raymond, I swear that's gonna stay with you for the rest of your life."

Ray picked up his daughter's picture and lightly brushed his index finger over her face. "She's still stationed stateside, Pop," he said as he looked over at his father's picture. "Thank God for that."

Since Ray's grandfather's enlistment in late 1916, all of the Silver family offspring had also donned the uniform—all except Ray. Not one member of the family had ever mentioned the physical "limitation" that had kept him out of the Navy. And as hard as he had argued the case that the slight defect in his lower spine was no real limitation, it would be to no avail. He had been denied the opportunity to carry on what had become a family tradition, and had felt cheated out of being able to share this special bond. A bond his grandfather had once had with his own two sons, or the bond his dad once had with his older son, Frank, and then shared with Ray's son and daughter. Not one member of the family ever said a word about it, but for the longest time it had bothered him that he hadn't been able to serve or to share that same connection.

He let out a big sigh as he slowly slid his hand across the top of his desk. The double layered three-quarter-inch thick boards had been cut evenly with seams that were both straight and tight. The holes he had cut to allow power cords and computer cables were perfectly round and sanded smooth so that no rough edges chafed at the wiring—the one- inch scar above the knuckle of his right index finger serving as a reminder of why he had chosen to be so meticulous. And he liked the fact that the desk didn't wobble or creek, betraying some unforeseen instability every time he rested his legs upon it. Legs that now ached like they never had before. "A nice, solid piece of work," he thought to himself, pressing against one of the outer support legs. There were two 4 x 4 support legs on either end of the desk. On the one to his left he had mounted a silver die-cast bottle cap opener with red painted lettering calling out to nobody in particular, "Drink Coca-Cola".

Even though almost every bottle of pop or beer had long turned to twist-off tops, Ray still liked the quick little whoosh of sound from escaping carbonation and the clinking of a bottle cap as it hit the bottom of the waste bin every time he opened another Pipeline Porter. Each week he squeezed out some time to kick back at his desk, take an ice-cold bottle from the mini-fridge that sat under the workbench, as the O'Banyon Factor played on the TV mounted on the wall behind him. While un-winding from the day, he'd sometimes stare at the surfer on the bottle's label and think about going back to Oahu. Especially since it was now more than just a passing thought.

Except for the occasional bottle of this unusual craft por-ter, Ray wasn't much of a drinker. Just like the majority of the people in Seattle, his preferred beverage was coffee. Not lattes or five-dollar grande, skinny wet, light on the foam concoc-tions, just a regular cup of joe. And that was one of the reasons why he had taken to the Pipeline. It was made with 100% Kona coffee, and there was something about that beer and coffee combination that just hit home for him. It always made him think of the islands with fond memories.

His first trip to Hawaii had been when the kids were very young. For as long as he had dreamed of going, and as much as he had enjoyed being on a family vacation, his fantasy of be-ing in "paradise" was met with the reality of being told by tour guides where to go, when to go, and how long to stay before it was time to move to the next attraction. By the time they got home all four of them had been exhausted. The one take-away "Kodak moment" he still cherished was the day he and the kids had snorkeled together in Hanauma Bay. After all the years that had passed, he could still see their smiles and hear their squeals of delight as multi-colored tropical fish swam in and out of their legs.

His second and more memorable visit was years later. It had been a combination 45th- birthday present along with a celebratory trip he gave to himself when his divorce was finalized. The trip was not so much a need to celebrate the end of a long relationship, though it had been a relationship that—he freely admitted—produced a number of wonderful memories as well as two great children. It was more of a gigantic sigh of relief that he was free from a slow, sad, and steady unraveling of a special friendship that had started out as a college romance. In spite of the attempts of both attorneys to turn their termination process into an all-out war, he was grateful they were able to walk away with civility still intact. Once it was all said and done, Ray had felt the need to finally start doing things just for him. He had wanted to go back to the islands for many years, and it had seemed to be the one place Mary Jo refused to go. So, as the cliché went, before the ink on the divorce papers had dried, he had donned an "aloha" shirt and was sitting in a first class seat on a flight to Honolulu.

He had dreamed of Hawaii for as long as he could remember. As a little kid munching on his first macadamias watching police dramas set in Oahu on the family's RCA Victor color TV, or while listening to his dad's stories of Uncle Jim's South Pacific adventures. But the one of how his uncle was killed at Pearl Harbor on December 7th 1941 as he lay sleeping in his hammock aboard the USS Arizona was the story he never forgot.

"And your Uncle Jim, " his dad always said, "wasn't afraid to die. He was the kind of guy who would've wanted to go out fightin' and not caught by surprise with just his skivvies on. If ya know what I mean. "

Ray had a number of pictures of his dad during his Navy days and even a few of the uncle he had never met. But whenever he had asked his father about his own experiences during the war, the few stories were either brief, or he quietly responded "I just did my time in the engine room of the 606 and then came home when it was all done. That's it. Pretty boring, if ya know what I mean. " Somehow those pictures of his dad hinted at a story or two the old man had never really wanted to talk about. Sometimes he would forget himself and begin to tell one. But every time, like clockwork, he would catch the wide-eyed stare of Ray or Frank and abruptly stop because of "something" he had forgotten he had to do.

"Aw come on, Pop. Don't stop now. You were just gettin' to the good part." *A young Ray Silver had pleaded.*

"Sorry, boys, I let the time get away from me and I promised old man Fischer I'd have those brass fittins' waitin' for him on the counter first thing in the mornin'."

"Just tell us what happened when that Zero started divin' on ya."

"Later, Frankie. Tell your mother I went over to the store."

"But, Pop, it's Sunday" Ray had said as his father, Ron, grabbed his plaid hunter's jacket and closed the kitchen door behind him. *"He stops every time he gets to the good parts, Frankie. Every time!"*

"Yeah, no kiddin', Raymond."

One of Ray's favorite pictures was of his dad standing on the starboard side of the crowded LCI 606 (a small ship classified as Landing Craft Infantry) as its crew helped evacuate sailors from what had been a damaged LCT (a landing craft that carried tanks). He had made two enlargements of that picture, pinning one to the corkboard over his desk in the workshop and hanging a framed version in his office at the Veterans Medical Center. He had two other pictures that hung in his office, one of his brother, Chief Petty Officer Frank Silver, posing with the other members of his SEAL team, and one of Uncle Jim's ship, the Arizona, exploding into a fireball as she sat tied up at Ford Island, Naval Station Pearl Harbor, Hawaii.

On the first day of his return trip to Oahu, Ray had dumped his bags at the Royal Hawaiian hotel in Waikiki and then driven out to Pearl to pay his respects to Uncle Jim and his 1,101 shipmates forever entombed at the bottom of the harbor. Standing on the memorial looking down at the droplets of oil that still bled from the ship, he had thought, *"If I came just four weeks earlier I could have been here on December 7th. Oh well, Uncle Jim, at least I'm here now. At least I'm finally here."* He remembered his disappointment with one of the young sailors he had talked to that day. The kid had been assigned to one of the motored launches that ferried tourists back and forth across the harbor from the visitor's center to the memorial site. In Ray's mind, this should have been an honored duty for the young sailor. Being stationed at the infamous Pearl Harbor, being able to watch over this hallowed site, and being in Hawaii of all places. What better duty could a person ask for? For the young kid though, having to be in his dress whites every day ferrying boatload after boatload of tourists was mind-numbing.

"No disrespect, sir," he had said to Ray, *"but I'd rather be on a ship in the Gulf."*

With a war underway after another sneak attack on America, Ray understood the seaman's point and wondered if he was being too much of a romantic.

In the days that followed, he had kicked it back a few notches and leisurely toured every bit of the island that he could, from Koko Head on up to the North Shore and from Waikiki over the Pali highway to Kanehoe and the Valley of the Temples. He didn't care that the local surfers laughed at the pale-skinned "haole" from Seattle. *"You'd think we'd be a common sight by now"* he had thought. *"Just like the giant sea turtles sleeping on the beach."* He just sat back in the warm, white sands of the North Shore and watched in amazement as those young kids effortlessly piloted their boards through a glass pipeline of turquoise blue. To him, the entire island was filled with awe-inspiring displays of both natural and man-made beauty.

There was a haunting serenity that had enveloped him at the Byodo-In Temple. He happened upon it shortly after a sudden cloud burst had sent tourists running for their buses and on to the next attraction. Watching them scurry through the rain had made him laugh, as he remembered being hustled around the island—on any one of several tours all those years ago. Now, he was on his own and free to come and go as he pleased. So as the rain let up, Ray slowly strolled over the footbridge and past the Koi-filled pond to the Buddhist temple nestled at the base of the Ko'olau Mountains. He felt at peace with himself. He looked up at the low-lying clouds and took comfort in the way they blanketed the mountain tops. Long, white wisps extended down and gently caressed the rigid folds of rock as if to coax them deeper into its soft white body.

For the first time in a long time, standing before that temple, he had felt the need to pray. As he made his way to the entrance he saw a woman waving him over to an ancient bell. *"She's young,"* he had thought. *"Twenty, twenty- one perhaps. Petite. Very cute."* He noticed her long flowing jet black hair as renegade strands danced across her face with the gentle breeze.

"Please, it is good to ring the peace bell before you enter the temple," she had said in a soft and comforting voice.

"The peace bell?" he asked, looking at the giant bell suspended from the ceiling of its own pagoda-like structure.

"Yes. It is good luck to ring it before you enter the temple. Please." She motioned with her hand to the rope-supported log that was used as a striker.

Ray carefully looked at the woman and noticed the serenity in her face. She smiled and motioned once more toward the bell. He hadn't noticed her when he crossed the footbridge a few minutes earlier and he certainly had not heard her walk along the gravel path. She spoke as he walked over to take hold of the rope on the large striker.

"It is said that ringing this bell will bring you many blessings. It will bring you joy and happiness. It will bring you an inner peace and a long life. It will also purify the mind of evil spirits and temptation."

Ray had pulled back on the rope and then pushed the heavy log to strike the bell. A low, harmonious tone rang out and slowly faded, as if being swallowed by the clouds. He turned to thank the young woman but she was gone. He glanced over toward the temple and then back toward the footbridge. Except for a lone calico cat sitting on the gravel path before him, he was all alone. He made his way into the temple, lit some incense, and placed the slow-burning sticks into a small rice-filled cup that lay before the giant statue of Buddha. *"There's so much going on,"* he had thought to himself as he bowed his head and closed his eyes. *"I pray that it all falls in to place, and I ask that your hand touch me and guide me while I am on this road. I pray and ask that your hand be with me and all my family members. Bless us and protect us. Keep us safe from evil and from harm. I pray and ask that you heal my mind, my body, and my spirit. I thank you for your patience with me, your tolerance of me, and your love for me, for that is the best of all. Amen."*

As he had turned to leave, that same cat was sitting just outside the temple's front entrance as if she had been waiting for him. He walked over to it and leaned down to rub its head. The calico looked up at Ray, squinted her golden brown eyes, and she purred at his touch.

He easily concluded that this was the best vacation he had been on in many years. After going to the Arizona at Pearl Harbor, hanging at Waikiki, watching the beautiful Kamaaina surf with reckless abandon, and spending the day snorkeling at Hanauma bay, he wished it could have lasted longer, and yet it was all over before he knew it.

He was however, very impressed with himself for doing something totally out of character. While having a quick bite at a small restaurant just off the beach in Lanikai—a restaurant he had passed by at first and returned to on a whim—he had summoned up his courage and made an attempt to meet a woman sitting alone at the bar sipping on a beer. It didn't even matter to him that she was quite a few years younger, or as it turned out, had been living in Seattle. There were beautiful half-naked women running around all over the island, but there was something about this woman that had grabbed ahold of him and wouldn't let go.

Perhaps it was the way her auburn hair had laid across her shoulders or how the bronze of her tan complimented her brown eyes and freckled nose and arms. It could have been the smell of passionflower as gentle, warm breezes danced across the palm- thatched overhang of the open air dining room. Perhaps it was the whole package. But it kept him stealing glances at her all through his lunch. Since his constant staring didn't escape her, he had figured *"what the heck?"* as he finally made his way over to strike up a conversation. He knew the encounter was something he would not have normally attempted but at the time he didn't care. That had been the amazing thing about it. Since his divorce, he had suddenly found himself willing to take more chances and willing to accept the outcomes.

In this particular case he remembered, "She was very alone, very attractive, very polite and very uninterested in a one-night stand with a guy fifteen years her senior." Admittedly, he had been slightly embarrassed when he had realized he was still wearing his wedding band. But she had been kind enough to indulge him with a little back and forth banter, and after all, she had suggested he try the Pipeline Porter. Thinking about it during his flight back to Seattle, he thought that perhaps if he'd taken off the ring, gotten back into the gym and took off a few pounds, maybe, just maybe, he would've had better luck. Fortunately for his dignity, the chances were slim to none that they would ever cross paths back home.

"That was such a great trip," Ray thought. Staring at the label on his beer he realized that it was no longer cold, but not as warm as the golden sky that bathed the surfer on the label. Hawaii, even that most recent trip, was for now just a memory, and the late winter rain that began smacking hard against his workshop windows brought his attention back to present time. He thought he heard his name, and turned around in time to see his picture at the upper right-hand corner of the television screen as Bill O'Banyon concluded his commentary

"So there you have it, people. An unlikely crew of genuine heroes, led by Ray Silver of Seattle, Washington, are true American patriots. And that concludes tonight's memo points."

"Aw, shit!" Ray said, picking up the remote and turning off the television. "Just what I needed."

To say he was glad to be done with *this* trip to the South Pacific was surely an understatement. The soreness, stiffness, and bruising across his lower back, in his knees, and on his arms were testament to that. This trip had not been what he had imagined it would be. It was not what it was supposed to be. But once the commitment was made, it was what it had to be. For the most part, he was glad he had been involved. Ray wasn't sure if he would do it all over again. Perhaps not, if he had known all the details beforehand. He wasn't exactly the action-hero type, although deep down in his younger days, he had briefly aspired to be. But it was done. It was over and he was now hoping that was the end of it. He had nothing left to prove now. In his mind, he had finally earned his place. He was glad to be home, but not quite certain of what lay ahead. Based on the most recent update from Casey, he had less than twenty-four hours to get back East, as everything was set to go at Arlington. He wasn't sure what he was going to do for a job, and except for voicemail phone tag, hadn't really spoken to Leigh Anne in over seven weeks.

His answering machine indicated a few unheard messages that he could have checked when he had gotten in late the night before. Given the numbers on the caller ID, they would have to wait until he made his flight reservations. Most likely the messages were from Peter McCain or some D.C. bureaucrat. There was a letter-size envelope with his name in Leigh Anne's handwriting on his desk. He glanced over the rest of the desktop and didn't see anything different or out of place since he had last been home. As he picked up the letter, Magic, a calico of unknown age, jumped up to greet him.

It was kind of eerie the way she had just showed up one day. During the weeks he had spent moving into his new house, the cat had started appearing on his doorstep as if by magic. He was taken by how she resembled the calico that he had seen that day at the Buddhist temple.

"Coincidence, or are you my guardian angel?" he had asked, walking right by her.

After repeat appearances at his door, and having no collar, he had begun letting her hang with him in the workshop as he built his desk and workbench. When it appeared that Magic had "adopted" him, he installed a small pet door leading into the garage and placed a food dish, self-filling water bowl, and a small box with a pillow underneath the workbench. She had been with him ever since. Whenever Ray took off for any period of time, a neighbor girl would stop by to feed her. He often thought about making an honest woman out of her by having her spayed, declawed, and sentenced to a lifetime indoors, but he didn't want to admit that his attachment to her had grown that much. "Besides," he thought, "why deprive the neighborhood toms?" Magic purred as she rubbed against him and Ray reciprocated by scratching her head. "You miss me? I missed you, Madge," he said as her golden brown eyes looked up at him and squinted several times.

Sitting at his desk, he looked up at the cork bulletin board and the list of men's names who had once been crew members on the 606. His eyes slowly scanned the list, stopping when he got to A.J. Lewis. Ray picked up a pen and wrote "KIA" next to the name. Then he picked up a red pen and circled it. He turned his attention back to Leigh Anne's envelope. The brief note inside was dated two weeks earlier. He shook his head, thinking of all the times over the past two months they hadn't been able to connect. "Damn. Just a little while longer, babe."

FYI, finally got the call from U of H, Oahu (right after you left!) I had to go or lose the opp. Also got your note. HAPPY! Still need to talk. If I'm not at the 'U' I'm at St. Philomena's. xo xo Leigh.

"Ok," Ray thought to himself. He was exhausted. He wanted, and definitely needed, a few more hours of sleep although he knew he wasn't going to get it. Not just yet anyway. He sat upright in his chair, placed his elbows onto the desk, and let out a sigh as he lowered his head into the palms of his hands.

2

Ray's small workshop and single-car garage sat at the end of the short driveway of his Magnolia neighborhood home. From his desk he could look west to Puget Sound and the snow-capped Olympic Mountain range that lay beyond the large body of water that sparkled in delight whenever the elusive sun made an appearance. The southern view gave him the Space Needle, Seattle skyline, and Elliot Bay waterfront. When the cloud cover wasn't low, Ray could see the majesty of Mount Rainer sleeping peacefully in the distance, and as long as she stayed asleep, he was happy to have her as part of the scenery.

It was a big house for him at 1800 square feet; certainly more than enough for his needs. He had completed the purchase of it just weeks after his return from the `02 Hawaii trip and right after he had gotten the phone call from the Veterans Medical Center congratulating him on his appointment to the medical staff. Newly divorced and with both kids away at college, he had fully anticipated that he would be alone most of the time. Not being a Washington native, the ties that now kept him in the Seattle area were his new position as staff chiropractor at the VMC and knowing—hoping, really—that the kids would keep coming back to their hometown for visits.

In some ways, that first day at the VMC seemed like it was almost yesterday, and in other ways it felt as if he had been there forever. Truth be told, in spite of certain events that made it seem intolerable, and which had him questioning his decision to work there, it was a position that he had wanted for the longest time. He had spent hours upon hours writing letters, sending emails, and making telephone calls to agency administrators, senators, and his Congressional Representative in a relentless effort to lobby his cause. He was adamant about being able to provide chiropractic care to vets and to be right-fully compensated for doing so, no different from any other health care professional employed by the government. But his had been a constant uphill battle, as the wheels of change in any government bureaucracy move extremely slow—and that's when they're running efficiently.

The inefficiency of the entire process should have given him a clue as to the red tape, cover your ass, done in tripli-cate banality of government that he eventually had to contend with. All totaled, he had tried to become part of the medi-cal staff for about ten years. Not that being in private practice hadn't had its perks. Still, he had never lost the desire to have some actual connection, if not with the United States Navy, then with the military in some form. By working at the VMC he had hoped he would finally satisfy his need to serve while achieving that special bond he had long desired. For that to happen, he gladly gave up private practice, taking care of peo-ple he felt took his services for granted, in order to provide care to those men and women who showed a greater apprecia-tion for what he did and how he did it. It had been more than an added bonus to have a guaranteed salary, benefits, no over-head, or the need to spend a good portion of his week fighting insurance companies.

Maybe it was his years of self-employment and fighting with those insurance companies that had given Ray the cour-age to occasionally display independence before his supervi-sors. A trait which was not appreciated in places like the VMC, and one that would get him into hot water on more than one occasion. All in all, it had been just one more new life experience since becoming single.

* * *

Ray was in private practice for a total of twenty years in Eastridge. He and his wife, Mary Jo, lived in the sleepy little hamlet of Eastridge Heights, which sat comfortably along the eastern banks of Lake Washington just a few miles from the city's fast-growing downtown. From their large cedar deck one could easily see the Seattle skyline. Ray had felt the "Heights" had changed since they had bought their house in '86.

"It's not the same here anymore," he complained to Jo. "The Heights has become artificial."

"Artificial? In what way has it become artificial?" Jo had asked, rather defensively.

"That feel of community is gone. If you ask me, we've become infested with narcissistic dot-com millionaires. I don't see any real participation in the community. Remember last Halloween? The kids got escorted off of, umm…oh, what's that guy's name from that vacation website? You know who I mean. Can you believe he won't even let the neighborhood kids come to his house and trick or treat?"

"These guys are harmless, Ray," Jo countered. "So what if they keep to themselves? They make big donations to the community. That's what's important."

"You may think they're harmless, but I see it differently. Instead of participating and being a part of the community, they're donating themselves to the head of the line. I noticed that after the school district received all new computer software, the city council renamed the downtown park for Phil and Belinda. Then they got the go-ahead to cut down those ancient evergreens that *you* fought so hard to protect so they could build their new estate. And did you notice Eastridge Elementary is now called the "Starfire Primary School" after Harvey Schwartz from Starfire Coffee made that big donation? Not very subtle, is it?"

"Ray," she said in frustration, "who cares what these things are called if the community still benefits from them?"

"Jo, do you remember when Steve Bowman held a fund-raiser for the President and the Secret Service came to talk to you because you make contributions to that environmental group? That's the kind of nonsense I'm talking about."

But even before the infiltration of the nouveau riche, the Heights was an upscale community that had been the place to live if you wanted to socialize with a smorgasbord of medical, legal, and financial professionals. Ray thought a good number of them were preoccupied with self-admiration and self-indulgence as they freely flaunted the spoils of their financial success. They spoiled their children as easily as they spoiled themselves, which passed on that sense of entitlement and privilege to the younger generation—and was all too often exercised without guidance and with little to no regard of any possible long-term consequences. This was something Ray had never understood or appreciated—perhaps a result of his blue-collar upbringing. Not to say the Heights didn't have a number of decent down to earth families that the Silvers' found to be kindred spirits.

It did. But the number of families sharing the same values that Ray had grown up with seemed to be getting harder to find.

* * *

Ray and his older brother Frank were the sons of self-employed parents who both worked at the family-owned hardware store. With the family as hired help, Ron Silver didn't have to rely on outside employees and was therefore better able to provide those little extras in life. But to do so required putting in long hours at the store. Regardless, Ray and his brother never felt neglected by their parents. They always made time for a family dinner, even if it meant having deli sandwiches while sitting behind the main counter at Silver and Sons Hardware.

"Raymond!"

"Yeah, Ma?"

"Frankie's back from the deli. Come eat."

"Coming Ma, just a sec," Ray said as he put a few more cans of paint on the shelf.

"Raymond!"

"Yeah, Pop?"

"Are you back in the paint section?"

"Yeah, Pop."

Walking down the aisle with a clipboard in his hand, Ron looked at Ray over his reading glasses. "Did you sell the last gallon of the all-weather fire engine red?"

"Yeah, Pop."

"Did you reorder any?"

Ray's eyes looked to the ceiling as he thought. "Yeah, Pop. I reordered it."

"Raymond, I don't see any on the order pad."

"Sorry, Pop...I guess I forgot."

"Again Raymond, you forgot again! And sorry doesn't put food on the table, if ya know what I mean."

"I know, Pop. I'm sorry. I wasn't thinking."

"What's that sign in the bathroom say? The one over the toilet?"

"Even in here, think."

"Exactly! Ya always gotta think. Understand?"

"Yeah, Pop."

"Come here," Ron said, giving his son a kiss on top of his head. "I love you. You know that right?"

"Yeah, Pop."

"God gave you a head. Please use it."

"Ron!"

"Yes, Mama, what?"

"Let the boy eat his sandwich before it gets cold. I want he should do his homework before it gets too late."

"But Ma," Ray said as he made his way to the front counter, "it's Friday night."

"Friday, schmeiday. You get your homework done before the TV."

"But Ma, if I miss my show I'll have to wait for summer reruns!"

"Good, you'll have something to look forward to. Now eat."

God, family, and love of country were the most valuable things in the Silver household. Doing one's part to support and defend those values were principles from which both parents never waivered, and doing the latter had made an impression on both boys since their very first visit to the aircraft carrier Forrestal when Ray was seven and Frank was eleven.

They had heard the stories of their grandfather stoking the boilers on the USS Texas, a World War I battleship. They heard the stories about Uncle Jim and the Arizona. They spent hours looking over the pictures of their dad as he told a brief story or two of himself and his shipmates on the LCI 606 as a flotilla of those mighty little ships landed the 1st and 5th Marine Divisions onto the shores of Peleliu and Iwo Jima. But it was that first trip to the Forrestal, decked out in all her grandeur during the annual Fleet Week in New York City, that made it all real for Ron Silver's two boys.

It was no surprise to the family when Frank, just out of high school, joined the Navy in '71 and went on to become a SEAL. It was a surprise, and a heartbreak that Ray's parents never got over, when Frank disappeared and was presumed killed on a "training" mission in the Philippines in 1981. There had been talk about Frank's SEAL unit working with Filipino marines in order to disrupt arms shipments to communist guerrillas. They had developed a strong presence on several of the inner western islands that lay between Luzon and Mindanao, launching terror attacks on government troops from their hidden bases on those islands. The Navy never did disclose any details other than it had been a night training mission with Filipino marines. Their Huey helicopter gunship radioed that they were having mechanical difficulties before all contact was lost over the Visayan Sea. Apparently, no wreckage was found and no bodies were ever recovered. For some reason though, Ron Silver insisted that Frank's SEAL team was not on a training mission with the Filipinos because SEALs worked alone.

He always maintained they had been inserted into Cambodia on a secret recon mission to look for MIAs—a claim that had quickly been downplayed by Pentagon officials.

Ray himself had been chomping at the bit to join when Frank did in `71, but until he finished high school he spent his afternoons working at the family hardware store. In doing so, he gave up participation in extracurricular activities. A trade-off he initially disliked, as he had wanted to chase after the records set by Frank during his days on the high school gridiron. Knowing that his folks did all they could to make ends meet, he rationalized that he wasn't the athlete his brother had been and that his classmates inevitably would have held him to a standard he could never meet.

Ray took pride in the work he did after school. He took pride in earning a paycheck, and with it the ability to purchase his own little extras without having to ask his mother or father for their hard-earned money.

* * *

Having learned the value of a dollar when he was a kid, he tried to teach those same lessons to his own children. But it wasn't always easy for his kids to understand, as their eyes bore constant witness to the glitter and other "toys" purchased with the easily acquired wealth within the neighborhood. So while Ray drove his kids to school in the new family minivan, the neighborhood kids were driven to school each day in new luxury cars, dressed in the latest designer fashions, and talked about zipping to Whistler for winter break or to the Grand Wailea Resort in Maui over Easter. For this and other reasons, Ray came to dislike living in Eastridge Heights.

Although they did not live the lavish lifestyle of their neighbors, Ray had developed a solid practice and made a decent living. The bulk of the income he brought home went toward household expenses, upgrades, constant repairs, or was invested in blue chip stocks and a college education fund for the kids that Jo had started and managed. But where Ray would have been satisfied with a smaller house in a middle-class neighborhood, Jo was more investment-minded. She saw the house with the view on the three-quarter-acre corner lot of 16th Avenue Northeast as a long-term investment with bigger dividends down the road. She was also more skilled in the social graces, relative to Ray, and knew that the kids would benefit later on from the friendships they made while in school. Since Jo had envisioned an Ivy League future for her children, she wanted her kids to have as many connections as possible. By developing those connections, she also built more of her own. Ray had a different path in mind for his children and was laying the groundwork, hoping for service academy appointments. And if that failed, at least there was ROTC.

Like any other married couple, Ray and Jo had their disagreements, but the course that Ray had mapped out for Jimmy and Casey always frustrated her. What made it worse for Jo was that both kids had shown an immediate interest in the Navy. When Jimmy and Casey made their first visit to the USS Enterprise, just like Ray and Frank visiting the Forrestal all those years before, they too were hooked. And if listening to their dad's stories while looking through the photo albums of their grandfather and Uncle Frank hadn't done the trick, seeing all those sailors dressed in their crisp formal whites during the visit to the "Big E" certainly had. The groundwork had been laid.

"It's in their genes" Ray would say each time the subject had come up.

"Defective genes if you ask me," Jo would respond. "I can't believe you would have our kids pursue a life in the service."

"What's wrong with that? It's not as if I want them peeling potatoes or scrubbing toilets."

"Ray, sometimes I just don't understand you, I really don't," Jo would yell knowing she was wasting her time. She was determined to plow ahead, convinced that as the children got older they would come to their senses and see things her way. But they didn't. Both would go on to attend the University of

Washington and participate in Navy ROTC, and for that she would never forgive Ray.

Always careful to pick the charities that attracted Eastridge's power elite, Jo made friends and connections with ease through her volunteer work. Ray never refused her requests to help with fundraisers, but detested all of the "willing" participants who were quick to supervise and delegate—but who never actually participated in the real work. "Unless of course," he said, "you consider real work to be seeking out reporters and photographers from the newspaper gossip columns and society pages."

Jo worked hard climbing the social ladder, and at times resented the fact that her husband was "only" a chiropractor and not a neurologist or orthopedist at the Lakeview Medical Center. She wasn't asking for a Nobel Prize-winner pioneering some ground- breaking procedure in thoracic surgery, "Although," She often complained to her mother, "it would make things so much easier for me." Ray's profession didn't have the same prestige in the eyes of her friends.

To Jo, it had been a stinging indictment of their standing in the social hierarchy whenever her husband was referred to as "Mr." Silver instead of "Dr." Silver by the local women on whom she focused her energies. She always felt she had to go above and beyond in order to be on the same level as, say, a Mary Jean Nathanson whose husband specialized in pediatric neurosurgery and was being considered for head of pediatrics at Lakeview. Or perhaps Emma Bowman, whose late husband Stephen earned a few billion in high tech and who now heads his charitable trust. Jo's feelings for Ray's profession didn't go unnoticed and would occasionally spark an argument between them.

But universal justice was soon dealt to those most deserving—by the year 2000 and the start of the new century, the dot-com boom of the mid to late '90s became the dot- com bust. And like vultures circling a rotting carcass on the blazing desert, local realtors soon swooped down, placing "for sale" signs in the front yards of the very same mega- homes they had sold just a few years earlier.

Ray never said a word. He never thought, "it serves them right". Although he lost some patients when several of his neighbors moved away, he felt bad for the ones who had worked for those former multi-millionaires. Now that they were out of work and left without a paycheck or insurance, he wondered what would happen to them. As some of these people came into his office for what would be their last visit, he spent time working out payment plans so they could take care of outstanding balances. In many cases, he cut the debt in half or forgave it altogether.

But while the dot-comers had to sell their mansions in the Heights, most still walked away with fairly large bank accounts. Even so, many of them could no longer afford the mortgage payments of the artificial Eastridge lifestyle. Gone were the leased Porsches, Bentleys, and BMWs. The yachts and luxury vacation condos were put up for sale, and memberships at the Lakeview Golf and Country club were terminated. Eventually, a good many of them packed their belongings and moved away. Mostly to save face, they let it be known to the town gossips that they were leaving for no other reason but for lucrative job offers in Los Angeles, New York and London.

As a result of the economic downturn that hit the local community pretty hard, much of the groundwork that Jo spent time developing seemed to have vanished in the same way as the once rich and famous of Eastridge Heights. She felt cheated. It changed the way she looked at life and contributed to the way she began looking at her relationship with Ray.

Over the course of that next year, before she filed for divorce, Jo's bitterness continued to grow. At first, Ray found refuge in an on-again off-again research project he had been doing on Frank's Navy unit SEAL Team Eleven. Reaching one dead end after another, he decided to set that aside and turn his focus to Landing Craft Infantry, the mighty little ships on which his dad had served. He soon found that obtaining information on LCIs was much easier than on the secretive special ops unit known as "STE". He began spending post-patient hours in his office researching the little ships on the internet.

At first it was to avoid going home to Jo and her increasing criticisms, but it soon became his obsession. He wanted to learn more about the 606, her different crews, and her missions.

Ray sometimes called his dad for information. It frustrated him that the old man would feign memory loss, claiming he couldn't recall names of shipmates or he would simply give vague details. But that didn't dampen his curiosity; it only served to fuel the fire. He knew there was something his dad didn't want to talk about. Rather than create another family problem, he just bit his tongue and did more research. Slowly, his list of 606 crew members grew. The more he searched, the more he wanted to know and the longer he remained in his office after hours. Even though he kept his sanity by taking comfort in his newfound sanctuary, this took a heavy toll on what was left of the relationship he had with the woman who had once been his best friend.

He was thankful that the kids were grown, in college, and neutral witnesses to the decline of their parents' marriage. He didn't feel responsible for the complete dissolution of their relationship, although he never denied that he could have been more proactive in trying to salvage it. By that point he had convinced himself that anything he attempted would have been taken the wrong way, so he attempted nothing. When he was finally served with divorce papers in late summer 2001, he had long since resigned himself to the fact that their relationship was over. This was his ticket to finally move out of the house without looking like the bad guy.

Jo was angry but reasonable, and willing to settle for a fifty-fifty split. With attorneys on both sides getting ready to dig in to fight for as much as they could get, Ray saw any prolonged fight as only benefitting the lawyers. He had just wanted to move on with his life and easily consented to letting Jo have the house and a sixty-forty split of their other investments. With that, her anger toward him eased. She demonstrated this by directing her lawyers to "heel" and bring the matter to a quick close. The fact that Jo's two closest friends had already introduced her to a newly widowed heart surgeon was incentive for her to move on as well.

When the process was finalized during the first week of January 2002, it was as if a cosmic chain of events had been unleashed, opening the doors for Ray to begin his new life. First, his trip to Oahu, then getting the position at the VMC, selling his practice to his two associates, and finally, finding the house in Magnolia. All unfolded one after another, as if it had been carefully orchestrated. When one of Jo's attorneys suggested they make an attempt to go after half of the proceeds from the sale of his practice, her parents, who had always liked their son-in-law, convinced her to leave well enough alone. Ray was thankful. Between the threat of having half of that money taken and his first few weeks at the VMC, the stress was starting to get to him. The one thing that gave him pause, the one thing in this whole scenario that evoked a sense of remorse, and maybe even a feeling that perhaps he should have tried a little harder, was Jo's freak car accident just after he began moving into his new house.

3

Ray slowly transitioned to his new place—from the small apartment he had been renting in Queen Anne—during his first weeks at the medical center. He had recently completed what he sarcastically referred to as his "orientation" at the VMC with the facility director, HR director, senior medical staff, head of orthopedics, the director of rehabilitative services and Washington State Senators Cathy Murphy and her polar opposite, Harmon Claremont.

Senator Murphy had been elected ten years earlier on a tidal wave of Democrat landslides across the country. Pledging to work for the "little" people, she was a hardcore tax and spend liberal who had never met a spending package she didn't like. Murphy continued to win re-election because of the many earmarks she attached to each bill that came across her desk. Directing hundreds of millions of dollars in government contracts back to her home state solidified the support she needed from state and local government employee unions. She did however, have some redeemable qualities, in Ray's opinion. She was one of the biggest advocates for national defense, veterans, and a big supporter of the chiropractic profession.

Harmon Claremont, on the other hand, was an "old-school" Republican war hawk who, like his liberal counterpart, catered to the economic concerns of a region once solely reliant on the military industrial complex. Where the senators differed was Claremont's steadfast adherence to his conservative values, which now alienated the younger high tech, eco-friendly demographic that had been growing by leaps and bounds. Murphy was fortunate enough to have been provided with key staff members, courtesy of the DNC, who recognized her limitations early in her first campaign. They kept her focused on the ever-changing hot button issues that insured her political health.

Of the dozens of letters and emails that Ray had sent to both senators over the years, all but one ended up in the hands of staffers whose only job was to match up the letter writer with their donor lists. Not being on either list, most of Ray's letters were tossed in the trash, while some—for profiling and security reasons—were electronically filed away. One day, while entertaining a visiting Seattle news reporter at her D.C. office, Murphy had wanted to show her constituents back home how she stayed in touch with the "common" folk. So, during a live report from Capitol Hill, she had walked over to a pile of letters on a staffer's desk and picked one at random to show to the reporter. As she did so, the staffer, caught off her guard, attempted to redirect the senator's hand to the "approved" pile but it was too late.

"And here's one from a Dr. Ray Silver of Eastridge, Washington," she began. As the reporter looked over the senator's shoulder and with camera zooming in on the body of the letter, Cathy Murphy had realized that she had to read on about the chiropractor who wanted to give up a lucrative private practice and go to work helping veterans. The senator's chief of staff sensed that she was about to step into another potential smelly pile, and decided instead that they could score political points by turning this into sweet-smelling success.

Over the next several weeks Murphy's staff—under threat of retaliation for her own blundering—was quick to put together a pilot project she now championed in spite of the resistance of VMC doctors and administrators. Since she chaired the Senate committee that controlled veteran's health and hospital funding, and since this was clearly going to be a vote-getter among the Independents back home; she would not be deterred. When staffers at Senator Claremont's Seattle office had seen the news story, they were quick to get word out to the local media that Claremont was already in the middle of crafting legislation to expand the availability of "alternative" medicine at veterans' medical facilities.

The day that Ray had first reported to work at the sprawling grounds of the Seattle Regional Veterans Medical Center he was greeted by the smiling senators, Veterans' officials, and a few local reporters who had received press releases from each senator's advance team. First, they posed for a number of pictures. Then Senator Claremont, being the senior member, gave a brief speech before turning the podium over to Senator Murphy. To his dismay, she spoke twice as long as he had, bragging of her efforts to lead the way for integrated health care options for "our deserving veterans who have sacrificed much to keep us free and safe." And then—as if on cue—she put on her famous sad puppy dog look and stared right into the cameras as she continued:

"You know, my dad was a veteran and I saw his suffering firsthand. He never had the options that our brave men and women have today, and as long as I have the ability and the power to make their lives better, then that's what I'm going to do. I'm also very happy that my Republican colleague has decided to join me in my ongoing efforts to spearhead better care for our veterans. That's why you sent me to the other Washington, so you can have *someone* there to stand up for all of you."

When she was finished, the reporters had a few questions for Ray that he never got to answer as Senator Murphy quickly turned the podium over to the VMC public relations officer while the group retired to the administrative offices. Once there, she took Ray aside for a few words of encouragement, mixed with a lot of caution to not let her down, as "I've clearly gone out on a limb for you with this project, Roy. Especially since there was strong vocal opposition amongst several members of the medical staff." Then Claremont had his turn with Ray, who was now more than a little pissed off at how they had used him for political theater. But he also knew that it was in fact Murphy who was responsible for him getting this job and it was definitely her that could make it go away. At the end of the day, they had all gotten what they wanted, and he let the politicking pass. Not that he had any choice, unless he was willing to walk away from this opportunity.

After their little meeting and another photo-op, Cathy Murphy was able to ditch Harmon Claremont and took off with reporters in tow to take a quick tour of the rehab wing at the medical center. Thanks to her professional handlers, she was never one to let a good PR stunt go to waste. Once Murphy and the reporters were gone, Claremont openly complained, calling her an "opportunistic bitch." Seeing no further need to be there, he signaled to his aide they were leaving—finally allowing Ray and members of the administration time to conduct their business. The medical staff laid down the law of how things were going to work.

During several hours of a private pre-meeting strategy session, Ray's new supervisors had decided that since he wasn't a medical doctor, he would be under the immediate supervision of the rehab department, and that *his* patients would be referred to him by the medical staff when they determined that chiropractic care was warranted. Ray protested, citing their lack of experience in chiropractic as well as his twenty-plus years as a licensed health care professional in private practice, examining, diagnosing, and successfully caring for thousands of patients with no need of anyone's approval or oversight. He even offered up the names of several orthopedists at Lakeview who had frequently sent patients to him for care or for second opinions.

In a less-than convincing defense, Peter McCain, the head of rehab services, countered that since Ray was the first chiropractor they had ever had on staff, his appointment was more of a learning experience for them then it was for him. As such, they needed time to understand how his role would be fully integrated into their system. "However," said McCain as their meeting concluded, "it would be best if you prepared an informational lecture, with a PowerPoint if needed. You can present it to the staff…let's say in about two to three weeks?" He looked at Ray to gauge his reaction, but there was none, as Ray was already lost in visualizing the best way to make his presentation to a room full of MDs.

"Oh and uh, Dr. Silver," McCain continued, "when you get your talk all put together, get with Stella Leone in orthopedics. She's one of the head nurses in that department, and she'll set the date and get the word out to the staff."

Ray thought McCain's explanation was bullshit. "Just the jerk's way of micro-managing what I do so he can report back to Senator Murphy without my input," he thought. He had to remind himself to look at the bigger picture. There were surely going to be territorial issues, as he was the new kid on the block—but this is where he wanted to be. He just had to remember that for the first time in twenty years he was no longer the boss. As hard as it seemed, he was going to have to pay his dues, so to speak, and put up with a little nonsense until he showed them what he could do. This was all part of the new life he was making for himself. And now that his practice had been sold, what else could he do? "Ok, it's no big deal," he thought. "I'm exactly where I wanted to be. I'm single and on my own…and I've got a new house… and I am going to make this work… I might have to tweak a few things here and there, but I will make this work… my way."

And his way of staying balanced was to focus on getting his new home up to speed. The Magnolia house was perfect for him. He had always liked being in the city and this location was close to downtown, the waterfront, the basketball arena, and the International District—or Chinatown, to the politically incorrect.

When the kids were young, every now and again the three of them would go to Chinatown for Sunday dim sum breakfast, sneaking out of the house as Jo slept in. Ray had also taken them to several Pilots basketball games each season. Perhaps now he would start going again to both basketball games and Chinatown.

* * *

Whenever he thought of the Pilots, Ray was reminded of Jimmy's youth basketball days. It used to frustrate his coach at the youth club when Jimmy would insist on wearing his number eleven Dieter Schmidt Pilots jersey on game day—a signed replica of which hung on the wall of a local tavern paying tribute to the city's sports legends. Jack, a patient from Ray's former practice, had told him about this popular bar and grill in lower Queen Anne, and it had soon become one of Ray's favorite spots. They didn't have the healthiest food, but the "homemade" chili and cornbread was actually homemade and quickly became one of his regular choices.

Kelsey's Bar and Grill had a number of flat screens mounted on brick walls that were thick with Seattle sports memorabilia. Ray liked the fact that he could watch several games at the same time. It seemed like a good place to go when he didn't feel like cooking for just himself and didn't mind being around some innocuous noise. He had heard from Jack, who bartended there a few nights a week, that sometimes a few of the Pilots players would stop in for a beer after a game. Ray knew the guy had a penchant for exaggeration; after all, a good bartender needs to be able to weave a good tale. But when he heard this, he had glanced up at the pictures of Patton, Schmidt, and Sikman and thought how cool it would have been to have met them. He could still hear the voice of the play-by-play announcer yelling out an "Achtung baby!" every time Schmidt made a spectacular play.

"Patton brings it up on the near side and dishes it to Dawkins at the top of the key. Dawk quickly sends it back to his point man. McIlerney sets a pick on Crippin as Patton breaks to the left. Schmidt

breaks along the baseline and cuts into the paint. Takes the pass from Patton and ACHTUNG BABY, SLAMS IT HOME!"

All in all, Ray liked the feel and the look of Kelsey's, so while making the gradual move from the apartment to the house in Magnolia he occasionally stopped for a quick bite after work or grabbed an order to go.

On one particular Saturday in mid-February, while running a last load of boxes to the house, he had stopped and picked up one of Kelsey's specialty chicken sandwiches and an order of fries. As he was leaving with lunch in hand, he caught the eye of an auburn- haired, brown-eyed, slightly freckled-faced woman sitting in the back corner with her long-time friend Kelsey, the bar's owner.

"What's up Leigh?" she asked, "You know that guy?"

"Not sure," she said, taking another sip of her Pipeline Porter. "He looks very familiar. I've seen him before but I just can't place him right now. Do you know him?"

Kelsey turned and watched him cross the street and get into his Jeep. "He started coming in a few months ago. Seems like a nice enough guy. Always says hello, and he is kinda good-looking. For an older guy, that is. Jack, one of my bartenders, knows him. Always calls him Doc."

Leigh Anne McMillen watched as Ray popped a french fry into his mouth and drove off. "I know that guy," she said to herself.

4

It was a rainy afternoon, and over in the Heights Jo had been cleaning and organizing the storage room when she came across a box of books belonging to Ray. At first she was just going to toss them, thinking, "had he wanted them, he wouldn't have left them behind." She decided she would be fair about it though, and call him to pick them up. But then again, she saw it as a great opportunity to see where his new house was and perhaps get invited in for a quick look-see. "Surely he wouldn't mind me stopping by to bring him his books," she thought. "After all, we are civil to each other." Wanting to look her best, she quickly freshened up and put on a brand-new dress.

Jo carelessly tossed the box onto the front passenger seat of her new Range Rover and hurriedly took off for Seattle. She had just finished leaving a voicemail for Ray when she rounded the sharp downhill turn of the freeway onramp. With her cell phone in one hand, she began to lose control of the steering wheel, and the top-heavy box flipped forward spilling several books across the center console and onto the floor. One book jammed underneath the brake, another on top of the gas pedal, and several more on her feet. Jo lost control of the car. The SUV bounced hard off the guardrail and swerved over to the right shoulder. She dropped the phone and with both hands, overcompensated by turning the wheel hard to the left. Accelerating from both the weight of the books and her foot on the gas pedal, the SUV flew across to the left lane, jumped the center divider, and smashed head on into a tractor-trailer.

The impact immediately separated Jo from the driver's seat, as the momentum of the car was instantly stopped when it made contact with the much heavier and faster truck. Within a millisecond, the combination shoulder harness/lap belt locked, instantly breaking the anterior ribs where they attached to her breast bone. The jagged ends punctured both lungs in multiple places. The force of her trunk moving against the vise-like grip of the lap portion of her harness snapped several vertebrae in her lower back, exposing and tearing the components of the neural canal. The sudden decompression caused by the tear immediately sucked the cerebral spinal fluid away from her brain. The front airbag exploded outward from the steering wheel with enough force to cause her head to snap back with such violent intensity her windpipe ripped like a busted zipper and the top-most vertebra in her neck burst into pieces. As her head recoiled in the opposite direction, a broken piece of bone cut her spinal cord in half. Another piece ripped through one of her carotid arteries, and she was dead before both vehicles came to a complete stop.

At that very instant, standing in his retro-styled kitchen unpacking a box of coffee cups and drinking glasses, Ray felt an icy chill shoot across his neck and shoulders. He went to shut the window but it was closed. Leaning back into the box, he felt something brush across the top of his upper back. Startled, he turned, but of course there was no one else with him. His heart skipped a beat however, when he caught a slight whiff of Jo's favorite perfume as he heard his name faintly echo through the house.

Ray froze and listened to the silence—for what seemed like several minutes—before resuming. He leaned his head into the carton one more time and decided that the smell had come from the box itself. He figured that it once held some of Jo's clothing. He had packed and sealed the box months ago, so it made sense that it retained her smell. Once again he felt a sudden chill, and an image of Jo flashed in his mind. He walked over to his jacket, hanging on the back of a chair by the small rectangular kitchen table, and dug into the pocket for his cell phone. He noticed one message.

"Ray? It's Jo. Don't wanna be a pain, but I was cleaning out the storage closet today and found a box of your books. I'm gonna be downtown anyway, just to do a few errands… Soooo, if it's alright with you I'm gonna stop by real quick and leave it on your doorstep. If your car's in the driveway I'll ring the bell. Maybe. We'll see. Ok then, see ya."

It had been about six weeks since the last time he had seen her, so he thought it would be nice, if for nothing more than to just say hello, receive his books, and perhaps give a quick tour of the little house that overlooked Puget Sound. The last time he did see her, both of them had had lawyers in tow. They had quietly signed the documents that were laid before them. And then it was over. They both stood and looked at each other in an uncomfortable silence, neither one knowing whether to turn and walk away, hug and say goodbye, or simply shake hands. Finally, it was Jo who had taken the lead, as she often had, and nervously shot out her right hand to shake. Ray took her hand in his, held it gently, and slowly caressed the back of her hand with his thumb.

"The other day I was thinking about the first time I brought you home to meet my folks," Ray said as he looked at her.

"I remember that. God, that was so long ago. I was so nervous," She said as she forced a laugh.

"My dad took a liking to you right away."

"Not your mom, though."

"It took her a little while longer. She needed time to get over the religion thing, but she came around."

"Now *my* folks, they both took an instant liking to you. They thought you were such a gentlemen. Little did they know how oversexed you were." Ray looked away and tried not to laugh.

"A lot of water under the bridge, Jo," he said in a more serious tone.

"Well, Raymond, I'm sure we'll see each other from time to time because of the kids," she said with a courteous smile.

"Yes, of course." Ray nodded. Their hands slowly separated and dropped away. As she turned to leave, he hadn't realized that this was the last time he would ever touch her. He hadn't realized that this was the last time he would see her alive.

5

Although the funeral had been a simple one, it took Ray almost two weeks to put it all together. He wanted to give Jo a sunrise graveside service, as a fitting send-off to the woman who had become a night owl. During the early years when the kids were young, Jo had often complained that there were never enough hours in the week to get all of her things done. Between school projects for the kids, grocery shopping, laundry, and her volunteer work, she soon found it much easier to delve into her projects and chores when the family had finally gone to bed. It didn't take long for her to realize that without interruptions, she was more efficient. But each morning as the sun would begin to creep above the Cascade mountain range to the east, her eyes would grow heavy. Summoning her last few ounces of energy, she would drag herself from her desk and make her way into bed. Jo's head no sooner hit the pillow than she was gone to the world until early afternoon. And even though this contributed to the decline of the intimate part of their relationship, Ray—a lifelong early bird—became the one who got the kids up, fed them, and brought them to school. Jo picked them up in the afternoon, chauffeured them to post-school activities, helped them with their studies, and got them to bed. Overall, it worked out pretty well for all four of them. Remembering this, Ray thought it should be no different now than it had been in life. It was only fitting she should be laid to her final rest with the morning sunrise.

He was thankful that Casey was close by, living just off-campus at the university. Between the two of them it had been easier to coordinate with the funeral parlor and the cemetery as they figured out the weather forecast trying to minimize the chance of rain or even overcast skies. Getting Jo's parents up from Scottsdale, Ray's dad from Florida, Jimmy from Georgetown, and dealing with his new responsibilities at work took a little more effort. Ray's dad had recently turned seventy-seven and his health was starting to decline. Even though he had insisted that his father didn't need to come, Ron insisted on making the trip. Jo had always been kind to Ron, especially after Ray's mom had passed away seven years earlier. Ron had appreciated her thoughtfulness in sending yearly birthday gifts and constant updates with pictures of the kids. So he felt that it was only right to come pay his last respects. He also didn't know how many more opportunities he would have to see his grandchildren, so he jumped at every opportunity—provided he was well enough.

Over the course of the twelve days from the time of the accident to the day of the funeral, there had been some stress in getting it to all come together. The most stress he experienced though, was from trying to come up with a eulogy. There were so many things he thought about. So many things he had wanted to say, but nothing that he had wanted to share. The memories, good and bad alike, were his. People already knew about the "public" Jo and they were free to discuss her at will. To talk publicly about the woman he had had to himself, who had confided in him her most secret of secrets would, in his mind be a betrayal of an unspoken trust they had honored all those years, even through their divorce.

So, feeling an obligation to say something, he shared a few things that people had already known and could easily relate to. He talked about how dedicated she was to her kids and how, regardless of motivation, when she committed to a school project or charitable event, she gave one hundred percent of herself until the project was completed. And almost as an after-thought, and with a little persuading from Casey, he decided to share one private thing. He talked about the time Jo had insisted they rent a motorhome to drive across the country on summer vacation.

"She said, 'It's about time the kids really see America'." He couldn't resist relating how she had slept most of the way because she always fell asleep whenever riding in a car for longer than thirty minutes. "I kid you not," Ray continued in response to the chuckles coming from the small gathering. "She was so determined that the kids got to see America up close and personal that she went ahead and rented this amaz-ing motorhome. It was loaded with more amenities than we had in our own house. I warned her that it was too comfort-able. Within minutes of hitting the freeway... I mean, we didn't even get out of the county and she was out like a light."

The night before, unable to sleep and still debating what to share, Ray had written a five-page letter to Jo, sealed it in an envelope, and tucked it away in the inside pocket of his overcoat. Later, driving behind the hearse through the dark empty streets from the funeral home, he had felt the fatigue slowly building. But as they drove, he noticed the city slowly awakening, with a random pedestrian here and there, a pass-ing car, a flickering neon sign coming on at a corner coffee shop. And as the snow-capped peak of Mount Rainier slowly turned from dark purple to pink the irony of a city coming to life—at the same time that Jo was being taken to her final rest—didn't escape him.

For the most part Ray's words were off the cuff and he kept them short. Jimmy and Casey also stood before the casket and the small group of Jo's family and closest friends. With the morning sun rising, they each delivered an emotionally heartfelt tribute to their mother that freely brought tears to all in attendance. When the services concluded and everyone had made their way back to the cars, Ray stayed behind, briefly studying the envelope he had taken from his overcoat. He summoned an attendant to help him gently lift the corner lid of the casket so he could place the letter inside. He stood for a moment longer, feeling a need to say something before he left.

"I got the kids, don't worry." He rubbed his hand across the top of her coffin and made his way back to the car.

The group gathered back at the house that Ray and Jo had once shared and in which they had once had raised their family. He had a lunch catered and received additional guests from the neighborhood. After a short while, formality gave way as one after another began to share their favorite memories of Mary Jo DeStefano-Silver. Casey commented how special the holidays had always been. With one Catholic and one Jewish parent the kids had gotten the best of both worlds, celebrating Christmas and Chanukah every year. Jimmy drew some laughs when he compared the toys and candy of Christmas to the eight nights of school supplies during Chanukah.

It had been a few years since Jimmy had spent any length of time in his childhood home.

Throughout his undergraduate years, ROTC had him traveling during his summers with classes and training sessions. He had always made it home for Christmas and Thanksgiving, though. His memories of growing up in that house notwithstanding, his attachment wasn't as strong as Casey's. Deep down, she wished her father would move back in, but it was no longer his. He wouldn't have wanted to anyway.

Ray never was too crazy about the house. To him, it was an endless project of repair, replace, and remodel that consumed too much of his free time and even more of his patience—especially when it challenged his ability. He did, however, find solace in his garden. The southwest location of the backyard allowed for maximum sun exposure during a short Western Washington growing season. He had taken pride in making homemade pasta sauce and salsa from his heirloom tomatoes, onions, and wide selection of freshly grown herbs. He delighted in coming home on late summer evenings and seeing little Casey sitting in the garden eating snap peas fresh off the vine. He wouldn't miss the house, but he wished he could keep his garden.

In her final will—which she had rewritten during their divorce—Jo left instructions to donate her clothes to the local church thrift shop and put the house up for sale. The proceeds and the rest of her possessions were to be shared equally between the children. Several months later, when the house did sell, Ray was taken by surprise when the kids gave him an equal share. It was not something he had asked for, but it was something they had known he deserved.

It had been a long two weeks, and the lack of sleep from the night before finally hit Ray. He excused himself and went to his former bedroom to rest. Within minutes of lying down, he was fading in and out of sleep. He hadn't been in that room for well over six months, and yet he felt as if he could have been between the sheets the night before. Jo's scent permeated the duvet cover and he half-expected her to come out of the walk-in closet complaining about a stain on her new white blouse. His body grew heavy as he drifted. In a stupor-like state he heard the echo of voices. He heard little children laughing as they ran in and out of the bedroom.

"Daddy, daddy" came the happy squeal. Ray smiled as he tried to lift his head. *"Daddy, come and play!"* He heard the call again. He felt a small hand pat his cheek and he smiled again. He heard the echo of Jo's voice calling out, *"Kids, stop making so much noise, your father's trying to rest."* Ray opened his eyes as he tried to pick up his head. Jo leaned over and smiled. He thought she looked so young. *"Don't get up sweetie,"* she said, placing her hand on his shoulder. *"You're tired, just rest. I got the kids, don't worry."* He put his head back down as he felt the coldness of her touch. He mumbled, "Ok, I'll lay ba…"

Ray bolted upright on the bed as he shouted out, "NO!" He looked around the room and realized he was alone. The hallway was quiet. He felt a shiver go through him. "It was a dream, it was a dream," he repeated, rubbing his face with both hands. "It was just a dream."

6

Later that evening back at the house in Magnolia, Ray threw another log into the stone fireplace. Ashes scattered and embers danced into the air as they were gently sucked up into the flue. The sizzle and crackle of steaming water vapor intermittently broke the silence. Ray's dad came out of the kitchen with a large mug of tea "warmed" with a shot of brandy. He settled into an easy chair close to the fireplace. Opposite, was a view beyond the picture window of a Seattle skyline lit up against the dark of the night. Late winter and early spring evenings in the Pacific Northwest came with a chill and provided a good excuse to make a fire. On the mantle, made of hand-rubbed old growth timber, were several native carvings from the Makah, Willapa and Chinook tribes depicting Salmon and Orca. Ray stabbed at the logs with a poker, enticing the flames to dance a little higher. He went over to the small desk in the corner, picked up a large book, and gently placed it onto his father's lap.

"Is that where you do most of your research work now?"

"For now. I'm building a workbench and desk in the garage. There's a wide strip of space that runs along the car bay. Has a window with a nice view."

"Want me to help you? When you were a kid, ya always seemed to cut yourself when ya worked with tools, if ya know what I mean."

"That was red paint that spilled on the floor in the hardware store, Pop," Ray said without smiling, and took a drink from his beer. "And it was only once or twice."

"Or three times?" Ron waited for a reaction. "Your kids look all grown up, Raymond."

"They look like their mother."

"Casey looks just like her. Jimmy has her colorin', has your frame and cheekbones though. He's so tall. What, about six-three?"

"Six-one. He only looks tall, Pop, because you're shrinking."

Ron laughed as he picked up the book that was lying in his lap. "Well, he's taller than both of us. I think he's got ya by three inches."

"Two," Ray said with a smile. "He's got me by two. Speaking of which, Jimmy heads back to Georgetown in two days. Graduation is the third week of May."

"And then my grandson's a Navy lawyer?"

"Yup. I understand he'll be in Bethesda at first and then maybe assigned to a carrier group, but it's just talk right now. We'll see. I think Casey's done... one or two weeks before him. Gotta check my calendar on that. No idea yet about her assignment. I'm hoping it'll be on a base here—stateside that is, rather than sea duty."

"There's gonna be a big demand for nurses in the Gulf region now that this war is underway."

"She'll be fine, Pop." Ray walked back over to the fireplace and poked at the logs a few more times. "She's a newly commissioned officer fresh out of school. It'll be quite a while before she'd be sent anywhere near the Gulf. And I'll bet this thing'll be over as quick as Desert Storm was."

"From your lips to God's ears." Ron looked into his white ceramic cup, took a sip, and looked back out at the city through the picture window.

"How would ya feel if one day Jimmy or Casey told you they'd wanna pursue their careers in the private sector?"

Ray stopped poking the logs and turned to his dad "What, have they said something to ya?"

"No, I'm just sayin'."

"I don't know, why, what's goin' on? Did one of them..?"

"No, no, not at all. But one day, one or both of `em just might wanna travel a different path, that's all."

"I never thought about it. I mean...it's possible...but they're so into this, I never considered..."

"Look it, did ya ever even give `em a choice? I mean, ever since they were old enough to listen to ya, that's all ya ever talked about, if ya know what I mean."

Ray put down the poker and sat down opposite his dad. "Yeah, I mean, I showed them the picture albums and told them about their Uncle Frank..."

"And you took them to see the ships during every Fleet Week, and on and on."

"Yes, I did all those things, but I never really pushed..."

"Yeah ya did. And Jo, God rest her soul, told me how you used to tell the kids about the 'family tradition' and how they were gonna be the first commissioned officers."

"No different from what you used to do...almost."

Ron placed his cup down onto the coffee table. "Look Raymond, your grandfather joined the service a few years after he and your grandmother emigrated from Eastern Europe just as the first war broke out. He wanted to prove that he was a good American. Your Uncle Jim left home and joined the Navy in the late thirties because of the Depression. He couldn't find work anywhere. He was desperate. The Navy gave him what he needed. A home, a job, and every adventure a young single man could hope for."

Ray had never heard this before, but he didn't see how this changed things. "And you, Pop? What about you?"

"I joined in `43 as soon as I turned seventeen. There was a war on. America was different in those days. Guys who got rejected for medical reasons went home and killed themselves.

I signed up because we all had a duty. The free world was going to hell."

"Ok fine, but you guys don't have a monopoly on patriotism."

"No, we don't, but things were different then is all I'm sayin'. We joined for different reasons. You and your brother were the ones who turned it into a tradition. During your brother's time, it wasn't common for kids to go runnin' off to fight in Southeast Asia."

"Is that what this is about? Frank?"

Ron sat silent for a few moments and stared into the fireplace. The burning logs broke the silence with a crackle here and there. "I think about him a lot, Raymond," he said, maintaining his gaze into the fire. "I think about whether or not I filled him with so much propaganda that he ran off in `71 to live up to an image that I created. Not just for him, but for both of you."

Ray leaned a little more forward toward his dad. "No, Pop. It's not that way at all."

"Isn't it though?" Ron looked over at his son, staring right into his eyes.

"God forbid, Raymond, I'm not worried about Jimmy. He's not gonna be in harm's way, if ya know what I mean, but if anything happens to that little girl, if she's flyin' in to a hot LZ on an evac and they take fire and somethin' happens to her, God forbid, Raymond, I swear that's gonna stay with you for the rest of your life." He leaned his head back into the chair and let out a sigh. "I think about Frank all the time, Ray. All the time."

Ray saw that his dad was upset. He decided to end the discussion.

"I know, Pop. I do know, I think about Frank too. But it's not your fault, I swear it's not. Frank made it through Vietnam. He came home. He could have stayed home. It was his choice to stay in, not because of you or the stories about Uncle Jim. He stayed in because he loved it. He stayed in because it was what he was born to do. I know this, Pop, because we spoke about it. Frank told me how much he loved it and could never see himself doing anything else. If not for anything else, you introduced him to something he loved more than anything. Would you feel any different if you had introduced him to the wonderful world of long-haul trucking and he ended up getting killed in a crash on the Interstate?"

"I guess you're right. But the thing that's bothered me all these years was that last secret mission."

"What secret mission?" Ray asked.

"Ya know, that final mission his team was on was a secret mission, not a training exercise like we were told. I told ya about it years ago."

"No Pop, you never mentioned anything about a secret mission."

"Your brother had mailed me a letter saying they were going on a mission and it was very hush-hush. He wanted me to know just in case anything went wrong. He wanted me to know... just in case...because if it did, the Navy was never gonna tell us what really happened."

"You never said anything before, Pop. I swear, this is the first I'm hearing this."

"I'm sorry, I thought I'd told you."

"That's why you were insisting they'd gone into Cambodia. I remember when we got final notification that there were no survivors from the chopper crash, you disputed the story."

"It was because of Frank's letter. But I couldn't tell anyone he had sent it. He was never supposed to have told anyone what they were up to."

"So you know the whole story?"

"No. he never gave me any details. I think...I may still have that original letter."

"I'd like to see it."

"I'll have to look for it when I get back home. I don't know where it is. After we got word that he died, your mother packed up all his things along with that letter and another package of papers he mailed to us. The box got put in the attic and I forgot all about it."

"What package of papers?"

"It was a big manila envelope. He asked that I leave it sealed and to put it in a safe place. So that's what I did."

"Well, at least they're easy to find, right?"

"I hope so. After your mother passed and when I moved down to Tampa I had all that stuff shipped and thrown into storage. When I get back home I'll look for it."

It was quiet for a few minutes although it seemed much longer. Neither said a word. Ray got up from his chair and walked over to the window.

"And you?" Ron said as he held the book up and waved it at Ray to get his attention. "Is this what you've come to love? Are ya still researchin' LCIs?"

Ray continued to look out at the city lights. "There's one here on Lake Union. You know, the 776. I told you about her."

"I don't remember."

"Yeah, I first saw her docked at the south end about a year ago, rustin' away. I stopped to check it out and met this guy Walters, John Walters. The guy's an old swift boat skipper, served in Vietnam. Says his dad served on LCIs. Anyway, the 776 was being used by a local fishing company as a floating storage locker. So Walters made an offer for it and for the last two years he's been workin' with some of his friends and some volunteers to restore her. I'm thinkin' about…maybe…helping out from time to time."

Ron sat up in his chair, his interest piqued. "Is she in good shape? Can we go see her?"

"No, not now. I mean she's not berthed here right now. From what I understand, she's out getting a new hull. It was pretty bad. Below decks you could see little pinholes of light coming through and the deck plating was pretty wet. They were lucky to raise enough money to get the new bottom. Good thing, too. The Coast Guard was threatening to tow her out to sea and sink her as an artificial reef."

Ron looked disappointed so Ray promised to fly him back out when the 776 returned to her slip. He slowly got up, stiff from arthritis in his hips and lower back, turned and gently tossed the big blue book titled "THE LCIs" onto his chair. "It's late, I'm gonna go to bed."

"Good night, Pop. Don't forget, the kids are comin' over around noon and we're goin' for lunch."

Walking with a limp, Ron slowly turned around and said, "Good, I'm lookin' forward to trying that homemade chili and cornbread you were tellin' me about." He turned to leave, stopped, and half-turned back to Ray. "Side ramps?"

"What?"

"The 776. Does she have side ramps?"

"Yes, as a matter of fact she does. And she has a round con."

"The 606 had side ramps, and she had a round pilot house too, not a square con like the older ones."

"Yeah, I know Pop. I saw... I have the pictures of her."

"Oh yeah, ya do. I forgot." Ron began to turn again and stopped. "Ya know, Raymond, I think it's great what you're doing, workin' at the VMC and all, if ya know what I mean."

"Thanks. That means a lot."

Ray was physically and mentally fatigued from the events of the past few weeks. The conversation he had with his dad had his mind churning, and it bothered him. He walked into his kitchen and looked around inside the refrigerator for something to eat. Foraging through some of the packaged leftovers he had brought home from the post-funeral gathering, he realized that if he gave in to his old habit of eating while stressed he would probably start putting back the weight he had recently struggled to take off. He closed the refrigerator, sighed, walked back to the living room, and returned to poking the logs in the fireplace. "What if dad is right?" he thought. "What if the kids are now leading a life that they might not have chosen if not for me always leading the charge?"

When he did finally go to bed, Ray tossed and turned the rest of the night, wondering what had given him the right to guide his kids into a lifestyle in order to fulfill a desire that he had been denied.

7

The next morning Ray got up at his normal five a.m. time. He threw on a pair of sweats, and before he headed out for his three mile walk, he stopped for a brief moment by the opened guestroom door and listened for his dad's breathing. Years of smoking and asbestos exposure had contributed to Ron's declining health, and it was evident to Ray as he listened to the heaviness of each draw of breath. Confident that his dad was doing ok, he headed out. He'd been carrying out this morning ritual for several years now. When the kids were in grade school, he ran three miles faithfully every morning—until a rear- end collision on the freeway had ended all that. The impact and subsequent injury had caused a positional shift to a lower vertebra that had previously been compromised by stress fractures. Although this condition hadn't prevented him from participating in youthful adventures, an x-ray taken in his senior year of high school had revealed the non- symptomatic defect. The only pain this had caused him prior to the car accident was the gut-stabbing rejection he had gotten from Navy doctors when they saw the diagnosis of "bilateral pars fracture-L5" in his personal medical file.

Remembering how he had tried to plead his case, Ray even offered to demonstrate his physical ability. He went back to the recruiter and insisted on telling him about his grandfather stoking boilers on the USS Texas and Uncle Jim and the Arizona, but found himself being escorted out to the street. *"Look, son,"* the recruiter had said, *"I appreciate your enthusiasm. God knows we need more patriots just like you, but there's just no way the docs will pass you."* The big Chief Petty Officer had headed back into his office, and as an afterthought, said, *"Write a letter of appeal and mail it in. Maybe they'll bring you in for an exam. Ya got nothin' left to lose, right?"*

After several appeals sent up the chain of command had been denied, Ray was heartbroken. He had found himself reliving that conversation since moving to the Magnolia house. Sometimes it was triggered by the sight of a ship heading out from the Bremerton Naval Yard and sometimes it happened when passing the occasional jogger, sparking his desire to run again, which then reminded him of how that could set off episodes of lower back pain. Deep down, however, Ray knew that being around all of the veterans at the hospital was the main catalyst for the recurring memory.

Except for an early morning dog-walker, he braved the chill of another moist February morning alone. Once in a while, he would pass a bicyclist or jogger, and he would always nod to them in an attempt at being a good neighbor. Only the men seemed to acknowledge him. The women would stiffen and trudge on ahead, pretending they hadn't seen his greeting. He thought there had been more people over in Eastridge Heights who were exercise-minded. Either that or maybe they were out walking or jogging so that they could be seen out walking or jogging by those who were out doing the same. Everything there was always about image. It seemed that the women as well as the men would go out of their way to wave to others as they passed. It was always amusing to him how they would all end up at the espresso place on Lakeview Drive, making a show of their new designer running outfits or talking about major stock deals while slowly sipping lattes and secretly hoping for a ride home.

He was looking forward to having lunch down at Kelsey's with his dad and the kids. Jimmy and Casey had been staying at the "old" house, keeping an eye on Jo's folks while having a nostalgic few days reminding each other of how the gash had gotten into the door of the guest bathroom, or how their mom had completely lost it when an endless river of thick suds poured out of the dishwasher after someone had tripled the amount of concentrated soap. It was their last two nights in the house they had grown up in, and the two of them stayed up late, savoring every last second. They told each other one story after another as they laughed, cried, and then laughed again. But neither one would claim responsibility for the river of soap suds that had warped a small section of the hardwood floor in the kitchen. Not wanting to face Jo's wrath, Ray never did own up to that mistake.

As the kids reminisced, they had to frequently remind themselves that their grandparents were asleep—giggling as if they were little children once again. Casey slowly thumbed through one of the many picture albums their mom had meticulously put together over the years. "So, you don't mind if I hold onto these?" she said, flipping another page.

"No, go ahead, take them. Just as long as you make some copies for me, I'll be fine."

"Mom really went overboard on these things. She used to stay up to all hours with her scrapbooking stuff. She was a woman possessed."

"And you used to give her the hardest time about it, too."

"Yeah, so did you," she said in protest, gently nudging his shoulder.

"Yeah, I think we all did," Jimmy said as he looked up at the framed picture of Jo and Ray that sat on the middle shelf of the bookcase. A lone tear ran down Casey's cheek.

"I'm gonna miss her, Jimmy. I really am."

He pulled his sister in for a reassuring hug. "Yeah, me too. Hey, do you remember the time in high school when you and Eric Hamilton were working on that 'school project'?"

Dropping her head into her hands, she laughed. "Oh God, how can I forget?"

"You guys were all over each other," Jimmy said as his laugh grew louder. "Then Dad walked into your room because of the noise and saw Hamilton on top of you."

"Grabbed the poor kid by the nape of the neck and scared the shit out of him. Me too!"

"Dad said he 'escorted' him out of the house, but he practically lifted him into the air, his feet barely touching the ground as he threw him out."

"I was scared shitless. Daddy says he doesn't remember screaming at him, but his face was beet red as he threatened to cut Hamilton's balls off if he ever came near me again. I was sooo mad at Dad. "

"Come on, admit it, he saved your butt that day and as it turned out, he did you a favor."

"Well, yeah, he did. I always knew Eric was a party animal. To think that it could have been me instead of Alyson Gordon who got killed that night he crashed his car."

"And he never got into any trouble for being stoned, did he?"

"A rich daddy who has connections can be your 'get out of jail free card'."

Ray was appreciative that the kids played babysitter to their grandparents during that week. All four of them had been busy packing up the house and thankfully—with Casey's help—the DeStefanos were heading back to Scottsdale as soon as they packed up the rest of Jo's belongings. Not that they were a bother, or that they didn't get along. In fact, they got along quite well.

With everyone in town though, things had ground to a halt for Ray and it was beginning to get on his nerves. He just wanted to get back to his routine. Jimmy would be flying back to school the next morning, and his dad would be flying back on the evening red eye to his retirement community in Florida. Then, he would pretty much be all alone. In addition to his new job, he had been getting more involved in his 606 research project, and the thought of putting in some time helping to restore that LCI at Lake Union was becoming more attractive to him. He would continue to meet up with Casey from time to time for a quick bite, but after her graduation in mid-May, she'd be off for training and then to points unknown. Their lunch that afternoon would be the last meal the four of them would ever have together.

Ray pulled up to Kelsey's and parked his Wrangler right in front. It was rare to get street parking in lower Queen Anne. One normally had to drive around the block several times and catch someone just pulling out of a space. The only other option was one of the private pay lots closer to the basketball arena. As he pulled up, he saw his old Honda minivan parked down the street. "Good," he thought. "They're already here." Since he had had a few errands to take care of after his morning exercise, he had the kids take the van to pick up their grandfather. On the way, they made a quick stop at the fish market in Pike Place, where Ron had picked up a few smoked samplers to be shipped back to his apartment in Florida and to Jimmy's place in Georgetown.

* * *

It had been two weeks since Leigh Anne McMillen had last seen Ray making that quick lunch pick-up. She had recognized the face, but couldn't place him. Jack, the bartender, had been able to give her some information, but it didn't help. Sitting at the bar with a cup of coffee and the morning paper, she didn't take notice of the older man with two college-aged kids in a back booth of the dining room. The flash of red that reflected off Kelsey's front window from the rare February sunshine did get her attention, though. She looked up to see "Doc" Silver— as Jack called him—get out of his Jeep and walk in through the front door. Ray stopped for a minute to let his eyes adjust to the darker interior lighting before noticing his dad and the kids sitting at the other end of the room. Seeing menus and drinks already on the table, he walked over to the front of the rectangular bar and ordered a Pipeline. Hearing this, Leigh Anne finally made the connection. "Lanikai. Of course!" she thought to herself. "That's where I know him from. He's the klutz that fell into me. Hmm, he grew a goatee and lost some weight!"

The bartender handed Ray a cold longneck, and pointing to the booth in the dining room, he asked her to add it to his lunch check. He didn't notice Leigh Anne—sitting off at the back left corner of the bar—as he went to join his family. Maybe the fact that she was hiding behind her newspaper had something to do with it.

From what little she knew of him, Leigh Anne found Ray interesting, from the clumsiness of his awkward attempt at meeting her at Kimo's to his sudden appearance at Kelsey's several weeks later. When she heard from Jack that he was recently divorced, his being older was now an asset. In her mind, he was not some married guy looking for a plaything on the side— although in Hawaii, he probably had been looking to play. Nor was he some younger guy looking for a casual 'hook up'. And although that had some benefits, she thought, "I'm not wasting my time with that nonsense. Nope, not me. I want nothing to do with that game. But this Doc Silver is a different story altogether. He's a professional guy, recently single, grown kids, and judging by the way we first met, he's definitely not in the habit of trying to pick up women. If he was, then he was certainly bad at it, which probably meant he hadn't met many, if any at all, since acquiring his freedom." She was convinced that he was a fish out of water, so to speak.

For the past couple of years Kelsey had been lecturing her to stop punishing herself. She had not allowed herself to get involved with anyone, and with Kelsey's help she had come to realize that it was finally ok to do so. "This could be good" Leigh said to herself as she got up from her stool. "at least this guy seems genuine." She slowly followed him into the dining room. "And, he's kinda cute."

As Ray made his way over to the back booth, Jimmy looked up to greet him. "Hey Dad, just in time. We already ordered."

"I went ahead and ordered that chili for ya," Ron quickly added.

Ray nodded and was placing his beer on the table when he noticed Casey looking over his shoulder. He turned around, coming face to face with Leigh Anne. She abruptly stopped to avoid crashing into him and hadn't quite thought about how she was going to say hello. Their eyes made contact, and it took him just a second to remember her face. He felt his heart rate increase. She looked a little different now that her tan was beginning to fade. Her brown eyes, however, were clearly the same. Her red plaid flannel shirt, jeans, and hiking shoes were a far departure from the t-shirt covered swimsuit she was wearing the last time they had met. For a moment, there was silence between them. Leigh Anne clearly felt the three pairs of eyes staring at her from the table.

"Oh, um, excuse me, I didn't mean to sneak up on you like that."

"No...not at all. I wasn't... I mean I didn't..."

"I recognized you from Kimo's," she said, waiting a few seconds for recognition. "In Hawaii?" Again, she waited, but Ray was processing a flood of information all at once. From the shape of her face, to the smoothness of her mouth to the curves accentuated by her jeans. He didn't know if he should respond or introduce her to the others. Then he realized he didn't know her name.

Now it was Leigh Anne who felt awkward. "Well," she continued as she stuffed her hands into her back pockets, "I recognized you and I just wanted to say hello." She glanced down at Ray's family and knew this was the wrong time. "I...I'm interrupting here."

"No...no. Uh...this is my dad, Ron, and my kids, Jimmy and Casey." Ray said turning an outstretched arm toward the table.

"And we're having one last lunch together," piped in a suddenly over-protective Casey.

Leigh Anne felt embarrassed. When he walked in, she had been so focused on him that she thought he had been alone.

"Well, again I just wanted to say hi…again. I'm sorry for the intrusion." She turned to walk away.

Ray quickly turned back to the table and glared at his daughter. She shrugged her shoulders and looked at the others for support. "I'll be right back," he said as he walked off to catch up to Leigh Anne.

Feeling foolish, she had walked back to her stool at the other side of the bar and was gathering up her newspaper and keys. She turned to leave, not knowing that Ray was practically on her heels. Her forehead crashed right into his face.

"Oh, jeez!" Ray blurted out, his hands going up to grab onto his nose.

Leigh Anne's head jerked back from the impact, her newspaper and keys falling to the floor. "Oh, man…damn, that hurt." She blurted out as she looked at him. "Oh you're such a klutz! And…you have a hard head, Doc."

He opened his eyes, not knowing if she knew who he was or if she was using "doc" as a generic expression. She rubbed her head still looking right at him. "Hey, I'm sorry," Ray said. "I didn't expect you to whip around like that."

"Seems to be a common theme here this afternoon."

"You ok?"

"Yeah, I'm just gonna have a bit of a headache, but I'll manage. You?"

"I'll survive." He bent down to pick up her things and placed them on the bar. Still rubbing his nose, he continued. "Hey, I'm sorry about…"

"No, not a problem. It was an accident, I think."

"No, not that. Well, yeah, about that, I…I'm sorry. It *was* an accident. I shouldn't have been so close. But I meant about my kid." Ray motioned to the dining room.

"Well, she was kind of abrupt. What's up with that?"

"We, uh…we buried my ex-wife yesterday. She was killed in a freak car accident about two weeks ago and yesterday was the funeral." Leigh Anne shifted her focus to the back booth in the dining room and then back to Ray.

"I'm sorry, I didn't know."

"No, how could you possibly...well, Casey—my daughter—is a little protective. Anyway, my dad's heading back to Florida late tonight, and my son and daughter are heading back to school, so we were just having a sort of last lunch."

There was an awkward silence that seemed to have gone on for at least a minute. Again Leigh Anne looked into the dining room. "Well, I recognized you and I...I thought it would be a nice thing to say hey, remember me? That's all that was about."

"I see. Well, uh... I do remember our meeting at that place by the beach...Kiki's? Kono's? Yeah, that's it, Kono's."

"Kimo's," she said.

"Kimo's," he affirmed. "Yeah, you already said that. Great place, really good food, and what a great location."

"Yeah, it is a great place. I'll tell my cousin that you liked it."

Ray look at her quizzically.

"You remember the guy who came out of the kitchen when you knocked over my beer?"

"Yes, I do. The gigantic Hawaiian guy, right?' Ray said as he lifted one arm up toward the ceiling to demonstrate Kimo's height. "That's your cousin?"

"Yeah, kind of. Not blood, but we're close enough." They looked at each other, and again there was silence. "Ask her, you fool," Ray said to himself.

"So, uh...listen, I think I'm a good judge of character, and I think you're feeling just as awkward as I am right now. So I was wondering, does it have to be just a passing hello, remember me? Nice to see ya, goodbye? I mean, after I met you that day I honestly never thought we'd run into each other again. No pun intended," he said as he rubbed his nose. "If it's ok with you...would you like to meet here for a Pipeline? Well, that is, if you want," he added half smiling at her. "I promise I won't butt into your head or knock your beer over...You don't have t..."

She cut him off. "Sure, that would be nice." She turned and leaned over the bar to grab a napkin and pen to jot down her number. Ray couldn't help but notice how nice she looked in her jeans. "Just as nice as when she was leaning over the bar at Kimo's," He thought. She sensed he was taking her all in—again—and smiled to herself as she took her time writing the information. Leigh Anne turned, and handing it to him, she said, "This week, ok?"

"Yes, absolutely. This week."

She smiled, rubbed her head, and headed for the door. "You've got a hard head, Doc."

He watched her leave Kelsey's and climb into an older model 4x4 pickup truck when he realized he had forgotten—again—to ask for her name. He quickly glanced at the paper napkin and relaxed when he saw it boldly written and underlined next to her number. He looked back up and saw her just sitting in her truck. She turned to see Ray standing by the big plate glass window with the hand-painted sign spelling out "KELSEY'S". He thought it odd that she was just sitting there. She thought it odd that he was just standing there watching her. Ray glanced over at the bar, and noticed that she had left her car keys and newspaper. Leigh Anne was just sitting there, tapping her fingers across the top of the steering wheel, waiting for him to rejoin his family. He gently folded the napkin and put it in his shirt pocket as he walked back to his table. Embarrassed at the sloppy exit, Leigh Anne got out of her truck, ran back across the street, and shot in to Kelsey's to grab her keys.

With one hand covering the bridge of his nose, Casey saw the redness in his face and had a laugh at his expense. Being the occasional wise mouth that she could be, she couldn't resist chiding her father. "Looks like your dating skills are quite rusty, Dad."

"Thanks, wiseass," he said as he slid into the booth right next to her. Ray looked at the others quietly returning to their lunch. He looked at his bowl of chili.

"Hey, listen, I didn't plan that, ya know."

"We're not saying anything, Dad," responded Jimmy.

"Your Mom and I hadn't..."

"Dad, it's ok. Really! We know your relationship with Mom had been over long before the divorce. I'm just giving you a hard time." Casey said.

"You're sure it's ok?"

"Totally." Casey assured him with a sly grin. "Besides, you probably struck out anyway."

Ray took the bar napkin out of his pocket and waved it at her. "Don't be so sure of yourself." They nudged each other playfully and laughed.

8

Dr. Leigh Anne McMillen had been contemplating moving back to Oahu for several months when she first met Ray at Kimo's in 2002. At thirty years old, she had returned to her native home three years after earning her doctorate in marine biology to interview for a future position at the Oahu Aquarium. Having worked there a number of years earlier she hoped that her past employment would help her secure a position, which were typically hard to come by. Leigh had moved to Seattle in the winter of 1994 with the goal of getting into graduate school while working part-time at the local aquarium on Elliot Bay. Her plan had seemed simple enough: temporarily live and work with her friend Kelsey until she began her doctoral studies and/or until she got hired at the aquarium. It took a year, but by the winter of '95 she had traded serving fish and chips to the patrons at Kelsey's to serving whole fish to the sea otters at the aquarium. And finally—after a few submissions—her application to graduate school was accepted.

During that time, she had been extremely focused on her studies and her job as if she was on a mission. Although Leigh Anne did not want to admit it, Kelsey knew that she had buried herself in her work in an effort to avoid any chance of getting involved in another relationship. For all intents and purposes, she had isolated herself from all but the most boring group-based social activities—and only doing those on rare occasions to get Kelsey to stop nagging her. Still, it didn't stop a number of very interested and good-looking men from being drawn to her beauty. As intrigued and enticed as they were by her willingness to engage in light-hearted small talk, they were soon frustrated and gave up trying to break through her impenetrable wall.

She was very successful in her graduate work, very successful at her job, and extremely successful at pushing away everyone who showed any interest in her. Since her self-imposed exodus from Oahu, she had purposely maintained her focus on everything but the question that had been raised by Father Dominick. Before allowing herself the comfort of companionship, she knew she would have to face and perhaps finally reconcile with her conscience. She was not, however, immune to the effects of avoiding a serious relationship.

One typical Friday evening, she found herself, yet again, sitting on her favorite stool at Kelsey's unwinding from the week with an ice-cold Pipeline Porter. The conversations with several couples who were regulars at the popular sports bar, were not much different from any other Friday evening. But when the talk turned to favorite movies to watch while cuddling and a "couples only" ski weekend at Crystal Mountain, Leigh Anne suddenly felt like the proverbial fifth wheel. Noticing the flush in her face, one of her friends had been quick to try to include her.

"No, that's ok" she said in an effort to brush off the well-meaning invitation. "I'm not much for the snow." Laughing off her embarrassment, she continued, "Now give me a longboard and some North Shore wave action and I'm with you guys." The group laughed with her, but the energy that had existed just seconds before was replaced with an awkwardness made even more obvious when Leigh Anne looked at her watch and excused herself.

Later that evening she found herself sitting alone on her couch in tears, watching one of those "great movies to cuddle to".

Seven years after leaving her home and avoiding confrontation with an issue she knowingly suppressed, she had come to accept the fact it was now time to do just that. Leigh Anne knew that the best way for her to do so, was to return to the scene of the crime, so to speak. She realized she truly missed her home, and maybe it was time to go back. She had contacted the HR director at the aquarium on Oahu and arranged a meeting in January. And with Molokai being an easy detour, she would also go to St. Philomena's—six months earlier than her annual visit.

During the years she had been away, she had periodically kept in touch with Kimo. So after her pilgrimage to Molokai and her meeting at the Oahu Aquarium, she headed up the highway from Makapuu to Lanikai. When she pulled up to the Oceanside restaurant a flood of memories came back to her all at once. She thought of driving off, but Kimo was quick to come out, excited to see her. He was a massive Polynesian who loved life, loved food, and loved Leigh Anne. She was family to him, as he was to her. They hugged and kissed hello and talked for quite awhile. She didn't ask, and he knew she wasn't going to, but he updated her on his cousin, Kenny. She showed no emotion as he talked. Well-meaning as he was, Kimo also told her that Tom Jackson had been forced to close his clinic a few years back. He had become too old to keep up and had been making too many mistakes.

"A few years too late," she said to Kimo.

"I'm sorry, Leigh. It was the wrong thing to bring up. I always do that," he said, looking at her for forgiveness. "Sometimes I just don't think."

"What do you mean *sometimes?*" she said giving him a big hug. "It feels so good to be back, Kimo. I've missed this place and I've missed you."

"I've missed you too, cuz. Now, I promised you a special homemade lunch."

"Yes, you did, and I've been waiting for this for seven years."

"I'm gonna make everything from scratch. So I hope you feel like taking a swim while I start to prepare everything?"

"Sounds great. I'll be back in thirty." She smiled and grabbed her bag to go change.

Any hesitancy that she might have had was forgotten as Kimo had always made her feel safe. Her swim in the aqua blue Pacific was therapeutic. It had been a long time since she had felt the warm, caressing massage of the sands of Lanikai under her feet as she strolled along the beach. She loved the taste of the saltwater on her lips as the spray from the surf gently kissed her face. Leigh Anne closed her eyes and leaned her head back toward the sky and tried to soak up every bit of heat from the sun. She felt at home and hoped that a position would eventually open up for her at the aquarium making her return all the more possible. Until one did, she was hesitant to make the move. That was going to be her focus from then on. She always felt, that by putting positive energy out into the universe, her thoughts could manifest into reality.

Her reality also included the need for her to find a way to atone for what she considered to be her great sin. The burden of which she had quietly carried inside of her over the last several years. Perhaps that was the biggest part of the burden. Ever since that talk with Father Dominick, she had felt a heavy guilt which brought her back to St. Philomena's each year during the last week of June. But the weight never seemed to fully lift from her conscience, no matter how many times she sat in his confessional. She knew that if she ever were to find redemption, it surely had to come from within herself. To do that, she knew she would have to allow herself to do something that she had not allowed in quite some time.

Leigh Anne sat at the bar eating mahi-mahi the way she had always loved it. She was flattered that Kimo remembered it was her favorite. "This is great, Kimo. You remembered everything."

"That's right, cuz. Jus' the way you like it." He motioned with his hands as if doing a hula. "I marinated the mahi in soy sauce and sweet rice wine. Then I covered it wit' crushed pineapple, garlic, ginger, and smothered that baby with whole green onion. I wrapped it all up in tender banana leaves and gently steamed it to perfection."

"And my favorite side dish of fresh sliced banana, deep-fried in macadamia nut oil and sprinkled with shaved coconut and powdered sugarcane. Now, top that all off with a frosty Pipeline and I'm in heaven, brah."

"Comin' right up," he said as he served up a cold one.

Save for the continuous staring of the lone guy sitting out in the open air dining room, lunch would have been perfect. Definitely a tourist, by the way he was dressed. It made her slightly uncomfortable, but then again, it was no different from what she often put up with at Kelsey's. "Oh god," she thought. "He's coming over here. This ought to be good...not."

Ray had been enjoying his lunch at Kimo's. He was nearing the end of a fantastic week and felt lucky to have found the place. He loved that grass shack feel and the fact that it was right across from the beach. He absolutely loved the food, but when he caught sight of the auburn-haired woman at the bar, he was completely distracted. Being a free man for the first time in a long time, he decided to throw caution to the wind. "After all," he thought. "She keeps looking back at me. I'm going for it. This ought to be good!"

The full extent of Leigh Anne's beauty became apparent as he got closer to her and he began to panic. He couldn't remember ever doing anything like this before, and now his adrenaline was pumping hard and fast. His heart was racing, his blood pressure started rising, and his mind went blank. "Quick," he thought to himself, "make like you're coming to the bar just for a beer." But his legs kept going straight for Leigh Anne as his torso twisted to the right to go to the bar. To the casual observer, he looked like he was starting to have a seizure. Leigh Anne pretended not to see him coming, and as she lifted her beer to her lips, he tripped over his own feet and fell into her, knocking the beer out of her hand. Her food splattered as the bottle hit her plate and flopped over onto the bar, spilling out its contents.

"Hey, what the heck!" She blurted out. "Get off me!"

"Oh geez, I'm sorry, I'm sorry. It was an accident." Ray pushed himself off of her and nervously tried to stop the beer from pouring out all over the bar.

"Hey buddy, if you're coming up for another drink, I think you've had too many," she said, looking at the splatter on her white t-shirt.

"No, really, it was an accident. I've only had one beer. I just slipped is all."

"Well, you ought to be more careful brah, your hard head hit my chest." She picked up her Pipeline and saw that it was empty.

Having heard the commotion, Kimo came out from the kitchen, "Hey Leigh, you O.K, you need help wit' dis guy?"

She threw him a shaka and he nodded, but watched for a few seconds more before going back into the kitchen through the swinging door.

"You owe me a beer, hoale." She leaned over the bar to grab a hand towel.

As her t-shirt lifted up to reveal her bikini-clad bottom, Ray blurted out, "Now *that* is nice."

Leigh Anne quickly sat back into her seat and spun around. "What was that?" she demanded.

"What was what?" he responded, realizing too late that his comment hadn't been in his head.

"What's nice?" She was instinctively attacking, while at the same time noting his interest.

"What's n...nice, what?" He felt and looked like a deer caught in the headlights of an oncoming car. "Oh god," he thought. "Stupid, stupid. I can't believe I said that out loud."

"Never mind." She continued mopping up the spill with the bar towel while firmly seated on the stool. "You owe me another beer."

"Uh, yeah, of course. No problem."

"Pipeline."

"Pipeline?"

"Yeah, Pipeline." She held up the empty longneck and showed him the label.

"Hmm, ok, Pipeline. Never heard of it."

"Look what you did to my shirt." Leigh Anne looked over at him and studied his face, "You *are* a tourist, brah! Where are you from hoale?"

He knew what "hoale" meant but saw a chance to ease the tension "Uh, no. It's Ray, the name is Ray, and I'm really sorry about your shirt. I'd wipe some club soda on it for ya, but you'd probably cut my hands off."

She didn't laugh, but she did crack a smile. "Ok Ray, where are you from?"

"Seattle."

"Oh," she said and shook her head in disbelief. The bartender came by. Ray held up the empty bottle and asked for two.

"How about you, where are you from?"

"I'm from here. But, I've been working in Seattle for the past few years." The words coming out before she could stop them. "Why did I just tell him that?" She scolded herself.

Ray's eyes widened, but she cautioned him, "Don't get any ideas, Ray." She pointed to his wedding band. "I don't play with married men."

He looked down at his left hand and realized that he hadn't taken off his wedding band. It had been on his hand for so many years he hadn't even thought about it until now.

"You probably wouldn't believe me if I told you I wasn't married."

"Heard that one a few thousand times."

"I'm sure you have."

The bartender returned with two Pipelines. Ray put them on his lunch tab while Leigh Anne carefully looked him over. Although she was still a little miffed at the way he had fallen into her, she did think he was attractive—and his clumsiness a tad on the boyish side of cute. He was definitely very different from the collection of men who had attempted to pursue her back in Seattle. "But I don't play with married men," she reminded herself. "so this ain't goin' nowhere." She couldn't resist one more little dig at him, though, "So did you enjoy the coconut-crusted Ahi steak with the pineapple salsa?"

"Yeah, I did. But how did you know that's what I had?"

"Ray, my Seattle friend," she laughed. "It's all over your shirt."

Ray looked down, saw the stains, and was clearly embarrassed. Leigh Anne almost felt bad for pointing it out to him. Almost. "Poor guy," she thought. "He's so lost."

"Hey Ray," she took her beer and got up to leave. "I hope you like your Pipeline, and I was only havin' a little fun wit' ya brah" she said in her best native slang, holding out her hand. "No hard feelings?"

"That's what I should be asking you," he said as he took her hand in his.

There was an unexplainable warmth and a tingle they felt at the same instant. What's more, each knew that the other felt it as well. Leigh Anne and Ray made eye contact for a brief moment as they both said, "Sure, no hard feelings."

He didn't want to let go of her hand, but he had already made a fool of himself, and deep down he was convinced this wasn't going any further. He would not forget her face or the sound of her voice, though. On his flight home, Ray had found himself closing his eyes to picture her smile, hair draping down over her shoulders, the bronze of her skin, and how her freckles dotted across her forehead and the bridge of her nose. But it was her eyes that he remembered most vividly. There was a complexity to her eyes that seemed lost and alone. He could sense it.

Leigh Anne, too, was somehow struck by him, but couldn't explain it. She just knew that there was something more to this guy. The sensation that she had felt from his handshake was definitely unusual. In spite of his clumsiness, she would have liked to learn more about him. "Too bad he was wearing a ring," she thought. "He could have been the one". But now it was time for her to focus her energies on getting that new job. "If that comes through, there's no chance of ever meeting Ray again anyway," she concluded.

Leigh Anne watched him pay his bill and head out to the parking lot. She watched him for several minutes as he just sat in his car, not making any attempt to leave. She could understand if he were parked facing the ocean, gazing out at the palm tree-lined beach, but he was parked facing the garbage dumpster. "What's this tourist doing?" she said laughing to herself. She saw Ray looking back into the restaurant, slowly tapping his fingers across the top of the steering wheel. Seeing that he had left his car keys and sunglasses at his table, she laughed some more and thought about running them out to him. Instead, she grabbed her Pipeline and headed back into the kitchen to talk to Kimo. That's when Ray jumped out of his car and ran back in to snatch his keys and sunglasses, trying not to be seen.

9

L eigh Anne had originally planned to go for her doctorate immediately after her undergraduate work, but a careless night of passion with her boyfriend, Kanoa, saw the arrival of their daughter Mahina just three weeks after she finished school. With a new baby altering their plans, but with help from the 'ohana—the family—she thought they both had taken this little detour in stride. No one denied it was stressful and Leigh Anne herself was somewhat disappointed with the timing; however, because of her Catholic upbringing, the thought of abortion had been unthinkable to her. Now that she had her baby, every time she looked into her eyes she felt blessed. They named their little girl for the full moon under which she was born. Translated, Mahina meant moonlight, and they both agreed that her smiles lit up the night as bright as any tropical moon.

Kanoa, or Kenny as everyone called him, had a year left at the university when Mahina was born. He liked Leigh Anne a lot and had been attracted to her from the very first time they met. She was intelligent, articulate, beautiful, and fun to be with, but he had never visualized a long term future with her. Kenny was a "player", and his friends found it unusual for him to suddenly be with only one girl. He had never known any-one like Leigh Anne before. She was different from his other girlfriends. She seemed more mature, and she made him feel that way, too. When he was with her he was happy to be with just one person, although the temptation to go back to his old ways never left him.

Having a baby was the last thing he had wanted. During her pregnancy, he had tried to convince her that it was not the time to start a family. He had hoped she would take the hint. But she was adamant about seeing the pregnancy through. Feeling pressured to step up to his new responsibilities, he worked it out with his cousin Kimo that he would bartend double shifts on weekends, and attend classes in the evenings during the rest of the week.

The way they had hoped it would work, Kenny could keep up with his studies at home and take care of the baby during the day while Leigh Anne worked at the aquarium. The hands-on experience would surely help when she resumed her studies. They also agreed that when he finished school, he would continue bartending nights until he found a "real" job. By then the baby would be old enough for daycare and Leigh Anne could start graduate school.

Overall, during those first few months of parenthood, life had been manageable for Leigh Anne, but barely tolerable for Kenny. Between both jobs and family help, they were just able to make ends meet. Kimo had always been more of a father figure to his younger cousin, and now loved Leigh and the baby just as much. He always made it a point to send extra food home with Kenny at the end of his shifts. If he needed to spend a little extra time doing research at the library, or if Leigh Anne had to stay a little longer at the aquarium to help out a coworker, there was always the extended 'ohana who happily watched Mahina for them.

It wasn't long before Kenny became distracted—both in and out of school. Once female classmates were aware that Leigh Anne was no longer on campus, they became aggressively flirtatious. He was also having a hard time with his senior year course load.

During the fall session, when Mahina starting cutting her teeth, she was irritable and inconsolable, making studying at home all but impossible. He began falling behind. As she got older, she was often sick. Never a fan of western medicine, Kimo had tried to tell them both that he thought her problems stemmed from all the vaccinations she was getting. He was insistent that it went against the laws of nature to put all those chemicals into a little body. Leigh Anne and Kenny both had a lot of respect for Kimo, but were convinced that western medicine knew what was best. There had been many trips to the local clinic during the baby's first year, and as a result of the increasing pressures of his new burdens, Kenny found himself "sampling" more often while working behind the bar.

Leigh Anne herself was often fatigued, working long hours during the day, staying up late with endless house chores, and caring for the baby. Sex had been the furthest thing from her mind for quite awhile and the one that was always on Kenny's. His frustrations and resentment grew, and he soon found himself longing for the days before he had "settled." He often considered pursuing several classmates who had shown interest. Leigh Anne suspected that his eyes were wandering, but some days she was too tired to worry about it. The amount of squabbles over the little things became more frequent, but their first—and last—real fight came on a Monday, when Kenny came stumbling home drunk six hours after Kimo's had closed for the night. It was six in the morning. Leigh Anne had been up most of the night with a feverish and inconsolable one-year-old. Half-dead on her feet, she now had to get herself ready for work.

The night before, the restaurant had been packed with locals and tourists alike. The bar had been busy for a Sunday, and a few of the local girls who knew Kenny from school were flirting, teasing, and buying him more drinks then they were having themselves. Kenny was a stud. Twenty-one years old with a movie star smile and a muscular torso to match. The more he drank, the more Kimo got worried. Several times, he took the boy aside and warned him to stop. He didn't want his young cousin getting killed on the way home, and he didn't want to see these girls talking the kid into giving them free booze. This was something that had happened quite a bit with past bartenders—once they started receiving lots of smiles and even more cleavage. What neither of them expected was Kenny being talked into a moonlit ride home after he got off work. It would be a ride that took six hours to go the five miles to where he lived.

Leigh Anne was no fool. She had sensed it the minute he stumbled through the door. The girl's smell cut straight through the booze floating off his breath and permeating his clothing. She saw it on his face and in his eyes. He had been sexually frustrated for some time. Many times before he tried—tongue-in-cheek—to convince an exhausted Leigh Anne that he was an "island man" and "an island man shouldn't be denied his natural desires."

His suitor for the evening had surely wanted to satisfy his natural desires, and fueled his fire by slowly stroking his ego with talk of how handsome he was and how great they could be together. The more she talked, the more excited he became. Because Kimo could appear at anytime, Kenny knew he had to be careful and play it safe. She was a classmate, but she was also a customer who was with her friends. And since they were spending money he gave them the attention that they wanted by laughing at their jokes and—with one eye on the lookout for his cousin—drank the drinks they bought him while eagerly pocketing his tips. As the evening pressed on and the alcohol worked its magic, the girl he was most interested in convinced him that he couldn't drive home by himself. She would be his "Good Samaritan." Kimo knew this was trouble and tried to intervene. At closing time he sat his cousin down and sent the oversexed, underdressed girl on her way. He saw that instead of leaving, she waited outside the restaurant, casually having a smoke as she seductively leaned against her car. After one final pass through the restaurant before lockup, Kimo had noticed that they were both gone.

Alone with her prey, she pulled off the main road and parked. Now she would zero in for the kill. Drawing herself close to him, her perfume was every bit as intoxicating as the alcohol. She rubbed his thigh and watched him become aroused. She pulled herself closer and breathed softly into his ear. Kenny closed his eyes as she lightly kissed his neck.

"We can…not do thish," he laughed. "I can not dooo thish."

"Why not, why can't we do this, Kenny?"

"I'm wish sumboody, I mean…I'm with Lei… I gotta girl."

"But you're not married to her. Are you?"

"No, weee are not married. Nooope. Not marrrrieed," he sang.

"Don't you think I'm pretty? I think you're so handsome." She whispered into his ear, making sure to touch her lips to his earlobe.

"Yesh, I…think yourrr pretty hot. You'rrrre a hottie. You got really great…" Kenny lifted his arms up to his chest and cupped his hands to mimic her breasts.

"Do you want to see them, Kenny? Would you like to touch them?"

He closed his eyes and turned his head away. Though his mind swirled, he had known he was on dangerous ground. His willpower, or what was left of it, was quickly deteriorating. He wanted to relieve himself so bad. When she thought he could no longer resist, she went in for the final shot. She climbed on top to straddle him and pressed and rubbed herself into him.

"I want you Kenny," she had whispered as she placed her hand right into his groin and gently rubbed. "I want you now and I know you want me. We're both natives, Kanoa. We're both Kanaka Maoli. Do you hear me, Kanoa? True Hawaiians. Not like your white Irish-Scottish girlfriend."

* * *

Leigh Anne just stood there looking at him. Her heart ached and she wanted to grab something and smack him with it, but she didn't have the time and he probably wouldn't have felt it. She quickly gathered her thoughts and went off to pack a bag for the baby. He was obviously in no condition to watch

Mahina, so she would drop off the baby at a friend's house on her way to work.

Later that evening when Kenny got home from school, they battled. He pleaded his case, claiming that he didn't remember a thing. He swore up and down that he didn't have sex with anyone, but the smell of another woman had been unmistakable. He took responsibility for drinking too much and then—sensing that his was a lost cause—he lashed out at her. He blamed her for ignoring his needs. Leigh Anne looked at him in disgust. His attack was as good as any confession, and she would have none of it.

"I never wanted this," an exhausted Kenny blurted out. "I never wanted any of this. I never wanted to have a family." Leigh Anne was stunned. "I never wanted to be a father, not now anyway," he continued. "I asked you to get an abortion. I didn't want…"

"Oh, I see. So all this is my fault. Is that it, Kenny?" She was calm but direct. "I'm the bad one here? Your life…is all fucked up…because of me? You fucking little prick. I hope she was worth it, you sonofabitch. Get the fuck out! Get your shit and get the fuck outta here!"

He grabbed his belongings and shoved them into a gym bag, an old duffle bag, and a few grocery bags. It was up to him whether he went home to his mother, to Kimo's house, or to his new girlfriend. Leigh Anne didn't care. She needed time by herself to sort it out. She wouldn't stay in their home, but she didn't want him there either. She didn't want him to have the freedom of being alone or to have the opportunity to drain his pent- up island manhood into one of his college cuties—at least not in her bed. She would take some time off of work and head over to Molokai. As a young girl, she had spent her summers working at St. Philomena's church. It had become her sanctuary, her home away from home. In times of great emotional stress, she went back there to pray in the chapel, work around the grounds and in the small graveyard, and sit by the ocean and write poetry. It was a place of comfort and security for her. She packed some things for her and the baby, and planned to leave the next morning—after she was sure that Kenny had gone.

Mahina continued to exhibit signs of illness. She had been irritable and running a low- grade fever for a couple of days, and by that evening her fever started to climb. She was oddly quiet through all the fighting, but Leigh Anne had been too focused on Kenny to notice. She wanted to leave for Molokai, but didn't want to travel with a sick child. She decided to wait a few days until the baby was better. But the next morning she was worse. Lethargic and with no appetite, her fever was rising as the thermometer now read 102.5 degrees. Leigh Anne was beginning to worry as little Mahina's face turned hot and red. She hoped a quick run to the clinic to have her looked at and to get some medicine would do the trick.

Dr. Jackson's clinic was old. Relative to the larger group practices in Honolulu, it was small and antiquated, but the kind of family practice people had been coming to for decades. Tom Jackson should have retired years earlier, but he had very few interests outside of his work. At this point in his life he was grandfatherly to his patients and although he hadn't kept up with the latest literature or the newest diagnostic tools, "Fifty years of experience can't be outdone by any fancy machinery," he could often be heard telling people when they questioned the absence of the latest technology. Most of the time all he needed was a brief description of the symptoms along with a quick look at the patient. He'd then write a script, tell a short joke, and everything seemed to work out fine. As far as he was concerned, this visit with little Mahina would be no different.

After a quick temperature reading and a check of her weight by the triage nurse, Dr. Jackson would enter the small exam room with his big, reassuring smile. He showed concern for the baby's lethargy. But a quick feel of the lymph nodes in her neck, a visual scan inside her ears, nose, and mouth, and he was done. In his younger days, his fingertips would have picked up the asymmetry and slightly increased size of the cervical chain lymph nodes, and his sharper vision might have picked up her bloodshot eyes or the subtle color changes of her lips and tongue. The advanced stages of osteoarthritis in his own neck, however, had put enough pressure on the peripheral nerves that innervated his fingers to the point where he had gradually lost the sensitivity in his hands. If the thickness of his reading glasses didn't affect his being able to detect the gradual color changes of the little girl's lips and tongue, then the early stages of his cataracts sure did.

"Looks like she picked up a viral infection of some sort," He said looking at Leigh Anne over his thick reading glasses. "There's really nothing to give for a virus, it just has to run its course is all." He asked the nurse to draw a little blood. "I just want to be sure that it isn't anything else," he added as he watched the sample being drawn. "I'll send this out to the lab and if there's anything significant, I'll give you a call. In the meantime, you go pick up some electrolyte water and get it into her with an eyedropper if she won't drink it on her own. Keep her hydrated, keep a cool, wet towel on her forehead and neck to make her comfortable, and this should run its course in, oh... I say about twenty-four to forty-eight hours at the most."

Leigh Anne took in every word. She was always attentive and very rarely had to hear anything twice. Tom Jackson looked at her and saw that she was extremely exhausted and stressed, so he gave her a big hug and asked her if she wanted him to write up a script for a sedative. She thanked him, but declined. Leigh Anne was exhausted but she was strong. She always had been. She tried to never let emotion get the better of her. But this was different. This was not about her. It was about her child.

For the next two days, the baby laid around like a limp noodle. Her fever rose to 103 even though Leigh Anne was keeping her cool with moist wet hand towels on her neck and forehead like she was told. She kept her hydrated with eyedroppers full of flavored electrolyte water. It had now been three days since the baby had eaten solid food. And then she noticed the changes in her daughter's hands and feet.

They were swollen to twice their normal size. The skin between her fingers and toes had begun flaking and peeling off. Her lips and tongue were also swollen and bright cherry red. Flop sweat was soaking her little undershirt. Leigh Anne hadn't heard back from the clinic with results from the blood draw, but she didn't have to at this point. She called them and said she was coming in with the baby. She called the restaurant looking for Kenny, but Kimo said he thought he was at his mother's place in Kaneohe.

"Kimo, Mahina is very sick. I'm taking her to Dr. Jackson's. Please find Kenny, please Kimo."

Tom Jackson took one look at the motionless one-year-old and finally realized that it was more than just a virus. He had seen this once, maybe twice before, but not this severe. He had forgotten about the blood results, which had come back early the prior morning—and had gotten misplaced in another patient's file. Had he remembered and asked for it, the receptionist would have recalled that the paperwork had been on her desk and would have searched for the report or called the lab to fax a duplicate. Kawasaki's disease—even amongst the Asian population on the islands—was very rare. He immediately had his nurse call for an ambulance to transport the baby to Honolulu General while he got her started on intravenous saline to replenish her fluids. Time was critical. If caught in the very early stages, Kawasaki's could be dealt with quite effectively. If not, the risk of coronary artery damage was very high. He hated to think he had missed his window.

1 0

The few months that Leigh Anne spent on Molokai at her "home away from home" was a true blessing. The change of scenery had definitely helped clear her mind. She spent many hours writing her poetry, working in and around St. Philomena's, and meditating. She began jogging again, which also helped her to focus. As Molokai was still not a tourist destination, she delighted in being surrounded by the native culture. And although not a Polynesian, she had been born and raised in Hawaii and considered herself just as much a native as the Kanaka Maoli.

She was growing restless and needed a change. She had been receiving invitations from old friends on the mainland who wanted her to come for a visit. Her childhood friend Kelsey offered her both employment and place to stay. The offer was tempting. She missed Kelsey and hadn't seen her since her move to Seattle. Leigh Anne had been there once as a child and remembered it as a good experience. She remembered the little aquarium right on Elliot Bay. Odd as it seemed, it had been there, and not at the aquarium on Oahu where she had come to realize that she would grow up to be a marine biologist. The more she thought about it, the more she prayed about it. The more she prayed about it, the more she was able to see it as a reality for her. Leigh Anne's plan was to apply to the University of Washington for her doctorate while at the same time—hopefully—work at the Seattle Aquarium.

"This is great, Kelse," Leigh Anne said. "Are you sure you don't mind?"

"Don't be silly, Leigh. I wouldn't have offered if I didn't mean it. It'll be fun. It'll be like we're little kids again and doing sleepovers. Plus, the bar has really started jumpin' and I could use another waitress."

"You do realize that it's gonna take some time for me to get accepted into the grad program?"

"Not a problem."

"And who knows if I can get a job at the aquarium?"

"Leigh, relax! Ok? Just get your ass here. You can work and stay with me for as long as you need to, or, for as long as you want to."

"You're the best, Kelsey. You really are."

With a plan in place and after several conversations with her friend, Leigh Anne decided that it was time to leave the islands—at least for a while, anyway. She knew that she would be coming back to Molokai at least. Her ties to this place were now stronger than they had ever been. Once that decision was made, she would go see Father Dominick.

On the morning of her last day, she woke up earlier than normal. Leigh Anne prepared a small breakfast and hiked out to the shoreline to eat and watch the sunrise. She was nervous. She had been telling herself that the best way for her to move on was to move away, but she struggled with that. Deep down, she wondered if she was only running away from the memory of her relationship with Kenny and running away from her guilt. She certainly had felt the frustration and heartbreak from his betrayal of her love and trust. There was no comparison however, to the anger and the deep hurt she held inside from when he had been nowhere to be found when their daughter was in the fight of her young life. Even then, she would have found forgiveness if it had turned out that his absence was simply because he had not known of the emergency.

For her, when Kenny didn't even have the decency to show up for his little girl's funeral, that was the day that he became dead in her heart. When Kimo found out that his cousin had spent the day getting stoned with his new girlfriend, he had let it be known that Kenny was unemployed and that the nature of their relationship would be forever changed.

The talks she had with Father Dominick had always comforted her. Always, until now. He had been her spiritual counselor since she first came to St. Philomena's church as a young girl. Father Dominick had always been her calm port in a sometimes stormy sea of parental turmoil, teenage issues, and most recently, with Kenny and the loss of her daughter. He wanted her to consider the possibility that perhaps she had allowed herself to become pregnant with Mahina in an effort to get a stronger commitment out of her boyfriend. Perhaps she had subconsciously tried to create the family that didn't exist for her as a child—due to an absentee father of her own. His intent was to allow her an avenue to forgive Kenny. If what Father Dominick said was indeed true, it raised questions in her mind that perhaps her daughter had been an innocent victim of her selfishness.

While talking to the Padre, he had agreed they could have a service to help Leigh Anne end one chapter of her life and begin a new one. She had spent the night writing out all that had been troubling her. She wrote a long letter to Mahina as well. After breakfast and watching the sunrise, she met with Father Dominick, a local Kahuna, and several of her friends by the little white headstone in the church graveyard. They formed a circle as the Priest and then the Kahuna led them in prayer. At the conclusion, Leigh Anne made a small fire and placed the letter of her grief into the flame. Of all the things she wrote, she decided that she would not include her new feelings of guilt. She would no longer allow anyone's actions against her to be a controlling factor in her life; however, the thing that she now felt responsible for she would hold onto—for now.

"I release this list of pain and anguish to be carried off into the universe for I do not own them and they no longer have any power over my life," she said as she knelt by the small fire. The letter burned, and she watched as the little flakes of black ash were carried off by the wind. She took the folded letter that she had written to her daughter, held it out to the sky, and brought it back and pressed it into her chest. "Mahina, my little angel, I thank you for the joy that your short life gave to my life. I thank you for the love that filled my heart when my heart was empty. Your memory will always be with me wherever I go. You will always be a part of me and I will carry you in my heart forever."

She placed the letter into the fire, and as it slowly succumbed to the flames, the ash that formed was pure and white as snow. A gentle breeze carried the pieces away. Leigh Anne walked over to the little headstone and lightly ran her fingers over the raised letters spelling out her daughter's name. Then, one by one, she received hugs and blessings from her friends to send her off to her new life.

11

During the first few weeks that Ray was getting settled into his new job at the Veterans hospital, he had to endure a series of prepubescent pranks from several members of the medical staff. It was either a rite of passage, or they wanted to send a message that he was not welcomed in the holy bastion of allopathic medicine. As some of his medical counterparts were prejudiced against any "alternative" health care discipline, their disrespect stemmed from an ardent reliance on old wives' tales handed down during medical school indoctrination, in spite of the fact that scientific evidence had failed to validate these suspicions. When it came to chiropractic, needless to say, the old wives' tales had been their first line of attack.

Ray found it all too amusing, as it reminded him of when he had first set up his practice in downtown Eastridge. At first, members of the local medical community rejected his overtures toward building a professional relationship. Then, over time and thanks to Jo's social skills, he had gotten to know some of the local doctors through fundraisers, the kids' school events, soccer games, and at end-of-season trophy dinners. When they met him on a personal basis, and after the barriers had begun to fall away, they had started asking questions about his profession. The conversations they had on anatomy, physiology, biomechanics, and nutrition not only put misconceptions to rest, but had made some realize that—in many areas—their own knowledge was lacking. Some were even mildly ashamed about what they had once said behind Ray's back. Over time, and after greater familiarity, the referrals started coming in. And some of those that had refused to even allow the word "chiropractic" to be mentioned in their own offices found themselves calling Ray late at night or on weekends, asking to stop by the house for a private "tune-up" after playing one too many rounds at the golf club. He knew that the doctors at the Veterans Medical Center were no different then their "country club" colleagues and that they too would eventually come around.

Childish antics aside, he also didn't mind that the double room at the very end of the basement hallway had been set aside for his two-room office—one for treatment and consultations, the other as his private office. He didn't care that he was the only health care provider along that entire hallway and that the other rooms were used for storage of either medical records or janitorial supplies. He didn't care that he wasn't assigned an assistant to help him with records or other clerical tasks. He was however, disappointed when he was informed that it would take several months for his exam equipment, treatment table, and other supplies to arrive—unlike the week to ten days when he had started his own practice. Whether it was intentional delay or typical government ineptitude, he didn't know. He just brought the equipment and supplies from his old "home" office that he had been keeping in storage.

Ray did win the sympathies of a part-time janitor named Abner Lewis and one of the head orthopedic nurses, Stella Leone. Abner, an African-American and a Navy cook in World War II and Korea, was all too familiar with feeling like the odd man out. He had overheard some of the other doctors conspiring to make things difficult.

"Jes like when ah was in the service," he said to Ray. "Ah can be in the same room wit' some guys an' they talk as if ah ain't even there."

With Abner's help, Ray changed the lock on his office door and made up extra keys so that only he, Abner and eventually

Stella would have access. Stella had been a nurse for twenty-three years. She started out as an Army nurse and after having served in the first Gulf War rose to the rank of Major by the end of her fourteen years of active duty.

"She's drop dead gorgeous," Abner would say rocking his head back and forth. "That woman's got a set a gams on her that could make ya heart stop, an' if it didn't it's `cause it probly was never beatin' in the firs' place. Those docs upstairs don't give her the respec' she deserve. Ya treat her right, Doc, an' she'll be an ally fo' sho'. Plus, she got a bad back. She'll be needin' ya help," he added with a sly smile and a wink.

Ray had already met with Nurse Leone to coordinate the educational talk that he was putting together for the medical staff. Abner was absolutely right, though. She was drop- dead gorgeous. He had easily been taken in by her smile, which somehow in spite of her fourteen years in the Army Medical Corp and nine years with the VMC, still had a seductive inno-cence. He calculated that they were the same age, and she looked better than women a decade younger. Fortunately for Ray, she already had a boyfriend. The last thing he needed was to get involved with a coworker. It's not that he was so sure she would have anything to do with him. But Ray was no different from any other guy who watched her walking down the hall-way—that is to say, Stella Leone had a body and sensuality that initiated an instantaneous hormonal rush.

His private office was very simple. Four whitewashed walls with a standard wall clock, gray government-issued desk, file cabinet, and a couple of free-standing book cases with six shelves each. In addition to the harshness of the lighting, the fluorescents in the ceiling made a continuous noxious hum-ming sound. Ray decided not to use them, opting instead for a free-standing lamp that he kept in the corner by the bookcases and a desk version with an articulating arm. The softer light from the specialty terrarium bulbs mimicked outdoor lighting, something he missed due to the absence of windows in the basement. It worked so well for him that he added two stand-ing lamps to the treatment room. He was thankful that both rooms were carpeted. It helped to add a bit of insulation from the cold that seeped through the concrete basement floor. The small space heater that Abner "liberated" from one of the physical therapy rooms was also greatly appreciated.

Next to the lamp on Ray's desk he had two small framed pictures, one of each of his kids. The walls remained barren except for three framed 8 x 10 photos: his brother Frank in camouflage with Seal Team Eleven, a black and white of his dad on the LCI 606, and the fireball that had been the USS Arizona. With Abner's help, the treatment room was all set up by the end of Ray's second week.

Abner had taken to Ray quicker then he had with anyone else at the medical center. Part of it was because of that odd man out factor. There was something else, though. At first he couldn't put his finger on it, but one morning before Ray arrived at work, Abner had stopped by to deliver several reams of printer paper. As he turned to leave, he did a double take at the three photos on the wall. He squinted and leaned his head forward. "Well, ah'll be…," he whispered and walked over to the wall.

The room was rather dark, lit only by the light from the outer treatment room that seeped in through the open door. Without taking his eyes off of the pictures, his hand reached out to the desk. Finding the small knob at the top of the lamp, he gently turned until it clicked and illuminated the pictures on the wall. "Oh Lord, if it ain't the 606," he said as he brought his hand up to his mouth. Ray's name had sounded familiar and Abner felt he knew his face. Now, seeing the picture of the 606—a picture that Abner himself had taken—he made the connection. All these years he had thought Ron Silver had been killed in action during the landing on the South Pacific Island of Peleliu. At least that was what he had been told.

"Maybe Ray's his nephew," he thought. "But jes maybe the guy wasn't killed an' Ray's his son. An' maybe…" Questions began to race through his mind. So much so that he couldn't think straight. He would have to sort it all out before he could mention it to Ray. Then he wondered if he'd ever dare to bring it up. He quickly turned when he heard someone enter the treatment room behind him.

"Good morning, Abner," Ray said turning on the other lights. Abner noticed the white ceramic coffee mug in his hand.

"Mornin' doc. Ah see ya went an' got ya mornin' coffee."

"Fresh brewed, courtesy of the nurses on the second floor. What brings you down this early?"

"Ah was jes droppin' off a few reams ah paper, like ya axed fo'. Couldn't hep notice ya pictures on the wall."

"Well, this one here...," Ray began, but was abruptly cut off.

"Don't mean no disrespec' doc, but ah gotta get up ta the fourf flo' ta fix a winda befo' they start complainin' again." And with that, the old man turned and was gone.

Ray didn't notice that Abner wasn't singing, as he usually did when walking down the long hallway to the elevator.

* * *

While trying to prepare his presentation to the medical staff, Ray had been visited by one of the orthopedists. William "Bill" Harrison had been with the VMC his entire medical career. He had learned early on in his residency that he would have a hard time making a living in private practice. Between his lack of bedside manner, the fact that he didn't care much for people, and the security of a lifetime government job, he cruised through his days on autopilot—never really varying from his routine. When a patient came to see him, he glanced over the notes from the triage nurse, briefly looked at the body part in question, performed a couple of cursory tests, and pre-scribed pain medication, an anti-inflammatory, and sometimes a muscle relaxant. Then he would send them off to physical therapy. Since patient care was therefore a chore and an inter-ruption for him, his only source of pleasure came from harass-ing the nurses and the custodial staff.

The nurses complained to Stella Leone—their supervisor. She brought those complaints to her supervisor, and those complaints would eventually end up in a file. That file would end up buried in a stack of files that eventually got boxed and stored in one of the many storage rooms in the basement level of the medical center. Stella, like the other female employees, hated Dr. Harrison, as well as some of the other docs who had a similar condescending attitude toward anyone with breasts or who did not have "M.D." after their name.

"Am I interrupting Mr...uh Dr. Silver?" Harrison said, coming in unannounced with a stack of patient files in his arms.

Ray stopped typing and glanced up from his laptop. "No, not at all, Doctooor..."

"Harrison. Bill Harrison. Orthopedist." He was slightly annoyed that Ray didn't know his name.

"Of course, Dr. Harrison. Please come in. Seat?" Ray motioned to one of the chairs by his desk.

'No... thanks. I only have a minute." As he carelessly dropped the files onto Ray's desk, several slid off the top of the pile and landed on his laptop keyboard. "Oh, hey, I'm sorry. That was an accident. I hope I didn't delete anything you're working on," he said without emotion.

Ray placed the files back on top of the others and quickly glanced at the monitor. "Nope, it's all fine."

"Maybe you can help me...help you." He said, looking at the photos on the wall. "I've got a bunch of patients here in this pile that may or may not benefit from choirpractics." Bill Harrison paused for a reaction to his intentional mispronunciation. Ray caught it, but let it pass. Harrison continued, "Since I'm not that familiar with what you guys really do, could you go through each file and then maybe give me an idea how you would be able to help these poor souls?"

The obvious answer to Ray was that all of them would be candidates. "Yeah....sure, not a problem," he said as he watched Dr. Harrison avoid eye contact. "You do know that I'm putting on an informational talk next week about this stuff, right?"

"What? Oh yes, your talk."

"Well, I'm going to cover the basics, which will give you the information that you're looking for."

"Oh…well, if you don't want to help me out…"

"I didn't say I didn't wanna help you, but this is gonna to be redundant."

Bill Harrison didn't answer. In fact, he was stumped and didn't know how to respond. Ray looked at him, wondering if he had just blown a chance to get this guy to start sending patients down to him.

"But hey, there's just a few files here," he said, breaking the silence. "I'll be happy to look through them and let you know what I think."

"Great," Harrison said as he stuck his hands into the big side pockets of his lab coat, avoiding a possible handshake. They nodded to each other and Harrison spun on his heels and headed out and down the hall, muttering to himself, "What a fucking asshole!" Ray wondered if Harrison had been sincere in wanting a better understanding. "But that could have been accomplished with a fifteen minute face-to-face over a cup of coffee," he concluded. He suspected that some of these docs were probably having a good laugh, thinking he was burning up the clock reading each file in order to make his case for having patients sent to him for care. "Maybe I'm just paranoid," he thought to himself. "Maybe this guy is sincere…We'll see."

Each morning during his first month, Ray had made a pass through the orthopedic ward on the second floor—just so the staff could see that he existed. He'd make a stop at the nurses' station to wish them a good morning. Most would smile and politely nod, some would return the pleasantry. He made it a point to grab a cup of coffee in the staff break room. At first, he noticed that conversations amongst the doctors would stop when he walked in. That had slowly changed as the weeks passed. In the meantime, he pretended to ignore them as he took his time preparing his coffee. Sometimes he even took the pot and offered refills to the women in the room. Although he had initially begun this ritual as a way of prolonging his presence, it was a simple courtesy that the male staff members never considered—and one the women appreciated. If present, Stella always obliged him and held her cup out to be refilled.

This annoyed Bill Harrison to no end—which made the coffee taste all that better to Stella. Accomplishing his mission, Ray headed to the elevator and down to his basement office.

Midway through his second week, while waiting for a patient—any patient—to be sent his way, he alternated between preparing his presentation and reviewing the thirty patient files that Harrison had given him. As he sat at his desk looking over one of the files, he heard the faint echo of footsteps from the far end of the basement hallway. Occasionally a file clerk, nurse, or janitor would be bringing another file box down for storage and the footsteps would stop somewhere along the corridor. Then Ray would hear the jingle of keys followed by the squeal of a door hinge in desperate need of oil. After a few moments of quiet, the hallway would once again echo with the slam of a door, a jingle of keys, and fading footsteps. It didn't take long for him to tell the difference between male and female. The male footsteps were generally a slower and heavier sound, while female footsteps were quicker and a higher pitch. He guessed that this was due to the lighter, more narrow feminine foot. Even when people wore cross-trainers instead of shoes, he could hear the spongy squeak of the rubber soles as they hit the linoleum tiles. He quickly learned the sound of Abner's slight waddle. But Abner also sang as he walked—a dead giveaway.

The echo coming down the hall as he reviewed Harrison's files was definitely a woman, and it wasn't stopping as the sound of each step grew louder. Then, it finally did stop. There was a knock on the door that led from the outer exam room to his private office. He looked up to see Nurse Leone leaning in.

"Am I interrupting?" she said with a slight smile.

"Uh…no, no." He quickly stood up, knocking some of the files off of the desk. "Please come in," he said, surprised to see her. "Have a seat?" he motioned to the chair as he came around the desk to pick up the folders.

"No, that's alright. Thank you. I'll just be a minute." She said as she looked at the pictures on the wall. "Who's the SEAL?"

"My brother, Frank. The other picture of the 606, that was my dad's ship, and the other one..."

"Is the Arizona," she said. "I know. Is that one special to you?"

"My Uncle Jim was on her that morning. My dad's brother." He laid the files back on his desk. Resting his hands on his back pockets he leaned forward to look at the picture. "She smells nice," he said to himself. She turned to look at him and he straightened back up, afraid he was standing too close. "Oh God, I hope I didn't say that out loud," he thought quickly.

"My grandfather was on the Oklahoma," she said as she turned back to the photos.

"Small world. Kinda."

"So your brother's a SEAL!" It was a statement rather than a question.

"He was a SEAL. He, uh.. he was lost on a training mission in the Philippines in `81."

"Oh, I'm sorry." She looked at the picture and then at Ray. He nodded. "You know, I see a resemblance between you two." They were both silent for a few seconds. "So, how's that presentation coming along?"

"It's getting there. I was racking my brain for the best way to present it to these guys."

"Just give it to `em as simply as you can. Trust me, there's no need to try to impress them. I've watched their eyes glaze over ten minutes into a technical lecture. I swear they're all ADD."

"Well, that's what I was thinking. Not the eye-glazing-over part or the ADD, but I'm just going to take one of my basic patient education talks that I've used for almost twenty years in private practice. It just needs a little updating is all."

"Ok... yeah, that's good," Stella said, hesitating for just a second. "So, I've got this thing going on with my lower back. Been bothering me for years now. The guys upstairs either write a prescription or they send me to PT."

"Not getting any relief?" he asked, knowing she wasn't.

"A decrease in the intensity, maybe no pain at all for a week at a time, but it always comes back. Think you could help? I'm tired of just taking meds all the time."

"Look, let's set up a time where ya come down for an exam. I'm sure ya have some films, yes?"

"Yes, I've got a set that's pretty recent. Six months ago."

"Ok, so bring your chart, we'll take a look at your films, I'll do an exam, and we'll go from there. Sound reasonable?"

"Yeah, that's sounds great. Speaking of charts, what's with the pile?" she pointed to the stack on his desk and started flipping through some of them.

"Harrison asked me to go through them to see who would be a good candidate for chiropractic and to help him understand why."

"What?" she said in disbelief. "That's ridiculous! No offense, but he could figure that out on his own, especially after your talk next week."

"I told him that, but I thought..."

"You shouldn't have to be wasting your time like this." She said scooping up the pile from his desk. "Besides, these guys are all deceased and Harrison probably got them out of a box that was getting sent down to storage."

"I noticed they were deceased, but did you notice the common link between them?"

She stopped as she was about to head out the door. "I'm not his triage nurse, so I never review his charts. What common link?"

"Well, I've only had a chance to review fourteen of the thirty files. Each patient presented to him with chronic musculoskeletal pain. Some neck, some back, some shoulders."

"Yeah, that's common with most of the guys coming through our ward."

Yes, but he put them all on the same prescription anti-inflammatory." He walked over to her and picked through to the fifth file in the stack. Again he couldn't help but notice her perfume. He opened the chart and flipped through a few pages. Stopping at one, he quickly scanned it with his finger.

When he found what he was looking for, he pointed. "Here, look at this. I'm not an expert in meds, but wouldn't you say this is a very high dosage?"

She looked at the chart and acknowledged that it was high. "Ok, but some conditions require an initial high dose."

Yeah…sure, but look further." he said slowly flipping the pages for her. "He never alters the prescription. In the fourteen files that I've looked at so far, not once was the dosage lowered over time." Ray knew that he had her full attention. "Look it," he said, "of the fourteen charts I reviewed, all fourteen patients died of either a cerebral hemorrhage or a myocardial infarct. Now what's that about?"

"Yes, but these guys were on the latest COX-2 inhibitor. It's supposed to be the best non- steroidal anti-inflammatory out there."

"Nurse Leone…Stella, uh sorry. Can I call you Stella?" She gave a slight nod and he continued. "Maybe it's a coincidence, I don't know. But fourteen cases of high dosage NSAIDs and all being taken for what, five, six months without a break? I'll bet if we look at the other sixteen files in this stack we'll see the same thing."

Stella knew in her gut that Ray was probably right in his suspicion. She realized too that she would have to look through more of Bill Harrison's deceased files to see if there was an ongoing pattern. If there was, she wondered what her next step would be.

Would she take her findings straight to Harrison—only to have him cover it up? Would she go directly to the head of the department and then explain what she was doing going through the medical records of deceased patients? She thought about the incident nine years earlier when she was stationed at Walter Reed. "This is not going to be good," she thought. "Ok, doc, I'll look into this. Let's just keep this between you and me right now, Ok.?" she said, looking straight at him.

"Sure, no problem."

"Ok then." She nodded and left with the stack of files.

Ray watched her leave the room and inhaled as deeply as he could in an effort to catch one last whiff of her perfume.

He wanted to stick his head out into the doorway to watch her 5'5" curvaceous frame walk toward the elevator, but he knew it wouldn't look good if she should suddenly turn around. As he stood there and listened to the echoes of her footsteps fade, he closed his eyes and pictured her walking down the hallway. He simply smiled and slowly shook his head back and forth. "Drop-dead gorgeous!"

1 2

The night before he gave his presentation to his new colleagues, Ray had a hard time falling asleep. He had a bad case of butterflies, and no matter how many times he told himself to relax, they wouldn't go away. He paced the floor of his living room, trying to visualize how his talk would go. He tried being his own devil's advocate and would imagine being asked questions that ranged from the innocent to the accusatory—feeling proud each time he sounded professorial. Once convinced he had this thing in the bag, he headed off to his bedroom, only to lie awake imagining the worst-case scenario. After fifteen minutes or more of self-torture, he jumped out of bed and headed straight for the kitchen for some comfort food. He couldn't eat, though. His stomach was twitching with nerves, as if hundreds of little bugs were crawling around inside of him. He went back to pacing the floor of the living room, stopping occasionally to look out into the dark of Puget Sound, watching the lights of a lone freighter slowly making its way from Elliot Bay. "She's heading north," he said out loud. "Most likely sailing through the San Juan Islands to the Straight of Juan De Fuca and finally out into the Pacific." As the clock drew upon 3 a.m. he sat down on the couch and watched a DVD—Clarke Gable and Burt Lancaster taking on the Japanese Navy—until he finally fell asleep.

At 9:05 he was standing alone at the head of the conference room with his laptop wired into the projector that Stella had provided for him. Although she had given the staff plenty of notice, the meeting wasn't mandatory, and they had known that a good number of them would not be able to attend. Besides Stella and three other nurses, there were just four doctors seated amongst the two hundred chairs. On one hand, Ray was almost relieved the audience was small. He had never been comfortable with his public speaking skills. Smaller groups always felt more intimate for him and that helped him to connect with people. On the other hand, however, he was somewhat insulted that only eight people were in attendance.

"Good morning," he said, looking out at his audience, noticing that they sat far apart from each other. He tried opening with a joke in an effort to slice through the tension. "The way you're all seated, it reminds me of that first junior high dance social." They just stared at him without emotion. "Ya know, boys afraid that the girls have cooties?" Still no reaction. "Ok then, maybe not." He looked out at the few people in attendance, thinking perhaps they were still asleep. "If that was the case, maybe it was better they weren't seeing patients," he thought.

"Hey, look guys…and gals, there's just a few of us here and really, I'm appreciative that you're taking the time this morning to be here, but it would be really great if you could all just move down closer to me." Some heads turned to look at the other attendees but nobody moved first. Then one of the doctors, Janice Peterson, got up from her back row seat and walked down the center aisle to the front and sat a couple of seats from Stella. "Thank you, doctor," Ray said as Dr. Peterson smiled and nodded at him. "Anybody else?" Ray scanned the audience once more.

"We're all good here, doc. We don't think you have anything contagious, it's just that the room is small enough that we don't need to be right on top of you," came a response from a doctor in the back row.

"I'm sorry, doctor, but I don't think we've met."

"Henry Thayer, orthopedist."

"You wouldn't be J. Henry Thayer, the developer of the Thayer technique for knee reconstruction?"

"The very same."

"Well Dr. Thayer, it's a real pleasure to meet you. Thank you for making the time to be here this morning." As an afterthought, Ray decided to walk down the center aisle to the back of the room and extended his hand to Thayer, who shook Ray's hand without hesitation. "This is good," Ray thought, walking over to the nurse sitting two rows ahead of Thayer and extending his hand to her.

"Candee French," she said as she took his hand.

Ray then made the effort to greet everyone else in the same manner. This simple act broke the ice, and one by one, people slowly moved a few rows closer to the podium. Ray turned to Dr. Thayer once more and gestured with his hands for him to join the rest. Thayer smiled, nodded and proceeded to take a seat up front.

He decided to forgo his Powerpoint and instead began with a brief explanation of the art, science, and philosophy of his profession. He then decided to open up the floor for questions, and for forty-five minutes, Ray and all eight of his guests had a meaningful discussion that made quite an impression. Especially when Bill Harrison—who had quietly come in during the tail end of the discussion—decided that he would try to put a chill on the warm glow of this fledging détente.

"Ah…excuse me. Sorry I was late, Mr., I mean, Dr. Silver."

"Not a problem, Dr. Harris." Ray said, purposely mispronouncing his name to the giggles of the other members in attendance.

"Harrison," he corrected Ray.

"Yes, of course, Dr. Harrison. My apologies."

"I don't mean to put a damper on things, as it looks like you are all getting along so nicely, but I had a few questions that I was going to ask you in private because, I guess, they might make you uncomfortable and I didn't want to embarrass you." Harrison was angry that his prank on Ray hadn't materialized and that the thirty files he had brought to Ray's office had wound up on Stella Leone's desk.

Stella turned around to look at Bill Harrison and mumbled just loud enough for the others to hear, "And yet here you are anyway."

"Excuse me, Nurse Leone, I didn't quite get that," Harrison said in a curt tone, having fully heard her remark as well as the chuckles from the other nurses.

"Nothing, Dr. Harrison," she said. "I wasn't talking to you."

"Please, doctor," Ray cut in. "Please go on. You have a question or two for me? This is the perfect venue."

Harrison continued to look toward Stella as he began. "Why is it that you guys always claim to cure everything from colic to cancer?" He said as he slowly shifted his gaze from Stella to Ray.

Quiet descended over the small audience as they looked to Ray, waiting for a reply to a question that they too had sometimes wondered. He thought for a moment and slowly smiled as a few more doctors quietly came in and sat down in the back row next to Harrison. In his own paranoid worst-case scenario, he had anticipated that something like this might happen. During his make-believe confrontations he masterfully silenced his imaginary critics. He knew he could do it again now. "Just keep your composure," he thought to himself. "Turn it around and put him on the defensive."

"Well, Dr. Silver?" Harrison boldly asked, sensing that he had wounded his target.

"That's a very good question, Dr. Harrison." Ray said slowly walking down the aisle to assert his control. "I've been in practice twenty years now. Was actually a chiropractic patient for... I'd say about thirteen years before earning my doctorate. I must know at least five...no, make that six, hundred chiropractors from all over the country as well as from Canada, England, Australia, Israel, and Spain."

"Sounds like you're gonna take us on a world tour," Harrison said, trying to get his colleagues to laugh. Everyone, even Ray, failed to react. He just paused, smiled at Harrison, and proceeded.

"In all the years that I've been doing this, and with all the colleagues that I know, I have never claimed, nor have I ever heard anyone else claim, that we can cure anything."

Everyone looked at Harrison for his response. "Yeah, well, I've heard it said by others..."

"Really," Ray cut him off. "By whom? If you have a name, doc, I'd like to go talk to the guy... or gal. If you read it in a journal, or if there was a study that came to that conclusion, I'd be appreciative if you'd provide the reference or perhaps you can give me a copy."

"Well, I've heard from patients who have gone to you guys and they said they had conditions cured."

"Now that's a little different, isn't it. It's the patient or patients who are claiming they've had diagnosed conditions resolve. And did they, doc? Did they have conditions that resolved while under chiropractic care?"

"I've had a few patients over the years, who...while under the care of a chiropractor, just happened to have experienced a spontaneous resolution of their condition."

Ray was sensing that he now had the upper hand. "So is that a bad thing, doc? Is that a bad thing, that while under chiropractic care, to have a patient also have a condition that you were treating with drugs....resolve?"

Harrison remained silent and searched for his next question. The other doctors and nurses were beginning to find their exchange a little entertaining.

Ray continued. "Dr. Harrison, In all my years in practice I've had a very large number of patients with diagnosed conditions, conditions that had been treated for years with nothing more than prescription medication, resolve during a recommended course of chiropractic care. I've also had a number of patients who came to me with health problems that didn't resolve. I assure you that I never took credit for the ones that did. I believe, as I'm sure you do as well, that the human body is an amazing living machine. That the human body, when allowed to function the way nature intended, is designed to express health...yes? The human body is, in fact, a self-regulating, self-healing organism. And sir, provided that there is no interference in the communication of the very intelligence that regulates every cell, every tissue, and every organ system in the body, this body has the ability to adapt to its environment, and to heal itself, just like when you cut your finger." Ray held up his index finger and slowly turned to show everyone, as if performing a show and tell. Then he turned back to Harrison. "Let me ask you, sir, what goes on inside your body when you cut yourself, and how does it know what to do and when to do it?"

It was a rhetorical question, but Ray waited a few seconds to see if Harrison had a response. "I'll tell you. Your innate intelligence kicks in and sends a host of chemical mediators to the injury site and begins to stop the bleeding, kill the germs, close the wound, form a scab, and as that healing process is finishing, doesn't that scab shrink and eventually disappear?"

Bill Harrison saw all the eyes that were upon him and knew that he was now on the defensive. "Well, that doesn't work for everyone. There are plenty of people who require a tetanus shot and a round of antibiotics, and you have to keep it bandaged, otherwise you risk infection."

"So I ask you, doctor, that while that is true in some cases, isn't that more the exception and not the rule? And that while washing a wound and dressing it to keep it clean is common sense, the other measures taken are done so because we, as a society, have long begun to lose faith in the body's ability to perform thousands and thousands of simultaneous functions—correctly I might add—without us even having to think about those processes. And when we think we know better then the very power that created us, isn't that when we begin to screw things up? Let's be honest. How many times have you had a patient with a sprain or strain type of injury for which you prescribed an anti- inflammatory, and then maybe a week or two later he began to complain of something he never experienced before...such as migraines. So then you wrote a prescription for that. Or maybe he or she began experiencing anxiety attacks or began feeling depressed so you wrote a script for an antidepressant. And now after a few weeks the patient tells you he's having trouble sleeping so you prescribe sleeping pills. If you take a good look at the long list of adverse reactions of these meds, then you know that what I'm talking about is drug induced—what we call 'iatrogenic' disease."

Ray looked around at the other members of his audience. "Now please, people, don't get me wrong here. I'm not bashing the practice of medicine, and please don't think that I am anti-medicine. I'm not. Well, not all of it anyway. I just have a problem with interventions that actually prolong or interfere with the healing process, or when, by the very nature of adding foreign chemicals to the process that we end up creating new problems. Look it, you guys know that where medicine really shines is when it comes to any intervention that's used to save a life or the procedures that you utilize to rebuild a blown-out knee or a busted shoulder. When someone strokes out, you guys have the skill to keep that person alive. The doctors, nurses, and emergency medical techs who work in the ERs, in the trauma centers, and," he said, looking at Stella, "in field hospitals in combat zones...you guys are the true life-savers. That's where medicine is at its best and nobody, especially me, has ever made any claim to the contrary. God bless you people for the kind of work that you do. But let's not confuse using surgery and drugs to save lives or to rebuild a face torn-apart in a grenade blast as the same thing as using those tools to restore health."

Bill Harrison was now visibly annoyed and defensive as he folded his arms across his chest. "We're getting new and improved wonder drugs all the time that help us treat our patients" he stated defiantly.

Ray turned back to him "Let's be honest here, doc. There's never been a pill, no potion, and no lotion that has ever cured anybody. Right? When a person is sick, is it because they lack a certain drug? Do people get headaches because they suffer from an aspirin shortage? Do they get infections because of low blood levels of antibiotics? Allow me to suggest to you, that if any living thing has gone from a state of health to a state of sickness, it's because it's either toxic with something or it's deficient in something. And that being the case, does it not make sense to look for that toxic substance and remove it or to look for that deficiency and then provide it so that there is sufficiency? In part, this is what I do. This is what I have always done with my patients."

People were quiet, looking at Ray and then Harrison as they waited for someone to say something. Ray continued. "If, Dr. Harrison, you really think that intervention to heal a cut is necessary, then I'd like to suggest that you go to the market and buy a steak. In fact, sir, don't just buy an ordinary cheap cut of beef, but get the most expensive cut of meat that they have. Take it home, lay it out on your kitchen counter, and take your very best steak knife and put a slice into it." People looked at him and wondered where he was going with this. "Then, I want you to wash the wound, swab it with alcohol, inject it with a tetanus vaccine, inject it with an antibiotic, stitch it up, put on a clean dressing, and then place it into your refrigerator and let it sit there for about a week."

Harrison, completely angered, interrupted him. "Now you're being totally ridiculous. Everyone knows that nothing is going to happen because it's a dead piece of flesh."

"Exactly my point!" Ray called out in excitement, causing everyone to flinch at the unexpected burst of energy. "The chemical makeup of that steak is the same as the muscle tissue in your own body. Proteins, right? Made of amino acids, right? Made up of carbon, hydrogen, oxygen, nitrogen, phosphorus, and a whole host of trace minerals, yes? So what's the difference between the two?"

"Life!" Stella said before continuing, "One is alive, it's part of a body that has a life force with an intelligence that directs an immune response."

"Exactly, Nurse Leone. Exactly." Ray looked around at everyone and then back to Bill Harrison. "My point, Dr. Harrison, is that healing does not come from a bottle of pills. It never has and it never will. Healing comes from within. It's when there is an interference in that life force that the natural healing capability of the body becomes impaired. It's when there is an interference in the self-regulating system of the body that the host's resistance to a germ becomes weaker, thereby making the host more susceptible. We have germs around us all the time. Why aren't we all sick? Do germs cause disease or is it a weakened host who provides the perfect environment for germs to thrive? Look it, chiropractors don't cure disease. Nobody can. We merely act as facilitators by finding and removing this interference… or by trying to identify the deficiency or even the toxicity. It's really as simple as that." Ray waited for a response, but Harrison was silent. The others mumbled amongst themselves.

"Dr. Harrison, chiropractic focuses on the spine because the spine houses and protects the nervous system, and the nervous system controls every function in the body. If there's an interference in the communication link between the brain and the rest of the body, does it not make sense to remove that interference so the body's allowed to function the way it was intended to? The ironic thing about all of this is that the father of medicine, Hippocrates, recognized this and also practiced spinal manipulation. Look at his writings. You'll see he said, 'look well to the spine, for here is the requisite cause of disease.'"

Dr. Brian Davis, Chief of Orthopedics emerged from the back corner of the room. "Ok people, time to get back to work. Very informative talk, Dr. Silver. Thank you."

Bill Harrison was first to leave the conference room, and as he headed down the corridor he mumbled, "What a fucking asshole." Stella looked at Ray, and they smiled at each other.

As Dr. Davis was leaving, he approached Ray saying, "Geez, Silver, I only wanted you to give an introductory talk about joint manipulation, not proselytize. And I surely didn't expect you to slap down one of my doctors."

"I'm sorry Dr. Davis, I didn't mean…"

"Yes, you did," Davis cut him off. "But that's ok. That guy needs to be bitch-slapped once in a while. Trust me, that alone just earned you points with the staff. Do me and yourself a favor, though. This isn't the place to go on an anti-drug crusade. Just stick to what you do and don't go rocking the boat. Clear?"

"Yeah, clear," Ray responded.

The room had emptied out except for Stella, who was packing up the projector. "That was quite some speech you just gave," she said as she wound up the extension cord. "You really slapped down Harrison but good." She looked at Ray. "That prick needs more of that from people around this place. You've got some fans now."

"Glad to be of service," he said, beginning to feel fatigued.

"Look, can I be straight with you?"

"Sure thing, go ahead."

"I get the feeling that you're out to prove yourself to the medical staff. Don't go there. You don't have to. From what I know of you, you had a successful private practice for twenty years and now you're here. The first chiropractor that Seattle VMC has ever had. You've already proven yourself and what you can do." She looked at Ray and felt the intensity of his full attention. "Just like when you were in private practice, there are always going to be those who hate you. It's not the messenger, it's the message. Got it?"

"Yeah, got it."

By the time Ray had gotten back down to his basement office, the adrenaline was wearing off and he noticed the nausea building inside of him. He had been so nervous when he woke that morning he couldn't eat. He had also been so tired from the lack of sleep that he had consumed several cups of coffee before arriving at work—the acid that was now churning away in his stomach. He realized suddenly that he wouldn't make it to the bathroom down at the other end of the long hallway. In a panic, he quickly looked around the room and saw the wastebasket in the corner by his desk—just barely getting to it before beginning to vomit.

13

Stella Leone often felt cursed by her beauty. As a teenager, she had matured early and as such had either been the envy of her female classmates or the subject of their ridicule. She was the most sought-after girl by the boys at school and the fantasy of several of her male teachers. On a number of occasions during her senior year at Charlestown High, her Spanish teacher had tried to convince her that private "tutoring" would help her ace his class. Being half-Italian and half-Spanish, Stella was already fluent in both languages though, and if she ever needed tutoring she could easily get it at home.

The Italian side of the family was where she had gotten her "in your face" attitude. Being an only child, her street smarts came from her older cousins, who never hesitated in coming to her aid. As soon as someone—anyone—tried to take advantage of her, she got her attitude in gear and set them straight. If that didn't work, the mere mention of her cousins did.

Stella was wise to Mr. Zaragosa and had known that he had more than just tutoring in mind. When his persistence became overbearing, she chose to bypass a typically unresponsive school administration and instead had brought in her cousins Anthony, Marco, and Ricky for an after school meeting with the teacher. It wasn't a long meeting. In fact, their business was concluded in less than ten minutes and without physical injury. Not another word was ever spoken of the incident, although rumors of the meeting spread like a wildfire in the middle of a summer dry spell. The boys were always there for her, but she was careful not to abuse their services. Having protective older cousins had been a double-edged sword. On the one hand, Stella had the benefit of her guardian angels. The neighborhood boys knew they had to be on their best behavior while on a date with her—with a heavy price to pay for any attempts on her virtue. On the other hand, after the Zaragosa incident most of her classmates had begun to keep a comfortable distance.

What few male friends she did have had known her and the family since grade school. It was easy for them to see past her physical attributes to appreciate her intelligence, strength, and sensitivity. Sadly, there would be very few men of that caliber in her future. When she did come across a man who had that rare ability to see her for the skills she possessed and treated her with the respect that she deserved, she was more willing to entertain a deeper relationship.

Her senior year in high school had been filled with other challenges which she faced head on and which helped shape her independent personality. Needing money for college, she began working in the evenings at the small Italian deli that was owned and operated by her father—and which was the life blood of her family. Working sixteen hour days—Monday through Saturday—her father would only take Sundays off out of respect to his wife, who insisted on observing the Sabbath. Sal Leone's deli was very popular in Boston's Charlestown neighborhood. There was always a line from the counter out to the street during the lunch hour. Local shopkeepers, mechanics, utility workers, cops, and firefighters from the Main Street station would file in one by one to order any one of his hot, homemade sandwiches.

His specialty was a meatball hero made from fresh ground pork, beef, and veal that he mixed with a variety of "secret" spices. But it was the smell of fresh garlic, oregano, rosemary, and parmesan that drifted out of the front door that grabbed passersby and held them prisoner. Sal prided himself on his tomato sauce, made from scratch, that he would spike with Chianti and let simmer for hours. Only then would he even think of ladling the thick gravy over his meatballs as they lay cradled in a still-steaming loaf of golden crusted Italian bread. The local moms would stop by on Saturdays and Sundays to load up on sliced lunch meats and cheeses of every variety.

Sal Leone lived for his deli, and as much as he would have loved for Stella to keep the business after he was gone, he knew that her dream was to become a nurse like her mom. His nephew Marco, however, practically lived at the deli. Like his cousin Stella, he had begun working with his Uncle Sal several years earlier when he was in high school. The both of them had decided that when it was time for Sal to retire, he would be the one to take over the business. Everyone in the family agreed that Marco was the best choice.

But it was not to be. In the early morning hours of a freezing cold late winter snowstorm, as Sal was preparing to head off to start another day, he heard a small explosion from several blocks away. The sirens wailed in the distance as Engine Company 9 and Ladder 32 raced up Bunker Hill Street to Leone's Deli. Marco had come running to the house and was banging on the front door. Sal felt his heart begin to race as he looked out of his kitchen window and saw the orange glow light up the pre-dawn sky. As the rest of the household started to stir, Sal and Marco ran down Auburn Street. Having spent the last thirty years of his life working sixteen hour days—giving in to the daily temptation of his own creations and never being able to give up his smoking habit—would finally take its toll on him.

By the time the two men got to the deli at the corner of Bunker Hill and Chappie the small brick building was completely engulfed in flames. The fire department could only pour water on it to keep the inferno from spreading to the neighboring businesses. Sal couldn't catch his breath. Watching in horror, his chest tightened as his life burned to the ground. Marco stared, unable to move. Stella and her mother finally arrived as Sal—in tears and gasping for breath—collapsed to his knees. Then, as if he had been struck by a lightening bolt, he felt the crushing, burning pressure of a massive heart attack consume his chest just as the flames were consuming his deli. He fought to bend his rigid arms up to his shirt and rip it open, as if that would help him to catch another breath. It didn't. He collapsed face down onto the snow-covered street as the walls of his deli collapsed in upon themselves. As he and the deli had lived because of each other, they died together as well.

* * *

Even with the money that she had saved up, Stella had still planned on working at the family deli while attending Bunker Hill Community College for a degree as a licensed practical nurse. Then, once in the workforce, she would continue to attend school on a part-time basis to fulfill all the requirements necessary to become a registered nurse. After the deli was destroyed, she had considered putting her college plans on hold in order to help her mother meet their household expenses. It had been her mother who then encouraged her to look into a career as an Army nurse.

"Estella, mi bebé dulce, they will pay for your school. You can get it your full nursing degree and you will have good paying job right away," her mother insisted. "This is 1975. You have been watching the news, yes? America is still angry over this Vietnam. Young people here want nothing of the Army. This is best time for you to do this. Esto es el mejor tiempo, se fía de mí."

Stella knew that her mother was right. With their financial situation being what it was, it made absolute sense. Both sides of the family also weighed in, encouraging her to take advantage of the opportunity. With everyone in agreement Stella went ahead and spoke with a recruiter. That Autumn, with an enlistment bonus check in hand, she headed off to nearby Northeastern University.

For the most part her Army career had been great. Right out of school and after successful completion of basic training, she had first been assigned to Fort Hood, Texas, and then to Madigan Army Hospital at Fort Lewis, just outside of Tacoma. She had quickly earned the reputation of someone who was not to be trifled with after an overzealous male colleague continued to make unwanted sexual advances. Stella had only needed to summon up her inner street child to put him in his place.

While stationed at Madigan, she had met and married her husband, a handsome career officer who was politically connected and on the fast track to a high-level Pentagon post. All he had needed to complete the perfect resume was a trophy wife with brains and several kids, and Stella had met his criteria. Her intelligence, along with her military-acquired discipline, had tempered the street attitude she had developed as a child of Boston. Her gift was being able to skillfully and diplomatically combine all three, making her a formidable opponent in many areas of debate. He had tried hard to convince her to give up her career for family life. Unfortunately for him, he wasn't going to win that battle. Several years later, and by the time she was deployed to a field hospital in Saudi Arabia during the Desert Shield build-up before the first Gulf War, the magic of their relationship had begun to wane. With her upcoming deployment, they both knew that any conversation regarding the future of their marriage would have to wait until she was far from any combat action.

Initially, she was not expected to be anywhere near live fire; however, one early morning her unit was hit by several Scud missiles. The first was a direct hit on a mess tent full of troops just sitting down to breakfast. By the time the second and third missiles had struck, Stella was already attending wounded soldiers and continued to do so throughout the additional strikes. At one point, she even hoisted a badly injured soldier across her shoulders and attempted to carry him back to the medical tent as the concussive force from a fourth blast knocked them both to the ground. A small piece of shrapnel barely grazed the top of her right shoulder as she was falling. Had it not been for the force of the explosion propelling them forward, that jagged piece of hot metal would have easily ripped through the neck of the already wounded private she was carrying.

When the invasion of Kuwait actually got underway, she had found herself on several helicopter evac flights during those first few days of battle—taking wounded off of the front lines and bringing them back to the rear area. On more than one occasion, her chopper had taken hits as they flew into live fire zones. By the time she rotated back to the States and an assignment at Walter Reed, she had been awarded the Purple Heart for her wound, the Bronze Star for heroism while under hostile fire, and a promotion from Captain to Major.

While she was stationed in the Gulf, her husband, Colonel Griffin Kelley, had been assigned to Army Intelligence at the Pentagon. Unbeknownst to her, it was Kelley who had pulled the necessary strings to get his wife transferred to Walter Reed Medical Center in Washington. Now that she was a decorated hero, he no longer had to pressure her about children, as her presence alone could still help his career. She played her part well, working at the medical center during the day and attending "inside the beltway" cocktail parties with him at night. Except for the fact that there was no longer any romance between the two of them, to outsiders, they were the perfect patriotic couple.

During her deployment, Stella had met a doctor from another medical unit who was stationed at the same base for several weeks before redeploying to set up operations further to the south in Jubail. While working together during that short time, they found they had similar interests and had quickly come to like each other's company. He too was married, and neither had any intention of taking their relationship to a physical level. They simply felt comfortable around each other, often spending time in their off-duty hours engaged in conversation, teaming up to play cribbage or hearts with other friends in camp, or simply sharing a meal. When his unit relocated, she missed him a great deal, but thought it best to not pursue the friendship. She often wondered whether the closeness that she felt with him was due more to the circumstances of their situation rather than to a natural attraction that might not have been there had they met back home. The fact that her doctor friend hadn't initiated any further contact during the rest of her deployment meant that he either felt the same, or perhaps that something bad had happened to him. Her curiosity did get the better of her at times when she found herself checking in on the location and overall well-being of his medical unit without attempting any direct contact with him.

After her return home, and to her surprise and delight, her Gulf War friend, Dr. Ted Cranston, was also on staff at Walter Reed. As it turned out, he had performed a surgical miracle on a Brigadier General who sustained a gender-threatening injury during a "non combat" operation. Upon his recovery and subsequent return to the Pentagon, he had had Dr. Cranston reassigned to Walter Reed so that he would be able to see him for his periodic follow-up exams. It was during this time their friendship was rekindled.

Outside of the obligatory cocktail parties and formal dinners, Stella found herself spending many evenings alone at home while her husband was often summoned to late night intelligence sessions, several of which led to consultations with the National Security Agency and meetings in the White House situation room. His was a rising star, and Stella knew that any appearance of impropriety would have a negative effect on his career. As her friendship with Ted Cranston grew, she was painfully aware that she could not be seen with him outside of the medical center. Even then, their relationship couldn't go beyond what it already was. But they were two friends who shared common interests, war experience, lifeless marriages, and a growing unfulfilled desire to be with each other on a deeper level. It was all too obvious to their coworkers that they spent every free moment at work together. Whether it was having lunch or coffee breaks, with or without fellow staff around, they seemed to be glued at the hip.

At the start of her second year at Reed, an incident occurred that would portent a significant change in Stella's personal and professional life. On several occasions, she had noticed discrepancies in the amount of narcotics inventoried relative to the amounts reported as having been dispensed. The miscounts had been consistent with night shift numbers that didn't tie out when compared to her next day beginning inventories. At first she had thought that the evening nursing staff was making errors in recording. Her evening counterpart had thought the same of her. When they finally put their heads together, they had noticed that the discrepancies were always consistent.

As they started to compare notes and continued to scrutinize every prescription written and dispensed, they realized that somehow the narcotics were disappearing right after the day shift ending inventory was completed. There was a ten-minute window during which the nurses from both shifts congregated in the break room or at the individual rooms of patients in order to review charts and update each other on any changes in patient condition or care. Although the drug cabinet was left unattended during this time, it was locked. When both Stella and her evening colleague decided they would begin to meet at the medication cabinet at the end of the day shift, they began to take note of one doctor stopping by at that very same time. The first time he came by, they didn't think anything of it. Noticing both nurses standing there, he had nonchalantly looked through his charts while sneaking glances at Kyla Shelbee, a supervising night nurse. When he had realized they weren't going to leave, he abruptly went on his way. The same thing occurred several days in a row, and it was then obvious to both of them that he was becoming more frustrated with each passing day. Stella also took note of the ongoing glances between Shelbee and Dr. Taylor each time he showed up.

On the fifth day, they decided to watch the nurse's station from a safe distance to see what he would do. Sure enough, when he came by and saw he was alone, he quickly produced a key to the cabinet and grabbed a box of pills. As he turned to make his getaway he had run right into Stella.

"So you're the one who's been raiding my drug cabinet," she said staring down her nervous drug thief.

"What are you talking about?" He tried to regain his composure.

"We caught you taking narcotics out if this cabinet without authorization. We got you red-handed," she shot back with authority.

"I hope you're not accusing me of stealing Nurse...." He slowly looked down at her name badge, taking time to observe the outline of her breasts. "Nurse Leone. And what do you mean 'we' caught you?"

Stella quickly turned around, looking for her fellow sleuth, but she was nowhere to be found. It became apparent that her colleague had stayed behind and then took off when Stella swooped in to nail their culprit. She turned back to her thief, and said "That's Major Leone to you, Captain Taylor! And I caught you taking drugs out of this cabinet without proper authority. I've got inventory records showing the same quantity of this drug disappearing now for several weeks."

"Well, Major, as a doctor dealing with chronic pain patients I have the right to check the expiration dates of the medications in this cabinet," he said, looking directly at her to gauge her expression, "And you don't have any proof to the contrary."

By this time the other staff members had heard the commotion out at the nurse's station and were soon congregating around them to see what was going on. Ted Cranston was making his way down the hallway when he noticed the gathering as well.

"Oh, and here comes your boyfriend," Dr. Taylor said much louder as he began to walk away.

"Dr. Taylor," Stella said very angrily. "Leave the medication."

He turned and tossed the box to her before proceeding down the hall. Stella had been furious for his blatant lies and disrespect, but most of all she had felt betrayed by her nightshift colleague and fellow witness, who abandoned her like a coward in the heat of battle.

In the excitement of the confrontation she had forgotten to question where he had gotten the key to the drug cabinet and whether he had access to other supplies throughout the hospital. Over the following weeks, Stella ran up against resistance from colleagues and superiors alike as she had tried to investigate the matter further. She was able to find out that the nurse who she had thought was going to help her had actually been romantically involved with Captain Taylor. In fact, it was from her key that he had made a copy. Although Stella had no hardcore evidence, she was almost certain that the Captain had an addiction to pain medication. She approached Shelbee, intending to determine the extent of her relationship with the Captain and to try to enlist her in getting help for him. No luck. Just like everyone else she talked to, she was in CYA (cover your ass) mode.

It seemed that everybody she approached was fearful of something. It was almost as if they all had a skeleton in the closet and feared being exposed in some way. It didn't take long before most of her nurse colleagues and many of the doctors were giving her the cold shoulder. Even Ted Cranston had begun to shy away, fearing repercussions. As the weeks progressed, she noticed that he was rarely around during their usual meeting times. Even when he was, he had become less engaged, less interested in their conversations. The glint that had once filled his eyes whenever they talked to each other had been replaced by guilt. He could no longer make direct eye contact. At one point he even told her that she should simply drop the matter altogether before both of their careers, and possibly the career of her husband were negatively affected. She was certainly disillusioned and felt abandoned. She wrestled with the idea of turning the matter over to the Army's criminal investigative unit and wondered how that might affect her career. "Would any further advancement ever be possible? What if they transfer me to a medical center in the Midwest or overseas? Will people talk about my friendship with Ted and portray it as something more than it actually is? But it's just a friendship and nothing more" she insisted to herself. "What if his career or marriage is affected? It'll be my fault. But what did I do wrong? I'm not the drug thief. I caught the bastard."

Her questioning went on for days. As little as they talked anymore, Stella decided to consult with her husband. She somehow thought, somehow hoped, that he would be supportive to some extent. At least he would be able to advise her. She was certain he would know the right thing to do. Just the opposite. He had seen the situation from one perspective. How it would affect him. He even scolded her for getting involved, as if she were a child. Stella's emotions ran the gamut from shock and outright disbelief to total betrayal. Betrayal from her coworkers, friends, superiors in the medical corps, and now her high-ranking, well-placed husband.

In the months that followed, they agreed to go their separate ways, She had soon realized that there was nothing for her any longer at Walter Reed or in Washington, D.C. She thought about transferring to another medical center, but where would she go? In spite of its enormity, the Army, and especially the medical command was like a small town. Although she had not pursued the matter any further than with her immediate superiors, she had made enough waves that she felt the incident would follow her. She would be a pariah no matter where she went. In spite of her military service and decorations from Desert Shield and Desert Storm, she would no longer be looked upon as a team player but rather as a trouble maker.

She walked away from the Army and began the transition process to the Veterans Medical Service, taking a position in Seattle. She never saw Ted Cranston again and refused to respond to several of his inquiries. He had wanted to tell her that he had come to learn that Dr. Taylor was the nephew of an Alabama Congressman who sat on the Defense Department appropriations committee. That was what had made her so "radioactive" and what had accounted for the isolation treatment she had received. Had she taken his calls, it would have answered a lot of her questions. Had she taken his calls, she would have also realized that Ted Cranston was trying to determine if it would have been worth his while to seek a transfer to Fort Lewis and try to salvage a relationship that had been easily progressing toward intimacy. Her refusal to respond to his inquiries had told him all he needed to know, and he retreated to the safety of his loveless marriage.

As much as Stella tried to put the incident behind her, she was left with those unanswered questions, along with the regret of not taking the appropriate actions regardless of the fallout that would have occurred. "After all" she said to herself, "look what it got me anyway."

14

It had been almost twelve months since the first time Ray had met John Walters on the deck of the LCI 776. At the time, Walters—a Navy veteran who did two tours of duty commanding swift boats on the rivers of South Vietnam—had been in the middle of pleading his case with a young Coast Guard Lieutenant regarding the rotting hull of the former World War II ship. Having rescued the vessel from a local fishing concern, Walters, along with a half-dozen fellow naval enthusiasts was slowly restoring the small ship to her former glory. Each man involved in the effort possessed a variety of skills that allowed them to tackle the myriad repairs including electrical, metal work, ventilation, engine restoration, and so on. The one thing they couldn't do on their own—replacing the original hull—was too big a job and too expensive. What little money they had contributed themselves had barely been enough to purchase paint, and donations were few and far in between. Needless to say, fundraising was not their forte.

John Walters had spent his entire post-military career in and around the maritime community, occasionally being contracted for "favors" from individuals within the military-industrial complex, he always seemed to come up with that rare mechanical part or the necessary funding when all seemed lost. Faced with having to come up with $500,000 dollars for a new hull or risk the Coast Guard scuttling the vessel, some of his band of volunteers had once again been stunned when he had the 776 towed from Lake Union to the Olympic Shipyards for the new bottom. He never said where or how he raised the cash other than, "I just know people." From that point on, some of the project volunteers were convinced he had been an agency man.

Just about a year after his first visit to the 776, Ray was ready to volunteer his Saturdays helping to restore the small ship to the way she was when commissioned at a Portland, Oregon shipyard in August 1944.

He had started to settle into a routine over at the Veterans hospital. As the weeks passed, he had seen an increasing amount of referrals from some of the medical staff and, thanks to the success that he was having with Stella Leone's chronic back problems, a growing number of the nursing staff regularly came down for visits. He had been on several dates with Leigh Anne and he was happy that they had gone well. Neither one expected too much from the other, which somehow made the mutual attraction they had all the more unexplainable. Their early dates had either started or ended at Kelsey's, which served as neutral ground. The first date had been spent entirely in the back booth of the sports bar's dining room, where they drank Pipelines, munched on finger food, and talked for hours about Hawaii, favorite foods, politics, sports, movies, and music. They found similar affinities toward Kimo's, snorkeling in Haunama Bay, grilled mahi-mahi, and ice cream made from coconut milk. They even found common ground in music, from Taylor, Henley and Alison Krauss to Frank Sinatra, which made Leigh Anne laugh.

"Sinatra was a staple in my house," said Ray. "My folks couldn't get enough of him. They not only played his records in the house, but also at my Pop's hardware store, they listened to this radio station that played him almost all day long."

"I'm surprised you didn't get sick of it." Leigh Anne said as she munched on some peanuts.

"Strange, isn't it? The more I heard him, the more I liked him."

"Favorite song?"

"What, by Sinatra?"

"Yeah, by Sinatra, but also do you have an overall favorite?"

"With Frank, I'd have to say '*The way you look tonight*.' Overall favorite? There's so many it's hard for me to pick just one. What about you?"

"'*Heart of the matter*'. The live version."

"Don Henley. Excellent song, I like it. But why that one, something personal?"

"No, not at all. It's just that it's very reflective, for me anyway. It's about learning from ones' mistakes, letting go, moving on and of course forgiveness. There's some irony in that, though."

"How so?"

"Sometimes forgiving is just not that easy."

Ray had sensed that Leigh Anne had some relationship baggage because the few times their conversations headed off into that direction, she quickly and skillfully changed the subject. It made him curious, but he was smart enough, and patient enough, to allow her the space she needed. He was sure that when she was ready to talk about it—and if she wanted to talk about it—then she would.

On one date, she had taken him to the aquarium after it had closed. He listened intently as she described the mating habits of sea otters. "Male and female sea otters are kind of like their human counterparts," she said watching them through the glass partition.

"In what way?" Ray asked as he watched her focus on her charges.

"First off, the females mature sooner than the males." She looked up into his eyes and continued. "A few years later, the males are finally ready to reproduce. And, much like humans, the female sea otter is more loyal to her mate."

"Are you saying the males fool around?"

"The male of the species seems to have no problem having multiple liaisons." Seeing his eyebrows raise, she smiled, took his hand, and they walked off to finish their private tour.

With each date she became more comfortable being alone with him. He was soft-spoken and comfortable with himself. He didn't constantly undress her with his eyes—at least, not that she could tell. And unlike men closer to her age, he didn't feel he had to prove himself.

"He's not a 'wow' kind of guy," she had said to Kelsey. "He's more of a 'woo' kind of guy."

"I don't get it," Kelsey said as she poured a draught for a customer.

"He's not trying to 'wow' me with expensive restaurants, fancy cars, and tales of masculine feats of bravado. He's woo-ing me. He listens to me, opens doors for me, asks my opinion on things, he walks me to my door, and asks before he kisses me goodnight. He's a gentleman," she said with a smile. "He's wooing me like men used to do in the old days."

"Wow, he sounds perfect," Kelsey said sarcastically. She pulled a Pipeline from a well filled with crushed ice, popped off the cap, and handed it to her.

"Well, he's not that perfect," Leigh Anne said pensively. "Politically, he does lean to the right."

Kelsey laughed and said, "Ok, so he's old, conservative, and it sounds like he's cheap."

"He's a little older, I agree, and you know me and politics. Where he's just to the right of center, I'm a little to the left. Makes for a nice balance, if you ask me. And I wouldn't be so quick to call him cheap."

"So he's a real gentleman, huh? Do you mean to tell me that after five dates he hasn't tried to jump your bones?"

"Nope, not once. I'm telling you, he's a gentleman."

Kelsey extended her hand to the air and stuck out her thumb. "So he's old," She chided, sticking out her index finger, "cheap," boldly extending her middle finger, "and he can't get it up?"

"We'll see about that," Leigh Anne said with a mischievous smile. "We will definitely see."

15

T he night before he went down to Lake Union, reintroduced himself to John Walters, and asked to help with the restoration project, Ray was doing his homework on the LCI 776. He wanted Walters to know that he was familiar with these little ships that had once served many roles, from troop carriers to gunboat configurations. At 158 feet in length they typically had a crew of four officers and twenty-four enlisted men. As he searched the internet from his workshop desk, his cat lay next to the keyboard and purred as much from the company as the heat coming from the articulating desk lamp. Ray would occasionally look over at her, and she'd purr even louder.

"Did you know," he said to Magic, "LCI stands for Landing Craft Infantry?" Magic just squinted and purred. "She can make four thousand nautical miles cruising at twelve knots with her eight GM diesel engines. Wow!" He continued reading and looking over schematic drawings of the ship. "And get this, Madge, she can do a sustained fourteen knots. Pretty good, huh? Yeah, I know. Pretty slow. All in all, they were under-armed, under-armored, and practically sitting ducks in battle."

He leaned over and kissed her forehead as she laid her head down on the desk. Her tail made a big sweep up into the air and back down onto his stack of papers. Ray closed his eyes, making sure he knew his nautical terms, reciting them several times as a schoolchild would recite his ABCs. "Starboard is right, port is left, bow is at the front, and stern is at the back." After repeating this until he was confident that he would not forget them, he had begun to read up on the battle history of the 776 when Magic began to stir. Her purring stopped at the same time she raised her head to look in the direction of the garage side door.

Ray stopped talking and listened intently, but didn't hear anything at first. He turned back to the computer monitor and then to Magic, who was now sitting up on the far right end of the desk, her tail slowly but firmly slapping against the plywood top. She clearly seemed agitated. Again, Ray turned his ear to the side door and this time heard faint footsteps along the gravel path that ran between the house and the garage. The footsteps stopped. Then they started again, going in the opposite direction. Again they stopped. It was quiet for a few seconds. Without taking his eyes off of the side door, Ray slowly reached to his left until his hand found the hammer lying on the workbench. He sat motionless at his desk for a few seconds more, then slowly slid the hammer closer to him. As he did, the claw end caught the corner of a small plastic tray of nails. He cringed as it crashed onto the floor and he froze. Magic turned to look at him. "It was an accident," he whispered to her. She turned back to the door. Then, a faint knocking and what sounded like Leigh Anne's voice: "Hey Silver, you home?"

Ray jumped up from his desk. Magic too stood and with a long, wide yawn, arched her back in a slow stretch before jumping down to follow him. When he opened the door, Ray looked out toward the house and saw Leigh Anne on his front step.

"Hey," she said with a slight upward nod of her head.

"Hey back," he replied surprised and yet happy to see her. He stood at the door, taking in every bit of her.

"You plan on using that thing?" she pointed to the hammer.

Ray looked down at his hand and then back at Leigh Anne. "Uh, no. I was just... just organizing stuff in the workshop."

Highlighted by the front porch light, she was dressed in tight, worn-out blue jeans and a sheer peasant-style blouse. Her auburn hair was pulled back tightly into a pony tail, and he could tell that she was braless.

"As you've noticed, it's a bit cold. You gonna stand there staring at me or are you gonna invite me in for a beer?"

"Oh yeah, sure. Just a sec," he said as he ran back into his workshop to return the hammer and shut everything off. The workshop and garage were now dark except for what little light was leaking in through the opened side door. Stepping quickly through the garage back toward the house, he tripped over the recycling bin and fell through the doorway and onto the gravel path.

"I take it you don't dance much," she said with a straight face.

With his ego bruised slightly more than his elbows and knees, Ray slowly got up, dusted himself off, and pursed his lips as he went to open the front door to let her in. She slowly walked past him, purposely brushing into his chest and abdomen. He deeply inhaled her scent as she went into the house. "I wasn't expecting you...but this is a nice surprise."

"I hadn't planned on coming by. Just a spontaneous thing," she said, stopping at the darkened fireplace in the large front room. Ray turned on a small table lamp and watched her survey the house. "I was just hangin' out at Kelsey's and had nothing to do." She turned slowly to face him. "I was hoping that you were gonna stop in. You didn't, obviously. So I thought I'd stop by to see what you were up to. I hope that's ok?"

"Yeah, well, I was...well yeah of course it's ok. I was just straightening up and doing some computer stuff in the workshop." He looked at the scratches on his palms and motioned for her to follow him into the kitchen. He washed his hands at the sink and when he turned Leigh Anne had a hand towel waiting for him.

"Give me your hands," she said holding out the towel. She gently patted them dry and he realized that though they had been on five dates, this was the first time she had been to his house. He watched as she carefully looked around the kitchen.

"Come," Ray offered, leading her with an outstretched arm back to the living room. "Give me a minute to get a fire going and then I'll show you the rest of the house."

She looked around at the wood trim, stone fireplace, and Northwest Indian artwork while he tossed some wood onto a pile of kindling and sparked a flame. He didn't feel nervous, and yet her being there made his heart rate increase.

"I think I'm all out of beer but, I can make…"

"Interesting interior design," she said cutting him off mid-sentence. "Who's your decorator, Eddie Bauer?"

"You don't like it?"

"No no, it's nice. Really, it is." She continued to look around. "But a little different. I mean, log cabin feel in the living room and 1950s in the kitchen?"

"The kitchen already existed. The living room décor is mine. It's a work in progress, I guess. Not quite sure where I want to go with this stuff yet."

Leigh Anne nodded and walked to the large windows at the southwest corner of the living room. She looked out at the city skyline and tried to locate the aquarium along the waterfront. "Nice view from here. Space needle always looks nice when it's lit up like that. I can see the ballparks way down there." Ray came over to the window and stood beside her. "I just can't seem to find the aquarium."

He got closer. "If you look right along Alaskan Way, can you see the Edgewater?"

Leigh Anne leaned over to sight through his outstretched arm, making sure the side of her face rested against it. "Yes, I see it."

"Ok, now just beyond that, where that cruise ship is docked, that's pier 66, and juuust beyond that one is you. I mean, the aquarium."

"Oh yeah?" she turned to look up at him.

"So, I was saying that I'm all out of beer, but I…"

Again Leigh Anne cut him off. "How many dates have we been on Ray, a half-dozen?"

"Uh…five?…Yeah, five."

"Five dates. And would you say you enjoy my company?"

"Yeah…Yes, very much so. Absolutely."

"I've enjoyed yours too. So you like being with me, right? That's good. That's good."

"Yes, of course."

"And…we seem to have a number of similar interests, right?"

"You goin' somewhere with this?"

"I'm the one askin' the questions here, buddy boy, ok?" she asked with authority and a smile—hoping her nervousness wasn't obvious.

"Yes, ma'am," Ray responded, not taking his eyes off of her.

"Ok, then. So…um…you're out of beer. Ok, how about… some tea?"

"Yeah, I've got tea," he said, walking back into the kitchen. He took the kettle from the stove and filled it at the sink. "Green tea?" he asked over his shoulder, startled to find that she was right behind him.

"Green is great." She tried to summon back the courage that had brought her to his house in the first place. "I must say, you've been the perfect gentleman. That's a hard quality to find in men these days."

"Thank you. I appreciate…"

"So is something wrong with you or are you just not attracted to me?"

"Whaddya…what?"

"Yeah, you heard me. Look at me!" she said, standing there like a department store display model.

Ray looked at her and swallowed hard. He had wanted her from the first time he had laid eyes on her that day at Kimo's. He had wanted her so bad that there were nights he lie awake thinking about her. Always having been a bit slow in the subtle hint department, Ray had wanted to make his next move very carefully.

"You've wooed me enough, Raymond Silver. Now it's time to wow me." Leigh Anne said with a devilish grin.

"Woo? I've been wooing you?"

"Shut up and come here." She pulled him close to her. He couldn't tell if it was his heart that was pounding or if it was Leigh Anne's. His hand came up, and he gently placed it on her cheek. She felt the heat coming off of his palm and closed her eyes as he leaned down to bring his lips to hers.

* * *

Leigh Anne woke slowly the next morning to the steady cadence of rain hitting the window pane and the gravel pathway along the side of the house. Drifting in and out of sleep, she imagined that the raindrops had actually been bacon slowly sizzling in a cast-iron skillet. She had been sleeping on her side facing the bedroom windows when her eyes finally opened—feeling at first betrayed by the sight and sound of the rain. But as she took her first deep breath of the morning, she knew that her nose had not been lying to her. "Yummy! That's definitely bacon." She quickly turned over to find that Ray was gone and smiled thinking of him making breakfast for the both of them. As much as she wanted to stay buried in the warmth of the down blanket, she was starved. Leigh Anne couldn't remember the last time she had woken up so hungry and smiled once again, thinking it was a result of her activity the night before. She grabbed Ray's pillow and hugged it with all her might. Looking around the room for her clothes, she remembered she had left them by the fireplace. She opted for one of Ray's button-down shirts and made her way into the kitchen.

"Hey Silver," she called out. "That bacon's smellin' real good. I hope you made some for me." She headed down the hallway, but when she walked into the kitchen she saw that she was alone. Ray had made her a breakfast of fresh-cut fruit, whole wheat toast covered with hummus, a big pot of Kona coffee, a freshly-cut red rose from the side of the house, and a note. She looked around the kitchen and then back at her breakfast, convinced she had smelled bacon.

"Now there's a first," she thought. "I've heard of guys ripping off a piece and then making their getaway before the sunrise, but this guy makes breakfast first and then runs off. From his own house!" Finally reading the note, she laughed and smiled.

Good Morning

I <u>didn't</u> want to get out of bed this morning. I can't tell you how nice it felt just to lie beside you. It did! I had an early morning meeting at Lake Union (LCI 776) and didn't want to wake you. Won't be back until later this afternoon. I made you breakfast. Coffee should still be warm by the time you get up. <u>DO NOT</u> worry about the dishes. I'll take care of them later. Dinner would be nice. Kelsey's 6 o'clock? let me know.

Ray

BTW, there's a small dish in the fridge for Magic. When you leave, could you put it next to her bowl by the workbench in the garage? Thanks

Leigh Anne poured herself a cup of coffee and walked over to the refrigerator for some cream. On the top shelf was a small plate of tuna for the cat, and it was sprinkled with "Bacon! I knew it!" she said out loud. The rest of the refrigerator looked like the health food section at the grocery store. "All kinds of milk in here," she said as she searched the shelves. "Soy, rice, coconut, but nothing from a cow." Leigh Anne grabbed the coconut milk for her coffee and sat down to eat. She was disappointed that Ray had left without waking her, but she felt certain by the breakfast, the rose, and the note that this guy was definitely different. She hoped she wasn't wrong.

1 6

LCI 776 was tied up at the old Naval Reserve Station at South Lake Union. Through his connections, John Walters was allowed to keep the ship there without having to pay for moorage. Except for Walters—who seemed to be on the ship all the time—most of the other volunteers had regular jobs. So, during the winter and early spring when darkness set in early around the Pacific Northwest, the majority of restoration work was performed on the weekends. They could have used the ship's batteries or run the diesels in order to light up the interior compartments at night, but the amount of fuel needed to recharge those batteries or to keep the lights burning was not worth the expense. Not to mention all the complaints they'd receive from the condo and houseboat residents about the constant heavy throated chugging of the eight diesels when they did run the engines.

As it was, the ship raised the ire of those living along the western shoreline of the lake. It wasn't so much the presence of a ship that bothered them, as the lake itself was mostly commercial in nature with large fishing vessels docked along the eastern shoreline. A number of the residents simply detested any military presence and had fought for many years to shut down the Naval Reserve Center. Now that the 776 called the vacant property home, an equally reactive but bureaucratic local government would occasionally entertain the renewed complaints of a "military ship" docked near their homes. Anytime the volunteers did find themselves working at night, it had to be done with the aid of a quiet portable generator, which worked well as long as they confined themselves to small areas such as the wardroom or one of several of the troop compartments on the lower deck. For the most part, however, the generator was used at night to allow Walters to practically live aboard the vessel—which was another thing that irked some of his less-than-tolerant neighbors.

By the time Ray showed up at the dock at 8 a.m. most of the volunteers had already begun their chores, while others lingered in the crew's mess. Ray walked up to the ramp on the port side of the small ship and waited to catch someone's attention to ask for boarding permission. Walters was rewiring one of two twelve-inch search lamps in the conning station above the pilot house when he noticed Ray.

"Well, you comin' aboard or are ya gonna stand around takin' pictures?" bellowed Walters with a cigarette dangling from the side of his mouth.

"I was just looking for someone to ask permission to board."

"Yeah? Alright."

"Alright as in it's ok to come aboard?"

"No, alright as in it's ok to wait for someone to ask permission," Walters said sarcastically before turning and heading down the ladder that led from the upper con to the gun deck. From there he entered the small bridge through the heavy steel hatchway of the pilot house and swung to the next ladder going down to the interior of the main deck. "Make a hole," he commanded as he flew down with the skill and confidence of an old salt. Without so much as a flinch, Steve Scott and Gordie Smithfield adjusted their postures as Walters reached the bottom of the ladder and slid between the two of them.

Ray stood at the portside ramp as Chuck Shimkin came up from behind carrying his tool box. "Behind ya, pallie," he said without breaking stride. Ray quickly stepped to the side to let him pass. Chuck turned around and asked, "You comin' aboard or what?"

"Yeah, if that's ok?"

Chuck laughed at him as he stopped mid-ramp saying "Sure it's ok. Come on up. I'm Charlie Shimkin, diesel mechanic. People call me Chuck."

"Ray Silver," Ray said, hopping up to the ramp and shaking his hand.

Chuck laughed again. "Oops, sorry pallie, I gotcha fullah grease. Come on up and I'll getcha a rag."

Ray looked at his blackened palm and followed the burly mechanic up the ramp to the main deck. Walters was there to greet him. Contrary to his gruffness, he was always happy to welcome a new volunteer—with a skill—to the crew. Ray was surprised that he remembered him from his first visit all those months ago. The former swift boat skipper had always had a keen ear and memory for anything Navy or nautical-related, and Ray had mentioned his father had been on the 606.

"John Walters, right?" Ray asked as he stuck out his now-greasy hand.

"Yeah, that's me," Walters replied holding back on the handshake. Chuck came back out of the main compartment and tossed a rag, which Walters grabbed mid-air and handed to Ray.

"You look familiar" he said studying Ray's face for a few seconds. "You came by a while back, didn't cha?

"Yeah, that's right. About a year ago, actually. My dad was on the..."

"606."

"Right again," Ray said, amazed. "You've got a good memory. Last time I was here you were being harassed by that Coast Guard Lieutenant."

"Yeah, that's right. You've got a good memory yourself." Walters said flipping his cigarette butt over the side. "So what brings you by today, pictures?"

"Actually, I was wondering if you guys needed any help. My Saturdays are pretty much open and..."

"Ya know anything about ships?"

"No, not really," Ray said as he worked at getting the grease off of his hand.

"Ya got any special skills?"

"Nope. Although I did build a desk at home...outta plywood."

"That's great." Walters was unimpressed by the offering. "I hope ya like ta paint?"

Ray was assigned the job of scraping rust, painting, and insulating. The rust was the hard job because it took a great deal of elbow grease, as power tools were in short supply. Setting the new insulating tiles in each compartment was a chore that all hands were happy to take part in, as the cold air and water easily penetrated the steel of the ship. The few portable heaters they kept onboard were only good when the generator was running. The painting, although equally boring and tedious, was easy with the primer and outer coat being two different shades of gray—thereby eliminating all confusion as to which stage each section was in.

As Walters gave him a quick tour of the bridge and gun deck of the small ship Ray was introduced to each member of the crew as they happened by. Steve Scott was a retired auto executive and self-proclaimed computer geek who had once owned his own yacht and who had years of experience navigating the coastal waters from Alaska down to San Diego. Like Ray, Scott was originally from New York, and the two soon discovered that they had grown up not too far from each other. Sam Lipton said he was a plumber by trade and a World War II weapons collector. He had already restored the 20mm anti-aircraft gun on the forecastle deck and was now working on the one just forward of the pilot house on the starboard side. There were five 20mm AA guns all together as well as a couple of .50 caliber machine guns. Unfortunately for Lipton, he wouldn't legally be allowed to install the firing pins, although he still restored the guns as authentic as possible. He also stowed the firing pins below deck. "Just in case we ever take her out to sea and get a chance to test them," he said with a wink to Walters.

Except for talking to Walters, Lipton pretty much kept to himself, one of a few odd behaviors that gave the other volunteers an uneasy feeling about him.

Gordie Smithfield was a veteran of the LCIs, having served aboard LCI 43 for the landings in French North Africa during Operation Torch in November of '42 and followed by the landings in Sicily eight months later. Gordie and A.J. were the technical advisors for the project. Gordie also helped with the painting when he had the energy. A.J., who was down below working in the galley was the only volunteer Ray still had yet to meet. He was their cook and had served aboard several LCIs, the 631 being his last and longest assignment. Tommy Gilmartin was a steel worker and small-arms enthusiast. He did all the welding onboard and had even fabricated parts such as hinges and support beams when necessary. Over the last year he had been busy strengthening the bulkheads and patching all the holes below decks until they finally had enough money to get a new hull.

Rounding out the crew was retired Chief Petty Officer Dennis Warren, aka "Tex," a Vietnam Vet who had served aboard the USS Edward McDonnell. He was the group's electrician and radioman. From photographs, old manuals, and what information he could get from Gordie, he was methodically replicating the radio shack and chart room. His biggest challenge had been locating old radio tubes. Tex had once spent an entire afternoon listening to the tales of an old radioman from the USS Nevada before he had been allowed to leave the old-timer's Lopez Island home with a cache of long-neglected tubes, dials, and other random parts. He would have loved for the ninety-year-old veteran to come see the radio shack on the 776—and perhaps provide some further help—but the old man had been frail and forgetful. Tex didn't want to take the chance of anything happening to his new friend.

With most introductions out of the way, John Walters brought Ray below to the galley to get breakfast and meet A.J. "So if I remember correctly, you said your ol' man was a motor mac on the 606, is that right?" Walters said lighting another cigarette.

"Yeah, that's right. Motor Machinist Mate 2nd class on the 606."

"Then you and A.J. should have a lot to talk about," he said as he led the way down the steel ladder from the bridge to the main compartment. "The 606 was one of A.J.s first duty stations before being sent to the 417 and then to the 631. Maybe your dad and A.J. knew each other. Go on in…" Walters stopped when he realized Ray was still negotiating his descent down the sharp angle of the ladder. "I hope you learn to navigate these ladders pretty quick."

"Just give me a little time, I'll get it."

"Well, when you get down here, go introduce yourself to A.J. and grab some breakfast before you begin work, if there's any left. He'll be happy to meet you."

When Ray got to the base of the ladder, he was facing aft. Looking down the passageway on his left—the ship's starboard side—he could see the officer's mess, wardroom, galley, and the door to the refrigerated food storage closet. At the end of the passageway there were twin bulkhead hatchway doors, one leading out to the stern and the other to the last two lower compartments. On the right side were the captain's quarters, officers' head, the ladder down to the engine room, and finally, the enlisted men's head and shower compartment. Immediately behind him and to his left, Chuck Shimkin, Steve Scott, and Gordie Smithfield were having coffee at one of the four fold-away tables in the crew's mess.

They were an interesting collection of individuals. Ray thought that Shimkin didn't look anything like a Navy man. He was not tall or muscular, but his broad shoulders and large waist still gave the impression that he would be a formidable opponent. The addition of the ponytail that stuck out of the red bandana covering his head along with the full beard made him look more like a pirate—sans the sword and a parrot. Most definitely not somebody you would want to meet in a dark alley. His easy nature and ability to accept people at face value however, betrayed his intimidating appearance. His laugh was infectious as he sat there drinking his coffee, smoking a Tareyton, and listening to Gordie tell stories of how he and the crew of the 43 couldn't wait to get their hands on the Sicilian girls after Patton's Seventh Army headed off to Messina.

By outward appearances, Steve Scott looked out of place too. But he knew his way around a ship and was one of those guys who could figure out a solution to almost any kind of problem. Scott was the epitome of a self-starter, quickly and easily diving into any project without having to be guided. In the late 70s, as an underfinanced freshman in college, he had been quick to pick up on the desire of his fellow college students to be able to acquire decent quality electronics at prices students could afford. He had established a business based on selling at wholesale prices, which he had appropriately named "Wholesale College Electronics." It wasn't long before he had the majority of the student body of twelve thousand purchasing low-priced calculators, stereos, and cassette recorders with a no-exchange, no return policy. By the end of his freshman year he had earned enough to pay for all four years of school, and by the time he graduated he had sold his little company to a couple of local businessmen.

For Gordie, being part of the 776 project was a homecoming of sorts. He had spent the most impressionable portion of his life living and fighting aboard an LCI at a time when the world was coming apart at the seams. From common experiences and mutual reliance, he had forged a number of friendships whose earthly bonds were only broken by death. Through time and attrition, those ranks had continued to thin and being aboard this ship allowed Smithfield to keep those memories alive.

Ray walked forward, stopping to look at the small room that had served as the junior officer's quarters and then moved on to the next compartment, which was almost twice as large. That one had four bunks for the officers of the troops whom the LCIs had often transported during amphibious assaults. He found it interesting that even on small ships such as this—and for the short journeys that their passengers traveled—officers and enlisted men still had separate eating and sleeping accommodations. As he looked around and heard the noise of men talking, laughing, and working, he tried to imagine his father as an eighteen-year-old kid walking decks similar to these during wartime. He would have given almost anything to have had an opportunity to be on the 606 itself. But this was close enough.

With all the work that had already been completed, Ray was impressed that there was still plenty more to be done. When Walters had acquired the 776, his first priority had been to remove all of the original asbestos insulation before full-scale restoration efforts could begin. Then, thanks to A.J.'s help, the galley was one of the first stations onboard that had been brought back to life. Walters spent many nights on the ship, so another early priority had been an operational head and cleaning up the captain's quarters—which he had clearly laid claim to and which was off-limits to everyone else.

"Hey, Ray," said Chuck, "I've got five more minutes before I head below to work on those engines. Why don't you grab yourself some coffee and come join us?"

Ray looked over at the three men sitting at the rectangular table in the mess area and nodded. "Coffee sounds great," he said as he headed down the passageway to the galley.

A.J. had his back to the galley door and didn't hear Ray enter. He was bent over the utility sink scrubbing a big aluminum stock pot, listening and rocking his body to a Glenn Miller compact disc. Except for the CD player, the mini-fridge and a microwave, everything in the small kitchen was either original or had been acquired from other vintage naval vessels destined for the scrap yards.

"Excuse me," Ray shouted as the sound of power tools began to buzz all over the ship. "Is there any coffee left?"

A.J. turned, singing *"Pennsylvania six five oh oh ooooh."* He dropped his steel wool to the deck when he saw Ray. "Hey, Doc," he said, looking like a kid caught red-handed—doing something bad.

"Abner Lewis! You're A.J.?"

"Abna Jackson Lewis," he said with authority. "Yessir!"

Surprised, Ray didn't know what to say. Thinking of the brief conversations they had had over the past few months, it dawned on him that Abner had never discussed his personal life. He handed Ray a fresh cup of coffee and noticed a hundred questions in his eyes.

"Ya go on an' drink that while it's hot. We can talk laytah, as ah'm sho ya wanna." He picked up his steel wool and went back to cleaning his stock pot.

Ray walked back to the mess area and sat down. "All the times he's been in my office, surely Abner must've seen the picture of the 606 on the wall. I wonder why he never said anything?" he asked out loud.

"Said what?" asked Gordie.

"What?" Ray asked looking over at Gordie. "Oh uh... nothing really. It's just that I know Abner. I mean A.J. We both work over at the VMC." He looked over at Steve Scott and commented on his baseball cap. "Yankee fan?"

"Yeah, ever since I was a kid. Sometimes I think I've been wearing this cap since then."

"It does look old enough. Pretty faded."

"Had it about twenty years. Picked it up on a visit to my old neighborhood in the Bronx."

"No kiddin'? Whereabouts?"

"Western and a 169th in Morrisania."

"No Shit! Small world. I was just south of Highbridge. On Gerard between 153rd and 157th streets."

"So you were over near the stadium."

"My building sat right above the entrance to the subway tunnel."

"You go to many games?"

"Not too many. It cost seventy-five cents to get into the bleacher seats. Who had that kind of money back then?" Ray said as they both laughed.

"Those were the days, Ray."

"Agreed."

Gordie opened up his three-ring binder and took out a couple of 8x10 pages with the scaled down schematic drawings of the 776. "Here," he said, tossing them over to Ray. "Use these until you get familiar with every inch of the ship. You'll notice that there are eight compartments down below. Four compartments carried troops, and they're labeled in order with the first troop compartment sitting behind the forward stores, then followed by troop compartment two, then troop three and then there's the crew's quarters."

Ray followed along on the diagram as Gordie spoke. "That looks like the engine room right behind the crew's quarters," he said to Gordie as he continued to look at the scaled-down print. "It must have been pretty loud sleeping next to that bulkhead?"

"Yeah, but not as loud as being in that engine room," added Chuck. "Which, by the way, is my cue to get to work. Come down later and I'll show you what powers this thing." He slid out from his chair and headed down the passageway.

"Yup, you got your engine room," Gordie continued, "and then behind that is troop four, more storage, and finally the compartment with the aft steering gear."

"Time for me to get some work done as well," said Steve Scott as he got up to begin his chores. "Let's get together sometime, Ray, and reminisce about the Bronx."

"Sounds like a plan, Steve."

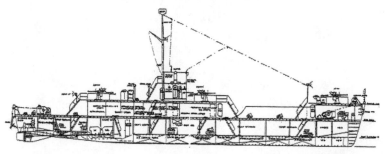

Schematic drawing of LCI from the book New Ship Of War and used with permission of Stan Galik and taken from the Stanley Galik website: www.galik.com/stanleygalik1922.

Ray studied the diagram a little longer as he finished his coffee. When he looked up, he suddenly became aware that he was the only one not working as the noise of power tools and banging hammers filled the ship. He picked up the coffee mugs the others had left behind and brought them back to the galley. Making eye contact with Abner, they nodded at each other. "That was a great cup of coffee Abner, I mean, A.J. Probably the best I've had."

"Thanks, Doc. Ah had a lot a practice," he said with a nervous laugh.

Ray looked at the diagram and picked out the ladder leading below to the crew's quarters. "Let's see where pop would've slept" he thought as he headed below.

17

For almost a week after Ray and Abner had come face to face in the galley of the 776, the janitor had been staying away from Ray's office as well as the entire basement in an effort to avoid having to tell him of his time on the 606. It was obvious to Ray that Abner was deliberately scarce all week and he had been debating calling his dad to see if the two of them had known each other. He opted to get Abner's side of the story first. There was something there, and he suspected that it could possibly explain why Ron Silver never went into any detail when discussing his war years. Even during his dad's last visit he had been quick to avoid discussing those days at any great length.

All that week Ray studied the photograph of the 606 on his office wall. In the evenings, while continuing to search naval archives on the internet, he also found himself looking over the duplicate photo he had pinned to the cork tiles on the wall above his workshop desk. By all appearances, the entire crew of the 606 had been on deck, and he was not able to identify anyone as African-American. He reasoned that it was possible Abner had been in the galley at the time the photo had been taken.

By Friday morning, Ray had still not seen Abner but once or twice. He seemed to be very busy with a project but promised to catch up with him later, although he never did. Worried that he also might not show up at the 776 the next morning, Ray decided he had to take matters into his own hands. He called up to the nurse's station on the second floor. "Stella? This is Ray," he announced with a growing familiarity. "I mean, Nurse Leone? This is Dr. Silver."

"Yes, Dr. Silver," Stella replied with formality, for the benefit of her nearby coworkers. "How can I help you?"

* * *

Abner Jackson Lewis felt betrayed by Ray's trick to get him to his office. But it had worked, and he was willing to give credit where credit was due. "Ah can't buhleeve ya tol' Nurse Stella that ya vennalation duc' was makin' noise an' that you'd be out all day. Ya knew no one else had a key but me an' huh," Abner said as Ray sat at his desk, proud that his little covert operation worked so well. "Ah can't buhleeve ya was jes sittin' in heyah waitin' on me. No disrespec' Doc, but thas jes low." He shook his head and looked right at Ray. "Ah' `spose ya wanna axe me some questions, since there ain't nuttin' ta fix?"

Ray apologized but got Abner to admit that he had been avoiding him since the previous Saturday. He half stood out of his chair, leaned over to the wall to remove the picture of the 606, and placed it between the two of them as they sat across from each other. Abner looked at the framed photo and let out a big sigh. The day he had dropped off supplies and spotted the photograph, he knew this conversation would eventually happen. After a minute of trying to figure out where to begin, a slightly nervous Ray stood up. "Can I get you something to drink?"

"Coffee'd be nice," Abner replied with a nod as Ray walked over to a small table that he'd set up in the corner of the room. He had a small coffee machine that he recently brought in, as making his morning stop at the second floor break room was no longer a necessity. He did, however, continue to stop in for a cup first thing on Mondays both because he liked talking to

Stella and the other nurses and also because it annoyed the hell out of Bill Harrison. Whenever he showed up for coffee Harrison would refuse to stay—which was just one more reason why the nurses liked having Ray on staff. Stella even began to come down to Ray's basement office from time to time under the pretense of grabbing a "fresh" cup of "good" coffee, while getting away from the gossip of the second floor.

"How do you take it, Abner? Or do you prefer A.J.?"

"Black's good, Doc. An' ya can call me which evah way works bes' fo' ya."

"I've got soy milk in the fridge if you want it?"

"Yeah, ah've seen ya bring that thang in. No, black's jes fine, thanks."

Ray poured two cups of Kona and added some soy milk to his own. He replaced the container, gesturing to the mini-fridge that he kept next to the small table. "I've got one at home just like this one. Keep it in my workshop." He walked back over to his desk, handed Abner his cup, and sat back down. "Except the one I have at home doesn't have soy milk in it."

"If ah had ta guess," said Abner, "it'd be beer." He looked at Ray and lightly chuckled. "An' not cans eithah. You's a long-neck kinda guy."

"Good guess. It is." Ray looked into his cup. "Do me a favor, Abner."

"Whas that, Doc?"

"When no one else is around, do ya think you could call me Ray?"

"If ya really wan' me ta, ah can try. It's jes…, well, ah'm a creatcha a habit an' at seventa-eight, goin' on seventa-nine years a age, it's not that easy gettin' riddah a lifetime a asperience an' habits."

Abner had not only grown up during the Depression, but also in the segregated Deep South. He took a sip of his coffee and nodded his approval to Ray. "Not bad…fo' a doctah."

"Thanks. I try my best." He replied watching Abner's eyes drift off to another time.

"Saw mah firss lynchin' when ah was only nine years old," he now told Ray. "It was mah cousin Thomas. He was five years olda than me. We walked in ta town one day, ah rememba it was hot. It was always hot in Missippi in the summah time. But we had a few extra pennies saved up from workin' an' hepin' people fix thangs here an' there. We'd even haul rubbish in the back ah mah uncle's wagon. He had this ol' horse that was blind in one eye, but she could haul a good load. Well, one day we hauled a load a trash ta the dump an' it was so hot. That horse was havin' one heckofa time. So when we pass by the Andersen farm, Thomas went up ta the Andersen's house ta ask em if he could watah the horse. But they wasn't home so he wen' an' did it anyways. He even took a couple a carrots too. Fo' the horse, that is. He took the carrots fo' the horse. It was hot an' she was havin' a hard time. Well, one a the Andersen kids was home an' was watchin' us from the winda. Ya see, they was told by Mista an Missus Andersen that if they wuzn't home, the only cullahed folk they could talk ta were their own field hands. Thas why the kid never come ta the doe ta talk ta Thomas. Well, the kid tol' his olda brothas that Thomas come ta the house an' stole their watah an' their food."

Ray was slowly drinking his coffee and listening very intently as the two of them sat alone in his office. "The kid didn't blame you too?"

"Ah was wit' the horse an' wagon down on the road outta sight from the front porch. So what the kid saw was Thomas walkin' up their path, pump their watah from their well into a bucket, an' then take a couple a their carrots as he walked back ta the road. Anyways, a few days laytah we was walkin' ta town. Ah had been wantin' a Coca-Cola fo' so long, thas all ah thought about as we walked. Ya know how on them real hot days how all those little drops a watah bead up on that cold glass bottle? An' then how it makes that swishhh sound when ya pop the cap off? Ah jes kept thinkin' 'bout how nice that looked. `Speshly when that little whisp a smoke come out the top a the bottle when ya firss crack her open. An' ah couldn't wait ta get me one. Then the olda Andersen boy, he was 'bout six years oldah than Thomas an' he was big. An' he was a mean sonofabitch.

He jes showed up outta nowhere wit' foe a his friends an' he started yellin' 'bout the watah an' the carrots. Ah was scared as hell. Then they drug us off inta the woods an' started beatin' on him. All five a dem. Hittin' an' kickin'. An' ah jes' stood there. Then they tied up his hands, drug him over ta a tree an' hanged him."

Abner became very quiet as the events of that day replayed in his mind. Ray sat silent, not knowing what to say. Then, staring off into his memory, Abner continued. "Jes befo' they kicked the box out from Thomas' legs, he jes looked at me. Tears was runnin' down his cheeks, his lips was shakin', an' his eyes was askin' me ta do sumthin'…But ah couldn't. Mah legs was…was like heavy bouldas. Ah couldn't move. Ah couldn't run ta hep him. Ah couldn't even run away. Ah couldn't charge at those boys. Ah jes stood there. Then one a those boys got right in mah face an' said ta me, 'Nigga, ya say one word 'bout this an' you'll swing like ya friend.' Then they kicked the box out from unda him. Ah remembah his legs was runnin' in the air an' he was twistin' back n forfh fo' 'bout a minute an then his legs jerked real sharp like…an' then he was still. The whole time those boys was jes laughin' at him an' ah jes stood there…an' pissed mahself."

Abner grew quiet as a single tear rolled down from the corner of his eye. He let out a big sigh, staring down at the picture of the 606. "Thas the firss time ah evah toll that storah."

"I'm sorry," Ray said as he looked at Abner. "You do realize that you were a nine-year- old little boy. What could you have done against five boys who were much older and much bigger than you?"

Abner looked back up at Ray and half smiled. "Oh, ya don't have nuthin' ta be sorrah 'bout, Doctah Silvah. Ah mean Ray. Ah could've…ah shoulda done sumthin' an' ah did nuthin'. But that was anotha place an' anotha time, an aftah the war when ah settled here in Seattle, ah didn't run up against any-thin' evah come close ta that again."

"Did anything ever happen to those boys?

"Ah know one who got hisself killed one night. He got real drunk an' real hornah. Ended up in the cullahed section a town lookin' fo' some trim."

"Trim? You mean he was looking to get laid?" Ray slowly took a sip of coffee.

"Yeah thas right. Funny huh? We wasn't good enough ta drink from the same watah fountain, but they could come `round at night wantin' ta fuck our women. But people there knew who he was an' what he'd done ta Thomas. He got what was comin' ta him is all. Ah heard he cried like a little baby. Pleadin' fo' mercy. Ah actually wish ah was there ta see it. Never did find his body. Mah guess is he ended up as gator bait. Ah tried ta stay away from the places those boys would always be at. Through the years we would cross paths here an' there an' they would do sumthin' ta `timidate me. Say sumthin' ta rem-ine me what would happen if ah ever said anythin'. When they was alone by theirselves they wasn't so tough, though. But still, come June of forta-one when ah turned seventeen, ah joined up wit' the Navy ta get the hell outta there. Ah joined up an' nevah looked back. But ah do think a Thomas often, though. Ah didn't do right by him an' as it turned out, some othas as well. An' there's some thangs in this life that ah still gotta make up fo'.

"What's the other things?"

"Ronnie, ya daddy." Abner said, looking right at Ray. He sat up in his chair and looked back at Abner. In the time he had spent searching for crewmembers of the 606, he had not come across Abner's name, but here he was now, face to face with the first crewmember of his dad's that he had met.

"Until ah saw that photo up there on the wall an' made the connection between you an' Ronnie, ah had thought he was killed at Peleliu in forta-fo'."

"What do you mean you thought he was killed? It's such a small ship and crew, surely you would have known?"

Abner hesitated, and slowly took a drink from his mug while he searched for answers. "Well, bah that time ah was already gone. Sent ta the fo-seventeen." He paused again, took another sip, and stared at the photo of the 606. "But we was all parta flotilla five. So ah had heard that ya daddy did some amazin' thangs befoe he got hisself killed. But ah guess he didn't get killed after all."

"What kind of amazing things?"

"Well ah don't know anymo' if thas even true 'cause the people that were tellin' the storah back then also said he was killed."

"Ok, so just tell me what you heard and then, tell me why you transferred off the 606."

"Ah didn't ask ta be transferred. The skippa wanned me off the ship."

"Why? What for?" Ray asked, leaning forward and anxious to hear more.

"Skippa was one a those typical Southern white boys is all," Abner said with a touch of anger. "Ah was a black man in the service in the forta's. War or no war, we was still bein' discrim'nated against. Ah was a cook, a servant. Ya get what ah'm sayin?"

Ray nodded his head. He had read a great deal about the segregation and mistreatment of African-American troops during the war. "Please, go on Abner. Tell me."

"The skippa was this arrogant, smart-ass, ninety-day wunda Secon' Lieutenant who treated me little bettah then the way ah was treated back in Missippi. Talked 'bout 'cullahed' folk when ah was in the room as if ah didn't exist. An' then talked 'bout us 'niggas' when he thought ah couldn't hear him. Damn, the galley weren't but fifteen feet away from the officeah's head. But the one thang he hated mo' than havin' a cullahed in his crew was havin' a cullahed an' a kike in his crew."

"And that would be my dad?"

"Yup. An' the one thang he hated even mo' than that was that the two a us become friends."

"What about the rest of the crew? How did they treat you? How did they treat my pop?"

"No offense, but ya daddy was, ah mean, *is* white. Ya know ah have ta `pologize, Doc, ah mean, Ray. But ah nevah axed ya if he was still wit us?"

"Yeah, Abner, he's still with us. His health is not so good these days, but he's still with us."

"Thas good. Now don't ya go sayin' nuthin' ta him jes yet. Ah'd like ta be the one who calls him. Ya know, ah wanna suprise him, if thas ok witcha?"

"Sure, no problem. So what was it like onboard for you two?"

"Oh yeah, well, some, not all the boys onboard talked `bout him when he weren't around. Jes like they did `bout me. He had ta listen ta his share a Jew jokes, but the majoritah a the crew liked us both. We all got along wit' dem jes fine. An' they knew the skippa was an ass. But ya daddy was not only good ta me, he was genuwine. Jes like you, Doc. He was a good kid, an' he was good ta me. When he wasn't on dutah he'd come hep me out makin'food or cleanin' up."

"Are you the one who taught him how to make griddle cakes?"

"Ya mean witta touch ah beer an' some vanillah?"

"Yeah that's right," Ray said with a laugh. "That's how he made it for us when we were kids."

"Thas mah secret recipe. Ya daddy was the only one in the service that ah shared it wit'."

"That was our Sunday morning breakfast for years. He even called them 'Navy flapjacks'. So he would come up and work with you?"

"Yup, an' when ah wasn't on dutah ah'd go down ta the engine room an' sometimes he even taught me `bout engines. It drove the skippa crazy. He hated it so much ah even heard him tell one a the junior officahs that it made him wanna throw up. `Ventually, he made it clear that he wanned one a us off the ship. The cook from the fo-seventeen had one too many fights so the skippas swapped us. That pictcha ya got here a the 606?

It's mine. Ah took it. We had pulled 'long side a badly damaged LCT an' we took on her crew. The skippa handed me a camrah an' ordered me ta go ta the highest point on that damaged tank transport an' shoot a pictcha a the ship wit' evraone on deck."

Abner took one last drink of his coffee and stood up. "Well, ok then ah guess we're done heyah. Ah got some work ah gotta do befo' ah can head home," he said turning to leave.

"So what did he do at Peleliu? Why do you feel you need to do right by him?" Ray said quickly before Abner could make his escape.

"Now, keep in mind that ah was in the galley a the fo-seventeen at this point so this is all based on what ah heard." Abner reluctantly walked back to Ray's desk. "It was the middle of Septembah in forta-fo' an' our flotilla was gettin' ready ta make a run on the beaches. There was a whole bunch a us. The 606, the fo-seventeen, the fo-sixta-seven an a whole bunch mo'. The shellin' a the island started 'round oh-five-thirtah hours. When that stopped, planes from the aircraf carriahs began ta make their run on the airfield. At oh-eight-hunred, the diesels powered up an' along wit' all the othah LCIs, we started headin' fo' the beach. We was carryin' the firss an' fifth marines. So as the 606 was makin' her run, an' keep in mind this is what ah was tol', ok?" he said, looking at Ray.

"Yeah, ok. I understand."

"So as the 606 was makin' her run up ta the beach she was strafed by a Jap plane. Ah guess one or two of them suckas got in ta the air. The crew mannin' the twenny-mil on the focastle deck was taken out right away. The skippa called ya daddy up from the engine room ta man that gun. Ya daddy was fast. He was one hellofa base-stealin' shortstop on our ship's baseball team. Ah even heard that he was bein' looked at by Brooklyn befo' the war. Was that true?"

"Yeah, it was. Before he joined in '43 they wanted to sign him. You want more coffee?"

"Naw, ah'm good," Abner said as he looked at the clock. "So, Ronnie goes flyin' outta the main compartment as this

Zero is makin' a nutha' run on the ship an' bullets is hittin' the watah an' the bow an' all over the place. Well, he doesn't break stride as he flies up the laddah ta the foward twenny-mil. He gets on this thang, sights in on the plane as she's flyin' off, an' he starts blastin' it with all he got."

"Did he get it?"

"I think he did. Sho' did look like he got a big piece a it, but there was a whole bunch a guns shootin' at this thang when it jes blew inta pieces. An' then Ronnie goes ta the guys that was all shot up an' he starts checkin' on 'em. He even carrahed one off on his shouldas an' brought him back inside."

Ray looked at Abner and wondered "So, that's it? What made you think he got killed?"

"Well ah ain't finished yet. The 606 pulled up onta the beach an' off-loaded the Marines. Meanwhile, ya daddy was workin' on the wounded guys an' carryin' the dead off a the deck an' back inside ta the crew's mess. Once the Marines was off an' on their way an' the ramps was pulled back, the skippa started yellin' at him again ta get back up ta the foward gun. So he runs back up, an' jes as he gets there the skippa shoves her inta full reverse an' Ronnie goes flyin' off the front a the bow right inta the surf. skippa jes kept on goin' an' left him there."

"Are you shittin' me? No way that could happen."

"Wouldn't have buhleeved it if ah hadn't seen..." Abner tried to stop himself, but it was too late. The words had come out of his mouth.

"You what? You saw it happen?"

"No, no, ah meant ta say ah wouldn't have buhleeved it had ah not heard it with ma own..."

Ray cut him off. "You were gonna say if you hadn't seen it with your own eyes. You were there, you saw it, didn't you? You were on the 606 when this happened."

"Now stop it, Doc. Ah tol' ya ah was on the fo-seventeen. In the galley doin' ma job." Abner was becoming very upset. "Now thas all ah know an' now ah gotta go. All this talkin', ya went an' made me late." Again he turned to leave.

"You guys were right in the middle of a landing operation. A couple of Japanese planes were making strafing runs and *all* hands would've been at battle stations," Ray said excitedly. He was confused and concerned. A number of questions began racing through his mind. "Was Abner holding back on something? Why would he lie about where he was unless he was someplace he shouldn't have been or doing something that he shouldn't have been doing?"

Abner didn't say anything more on the topic. He was taken aback and he knew that he just got caught lying. He stood there and looked at Ray. "Ah've gotta get back ta work. Ah've been down here too long an' the lass thang ah need is a supavisah bustin' on me."

"I hope you'll be willing to tell me the rest of what happened. After all, you took me this far."

"Yeah, well...obviously Ronnie sahvived, an' ah'm glad he did. Maybe ya should get him ta tell ya what happen' ta him. After all, he's the one that asperienced it firsshand. Ah didn't see it."

"Tomorrow's Saturday, A.J. You gonna be at the 776?"

"Yeah, ah guess so. Maybe. Ah don't know. Ah gotta see how ah feel in the mornin'."

"So what are the other things?"

"Whas that?" Abner stopped again, turning around and wondering if Ray was ever going to stop asking questions.

"You said that there were some things that you had to make up for? What other things, and how are you gonna make up for them?"

"Some othah time, Doc. Ok? Ah'll tell ya some othah time. Jes know this. A man has ta be able ta cleanse his soul, he's gotta clean the slate. Make up fo' what he did wrong or didn't do what he shoulda done. He's gotta seek redemption befo' he can move on."

"And how do we know when we get it, if I can ask?" Ray said as he looked up at an exasperated Abner Lewis.

"When it comes down ta it, Doc. A man has ta be able ta look at hisself in the mirrah. So ah guess ah need ta get right wit' mahself. Ah need ta seek redemption fo' mahself, from mahself. It's in my own eyes that ah am my own redeemah. An' when ah figure out how ah'm gonna do that…well then, ah'll let ya know."

Abner turned to leave and Ray was left with more questions than answers. Should he press Abner about what he did or did not see during the landing at Peleliu? Having seen how upset Abner had become, should he risk getting his father just as upset? Should he even mention to his dad that he now knew Abner? He did know one thing, though. He was going to spend even more time searching the naval archives every chance he got. He walked over to pour himself another cup of coffee and noticed that Abner wasn't singing as he normally did when walking down the hallway. In fact, by the sounds of his footsteps, he was walking at a faster and more deliberate pace. Ray pissed him off and he knew it. And now he was pissed at himself for having done so. He walked over to his desk, picked up the coffee mug that Abner had used and was about to throw it against the wall when there was a knock on the outer door.

"Yeah?"

"Dr. Silver?" asked an apprehensive patient, looking at Ray, who was gripping a white ceramic mug and cocking his arm in the air like a pitcher about to release a fastball. "Dr. Thayer sent me down here for you to take a look at my neck and back, but if you're busy, sir, maybe I should come back."

18

In the weeks that had passed since his presentation to some of the medical staff, Ray began to slowly see an increasing number of patient referrals from several of the orthopedists on the second floor. Stella, as his biggest advocate, had become a firm believer in the benefits of Ray's expertise in musculo-skeletal care after personally benefitting from the sessions she had with him. She and Ray were fast becoming friends, and she was quick to bring up his name to the doctors when their first inclination was to write orders for physical therapy. A growing shift in the referral patterns had surely been noticed by the physical therapists. While some welcomed Ray's addition to the staff and a lighter workload, others remained territorial and continued to challenge the need for his services.

Stella's colleagues had noticed her increased interest in him and occasionally teased her about it. In turn, she was always quick to remind them that she was already in a relation-ship and had no romantic interest in Ray Silver. The busier he became, the less time he had to wander up to the second floor. This prompted Stella to begin taking some of her coffee breaks down in Ray's office, claiming that the freshly ground Kona he brought from home was worth the walk. They found themselves getting into debates about holistic versus allopathic healing principles that often led nowhere, as neither one could convince the other that they were right. He felt she was passionate, yet stubborn about her positions. She felt he was sometimes arrogant about his. She was even more convinced of this when he stated, "It's not arrogance, but rather confidence, because I know I'm right. But prove me wrong, Stel, and I'll buy you dinner."

"No, that's ok," she countered. "I don't get off on tofu and sprouts." At which point they had a good laugh. Especially when Ray not-so-innocently queried "Don't suppose you'd tell me what would get you off?…Gastronomically speaking, that is."

When he really wanted to ruffle her feathers, he brought up the Yankees-Red Sox rivalry. Their verbal sparring was fun and lighthearted for the both of them. Increasingly, Stella looked forward to the time they got to spend together, and began to wonder if the relationship she was slowly building with Ray wasn't a repeat of the friendship she had once had with Ted Cranston.

She had liked Ted because of the way he talked to her and treated her. He talked *to* her and not at her. When he looked at her, he didn't look at her as a sexual object, but as a person. And whereas most other men undressed her with their eyes as they pretended to agree with her positions, Cranston had listened to what she had to say and challenged her opinions when his differed. Ray was the same way in that respect, but different in that he, unlike Ted, had demonstrated that he wouldn't run away from controversy. Still, she wondered if she hadn't been gravitating to Ray, as she had to Ted, because of what was lacking for her at home. And just like her marriage, the relationship with her boyfriend had long ago reached a plateau and was now on a slow and steady decline.

At first it had been fun, exciting, and very different. Robert was an international entrepreneur who had been immediately taken by Stella's beauty when they met at the dedication of a new outdoor garden he had built and donated to the medical center. She admitted that she had been attracted to him, as well as intrigued by his purported exploits, reported in the local media. Every time she turned her head it seemed he was flying off to New York, Europe, or the Middle East with a new trendy start-up venture or some strange deal that he had brokered. She had even gone along on several of his trips when she was able to manage time off from work. But for her, it had gotten old fast. Once again, she felt as if she were a piece of eye candy, a fashion accessory to be dangled in front of prospective investors.

Everything Robert did revolved around making money—and getting the attention that came along with it. It was the center of his universe. As time passed, they had less to talk about. His business trips were occurring more often and for longer periods of time. Somewhere along the way he had stopped asking her to accompany him. Most days, Stella went home to a cold, empty high-rise condo, and it was all too reminiscent of her time in Washington, D.C. When Robert did return from one of his extended trips, he still brought home thoughtful and expensive gifts, they dined out with his friends and business partners at Seattle's finest establishments—but soon he buried himself in yet another one of his projects.

Long gone were the early days of a relationship that had consisted of Friday night dinner and movie dates, cold rainy Saturday afternoons cuddling on the couch with a roaring fireplace while watching an old movie classic and lazy Sunday mornings lying in bed as they swapped sections from the Sunday Times. Stella freely admitted that Robert was good, kind, and respectful of her but he was often distant and took little interest in what interested her. She was lonely, and soon found herself finding ways to spend increasing amounts of time with Ray while at work—once again filling that void.

But she knew she had to be careful. Ray had openly talked about his budding relationship with Leigh Anne and she had quickly noticed how his eyes got excited when he talked of their first meeting in Hawaii. And yet at the same time, she felt his penetrating energy, as his full attention was always on her as they talked. As much as she could see herself with Ray, she wasn't sure if she should be the one to pursue anything beyond their current work friendship, or what she would do if he did.

Ray Silver wasn't her only preoccupation though. Ever since he had pointed out an apparent link between Bill Harrison's excessive prescribing of non-steroidal anti-inflammatory medications and patient deaths, Stella had been carefully and quietly reviewing his patient files, compiling information, and reviewing all of the available research as she slowly built a case against him.

19

By late April, Ray and Leigh Anne had pretty much settled into a comfortable routine. Still adamant about not making a big commitment, neither wanted the other to feel any pressure to end each date in bed. Ray usually let Leigh Anne take the lead when it came to that, and he was only too happy to oblige her when she did.

On a Sunday morning, while sitting at the kitchen breakfast table, they were surprised to see Casey, who had stopped by unannounced. As she came in through the front door she was followed by Magic, who after a night of carousing had made her way over to the fireplace and curled up to the heat of the still-burning embers.

"Hey Dad" she called out. "You up yet?"

As she turned the corner into the kitchen, she came to a sudden stop when she saw Leigh Anne and her dad sitting there sharing a newspaper with their morning coffee. Ray, dressed only in sweatpants, and Leigh Anne in a thigh-length football jersey, smiled at Casey. "Grab a cup and join us," she said, pointing to the coffee machine on the counter. To Ray's relief, Leigh Anne and Casey had talked a few times since their first meeting at Kelsey's. Given the circumstances of that brief encounter, both had easily considered it water under the bridge. Casey walked over to the counter and grabbed the mug emblazoned with the dark blue initials "USN." She poured herself a cup and spied the frying pan on the stove.

"Hey, Matzoh Brei! Are you guys done with this?"

"Sure kiddo, It's all yours." Ray said motioning to the stove. "Just scoop out a little for Magic."

"I haven't had this in a long time. What a nice treat. Thanks, Dad." Casey filled a small bowl and sat at the table. She ate a forkful of the egg and matzoh combination and closed her eyes in delight. "Oh, man does this bring back memories. Glad to see you haven't lost your touch."

"That's not the only thing I'm still good at." Ray said, looking at two suddenly red-faced women. "I meant, that there are other things that I can still cook well. What didja think I meant?" Casey shook her head as she briefly looked up at the kitchen clock. Ray caught a wink and a quick smile from Leigh Anne. "So anyway, Casey, what brings you by this morning?"

"I was able to pick up two tickets for graduation," Casey took an envelope from her back pocket and handed it to her father.

"Two tickets?" Leigh Anne asked, turning to Ray. "Is your son or your dad flying out?"

"Neither," he said. "I got the extra ticket for you. That is, if you'd like to come."

She looked at Casey, who smiled and nodded saying, "Yeah, that would be great. I'd love to have you come with dad. That is, if you want to. It's completely up to you."

"Graduation is in two weeks. Jimmy's in three," Ray said as he flipped a page on the wall calendar. "My pop's not gonna come. He just doesn't have the energy to do both, so I thought it best if he made just the one trip up to Georgetown. It'll be a lot easier on him. Unfortunately, Casey, you've got to report for duty a few days after your graduation."

Leigh Anne was remembering the four-hour long ceremony that she had to endure when she graduated from school. She looked over at Casey, while taking a long drink from her mug. "Leigh," Ray continued, "I know I should've asked you before ordering the tickets, but I was hoping you'd keep me company."

"Sure, Casey" she said, "I'd love to come to your graduation. And after the ceremony your dad can take us out for dinner on the waterfront."

Casey smiled glancing at Leigh Anne and then at her dad. "Good. I've got just the place, too. It's a little pricey, but what the heck."

"Sounds good to me, ladies." Ray reached for the sports section before his daughter could grab it.

2 0

Ceremonies for the University of Washington graduating class of 2002 were set for a Friday morning on the playing field of Husky Stadium. A full month before Casey's graduation, Ray had made an official request with his department head to have that day off—but didn't find out that it had been denied until a few days prior to the ceremony. He was furious as he reread the letter in disbelief. "What kind of fucking bullshit is this?" he yelled out to his empty office after reading the note a fourth time:

"Your request for a day off is denied, as you are the only chiropractor on staff and as such, we do not have a qualified individual to administer chiropractic services on that day. If you have any questions please feel free to call me at ext. 2132.

Peter McCain, Director of Rehabilitative Services, VMC."

Ray called and pleaded his case to McCain, a career administrator, Or in other words, a lifelong bureaucrat who never let the human factor get in the way of any decision. No matter how Ray tried to argue his case, McCain's mind had been made up and he wasn't going to change it. After Ray had hung up the phone, he found himself pacing his office trying to think of his options. He walked over to his desk, picked up one of his white ceramic coffee mugs, and was about to throw it against the wall when there was a knock on the outer door.

"Yeah?"

"Dr. Silver?" asked an apprehensive patient looking at Ray, whose hand was gripping the mug, his arm cocked in the air like a pitcher about to release a fastball. "Dr. Araghi sent me down here for you to take a look at my neck, but if you're busy, sir, maybe I should come back."

"Nah, that's ok, come on in and have a seat," Ray said as he took a good look at the coffee mug before setting it down on his desk. He walked into the exam room, took the patient's medical chart, and carefully looked through several pages of the one-inch-thick folder.

"Hmm, Benjamin Center?

"Yes Sir. That's me."

"It says here that you've been having constant neck pain, stiffness, and chronic headaches for several years now."

"Yes sir, that's right. It's kinda stupid, but I fell outta the back of a humvee during a training exercise. Landed on my back and smacked my head. Been having problems ever since."

"I see you just recently started seeing Dr. Araghi."

"Yes sir."

"I really don't see any of his notes in here other than your exam. What's he been doing for you so far?"

"He just took over my case last week, and after his exam and a new set of x-rays he just said I should come down to see you."

"I see," Ray said as he took the x-rays from the big yellow envelope and put them up on the view box. "What had you been doing before being sent to Dr. Araghi? As far as treatment goes, that is?"

"All my other docs just gave me meds and physical therapy, sir."

Ray studied the x-rays and turned to his new patient. "Well, Mr. Center, let's have a look at you, shall we?"

* * *

Regardless of having been denied a personal day, Ray was absent on the Friday of Casey's graduation. He had talked to Stella, who in turn had talked to the orthopedists who were sending their patients to Ray. They all agreed that on that Friday, they wouldn't send anyone down to his office. That is, all except Bill Harrison. Until he heard some of the other doctors talking about this during a coffee break, he had refused to refer any of his patients for chiropractic care. That Friday, however, he referred several of his patients to Ray, knowing that they would only find a locked basement office. One of those referrals had been having intense pain traveling from his lower back down both of his legs. By the time he had walked the entire length of the basement corridor to Ray's office, his pain increased so much he had tears running down his face. Fortunately for him, Abner was working in one of the record storage rooms and heard the man whimpering as he lay on the floor in the hallway. Using his wireless, Abner had called for an orderly to come to the basement with a wheelchair.

While Stella couldn't openly question Harrison's motive—as that would reveal her complicity—she did question his judgment to send a patient in acute pain to walk that long distance without the benefit of any kind of assistance. And regardless of how he appeared, Bill Harrison had used the opportunity to lodge a complaint with the department head.

The next day, Peter McCain was waiting for Ray with his first official reprimand. He got his second reprimand, along with a three-day suspension, after he attended Jimmy's graduation from Georgetown Law. The irony of not being allowed a few days off, but suspended for three, wasn't lost on Ray as it was on McCain.

"Rules are rules," McCain rationalized. "If I let you have your way, then everyone else would follow suit."

While Bill Harrison was quite proud of himself, Stella diligently continued gathering evidence against the orthopedist, and Ray was slowly losing his patience with him.

21

Even though Abner showed up at the 776 the Saturday after the unsettling conversation he had with Ray, he had avoided all but the most courteous exchanges whenever Ray came by the galley for a cup of coffee. In fact, Abner cleaned up and shut down the galley two hours earlier than normal and had left the ship without saying goodbye to anyone. Over the next five weeks at the medical center, he continued to try to avoid Ray as much as possible, even asking another janitor to deliver assorted office supplies, something he had previously looked forward to doing himself.

With his three-day suspension starting on a Wednesday, Ray now had a five-day weekend all to himself. Leigh Anne was off with a team of fellow marine biologists studying a sudden large red algae bloom that had caused a fish kill along the southern Washington coastline. He spent the first couple of days glued to his workshop computer, continuing his research on the 606. As he dug through page after page of online documents, he slowly added more names to his list of crew members who had served on that LCI at one time or another. Even though not all World War II era Navy records had been fully digitized, at times it seemed easier to locate a name than it was to track down the present-day whereabouts of these guys, living or deceased.

Then Ray found a partial ships log from the 606 on file at the National Archives. First entry: **30 September 1944 relieved Lieutenant Robert Lee Johnson of command of LCI(L) 606 @ 14:30 hours**. Below that, the second entry: **30 September 1944 assuming command of LCI(L) 606 @ 14:30 hours Lieutenant Everett Wendall.**

As he read through the log entries, he thought it curious that there was no information prior to Everett Wendall taking command of the 606. "Perhaps Robert Lee Johnson kept a separate log and never turned it in, claiming it had been lost," Ray thought. Based on the accounts Abner had told him, it was Johnson who had been in command during the Peleliu landings, and the first dates recorded in Wendall's log showed that to be the case. He continued to browse through the entries when he suddenly stopped at his father's name. Entry: **2 October 1944 @ 09:45 hours received communiqué from LCI(R) 705 re: 606 crewmember MoMM 2nd class Ron Silver. Recovered from Peleliu 22 September 1944 by LCI(R) 705. Condition good. Will rendezvous with 705 and retrieve.**

Ray was intrigued and excited to make this find. He leaned over to the small refrigerator sitting under the workbench next to his desk to grab a Pipeline, but there were none to be had. Having finished the last one prior to taking off for Georgetown, he had forgotten to restock. Looking up at the clock, he decided he was not only thirsty, but hungry as well. He started a download of the ship's log so he would have it on his hard drive and began thinking about dinner. He thought about calling Leigh Anne to meet him at Kelsey's before remembering she wasn't in town. He reached over to rub Magic's head. She began purring.

"Sun's going down soon," he said. "I suppose you have a date tonight?" He rubbed her neck and made his way to the house to see what he had in the fridge. Abner was standing by the front door—grocery bags in both hands.

"Ah was jes 'bout ta leave. Rang the bell five times."

"Bell doesn't work."

"Ah can fix it fo' ya, if ya want."

"If you want to, sure." They looked at each other for a few seconds.

"Nurse Stella hept me look up ya address. She didn't really wanna, but she's the one that convinced me we needed ta talk."

"Nurse Stella, huh?"

"Yeah, Nurse Stella. Ya gonna open the do'? These bags is gettin' heavy."

Ray looked down when he felt Magic rub between his legs and then back at Abner. "What's in the bags?" he asked, walking past Abner to open the front door.

"Ah figured we could talk ovah summa mah home cookin'," Abner said as he handed the bags to Ray. They walked into the house. "Nice place ya got here, Doc." Abner looked around and followed Ray into the kitchen.

Ray set the bags on the counter and went to the fridge for a beer, but again remembered he was out. "You want something to drink?"

"There's soma that Hawaiian brew that ya like. In the bag ta the right," Abner said as he washed his hands at the sink. "I think it's the kind ya like, I wasn't sure."

Ray tossed him a hand towel, then looked into the grocery bag beneath the greens and the box of cornmeal finding a six-pack of Longboard. "Just as good" he thought. Leaving two on the counter he put the rest into the refrigerator. "Yeah, this is good, thanks."

"We gonna have some pan-fried catfish, collards, an' some hush puppahs. That ok wit' ya?"

That was more grease in one meal than Ray would eat in a few months, but he appreciated the effort Abner was making. "Abner, that sounds downright delish." He grabbed an opener from the utensil drawer, popped off the bottle caps and handed Abner a cold Island Lager.

In spite of the deep-fried balls of flour and cornmeal along with the onions and collards sautéed in a mixture of bacon fat and butter, Ray had to admit that the meal Abner whipped up was not only delicious but extremely satisfying. He felt so stuffed he couldn't move. As comforting as this food was though, he knew that the next morning he was going to feel bloated, heavy, and sluggish. "You eat like this all the time?"

Abner laughed. "Nah, course not. Ah'd like ta, but mah cardaologist ovah at the VMC, Doctah Vincent, ya know Doctah Vincent?"

"No, I haven't met too many of the heart guys yet."

"Doctah Vincent don't wan' me eatin' this stuff at all. Hell man, ah gotta have it once in awhile. Otherwise ah jes might as well go an' die."

"Well, as long as it's just once in awhile I think it's ok." Ray forced himself up from the kitchen table and looked at the stack of dirty mixing bowls, frying pans, and cooking utensils as he brought their dishes over to the sink.

"Lemme hep ya clean up," Abner said as he started to get up.

"No, that's ok. You did all the hard work. I'll take care of this...stuff." Ray looked at the grease-splattered stove and back at Abner. "Tomorrow. After all, I've got a few more days off."

They walked into the living room and sat by the picture windows looking out at the view. Now that it was May, and even though there was still a slight chill in the air, it was definitely too warm to start a fire. "Want another beer?" he asked Abner, holding up a cold one that he had brought in from the kitchen.

"Nah, two's mah limit. Ah'm stuffed wit' catfish an' grease an' ah still gotta drive home. Although, ah could call in sick in the mornin'. They ain't suspendin' part-time janitors lass ah heard." He chuckled as he looked at Ray. He looked at the bottle of beer and thought Abner had a point.

Ray opted for a bottle of mineral water instead and rejoined him in the living room to point out the different landmarks as the sun disappeared behind the Olympics. They had made small talk over dinner, with Abner mentioning out of the clear-blue how obvious it was that Stella and Ray had taken a liking to each other. Ray listened and nodded, but refrained from commenting as he patiently waited for Abner to get down to what he had wanted to know for the previous five weeks.

They sat opposite each other as the old man looked out at the water and then toward the city. The tension was evident. The quiet even seemed loud as Ray, waiting, kept from pressing the issue, and Abner wanting to say something but not knowing where to start.

"I've missed…," they said simultaneously, then stopped, each waiting for the other to continue on.

"I've missed having you come around to my office," Ray finally said.

"Yeah, me too. Ah've been silly."

"No, you haven't. I obviously brought up some stuff that you weren't ready to discuss, or perhaps didn't wanna discuss, and it upset you. I understand that, and if you don't wanna discuss it…well…then, I'll respect that."

Abner looked at Ray and got up, walking over to the large picture windows. "Actually, ya bringin' all this up made me remembah thangs that ah didn't wanna remembah. It made me remembah thangs that ah had completely foegot. Ah needed some time ta think 'bout it all. Ah needed time ta get mah head straight an' face somethin' that ah been needin' ta face fo' a long time." Ray took a sip of his water and placed the bottle down on the small cedar table that separated the two brown leather chairs.

"Ah was there," Abner said without turning from the window. "Ah was on the 606 when the flotilla took the firss an' fifth Marine divisions inta Peleliu. Septembah fifteen, nineteen forta-fo'. Oh-eight-hunred. Hadn't thought 'bout that day in a long, long time. Well, not til ya brought it up lass month, that is." He looked at Ray and they both nodded at each other. Then he turned back to the window and looked out again at Puget Sound. "Hadn't thought 'bout it in so long, an' the lass few weeks it's all ah been thinkin' 'bout. Jes as well, ah ain't gettin' no younga so its time ta face this once an' fo' all. Ya know, Doc, think ah will have that Longboard." Abner turned and headed for the kitchen.

"Light switch on the right when you walk in," Ray called out, not moving from his chair.

"Ah like this kitchen, Doc. Sho do take me back. It reminds me a mah firss apartment in Seattle, after mah time in Kohreah." Abner flipped off the kitchen light and sat in the chair next to Ray. He took a long drink and then studied the label, letting out a deep sigh. "The skippa called all hands ta battle stations. The motor macs alreada on dutah had ta remain in the engine room an' the res' a us took up positions on each a the AA guns. Mah position was at the ammo lockah by the foward gun. Ah was what we called 'the secon loada'. Ah gave canistas a 20mm ammo ta the firss loada an' then he'd load the gun. As we was makin' our run ta the beach ah saw this Zero bearin' down on us off the starboard beam. Now, ta this day ah swear that ah yelled out ta the res' a the gun crew 'Zero, three o'clock!' befo' ah jumped down from the foecastle deck an' took covah. But they nevah swung that gun around ta face off wit' it. They was firin' straight ahead on ta the beach, at a pill box. Next thang ah know, the Zero took `em all out. Two guys was killed right away, the otha two was tore up pretty bad, an' they was jes layin' there. A hand from one a the guys was layin' there on the laddah. Thas when ah froze. Ah swear, mah mind kept sayin' 'Abner, get ya ass back up there' but mah legs was like lead weights. Ah couldn't move an inch. Ah hadn't felt like that since mah cousin Thomas…" Abner looked out the window and lifted the bottle to his lips. Ray sat silent and continued to listen.

"Ah looked up at the connin' station above the pilot house an' saw the skippa yellin' an' screamin' an' lookin' right at me. Ah couldn't hear what he was sayin' cause a the other twennah-mils was firin' away an' a'course the guns from the other ships an' all that. But ah could read his lips. 'Nigga,' he was yellin,' 'Ya getcha black ass on that gun or ah'm gonna kill ya.' Man o' man his face was so red ah thought he was `bout ta esplode. Almost wished he did, that fuckin' sonofabitch. Next thang ah know, ya daddy come flyin' outta the bulkhead hatch an' headed fo' that foward gun jes as a second Zero was makin' a run on us an' started shootin'. Bullets was hittin' all ovah the place, but Ronnie didn't flinch one bit. He was screamin' at me ta get up there an' feed him ammo. As that Zero made its pass ya dad swung that twennah-mil around an' started firin'. Ah got up there, but each step seemed ta take me foever. Ah was able ta reload a canister fo' him an' Ronnie was blastin this guy an' took him out. Ah know he did. Ah saw the traceahs hittin' it as it blew. Skippa never gave him credit fo' the kill, though. Said it was the otha AA guns that took it down. We was at the beach then, an' the Marines was done off-loadin' down the ramps. Me an' Ronnie started tendin' the wounded. At firs' right there where they was layin', an' then we brought `em inside. As we was carryin `em in, anotha plane made a pass on us. Evraone ducked as it fired, but Ronnie kept runnin' with a guy on his shoulda an' bullets was hittin evrawhere. He carried the dead guys too. Ah was back an' forth ta the galley gettin' watah an' rags an' stuff. Then the skippa started screamin' down the laddah outta the pilot house. He was screamin fo' us ta get back ta the foward gun. Again ya daddy went flyin' on up there. Ah hesitated at firss, but started ta go. Ah got outside in time ta get knocked backward on mah ass as the 606 jerked hard inta full reverse. Next thang ah know, Ronnie went flyin' off the bow inta the surf, an' the 606, well she jes kept goin'." Abner became silent for about a half-minute, but it seemed like five to Ray.

"That was the lass ah saw him," he slowly continued. "Ah got mah ass chewed out fo' bein' yella', an' the skippa threatened ta bring me up on charges. Instead, `bout a week laytah ah was bein' swapped wit' the cook from the fo-seventeen. Ah felt bad `bout Ronnie. Ah thought he was dead. An' gettin' sent ta the fo-seventeen? Well, that was a blessin' fo' me. That was a good ship wit' a good skippa an' a good crew." Abner took a deep breath and a longer exhale. He felt a sense of relief. After all those years, he finally felt that a part of his burden had been lifted from his back.

Ray got up and placed a hand on Abner's shoulder. "Thank you. From what you just told me, you did nothing wrong, and you have nothing at all to be ashamed of. As it turns out, I suspect there were other LCI skippers or officers who witnessed what happened. Two weeks after that landing, Lieutenant Johnson was relieved of his command of the 606. From what I read in the logs of the new skipper, my dad was picked up about a week later by the 705 and rejoined his ship when the two eventually rendezvoused." Ray walked over to the window and glanced out at the now darkened western sky.

"Well, Doc...ah mean, Ray, thas very kind a ya ta say, an' no disrespec', but ya weren't there an' ya was never in a situation like that so how would ya know? An' besides, when that Zero made its firss run on us, ah jumped an' took covah. What ah shoulda done was ta stay at mah station wit' them other guys."

"You're right, I wasn't there, and I was never in battle. And as far as that goes, I wasn't even in the service. So I guess you can say that I'm on the outside looking in. But sometimes you have to be on the outside in order to be free from emotion. And sometimes you have to be free from all of the emotion in order to see the facts as they really are and not the way we think we see them. From what you told me, had you stayed at your post, you would've been taken out by that Zero just like those other guys."

"Maybah so. Or maybah ah coulda warned `em again an' pahaps they woulda swung that twennah mil an taken the sucka out."

"Well, that's something we'll never know. To this day my dad doesn't talk much about things that happened on the 606, but now I think I understand why. I can tell you this much, like I told you once before, that when me and my brother Frank were kids, Dad made us 'Navy pancakes' almost every Sunday morning. He was making us the pancakes that you taught him to make. And I know now that whenever he made them, he was thinking of you. Would he have been doing that if he thought you hadn't stepped up that day?"

Abner looked out of the south window toward the Space Needle and the city skyline. He grunted slightly as he pushed himself up and out of the chair and walked toward the window. "Ah hear whatcha sayin' and ah do `preciate it. An' don't get me wrong now, jes talkin' `bout it after all these years actually feels good. But ah need ta reconcile this in a way tha's right fo' me. Ya get what ah'm sayin'?"

"Yeah. I hear ya."

"Well, thas it. Thas the whole storah. We good now?"

"Yeah, Abner. We're good."

"Listen up. There's sumthin' ya should know 'bout Walters."

"John Walters?"

"Be careful wit' that guy. He's a spook."

"A spook? Whaddya mean?"

"Don't ya evah watch TV? He's a comp'ny spook, an agency man. CIA."

"Go on, get outta here," Ray said in disbelief.

"No man, ah ain't messin' wit' ya. This guy commanded a swiftboat in 'Nam, but he wasn't attached ta a reglar Navy unit. He was black ops. Walters was runnin' undah covah missions on the rivahs inta Laos an' Cambodia befoe Nixon even thought a conductin' bombin' runs ovah there. In fact, it was some a those missions that set up those bombin' runs."

Ray thought for a few minutes before responding. "How do you know this?"

"Nevah ya mind how ah know. Trust me, ah know."

"Ok, so what if that's what his role was? That was then. What does that have to do with now or with the 776 for that matter?"

"He's still involved in some way. Once a comp'ny man, always a comp'ny man."

"Nah, come on, Abner."

"Ah'm serious, Doc. Evera now an' then he gets visitahs at the ship. Same two guys evera time. They come by at night when no one's 'round."

"Yeah, well, that doesn't mean anything. They could just be friends of his."

"Doc, one Friday night ah stopped ovah there ta drop off a bunch a stuff that ah picked up at the grossry sto'. We had a big day planned fo' Sataday an' ah wanna ta get cookin' break-fass real early. Those guys was wit' Walters down below in troop two an' ah heard `em talkin' `bout gettin' mo' information an' stuff like that."

"I'm not saying you're wrong, but they could've been talking about anything."

"Look, evera time they pay Walters a visit, they *pay* Walters. I mean he magically comes up wit' large sums a money fo' the restoration projec'. The new hull we jes got? The money was magically donated right aftah one a their meetin's. Ah jes don't think they're good hearted naval enthusias', if ya know what ah mean. All ah'm sayin' is that if ya enjoy spendin' time on the 776 then jes leave it at that an' don't let yaself get too close ta Walters or his biznus. Thass all ah'm sayin', ok?"

"Yeah, ok. What about the rest of the guys volunteering?"

"Ah'm not so hot `bout that Lipton charactah. He kinda gives me the creeps. Chuck Shimkin, the diesel guy? He's good folk. Makes a good dry rub too. Steve Scott is anotha straight-up guy an' so's Gordie. Them other guys is ok as far as ah can tell."

Ray nodded, looked at the small clock sitting on the fireplace mantle, and noticed it was getting late. He knew that Leigh Anne would be calling soon but didn't want Abner to feel he had to leave. "Ok then, I'll keep it all in mind. Look it, I've got some things to wrap up in my workshop. Dinner was great. Thanks so much for doing all that. If you're too tired to drive home, the guest room is down the hallway, second door on the right. Linen closet by the hallway bathroom has fresh towels. If you need anything else let me know. Oh, and don't you dare touch the mess in the kitchen."

2 2

John Walters carefully flipped through one large sheet after another until he came to the correct chart of the Southwest Pacific. He looked up at the single bulb that lit the small radio shack of the 776 and shook his head. "I've got the chart, but it's not bright enough in here," he yelled out toward the wardroom. "I've gotta remember to get Tex to take care of this. For the life of me, I don't know how he works on these radios in such dim light." Walters slid the sheet out from the stack sitting atop the gray painted chart table and crossed the passageway to the wardroom—laying it out in front of his guests. "Are you guys absolutely sure about this?"

"Yeah. No more guesswork at this point. We have solid confirmation from our guy in Luzon," said the smaller of his two visitors, who went by the name of Jeffries.

"Francis?"

"Yes. New code name is Rat Pack. As you already know, he's been working on this for almost a year now."

Bringing one leg up onto the seat of the outermost chair, Walters rested his elbow onto his thigh and rubbed the top of his head as he leaned forward to look at the chart. "When you first mentioned the possibility back in January, I thought it was nuts. When you guys came back in May with more info and this blurred photo," he said, tapping the grainy black and white picture on the table, "I toyed with a few different scenarios, but all of them were too farfetched. Now that you have confirmation, I don't know why you're not taking care of this on your end?"

"All the options were considered, John," Jeffries answered matter-of-factly. "If any of them were viable at this point we wouldn't be here talking, you know that. What it comes down to is that they've got eyes and ears all over the place. Any hint of an action could force them to relocate those packages or they could move up their timetable. Obviously, either case is not good. But what we really don't want is for them to get spooked to the point that they decide to send the stuff to their friends in Afghanistan, or still worse, offer it up for sale to the Iranians. The boys at Langley decided they wanted to do something so unlikely that no one would ever suspect anything. I floated this idea and they liked it. We figure with this plan, we have the best chance of catching them with their pants down." Walters looked at both men as he lit a cigarette. He inhaled deeply and blew a thin stream up toward the overhead light, watching the smoke as it deflected off the fixture and drifted toward the open starboard side porthole.

"What doesn't make sense to me is why they're willing to sell this damn thing in the first place." He picked up the blurred photo of a ship. He tilted the glossy paper back and forth in an effort to reduce the glare—trying to make out the faded bow numbers.

"We had Francis approach them with the offer. Who knew they'd take the bait? From what we can tell, it served its purpose, and now that they know what targets they're gonna hit, they not only need stealth getting in but also speed getting out. Plus, they've been hard up for cash. Otherwise my guess is they would have just left it to rot. Ever since the North Koreans stopped supplying them, they've been counting on the extremist nuts in the Middle East for funding. And since the start of the Afghanistan offensive and with rumblings of us going into Iraq, Al-Qaeda has all but forgotten about these guys. What little help they were getting is all but gone at this point."

"Which is probably why they've been so quiet the past couple of years," Walters said as he flicked an ash into his coffee cup. "Funny though, thinking of an LCI as stealth."

"Well, a lack of money and the lack of ammo are two reasons. I'd also say they were hoping that we, and the Philippine government, would forget about them if they just laid low for a real long time while quietly putting all the pieces of this plan together."

"And they were forgotten about, weren't they?" asked Walters.

"Not entirely. They did have all that time to plan, thinking of course that once we had our guard down, they'd strike us just like we were hit on 9/11. But Francis has been keeping a close eye on these guys. He says that if, or more likely when, we invade Iraq, that's when this splinter group, the Filipino Liberation Brotherhood, is going to strike. They're also hoping that it catches the attention and respect of Al-Qaeda in Southeast Asia."

"Exactly. Provided the damage is extensive enough," Peters—the larger of the two visitors—finally spoke up.

"Rest assured, it will be if they're successful," Jeffries agreed as he looked at the chart.

Walters looked at the chart as well and then back at his guests. "So the President has decided to go into Iraq?"

"It's inevitable," said Jeffries. "All the intel for WMD is there. From NSA, CIA, MI5. I think if he gets full UN support..."

"Which he probably won't," Peters cut in.

"Five, six months from now *if* he gets support," continued Jeffries. "If not, then he's gonna go in anyway. My guess? Shortly after the new year. Eight months from now at the latest. And that brings us to March. A winter or spring offensive is best in order to get it all done before the hot weather sets in. So, as you can see, time is short on our end." he said as he picked up a small black canvas athletic bag and placed it onto the table. Peters grabbed it and slid it over to Walters, adding "That's why we have to get in there and do our thing so the FLB can't do theirs. So, John, is she seaworthy?"

Walters unzipped the bag and without reaching in, looked at the neat stacks of crisp one hundred dollar bills. "As it stands right now, she's not one hundred percent, but she's very close. I was hoping we wouldn't have to use her. I've got a bunch of dedicated volunteers who've been busting their butts trying to turn this into a floating museum."

"You're kidding me, right?" Jeffries said in disbelief. "You don't think we've been financing all these repairs just to make this a tourist attraction, do you?"

"I haven't forgotten why we bought her. We've got a lot of hours into this thing, and I was just thinking what a waste it would be if she became a casualty. I'm just hoping there's another option."

"I think you're getting old, John. You of all people should know that the outfit doesn't do anything just for the hell of it. If it wasn't this operation, we would have found another use for her."

"No, I'm not getting old, Jeffries. Maybe just a little tired."

"If that's the case, maybe after this you should think about hangin' it up."

"I have been thinkin' about it. And…after this one, I am done," Walters said dropping his cigarette into what was left of his coffee.

"I wouldn't worry about it, John. Honest. She's not gonna be in any trouble if we play this one as it's written up. Besides, she's the perfect decoy," assured Jefferies as he pulled the chart closer for a better look. "I took the liberty of charting a course that would fall within the 776's sailing ranges. This would allow for…"

Jefferies was interrupted by the squeal and the deep metal clunk of a bulkhead door latch being opened at the forward end of the main compartment. All three men stopped talking as Peters grabbed the athletic bag and placed it back below the table. Walters—with his right hand on the 9mm Ruger that he kept under his jacket—leaned out of the wardroom and looked forward down the main passageway. As Abner and Ray came through the bulkhead hatch, each with grocery bags in both arms, his empty hand came back out and rested against the doorway.

"It's nine o'clock on a Friday night," Walters called out. "What the hell are you guys doin' here?"

"Hey, skippa," said Abner. "Ah jes did ma Sataday shoppin' so ah could get an early start in the mornin'. Ah was real low on supplies."

As Ray passed by the wardroom on his way to the galley, he and Walters exchanged cautious nods. From years of training and on-the-job experience, John Walters was always suspicious of people when they acted out of character or did things outside of their normal routine. On occasion, Abner would show up late on a Friday night with groceries or other galley supplies, but in the four months that Ray had been volunteering on Saturdays, he had never come to the ship on any other day.

"Since when do you need a helper, A.J.?" Walters asked in a light-hearted tone while his two guests silently organized the papers on the wardroom table.

"Oh, ah showed mah list a stuff ta the Doc while we was at work taday," Abner called out from the galley while unloading his bags. "An' since his girlfrien's off on biznus fo' the week, he offered ta hep me."

"Is that right, Doc?" Walters asked. "You goin' stag this week?"

"Yeah, it seems like," Ray responded, coming out into the passageway. "Don't let us interrupt you guys, unless of course you're planning some covert operation?" Simultaneously, Abner dropped a large can of beans, startling everyone when it hit the steel deck plating, and Peters and Jeffries quickly looked at each other and then at Walters. Suddenly, all went quiet onboard the 776. Meanwhile, Walters just stared at Ray.

"Ah'm ok in heyah, in case enabody was wunderin'," shouted Abner. "A big can a beans jes slipped outta mah hands is all."

"Hey, I was just kidding," Ray said as he glanced first at Abner standing frozen in the galley and then back at Walters. "It was a joke."

"No sweat, Doc," Walters said, glancing over to Peters and Jeffries seated in the wardroom. He looked back at Ray and half-smiled. "Come here, I wanna introduce you to some friends of mine." The two men once again looked at each other and then at Ray. "The big guy is Peters and that's Jeffries," he said as the two of them just barely nodded at him without attempting to get up for a handshake. "These guys run an import-export marine supply business out at Harbor Island, and they've been helping me track down parts from old Navy ships for the 776. They've also been very generous with personal donations to help pay for a lot of the supplies and other work onboard."

In spite of their questioning of Walter's mixed emotions, Jeffries and Peters were quite pleased with his ability to think on his feet. Ray thanked them for their generosity as he noticed the old photo on the table. "What's that?" he asked Walters.

"Oh...that's what I really wanted to show you. Check this out. It's an LCI that these two guys got wind of in the Philippines. The picture quality sucks because we had to enlarge it from an email file. It's owned by a small fishing company that's been using it for almost forty years, maybe more. Now check this out," he said to Ray as he leaned in closer to the photograph. "Check out these features. Round pilot house, see that?"

"Yeah, I see it."

"Starboard and portside gangway ramps. See that?"

"Yeah, I see that too."

"Now look at the number on the bow."

"It's pretty faded, it's hard to see." Ray said as he leaned in closer. As he did, Walters looked over Ray's back and winked at his guests seated at the table.

"Obviously the first number is gone, as you can barely see any trace of it. The middle number is also pretty worn off, but these guys here will agree with me that's definitely a zero. Now look at that last number." Ray's eyes widened as he figured out what Walters was getting at.

"That's definitely a six," Ray said, staring a little harder.

"Exactly. We're looking into it, but we think it's the 606."

"No way, can't be," Ray said in disbelief. "The 606 was struck from the record in '47 and then sold to Argentina. Nav Source lists that the Argentine Navy used her until '67 and then scuttled her."

"Not true," said Jeffries as he realized what Walters was doing. "Officially, the 606 was struck from the record, and yes, it was listed that it went to Argentina. Unofficially, the 606 along with a couple of other LCIs went to the CIA and were used in the Bay of Pigs invasion."

"That's right," added Peters. "After that, they just dumped her. No one knew where, but based on this photo taken a few months ago in the Philippines, we think it's her."

Ray studied the photo again. "CIA? Bay of Pigs? Look guys, no disrespect, but how would you know that?"

"Through their contacts in import and export, these two are always coming across leads on old naval vessels and the like. That's how we're getting a lot of parts for this old thing," answered Walters.

"That's right," agreed Jeffries. "You'd be amazed at the stories one hears."

Ray looked at all three and then back at the photo. "Well, how can you be sure it's not the 506 or the 706?"

Walters looked at Peters, Jeffries, and then at Ray. "We're not sure. Like I said, we think it *might* be. But here's the thing. The fishing company that owns her wants to sell her. So we're thinking about maybe taking a trip out there to check it out. If it's in decent condition and if it's not too expensive, we may just buy her and sail her back here."

The possibility that the 606 still existed excited Ray. So much so that he was distracted from the possibility that Walters and his two "friends" might actually be up to no good—which was what Walters had counted on. "What if you get out there and find out that she's just a piece of junk?" Ray said as he alternated looking between Walters and the photograph.

"Well, if she's a real rust-bucket not worth saving, I suppose for a reasonable price they may let us strip her of anything salvageable. But, to know for sure we're gonna have to make a trip out there to see for ourselves. You wanna come with us if we go?"

Ray thought about it for a moment. He thought about the look on his dad's face if it did turn out to be the 606 and if he could get pictures of himself in her engine room or standing in front of the pilot house. Ron would surely get a kick out of seeing Ray on his old ship. "Yeah, that would be an amazing experience," he said as Abner listened intently from the galley. "But after what happened to me last month at work, there's no way I'd be able to swing that kind of time now."

"Not a big deal. But if we do decide to make the trip, we'll just video the whole thing and I'll make a copy for ya. Ok?" said Walters.

"Yeah, that'd be great. Thanks."

Abner finished putting away his supplies and was shutting down the galley when Walters asked him to leave the door open. "I'm gonna be up late tonight, A.J., so you might as well leave it open for me." As Abner passed by the wardroom he stopped and dug through his pants pocket. He pulled out a balled-up slip of paper and handed it to Walters. "What's this?"

"Thas the receipt fo' the stuff ah jes put away."

Walters unfolded the register slip and looked at it. "One hundred and seventy-three dollars?"

"Lemme get a look at that," Abner said as he took the slip back and quickly scanned to the bottom of the receipt. "An' thirta-three cent." He handed it back to Walters, smiled, and turned to leave. Ray and Abner said their goodbyes and headed down the port side ramp to the dock. "Didn't ah tell ya he has late night meetin's wit' these guys? An' those were the guys ah saw the lass time ah showed up on a Friday night," Abner said once they had gotten far enough away from the ship to not be heard. "An' what the hell was that remark 'bout plannin' a covert operation? Ya wanna get us killed or sumthin'?"

"They know that anyone in their right mind wouldn't mention covert, black ops, CIA, or anything else like that if they openly suspected that stuff was going on. And besides, I wanted to see the look on their faces."

"An' what look did ya see?"
"They looked like little kids getting caught with their hands in the cookie jar."

* * *

'That was close," Jeffries said once he was sure their surprise visitors were gone.

"They're harmless. I wouldn't worry about them," responded Walters.

"I hope you're right." Jeffries said bringing the black canvas sport bag back onto the table. "We know who the old man is. He's stopped by before. Who's the other guy?"

"Ray Silver? He's a chiropractor at the Veteran's Medical Center. His dad was on the 606. That's his connection to this restoration project and why I brought up that hull number."

Jeffries nodded and pulled out a folded yellow sheet of paper from his jacket pocket. "Here's a list of items and modifications you'll need to make over the next couple of months. We'd like to see this thing ready to sail by December, January the latest. Does Lipton have all that hardware in working order?"

"Yeah, he does. The firing pins are all stowed below. He can have those put together in a matter of minutes. We have some ammo, but we'll definitely need more."

"That'll be waiting for you when you get to Midway. There's also a stash at Guam…just in case" said Jeffries.

Walters continued to look at the list. "Chuck Shimkin is gonna need help getting those diesels turbocharged and automated so that they're fully controlled and monitored from both the bridge and the conning station. I'll get the doc to help him on that project. GPS units, no problem. Sonar? We can use the same units the fishing boats use."

"We're gonna give you the GPS units. They'll have a built-in tracking device so we can keep tabs on you. That way, if we do have to send in the cavalry, we'll know where to find you. And don't worry about the radios," Jeffries added. "We'll get those to you as well. Now, as I was sayin' before your friends showed up, I charted a course from here to Lamon Bay in the Philippines with refueling stops at Midway and Guam. We'll have people at each port who'll know to look out for you and get you whatever additional supplies you may need. Fuel, food, weapons, whatever. When we get closer to departure we'll have radio frequencies and call signs for each waypoint. Depending upon weather conditions and your speed, you might be able to bypass either Midway or Guam going and coming back. Obviously that'll be up to you."

As they got up to leave Jeffries turned again to Walters. "The more this trip looks like a bunch of amateur naval buffs looking to buy an old ship, the better chance you'll have at pulling this off. That was a good idea, asking Silver if he wanted to go along. Besides the small crew we're giving you, see how many of your volunteers would be willing to come along for the ride and let me know as soon as you can. Otherwise we'll have to provide you with a few more people."

"I don't like the idea of using amateurs. It's crazy and it's way too risky," Walters said.

"John," Peters said, "I think Jeffries is right. You are getting old, and perhaps a little soft. We're not asking these guys to be anything more than window dressing."

"As long as they think we're going to retrieve another LCI, I'm sure I can get four, maybe five," Walters conceded as he mentally went through the faces of his Saturday sailors.

"That should be fine. Maybe we'll add one or two more. Just to be safe." Jeffries said.

"What about outside communications? My guys are all going to have cell phones." Walters pulled one out of his pocket and waved it at Jeffries.

"That's a good point." Jeffries thought for a minute. "We really don't want them calling anyone. It's risky to have people on the outside knowing where we're heading. Then again, the only time they'll be able to contact anyone is when we're within range of a cell tower."

"Once we get well out into the Pacific that shouldn't be a problem. But what about when we're within range of Hawaii?" asked Walters as he looked at a map.

"Let's just tell them the cell phone signals will fuck with the navigation equipment like they do on airplanes." He patted Walters on the shoulder as the two men quietly started to leave the ship.

As they headed down the ramp, Jeffries turned to Peters. "One of us, or maybe both of us are gonna have to go along on this thing to keep an eye on Walters. I think you're right that he's getting soft. He was never like this before. Oh, and I almost forgot. I want this chiropractor checked out."

"I'm on it."

2 3

Ray slowly woke to a warm breeze flowing through the open window, gently lifting and releasing the sheer white curtains as if they were inhaling and exhaling on their own. As Leigh Anne's backside pressed into him, the warmth and softness of her flesh aroused him as they spooned. Her eyes still closed, she smiled as she playfully scolded him, "Damn, boy, doesn't that thing ever get tired?"

"Can you blame me?" he asked softly pressing his lips into her shoulder. "I haven't seen you in three and a half weeks, and in another few days you're heading off to Molokai. I'm beginning to think you're getting tired of me."

She didn't answer as she was reminded of her annual pilgrimage to St. Philomena's. She tried hard not to think about the trip she had made during the last week of June for the past seven years. But like clockwork, and as if innately programmed into her genetic coding, when most people celebrated Memorial Day weekend, her melancholy started setting in and she would think about her daughter. She would think about all the things they would have done together as she reached each milestone in her life. She imagined the expression that she might have had the first time she tasted Kimo's pineapple mango salsa, or the joy she would have known on her first swim with a dolphin. She wondered what thoughts she would have had upon receiving her first valentine.

It had always been hard for her to make the trip back to Molokai, as being there fueled her conflicted emotions and rekindled her guilt. She had anticipated nothing less when she had returned earlier in the year, but that trip had been different. Once she was there, once she was back where she knew she belonged, she felt the burden dissipate with each successive sunrise. Maybe it was the time she spent at the church in prayer and taking counsel from Father Dominick. Maybe it was the time she spent in solitude as she cared for the graves in the parish cemetery or walked along the trails as she returned to her poetry. It could have even been Kelsey's persistent—and at times annoying—badgering over the years. Whatever the reason, when she had finally accepted that she had been punishing herself by not allowing the possibility of companionship, things began to change. Having acknowledged that, her guilt and anxiety began to ease, and she was finally able to give herself permission to love again. Having Ray in her life certainly helped—and definitely made it more complex.

"Hey," Ray said as he gently rocked her back and forth. "You're pretty quiet. Maybe you *are* getting bored with me. Didja meet some young stud or something?"

"No, no young stud. Just thinking is all." She lay there watching the curtains drifting away from the window, while savoring his touch. She wondered how many more times she would wake up in his bed as another warm breeze blew in.

Ray closed his eyes, leaned in to bury his face in her auburn hair, and slowly breathed in her scent. His hand slowly exploring the curves of her body, he laughed to himself at the irony of it all as he recalled when they first got together. Both had agreed that their relationship was not going to get complicated. They weren't going to be one of those couples who needed to be with each other night and day. Sometimes they got together on a whim, sometimes it was planned, and sometimes they didn't see each other for several days or longer. If there was a long period of not seeing each other, they still kept in touch—if not for any other reason than to let the other one know they had been in their thoughts. There were times, however, that because of prior obligations, one or the other had to cope with an unfulfilled physical desire. There had never been promises of monogamy and yet they both were—not that it was easy. There were still plenty of young, handsome, and professional men who were completely infatuated with Leigh Anne's beauty and would have done anything to bed her. Some had even come on to her at Kelsey's with Ray seated right by her side.

"Hey there. I couldn't help but notice that your beer's been empty for quite awhile," said her most recent come-on. "The name's Bob, and I was wondering if I could get you...," he waited for her reaction. "Uh, a refill that is?"

"No, that's ok. I'm good," she responded without looking over at him.

"It's really no trouble. Whaddya drinkin'?"

"I'm doing just fine, thank you." Leigh Anne said to the hopeful suitor who had approached her on a dare by his buddies.

"No, really, let me get you a refill."

"No, really, I'm doing just fine, Bobby."

"Well, I also couldn't help but notice that you were looking kinda bored just sittin' here by yourself." He looked back at his buddies and smiled. "I'm sure a little friendly conversation would make the evening a lot more interesting. Come on, let me get ya a refill." He continued as he inched a little closer to her.

Ray, sitting on the other side of Leigh Anne and knowing she could easily handle herself, had stayed out of it. Yet it was not lost on him that younger, more athletic-looking men never considered that the two of them could be a couple. She took a hard look at what she considered to be an over-confident, ego-driven jock looking to chalk up one more conquest. She also took note of his buddies at the far end of the bar, snickering like little schoolgirls.

"Nope, I don't want a refill, and as you can plainly see, I'm not alone and I'm definitely not bored. So Bobby, please leave us alone and go back to your friends." She exchanged a quick look and a smile with Ray.

"Oh, excuse me," he said, loud enough for Ray and everyone around the bar to hear. "I didn't know you were here with your father."

A number of people stopped their conversations and focused their attention on the intended insult. From behind the bar, Kelsey slowly put her hand on the Louisville Slugger that she kept for times like this. With her hand on his thigh, Leigh Anne knew from his tightening muscles that Ray was about to stand up. She also knew that he would get his ass kicked if he went toe to toe with the guy. She quickly pressed down on his leg and got up before he could. Circling around to Ray's other side, she placed her hand on his opposite cheek, guided his face to look right at her, and proceeded to give him the deepest, wettest and longest kiss that anyone in Kelsey's had ever witnessed.

"Let's go home, babe," she said to Ray, while looking at Bob. As they started to leave, Kelsey rang the brass bell behind the bar and yelled out, "You go girl!" before pointing to Bob as he brushed off the rejection and returned to his friends.

Ray too had been dealing with his share of potential suitors, as several of the nurses at the medical center had suddenly developed a need to come to his office for "treatment." Even Stella had started to seem more interested in him as their conversations began to take on a more personal tone. He couldn't explain it, but sometimes it did make him feel a little uncomfortable. Still, he looked forward to their get-togethers and didn't discourage the growing friendship.

The longer he and Leigh Anne continued their "uncomplicated" relationship, the more he found himself thinking of her—and missing her when she was away. Leigh Anne also found herself thinking about him—sometimes to distraction. She began questioning whether or not the relationship could continue. She had admired the bravado he displayed the very first time he approached her. His unintentional clumsiness when he was just being himself. The way his eyes burned right through her whenever he watched her as she talked about her day. The way he made love to her, especially the night she had used his spare key to sneak into the house and wait for him under the sheets while he had been in the shower. When Kelsey had asked her what she saw in him, she had commented that she appreciated his maturity, his sense of stability and that he made her feel safe and secure. And when she heard those words come out of her own mouth, she wondered if she liked being with Ray because he was the father figure that she had never had growing up. There were times when she certainly felt his awkwardness when they were at Kelsey's with her friends. The fifteen years that separated them had, at times, created a disconnect for him. There had been occasions when he had certainly felt left out as group conversations veered from current events to social and entertainment interests that he couldn't relate to.

"Why so deep in thought this morning?" he asked as he slowly slid his hand up and down her arm and shoulder.

"It's that time of the year, I guess," she said staring off toward the window. Ray wanted to joke about her "time of the year" comment, but thought better of it.

"As 'uncomplicated' as we're trying to keep what we have, I think we're progressing into that 'no fly' zone. You know I care about you. There's a lot you still haven't told me…about you, about your life…stuff like that. And you know I haven't pressed you, and I'm not pressing you now."

"I know. There's a lot I want to be able to share with you. In time. Maybe if you came with me to Molokai. The energy there is amazing."

"If only I could. You know how much I love the islands. You also know that they'd suspend me again if I took off so soon after the last incident."

She half-turned to face him. "I'm thinking of going back there, Ray. Not to visit, but to live." He looked at her but didn't say anything. "When we first met at Kimo's last January, it was my first trip back to Oahu in almost eight years. That's my home, Oahu. I was born and raised there. I'd gone back to apply for a job at the aquarium."

"I had no idea. I mean…I had no idea you felt that way… that you've been feeling that way. Why didn't you say anything?"

"Because I…I'm not really sure why. I just know that this desire I have is overwhelming me, and I thought you'd better know how I feel."

"Hmmm, I guess that does complicate things."

"Just a little, right?"

He noticed a small tear as it slowly rolled from the corner of her eye over the bridge of her nose. He caught it with his index finger and wiped it away. "I can't believe they didn't call you. It's over five months."

"Apparently the guy who was supposed to retire, hasn't. Otherwise, I'm sure I would have been there by now."

"Lucky for me, eh? And what if they do call you? What if they called tomorrow and said the job just opened up? Then what?"

"Then I'd go."

"Really? Just like that?"

"If this were back in January or February, yeah, just like that."

"But this is June and…"

"And things are now where we didn't really want them to go. Right?"

"I don't want to pretend that my feelings for you haven't become stronger. You know they have."

"Same here."

"I know. So, if they called you tomorrow, would you go?"

"I think it's obvious that they're not calling me tomorrow and I don't think they will. But, if they did…yes…I would go. It's time for me…I want to go home."

"But you hesitated."

"Only because of you," Leigh Anne said as Ray's eyes examined hers. She turned onto her back and placed a hand on his cheek. He lowered himself to kiss her as she pulled him tight. "Damn, boy, that thing never does get tired."

24

Ray sat at his desk staring out at the glistening water of Puget Sound, the July sun slowly disappearing behind the snow-capped Olympic Mountains. With Leigh Anne unexpectedly extending her Molokai trip an additional week to interview for a professorship at the University of Hawaii's School of Marine Sciences, he was distracted and hadn't been able to stay focused on his research project for a number of days. This night was no different. He had spent hours searching for information about Robert Lee Johnson, the 606's skipper, during the Peleliu landing in 1944. Every naval related website that he searched was a dead end. Every possible lead had turned out to be nothing. Not being able to focus, he just kept replaying the conversation he had had with Abner. The words echoed in his head:

"As that Zero made it's pass ya dad swung that twennah-mil around an' started firin'. Ah got up there, but each step seemed ta take me foever. Ah was able ta reload a canister fo' him an' Ronnie was blastin' this guy an' took him out. Ah know he did. Ah saw the tracers hittin' it as it blew. Skippa never gave him credit fo' the kill, though. Said it was the otha AA guns that took it down. We was at the beach then, an' the Marines was done off-loadin' down the ramps. Me an' Ronnie started tendin' the wounded. At firss right there where they was layin', an' then we brought 'em inside. As we was carryin' 'em in, anotha

plane made a pass on us. Evraone ducked as it fired, but Ronnie kept runnin' with a guy on his shoulda an' bullets was hittin evrawhere. He carried the dead guys too. Ah was back an' forth ta the galley gettin' watah an' rags an' stuff. Then the skippa started screamin' down the laddah outta the pilot house. He was screamin' fo' us ta get back ta the foward gun. Again ya daddy went flyin' on up there. Ah hesitated at firss, but started ta go. Ah got outside in time ta get knocked backward on mah ass as the 606 jerked hard inta full reverse. Next thang ah know, Ronnie went flyin' off the bow inta the surf and the 606, well she jes kept goin'."

He glanced up at the picture of the 606. On the starboard side of the ship, his dad was clearly visible. Shirtless and no hat—like a number of the other crewmembers onboard—Ron Silver was pulling on a rope looking over the side.

"Ah got outside in time ta get knocked backward on mah ass as the 606 jerked hard inta full reverse. Next thang ah know, Ronnie went flyin' off the bow inta the surf and the 606, well she jes kept goin'."

Ray leaned over to his left and opened the small refrigerator door. Without taking his eyes off of the Coast Guard frigate sailing into Elliot Bay, he located a cold Pipeline and angled the top of the longneck into the die-cast bottle opener next to his desk. As the bottle cap hit the bottom of the metal wastebasket, he heard Abner's voice again:

"Next thang ah know, Ronnie went flyin' off the bow inta the surf and the 606, well she jes kept goin'. She jes kept goin'."

Between work, researching the 606, volunteering at the 776, helping Stella to gather information on Bill Harrison, and worrying about Leigh Anne, his kids, and his dad, Ray was slowly becoming stressed and fatigued. Not exactly what he had envisioned for this stage of his life. He thought about Leigh Anne being away and more importantly, about her interview at the University of Hawaii. She had made it perfectly clear that she wanted to move back there and obviously she wasn't going to wait for the aquarium position to materialize. As much as it bothered him that she would leave, he admired how proactive she was. He considered his options should she go.

"I could try to transfer to VMC Honolulu" he thought. "Yeah, but would she want me to follow her? Well, she did want me to come with her on this trip…but maybe she just said that because she knew I couldn't go." He kept wrestling with himself and then thought of Stella. He was equally as comfortable around her as he was with Leigh Anne. "But they're so different from each other," he thought. "She's older than Leigh, my age, and has different tastes. She's lingerie and heels for sure, whereas Leigh is worn-out jeans and peasant blouses. What the hell am I thinking about? This is silly. Stella's got somebody and Leigh is only interviewing. What's wrong with me? I can't believe I'm even thinking of someone else…damn, I'm tired."

Ray felt a little guilty, but still imagined Stella lying in his bed dressed in nothing but a black lacy bra and panties with sheer black stockings. "Definitely a Vargas girl," he thought. He sucked hard on his beer as a passing freighter sounded its horn and he heard Abner once again: *"Ronnie went flyin' off the bow inta the surf and the 606, well she jes kept goin'."*

He picked up his cell phone and hit number one on the speed dial. It rang a half-dozen times before going to voicemail. He hung up and redialed—surprised when a sleepy female voice answered. "Oh I'm sorry, I think I have the wrong number," he said, hanging up quickly. Ray looked at the number he just dialed and knew he had it programmed correctly into his phone. He hit number one on the speed dial again, and again a woman's voice answered.

"Yeah, who is this? Don't ya know it's after midnight?"

Ray looked up at his wall clocks and saw that it was 9:15p.m. 12:15 a.m. on the East Coast. The longer summer daylight hours in the Pacific Northwest always made him forget the time difference back east. "I'm real sorry, I didn't mean to wake you."

"Who is this?" she demanded

"Excuse me, but who's this?"

"Caroline."

"I'm sorry to wake you, Caroline. I was trying to reach my son."

"Hold on." Ray heard her muffled voice in the background.

"Hello, this is Jimmy. Dad? Is that you?"

"Hey, kiddo. I'm sorry for the late call. I forgot about the time difference. Go back to sleep, I'll call you tomorrow."

"It's no problem, now that I'm up. Everything ok? Is Casey ok?"

"Yeah, everything's fine. Casey's fine too. We're all ok. You alright?"

"Yeah, Dad, I'm good. Everything is good."

"I know you've only been there six weeks, but any word on whether or not you're going to ship out anywhere?"

"No, nothing yet. I hope that's not why you called."

"No, it's not. I was actually wondering if there was any way you could do a little research for me? That is, without getting into any trouble."

"Depends on what it is."

'I've come across some new information about your grandfather during the war. From an eyewitness. I think, because of a racist and anti-Semitic skipper, your grandfather was denied some sort of official recognition, like a Bronze Star or maybe some other sort of commendation for heroism."

"Serious?"

"Yeah, very. You got a pen and paper?"

"One sec" Jimmy said, as Ray again heard a woman's voice in the background telling Jimmy to come back to bed. He wanted to ask him all about it but it was definitely not the right time. "Ok, go ahead."

"Robert Lee Johnson. Got that?"

"Yeah, got it."

"He was the skipper of the 606 and got relieved of command after the landings at Peleliu in September of `44. Find out what you can about him. He never turned in his log book after he lost command. It disappeared. Maybe he kept it. Find out if he's still alive, and if not, where his family lives. That is, if he had any family. Can you do that for me?"

"I'll try. I can't make this a full-time thing, ya know. I'm loaded down with real work."

"Yeah I know, kiddo. It's for your grandfather though. If he was cheated out of something that he truly deserves, I'd like to see him get it. Ya know?"

"Yeah, dad. I know."

"Ok, thanks. Sorry I called so late. You better get back to your 'real' work. She sounds lonely."

"Cute, dad, real cute!"

25

Food had always been a great source of comfort for Ray. From the time he was a little kid, watching both parents turn meal preparation into a labor of love to the music of Sinatra, right up through his adult years. With every stressful time in his life, he always found refuge in food. If not for his commitment to an exercise routine, he would surely be twenty, if not thirty, pounds overweight. He not only loved food, he loved the whole process involved in the preparation of the meal. Spending time in the kitchen was a creative outlet for him and it often took his mind off of his problems.

When Jimmy and Casey were growing up, the three of them often spent rainy Saturday and Sunday afternoons making pizza and calzones from homemade tomato sauce and hand-kneaded dough. He taught Casey to make her first Thanksgiving turkey when she was only eleven. Sunday dinners had always been a family event, with Jo gladly pitching in as Jimmy often became distracted by a televised football or basketball game. The smiles and laughter that he had shared with his family remain married to the fragrances that had once freely flowed through their home. To cook those recipes again surely ignited a pleasant memory. Now that he was alone, he didn't spend much time in the kitchen. As much as he loved food and the ritual of preparation, he took more pleasure out

of watching people enjoying his many creations. And now—
except when Leigh Anne stayed for dinner—there was really
no one to cook for.

Ray was feeling somewhat depressed. His kids were grown
and onto their careers, and Leigh Anne was putting the pieces
into place for an eventual move back to Oahu. He felt an empti-
ness he had not known before. "Geez," he thought. "If I feel like
this now, what's it gonna feel like when she actually leaves?" He
wanted to talk to someone, but didn't know who. He couldn't
talk to Leigh Anne until she returned from Hawaii, and even
then, he didn't know what it would accomplish.

After mindlessly flipping through all the cable channels
and finding nothing to distract him, Ray tossed the remote
onto a chair and headed straight for the refrigerator. "Nothing
here," he said as he closed the door and then wondered out
loud, "Ok, what if she does leave? She is going to. Ok, then.
But even if she stays, we're not committed to each other right?
Yeah, right. So, ok then. So I can see other people, women.
There's nothing to stop her from seeing other men. Right? So,
ok then." He walked back into the living room and picked up
the remote. It would be a few more days before Leigh Anne
returned from her trip. He knew he would have to talk about
how he felt. "God! This sucks so much. I feel like such a teenager!" He tossed the remote again, and walked back into the
kitchen, and found himself foraging, but nothing looked
good. "Just as well, damn it," he mumbled to himself. "Can't let
myself get back into the habit of eating when stressed. I've got
a few hours, might as well just cook up something for dinner."

He looked up at the kitchen clock and thought of the
time that he had set up an assembly line operation for him
and the kids to make meatballs. Jimmy was first in line, taking
three different kinds of meat along with the seasonings that
Ray had added and mixed them together with his hands. He
always took delight in grossing out his sister as he squished
the ground beef, pork, and veal through his clinched fingers.
Casey then scooped up small portions of the seasoned mixture
and carefully rolled a perfectly round ball out of each scoopful

before dropping them, one by one, into the skillet. Ray then slowly browned them before dropping each one into a pot of simmering tomato sauce. The memory brought a smile to his face, and made him all the more hungry. He made a list of ingredients and headed off to the market.

* * *

With Sinatra singing in the background, his one-man meatball operation was in full swing. He had a big pot of sauce simmering on the stove while a few dozen meatballs sizzled in a big cast iron skillet. In between stirring his sauce and transferring meatballs from skillet to paper towel, he sipped from a glass of his favorite Chianti. At first he didn't hear the timid knock at his front door. Sinatra was too loud, which was just the way Ray liked it. But then, through the chorus of *The Way You Look Tonight,* he heard a loud repetitive knock. "One minute," he yelled out, turning the heat down under both the skillet and the pot of sauce and headed toward the door, singing, "*Just the way you look to...* Stella!"

"I hope I'm not interrupting," she said as she angled her head to look inside.

"No, not at all. I was just working on dinner. Are ya hungry? Didja eat yet? Please, come in."

"Actually, I've been working all day. I pulled a Sunday shift since Robert's been off on another one of his European business trips." She walked in and carefully looked around— instantly smelling the garlic, rosemary, and oregano drifting out of the kitchen. "Smells good."

"Well then, please join me for dinner. I got a little carried away with myself and cooked up a ton and there's no one else to share it with."

"Sure, I'm starved, and I'd love to. As long as you're sure it's ok."

"Wouldn't offer if it wasn't. Come, this way." He led her into the kitchen, and she smiled at the sight of the meatballs and large loaf of Italian bread still sitting in its brown paper sleeve. She was immediately transported back to her father's Boston deli.

"Those meatballs smell amazing. They smell just like my dad's."

"Did he like to cook?"

"I'll say! He owned a deli in Boston and cooked everything from scratch. Meatballs, eggplant parmesan, everything. Gravy, too." She walked over to the stove and looked at Ray. "May I?" she asked as she picked up a fork and pointed to the skillet.

"Be my guest," he said, watching her decide which one to pick. Stella gently pierced one and cupped a hand under it as she brought it up to her nose and smelled. "Hmm. I smell garlic, rosemary, basil." She took a bite, closed her eyes, and smiled again. "Oh, Ray. Are you sure you're not Italian? I'm tasting beef and pork and...veal! Am I right?"

"Right on the money," he said, smiling back at her.

"That's how my father used to make them. I can't believe it." She looked at the bottle of Chianti on the counter. "Oh my God, tell me you didn't put Chianti into your gravy?"

"Gravy? Oh, you mean the tomato sauce?"

"Yeah, sauce, gravy, same thing."

"Yeah, I've always put Chianti in my sauce."

"Amazing, Ray Silver. Simply amazing. Pasta?" She asked as she looked around the countertop.

"No, sorry. I was in the mood for a meatball hero."

"Hero? You mean a sub?"

"A sub?" He laughed. "I thought you guys up in Mass called them 'grinders'?"

"Grinda?" She asked with an exaggerated Boston accent. "That's Rhode Island."

"Hero, sub, grinder, whatever. Let's eat!"

They sat in the kitchen and savored every bite of Ray's meatball heroes. He was thrilled that Stella completely enjoyed his cooking. They made small talk during dinner. He talked a little about Leigh Anne, but didn't want to say too much. Mostly, he talked about his kids, or he listened to her talk about her teenage years, her protective cousins, and about her father's deli in Boston. As she talked, smiled, and laughed, he watched her dark brown eyes and how they lit up as bright as her smile. Ray thought about how great she looked—even in her blue hospital scrubs. In spite of his feelings of guilt, he imagined what it would be like to kiss her and to hold her body close to his.

Somewhere during their conversation of her high school and college years, she had changed gears and begun talking about Bill Harrison and the information she'd been compiling. "So, as soon as I saw that letter, I knew I had to make a photocopy." She looked at him waiting for his response. "Did you hear what I just said?"

Caught in the middle of his fantasy, he quickly tried to recover. "Yeah, I…I was just thinking."

"About what?" She asked with a doubting look.

"No really. I was. Come." He stood up and grabbed their wine glasses. "Grab the Chianti and let's go sit in the living room. I wanna hear everything you've been able to find so far."

She looked at her watch and noticed they had been talking for hours. "It's getting late, I really should be going."

"Are you working tomorrow?"

"No, I'm off."

"Then fill me in on what you've got on Harrison. You know how hard it is to discuss this stuff at the VMC. Come." He motioned his head toward the living room.

They sat close together on the couch, sharing the wine as Stella leafed through the pages in her file folder. She had been keeping notes and other documents on Harrison ever since Ray had alerted her to what seemed like the orthopedist's careless prescribing practices.

"Listen, Ray. The more I dig into this thing, the more I'm beginning to suspect that there's something more going on here than just this guy's incompetence or disinterest in his patients."

"Whaddya mean? Are you saying that what he's doing is intentional?"

"I don't know. I can't be sure. But I'm getting an uncomfortable feeling that what's going on is not by accident."

"As much as I think this guy's a jerk, I can't see him intentionally over-prescribing to hurt his patients."

"I know it sounds nuts but I've overheard parts of conversations that he's had. On several occasions, I've seen him meet a pharmaceutical rep out in the parking lot and he was giving her large envelopes."

"Medical records?"

"Possibly. I can't be sure. I even found this torn up pay envelope in his trash bin."

"How is a torn up pay envelope evidence?"

"Ray, the VMC doesn't use a payroll service and we don't get pay envelopes. Our pay is a direct deposit straight from administration offices in D.C."

"Yeah, you're right." He thought about the possibilities. "But this doesn't mean that the envelope belongs to him."

"No, that's true."

"What are *you* doin' looking through his trash bin? You can get caught, ya know."

"When Abner makes the morning rounds changing out the trash bin liners, he sets Harrison's aside for me. Look here, see the payroll service initials printed on the back of the envelope?"

"A.P.S? yeah?"

"The sales rep that I saw him talking to works for Visor Pharmaceuticals. I'll bet a company that big uses a payroll service. All I have to do is find out which one."

"Assuming they don't do direct deposit like the VMC does, how you gonna do that?"

She sat silent for a moment as she took the torn envelope back from Ray. "I'm not quite sure. I'll have to think about that."

"Why wouldn't they pay him in cash? Ya know, so there's no paper trail."

"Unless of course, they want a paper trail." She said

"To what end?"

"My guess is that Visor wants to have a paper published showing how safe and effective their drug is with long term use. Harrison's writing the prescriptions and supplying them with the raw data, they publish the study as if he wrote the darn thing and he gets a check."

"Ya mean they ghost-write it."

"And he's only too happy to let them use his name because he's thinking it's gonna make him look good. Plus, he's probably getting paid pretty well."

"Ok, call me naïve, but the data is still gonna show that his test subjects are dying from stroke or cardio-vascular injury."

"True." Unless they ignore it and manipulate the data to reflect the results they want. And then when sales start to skyrocket...,"

"Then so does the stock price. And when the FDA and CDC start to see a rise in strokes and vascular injuries?"

"Visor throws up its hands claiming that they're victims of Harrisons' incompetence. And you can bet that they have docs at other facilities doing the same thing. This way they can show they didn't rely on just one guy."

Ray shook his head. "I can't believe it. This really goes on?"

"What, ghost-writing? I've heard that it does, but there's no way I can prove it. Ray, I need to ask you a favor."

"Sure, go for it."

"When I started looking into this thing, I didn't want...I didn't want to involve you."

"Whaddya want me to do?"

"Maybe I'm being a little paranoid, but if anything happens to the stuff I've been gathering, I'll have no case against Harrison. I've scanned all these documents into my home computer and I also burned them onto this disk." She reached into her small backpack and pulled out a CD. "Would you mind keeping this in a safe place? Just in case? As I get more information, I'll give you updated disks. Ok?"

He took the CD from her and noticed the seriousness in her face. "Sure thing, Stella."

They found themselves talking past midnight, strategizing about how much documentation would be enough and to whom they would be able to bring their information.

"I can't believe how late it is," Stella said as she tried to stand up. She felt off-balance—slightly dizzy from all the wine they had shared—and quickly sat back down. "I don't think...I don't think I'm gonna be able to drive home, Ray."

"Then don't," he said, getting up. "Whoa." He swayed briefly before regaining his balance. "I think I drank too much too. I didn't realize how big that second bottle was."

"We finished both? That was a lot of wine. I really can't stay here. I...I should go home." As she tried to stand a second time, she laughed as she leaned into Ray to keep herself from falling. His arms reflexively came up to support her shoulders and steady her. She stopped laughing and looked up into his eyes. He slowly studied her face for a minute and was tempted to kiss her. She sensed that he wanted to. Stella pressed herself forward, and his arms relaxed, allowing her body to make contact with his. Ray closed his eyes when he felt her up against him.

"You're in no condition to go home. I'm not letting you drive like this. You're staying," he said as he placed his arm around her shoulders and led her down the hallway toward the bedrooms.

* * *

Ray couldn't remember the last time he had had such a killer headache. But when he drove off to work the next morning, he certainly did have one. Too much wine always did that to him. He had also woke-up late and was unable to do his 5 a.m. walk. His head and his body felt heavy, and his thoughts were clouded. Had he had the time, he would have prepared a nice breakfast for Stella. He didn't think she'd mind that he hadn't though, and could easily make something for herself if she really wanted to. In short, he felt like crap and prayed for a hassle-free day—which meant a day of no Bill Harrison.

By the time she slowly opened her eyes, Ray had been long gone. Stella carefully looked around the room and shot upright when she realized she was not in her own home. Her head hurt from the after-effects of the Chianti. Lifting the comforter to get out of bed, she noticed she was only in her bra and panties. Stella quickly covered herself, again looking around the room until she located her hospital scrubs on the chair by the side of the bed. The house was quiet, and judging at the time on her cell phone, she knew that Ray had already left for the medical center. "Bad girl, Stella. Bad, bad girl!" She gathered up her clothes, dressing quickly. "Ray?" She called out, making sure he really was gone. "Ray, you still here?"

There was no answer. She walked down the hallway and peaked into his bedroom. His unmade bed abandoned, she smiled at the thought that he had put her to sleep in the guest room, and yet was disappointed that he hadn't spent the night with her. "Sometimes, chivalry can really suck," she said as she made her way into the kitchen.

2 6

Leigh Anne had been back from Oahu for four days
before Ray saw her. He had thought she would have
come to the house. In fact, since she had a key he had
assumed—hoped—she would have been over by her second
day home. By the fourth day, without even a phone call to
return his messages, he was worried about her.

His afternoon had been very quiet. No patient visits in
almost two hours and nothing but a stack of unfinished reports
sat on his desk. Working for the government had turned out
to be everything he had feared. Tons of red tape, requests that
went unanswered or got passed on to a faceless bean counter
somewhere, and of course the weekly, monthly, and quarterly
reports. He looked up at the clock on the wall in his office.
"Five o'clock, thank God!" He said out loud. He picked up his
cell phone and pressed number four on his speed dial. Leigh
Anne's cell was number three but she hadn't been answering
that one. Number four was to her apartment.

"Leigh? Hey, this is Ray...again. Leigh, if you're home pick
up...ok, listen. I don't know what's up, but I'm pretty sure you
were supposed to be back a few days ago. If you don't wanna
see me or talk to me for some reason, that's fine. But just let me
know that you're alright...It's five on my clock and I'm leaving
work now. I'm gonna stop by Kelsey's to see if you're there."

In the five months they had been seeing each other, it was not like her to blow him off—if in fact that was what she was doing. She had always been a straight-shooter with him, and he with her. Ray's concern for their relationship was growing. He left the building through a side door to avoid running into anyone who would delay him getting to Kelsey's. After having been in his cool subterranean office all day, the late afternoon heat smacked him as he pushed open the heavy metal door. Pulling off his tie and unbuttoning his shirt, he double-timed it to his Jeep.

Ray was just a few feet from freedom when he heard Peter McCain's annoying voice wheezing out his name. "Not so fast, Dr. Silver. Hold up there."

Ray broke stride and looked up at the sky. "Fuck me, man. Just fuck me already!" he mumbled.

"Dr. Silver," McCain called out again, in between gasps for air as he did his best to catch Ray.

"Slow down, Mr. McCain. You wouldn't want to have a heart attack, now would you?"

"Well, doctor," he said as he finally caught up to him—all out of breath. He took a little time before he could continue. He was roughly the same age as Ray, but extremely overweight and a smoker. "Well," he said after about thirty seconds of heavy breathing, "if you weren't trying to…sneak away…I wouldn't have had to come…running after you."

"I wasn't sneaking away. It's after five, my shift is over, and I had nobody waiting for care."

"Well, why did you run…out of the side door then?"

"Mr. McCain, are you tracking my movements when I'm on my own time? Is that why you chased me down?"

"I just think that it's unusual for someone…to sneak out of a side door. Unless of course…they didn't want to be seen."

"Like I said, I was not sneaking. That side door is closer to the parking lot, and I'm late for a personal appointment. Now, if there's nothing else, I really have to get going."

"Actually Dr. Silver, there is something else. You haven't turned in your last two weekly reports."

"You're kidding me, right?" He knew his reports were delinquent, but still looked at McCain in disbelief. "You chased me down because I'm late on my weekly report?"

"Reports. Not report. Reports. As in more than one. And you haven't turned them in."

"You chased me down in your condition to tell me I'm late with my reports. Ya know you're probably gonna have a heart attack, getting all worked up over something like this. Why didn't you just call down to me during the day?"

"Never mind about that," He said angrily. "I'd appreciate it if you went back to your office now, completed those reports, and got them to me."

"You'll forgive me sir, but no. Not tonight. I've got a personal matter that I have to attend to and right now I'm off the clock. I'll do them in the morning and you'll have them on your desk before noon."

McCain was visibly angry. Ray couldn't tell if his face was still red from running the one hundred yards from the building to the parking lot or if it was because he was so mad at Ray that his blood pressure was through the roof. After having been suspended by McCain for taking time off to attend Jimmy's graduation, Ray hoped his face was red because his blood pressure was sky high. "You're off the clock now, are you? Ok then. I want them on my desk tomorrow, before noon!" McCain demanded. Turning on his heel to march back to his office, he shouted out, "And this *is* going into your personnel file!" Ray was beginning to think that he had made a mistake, coming to work at the VMC.

* * *

Kelsey's was packed for a Wednesday night. All of the big flat screens had the Yankees-Red Sox game on, and it seemed as though every transplant from the Northeast was at this local sports bar watching the contest. When Ray walked in, he immediately looked to the left side of the bar where he and Leigh Anne always sat. There was a wall of people in every direction.

Kelsey and two other bartenders were working full speed, pouring Boilermakers and other drinks as if Prohibition had just been repealed. Slowly making his way through the crowd, he began to spot what looked like the back of Leigh Anne's head. When he saw the bottle of Pipeline Porter in the woman's hand, he pushed his way through with more intent. He squeezed and sidled through the sea of bodies. When he got closer to the bar, he caught Kelsey's eye. She motioned to him with the raise of her eyebrows and a nod that it was indeed Leigh Anne sitting at her usual spot and that he should go on over. He nodded back. Just as he got behind her he held up his index finger and called out to Kelsey, "Pipeline?"

Leigh turned around, greeting him with a half smile. "Hey."

"Hey back. You get in on Sunday?"

"Yeah, around noon."

"I wish you would have let me pick you up at the airport."

"I didn't wanna bother you. Besides, Kelsey wanted to do it. Girl talk, ya know?"

"Yeah, I know. But I didn't hear from you…I was worried."

"Sorry. The minute I got off the plane I had a bunch of frantic messages from the aquarium and I had to get over there right away. One of the big re-circulating pumps failed after a generator blew. It was a mess. I was there for three days straight. Didn't even get to unpack until this morning."

"I left a couple of messages on your cell and one at your place."

"Yeah, I'm sorry. Really, I am. My cell died, and I didn't realize it until a few hours ago. Look behind the bar by the cash register. See it over there? Kelsey's letting me recharge it."

"Yeah, ok. But I was still worried…about you. That's all. But you're ok, and that's good. You do look a bit tired."

"Yeah, I'm good and…definitely tired. Could use another vacation," Leigh Anne said as she turned back to the bar and raised her empty bottle to get Kelsey's attention.

Ray picked up his beer and without taking a drink, placed the bottle back down. For the first time since he and Leigh Anne had met he thought her tone was somewhat dismissive, and as such, was feeling slightly annoyed with her. He was already in a pissed-off mood because of Peter McCain, but in the few months they had been together, he had never had this kind of vibe from her before. It could have been as she said, that she was exhausted. Maybe she just wasn't in the mood to see him. Or perhaps she had become comfortable enough with him and their relationship that she felt safe enough to be herself when she was feeling like crap. He didn't consider that his fear of losing her was making him a bit too sensitive—to the point that he was being a little insensitive.

"It's been a long couple of weeks, Leigh. I've been anxious to see you, hoping you wanted to tell me about your trip and the interview. But if you're too tired and need time to unwind, I'll understand." He waited for a reply and when there wasn't one, he looked over at Kelsey. She shrugged her shoulders. "Ok look it, I've had a long day and I'm beat. So I'm gonna head home. Call me when you're feelin better," he said to Leigh Anne as he dug into his pants pocket and pulled out a twenty-dollar bill. He tossed it onto the bar for their beers and turned to leave.

"Yeah Ray, look. I am tired, ok, I'm exhausted." Ray turned back to face her as she continued. "I'm sorry, I've got a lot on my mind, and I just want to…"

"Ok then, not a problem. It's your call. Tell me what you wanna do. But unless I'm reading things wrong, I'm sure some of this has to do with me. You wanna talk about it? I'll listen. You don't wanna talk…"

"No, I don't wanna talk about it. Not just now… and not if you're gonna act like this."

"Ok then. That's fine. I'll let you have your space. Just come talk to me when you sort it all out. And if you need help sorting it all out, I hope you'll…well, you know where to find me." Again he turned to leave, but the wall of people was nearly impossible to squeeze through.

She sat there looking across the bar and caught Kelsey's angry look as she mouthed, "Don't do this to him."

"It's a two-way street," Leigh Anne mouthed back.

"Ya could have called him when ya got back!" Kelsey said as she came closer to Leigh Anne.

She glanced away from her mothering friend and lifted the longneck to her lips—putting it back down before she drank.

"Hey Silver, wait up a sec." Leigh Anne spun around on her stool and stood up. "I'm super hungry. How about you? Didja eat yet?"

There were so many people vying for real estate that she was pushed into him as somebody went for her now empty stool. Her arms automatically wrapped around Ray's body in an effort to keep herself from falling. He pulled her in tight as he helped her to right herself. "Yeah, I'm starved. Let's go someplace a little more quiet, ok?"

"Sure, sounds good."

2 7

The view from Kerry Park in Queen Anne had always been one of Leigh Anne's favorites. When she was in graduate school, she often went there to meditate, study for a test, or whenever she just wanted to be alone with her poetry. Ray and Leigh Anne both sat on the stone wall as they finished their sandwiches and looked out at the city below. She had finally decided to tell him about the relationship she had when she was in college. She told him all about her daughter and how her trips back to Molokai every year coincided with the anniversary of Mahina's death. She told him how she had originally come to Seattle to get away from Oahu and the mistakes she had made—how moving back would finally help her deal with the guilt that she had carried all these years.

Ray didn't say much in response. In fact, he now felt ashamed for having been annoyed at her. "So, my coming along when I did is more than a coincidence?"

"Yes, very much so. You came along at the same time that I was finally ready to allow someone back into my life. Don't you see the connection?"

"Divine intervention?"

"Something like that. It's the way the universe works."

"So now the universe is directing you to go home?"

"No, not the universe. Me. I'm the one that needs to do this…to finally put it all to rest. As I take my action steps, the energy that I put out to the universe will influence the energy that comes back to me. In essence, giving me what I'm asking for."

Ray repositioned himself on the wall so that he was sitting behind her, and pulled her close so that she was leaning back into him. She reclined with ease, wondering why it was Ray who had come along when he did.

"Are there any other loose threads hangin' out there?"

"You mean like unfinished business?"

"Unanswered questions, roads not traveled, stuff like that?" he asked and then thought he heard her mumble that she had a blister. "What's that, you have a blister?"

"No, silly, I said I have a sister…somewhere."

"Whaddya mean you have a sister somewhere?"

Leigh Anne's chest rose with a deep breath, then slowly exhaled.

"I had…have a younger sister. I haven't seen her since I was eight. My dad was a Marine and he was away a lot. When he was home, he and my mom fought all the time. When he left the service it just got worse. So whenever he went to California on business, his trips continued to get longer. Mom later said he had a girlfriend there. Eventually they split up and divorced. Somehow he got custody of my baby sister, Jennifer, and they moved to San Francisco. My mom never wanted to talk about it and by the time I was old enough to start asking questions…I tried to track them down I… couldn't come up with anything."

"What's the age difference between the two of you?"

"About six years."

"And your mom hasn't been able to give you any information?"

"Now that's another loose thread, I guess."

"You guys don't talk?"

"It's been a few years. After my dad left, she became withdrawn and somewhat bitter. Let's just say we had… have our issues."

"Then, maybe I shouldn't go there."

"No, that's ok. I heard from Kimo that she's been asking about me. I think I'd like to deal with that issue as well, but one thing at a time."

"Maybe when you do, perhaps you just might get some more information about your sister and then, who knows. Maybe you'll be able to track her down."

"That's not a bad idea, Ray."

"Ya know, it's amazing how on some nights Mount Rainier looks so much bigger. I can never get over how when the sun sets it makes all the snow up there look so pink." Ray slowly and methodically massaged the knotted muscles in her shoulders.

"If you watch it long enough," she said as she tilted her head back and looked up at him, "you'll notice that as the sky gets darker, the pink slowly becomes a deep purple."

"I don't know if you want to hear this just now, but…"

"Then maybe you shouldn't say it," she quickly said fearing something bad.

"No, I want to. I've got to. It's been on my mind for quite awhile, so maybe it's time I did. You need to know what I'm feelin'. When you were away, I thought about you. I thought about you a lot. Damn, Leigh, I thought about you every day. I thought about you leaving, and how I'd feel about it. Quite honestly, I know it's not gonna feel good."

"I thought a lot about you as well these past two weeks, and this is really difficult for me. Ray, I really want…to go home, and at the same time, I wanna stay here with you. I just can't explain it, but I feel like I have a million things going through my mind and it's driving me nuts." On one hand, even though she could sense he felt the same way for her as she did for him, she had wanted him to say he loved her. On the other hand, if he had, it would make things that much more difficult. She would have welcomed the difficulty.

He hugged her a little tighter and she leaned her head back into his chest. He lightly pressed his lips to the top of her head. Her hair smelled like Kelsey's bar and grill. It made him smile.

"You interviewed for a job at the university. How'd that go?"

"I think it went well. But I was also one of several candidates."

"When do you think you'll hear anything?'

"Well, if I'm a serious contender, I'll get called for a second interview. Most probably in the fall. They're looking to fill that position for the spring semester."

"That's pretty quick."

"Exactly. If they want me, I'm gonna go. I know we've had this conversation before. But now, even if they don't want me, I'm sure I'm gonna go back. Maybe not as soon as I would if I got that job, but I know it's the right thing for me to do. The struggle that I'm having has to do with you."

"Well, maybe the universe has brought us together as part of the process that you're going through. Maybe I'm in your life just to help you get to the point where you can finally forgive yourself." Ray sat without moving and looked out at the city and across Elliot Bay. A pill-shaped elevator slowly climbed to the top of the Space Needle as another ferry headed out of the Coleman dock on its way to Bainbridge Island. "And if that's the case, then you should go," he finally said.

"What?" She sat up and looked at him.

"What, you want me to ask you to stay? Sure, I want you to stay. You must know that by now, right? But then, if you don't go back, I'll always be the guy who kept you from going home. And I'll be the guy who kept you from finding what you're lookin' for. I'll be the one who kept you from finding your redemption. And when the pain of not being there gets real bad, you're gonna get angry, and you're gonna get angry at me. No, you should definitely go. If it's in your heart, if it's what keeps you up late at night, if this is what you deep down truly want…then you should go."

"And what about you, Raymond Silver? What keeps you up late at night? And what about us? This is what's driving me nuts."

"Well, thinking about you when you're away. That keeps me up late at night. But in a good way," he said, to her approval. "Having you naked in bed next to me. That definitely keeps me up at night." They laughed as she playfully hit his shoulder. "We've got this thing in my family going back to my grandfather. It's this Navy thing. I'm probably making more out of it then I should, at least that's what my father tells me. But then again, out of seven of us Silvers, I'm the only one who's never served. I don't know, maybe I'm nuts, but I guess what's been keeping me up late at night, figuratively speaking, is trying to find a way to do my part. I thought that by working at the VMC I could satisfy that desire. Don't get me wrong, I like being able to help those guys. But deep down, that void is still there. But more importantly, Leigh Anne McMillen" he continued as he took her hands in his. "About us? If you do go, as long as you're interested in me, and as long as you continue to wanna be with me, I'll come out every chance I get. And then we'll see where that takes us. That's fair, isn't it?" He looked at Leigh Anne and now she was the one gazing out at the view.

A part of Ray would have loved to have been able to just walk away from everything and move to the islands with her. He had dreamt of living there almost his whole life. He wanted to believe that it was his practical side telling him he couldn't just sell the house and walk away from his job. "And what if I did?" he wondered to himself. "What are the chances that Leigh would eventually grow tired of me or what if she got to the point where she wanted to have a family? What would I do then?"

Leigh Anne, on the other hand, wasn't sure if she wanted Ray to walk away from his job and his house. She wondered if she hadn't just blurted out the question because he really had been her security blanket, and after having found that security, perhaps she was afraid to lose it.

"After all," she thought, "didn't I admit to Kelsey that I appreciated his maturity, his sense of stability, and that he makes me feel safe and secure? Oh God, what would he say if he knew I'd like to have another child?"

"Yes? No? Isn't that a reasonable approach?" Asked Ray as she became lost in the 'what if's.'

"Yes…I suppose it is."

"Hey, I'm the one that's taking the big risk here."

"Oh, and how do you figure that?"

"With all the young sun-tanned studs roaming the campus at UH? Tell me you won't be tempted?"

"What? A girl can't have a little fun?" She watched Ray furrow his brow. "Geez, guys really are insecure. I'm only havin fun wit' ya, brah." She laughed and then turned around to lean back against him. "It's a reasonable plan, Ray. And I can come here whenever I get time off. To be with you, that is."

Ray noticed that she had long finished her food. With one hand holding on to Leigh Anne, he leaned over to gather up all the trash and placed it back in the bag that had come from the deli. "I owe you an apology, Leigh. I was a little annoyed at you earlier because I thought your attitude was shitty. I was annoyed at you because, as it turns out, I was the one being selfish by only thinking about how I was feeling when I couldn't get in touch with you. I hadn't thought about what was going through your mind or why. I was worried about you though. I'm sorry." Again she sat up and turned to study his face. She smiled at him as he brushed the loose strands of hair away from her eyes. "You look exhausted, Leigh."

"I am."

" Come, I'll drive you home"

"No...let's go back to your place."

2 8

Ray stood in the conning station atop the pilot house of the 776 soaking up the afternoon sunshine. With float planes passing low above the ship and landing on Lake Union, he visualized a time when Japanese fighter planes made strafing runs on these small ships. "It must have been hell," he thought. Under-armed and lightly armored, they were easy targets as they off-loaded their cargo of Marines onto Pacific Island beaches.

It was hot. Hotter than it usually was for August in Seattle—but welcomed by all after a long, cold, rainy winter and spring. Although the others sat below in the crew's mess eating lunch, Ray had wanted to get some sunshine and fresh air after spending his entire Saturday morning breathing in diesel and cigarette fumes in the engine room with Chuck Shimkin.

With eight GM diesels lined up in two parallel banks of four, the two of them had been working hard installing a turbocharger to each engine. "Having these turbo units will give us more power and better fuel efficiency," Chuck had explained as he wiped the grease from his hands. "With these little puppies forcing air into each engine, we should be able to cruise at a sustained seventeen to eighteen knots and use the same amount of fuel as if we were cruising at only twelve." He walked over to his cooler and removed a half-empty liter bottle of

Pepsi from the ice. "And, if you do the math, we'd save six, seven days sailing in each direction. Assuming of course that Walters is taking her all the way to Luzon. Not bad, huh pallie?" He offered the bottle to Ray, who politely refused.

"Nah, that's ok. Thanks anyway."

"What? You afraid of my joims?" He laughed and sucked down the rest of the cola in a few big gulps. "Ahhhh. Good stuff!"

Work on the 776 had taken on a more urgent pace once Walters, Peters, and Jeffries had called a meeting a few weeks back and announced to Ray and the others that they had decided to try to purchase the LCI that had been found in the Philippines. The plan, as told by Walters, didn't sound as if it was a sure thing. Plus, it sounded risky since they now wanted to take the 776 to the South Pacific without the benefit of a preliminary ocean voyage to check everything out. It explained why work on the ship over the past few weeks had shifted from restoration to modification. LCI veteran Gordie Smithfield along with Ray, Steve Scott, and Tex Warren had each voiced concerns about the sudden redirection of the project. They were assured that the modifications—although necessary for the voyage—were temporary.

"Seriously," said Walters, "the owners of that LCI definitely wanna sell her, in whole or as parts. Taking the 776 makes sense for several reasons." He had everyone's attention. "First, if we just flew over there and bought her outright, we'd have to sail her back. So the question then becomes, what if she has mechanical problems while we're in the middle of the ocean? With our ship alongside for the journey home, we could provide equipment for making repairs or even tow her if necessary. Second, once we're there and if we decide she can't make the journey, we can still strip her of any or all of her parts. And what better vessel to transport all that stuff back home then the 776, right? Third, we've all been talking about getting this ship out into the open ocean to see what she can do. This trip will accomplish that, but, we need to add these temporary modifications in order to safely make that kind of a crossing."

"What about costs?" asked Ray. "Fuel, food, purchase price for the ship?"

Jeffries stood, looked at Peters and then Walters, before addressing Ray's concerns. "Food is not a problem. Once we figure out how many of you guys want to join us, then we can get an idea of how much food we'll need. I'm sure you guys wouldn't mind making a small contribution toward that effort." He looked around as most of the guys nodded in agreement. "With all of the modifications we'll be making, we figure it's a two-week trip back and forth if they meet us at Midway Island. We're still working on that. But if we have to go all the way, then we're looking at four weeks round trip." The group started talking amongst themselves.

"Shit," Tom Gilmartin protested. "At best I can swing two weeks off from work. No way I can do four."

"Hey, guys, settle down," Walters jumped in. "Look, we know that a four-week trip is a big commitment. That's why we're trying to get these guys to meet us halfway. They're considering it. The thing is, if they do come to Midway, we're gonna have to come up with the extra cash for the fuel they use to get there and to pay for their guys to fly home.

The other option is that Jeffries and Peters will have some of their guys...uhm, employees, come along. They're experienced former sailors, so that'll actually be better. We just wanted to give you guys first crack at it since you've been working so hard on helping put this ship back together."

Walters took an initial head count and wrote up who would be coming along. He was first on the list followed by Jeffries and Peters, who—after acquiring more intel—had decided that they needed to personally direct the mission. Chuck Shimkin was in, as he was part-owner of a diesel repair business and would have no problem taking the time off. Tex Warren was off of work due to a slight disability, and Sam Lipton always seemed to be out of a job, although it was rumored that he had been working for Jeffries running errands. Steve Scott was retired, divorced, and looked forward to the adventure. Bowing out were Ray, Abner, Gordie, Tom Gilmartin, and Danny McKay.

All totaled, Walters counted up seven members that would be making the trip. He had wanted to sail with at least fifteen.

"Just as well" Jeffries later said to Walters. "The way things are shaping up, we're gonna need more company men on this gig."

As the meeting broke up, Peters took the list and added in black marker at the top 'Operation LCI Recovery: ETD 06:00 January 1, 2003.' Little did anyone know that although they would be embarking on a recovery operation, Walters, Peters, and Jeffries did not have any intention of purchasing the Filipino LCI.

"What's in the envelope?" Walters asked Jeffries, once they were alone.

"Just a little information Peters dug up on your chiropractor."

"Anything interesting?" Walters asked as he pulled out several sheets of paper.

"You could say that. Take a look at the second page."

Walters quickly read through the material and studied the attached picture. "Are you shittin' me?" He flipped through the other pages.

"Nope."

"Does Rat Pack know?"

"We got word to him as soon as we found out. He'll be glad to hear this guy won't be coming along with us. And he said, that under no circumstances can we let him go. So he better not suddenly change his mind." Jeffries reached over to Walters' breast pocket and took out his pack of smokes. He watched Walters' eyes continue to scan the material as he lit a cigarette, tucking the crinkled soft pack back into his own shirt pocket. "John, this is important. Are we on the same page here?"

Walters looked up at Jeffries and nodded his head.

Ray closed his eyes and leaned his head back to catch the warmth of the afternoon sun. He could smell the smoke from Chuck's cigarette before his foot hit the bottom rung of the ladder that lead from the gun deck up to the conning station.

"Hey, there you are. What are ya, anti-social or somethin'?"

"Nah, just working on my tan and enjoying this rare summer heat. And anyway, I don't see how those guys can sit inside on a day like today. It's roasting down there."

"It's not that bad. They got the forward and aft hatchway doors wide open, so a nice cross flow is cooling it off."

"Well, there's nothing like a little vitamin D and a lot of fresh air," he said, in reference to Chuck's cigarette—a reference that was quickly noted.

"Peters just added two more names to the list down below. So that makes five more in total since they posted the original seven a few weeks ago," Chuck said as he blew a stream of smoke in a direction opposite of Ray.

"They're Jeffries' boys, right?"

"Yeah, I suppose." He extinguished his cigarette. "I sure wish ya could come along. You've been a big help to me these past few weeks. I know ya learned a lot about those engines. It'd be good to have you splittin' shifts with me in the engine room."

"Thanks, but there's no way I could swing time off of the job. I've got two guys there who are looking for more reasons to have me canned. I even got a personal call from Senator Murphy about some of the reports she's been getting on me. She won't even listen to my side. All she's concerned about is how it makes her look. Don't get me wrong, Chuck. I wanna go real bad. If it is the 606, it would be a thrill to sail her home. Besides, now that we got those engines modified, can't everything be done from up here or on the bridge?"

"Still gotta monitor oil and manifold pressure, fuel flow. Keep an eye out for leaks. All that shit. The good thing is that ya don't have to be down there continuously."

"Oh, I didn't know." Ray now pictured his dad working in the engine room of the 606. "The other thing is those two guys, Jeffries and Peters. You know anything about `em?"

"Just what Walters had told us."

"They kinda give me the creeps, the way they seem to be taking over around here," he said carefully—not wanting to say anything about suspicions he couldn't prove.

"Ahh, they're harmless. Just two guys who don't have any-thing better to do with all their money. I wouldn't worry about `em." Ray just nodded in agreement. "Well, don't let it get ya down. With all the stuff you helped me with, even if you're not here with us, you'll still be a big part of this journey. Just look it, by the end of the day we'll have all the engines turbocharged. They can be controlled from up here in the conning station or below on the bridge. Ya did a nice job mounting and runnin' those throttle cables. At least you'll be able to come with us next month when we take her out into the Sound for her first shakedown, right?"

"I got it marked on my calendar. Third week of September. Even though the Sound is not like being out on the open ocean, I'm still looking forward to it."

"Good, we'll have a blast." Chuck said as he began to head down below to get back to work. "Oh, before I forget, I'm hav-ing a little get-together at my house tomorrow afternoon. Got some good folk comin' over. Gonna crank some tunes, and fire up the Weber, and grill us some good eats. I make a mean German-style potato salad. If you're not doin' anything, bring that little cutie of yours over around five, ok?"

"Yeah, sure. Sounds fun."

"Good. Don't take too long up here. Still need your help."

29

Just off the kitchen in the condo that Stella shared with her longtime boyfriend was a small room that she used as her private study. Situated on the twenty-first floor of a downtown luxury building—one among several that had sprung up during the construction boom of the late `90s—she never felt comfortable with the embellished accoutrements of modern architecture. The heavy reliance on glass, marble, granite, and stainless steel left her feeling cold. No matter how much furniture they purchased, the apartment still echoed with every footstep. It was a stark contrast to the coziness and warmth she had felt at Ray's place. Besides her small study, the only other feature that she loved about the two and a half million dollar apartment was the western view of Puget Sound and the Olympic Mountain Range. To the north, the view of upper and lower Queen Anne and the Magnolia neighborhoods were just as pretty. On more than one occasion she found herself gazing through the powerful telescope that Robert had kept on the wrap-around terrace of their corner unit on the slight chance she might find Ray's small house among the ones she had secretly desired. Even when Robert wasn't away on one of his many business trips, she found herself secluded in her small room, keeping up on the politics of Washington, D.C.—A habit she had gotten into when her 'ex' had been with Army

Intelligence and keeping current on all the dirt had been a pre-requisite for cocktail parties.

As summer had slowly drawn to a close, she reached a dead end in her investigation of Bill Harrison. She hadn't been able to find out anything further about a possible connection between him and Visor Pharmaceuticals. Abner had found one excuse after another to get into Harrison's private office, but she had to ask him to back off after he came close to getting caught looking through the stacks of papers covering the doctor's desk.

She stared into her computer monitor trying to think of how to proceed when she heard the door to the apartment open. "Robert?" she called out.

"Yeah, it's me" he said as he placed his attaché on the bench in the foyer and headed straight for the kitchen.

"You're home early." Stella didn't move from her desk. "Wasn't expecting you `til the end of the week. Everything ok?"

"Excuse my French," he said, grabbing a tumbler from one of the cabinets above the granite countertop, "but the fuckin' State Department is making it harder for me to conduct business overseas." He scooped a handful of ice out of the freezer, dumped it into his glass, and poured two fingers of Black Label.

"Wanna talk about it?"

"Nah, too pissed off." He took a slow sip, then walked over to Stella's private study and asked to come in. One thing about Robert that she had always liked, in spite of how distant he had become over the past few years, was that he was a gentlemen and respected her space. He leaned against the door frame, undid the top two buttons of his monogrammed shirt, and smiled. "I had this meeting in Bahrain set up for months. The State Department knew all about it. I gave them full disclosure. I can't believe they wait until I get there to tell me that they had intelligence reports from the CIA, the NSA, I don't remember which agency that stuffed-shirt, career diplomat said. Anyway, he said they got information that one of the Arab guys I was dealing with was an Al Qaeda operative, and if I tried to go ahead with the transaction they were going to arrest me under some homeland security thing. Total bullshit! Anyway, I'm starved. Care to join me?"

"Sorry, I've eaten already." Stella lied—not wanting to listen to his endless comparisons of Seattle cuisine to the bistros along the Champs-Elysees.

"It was a long flight. I'm going to get cleaned up and then go grab something at the Harbor club." Robert walked off to the bedroom to shower—never once asking how she was. It didn't matter to her as she heard what she needed to hear.

"The NSA, of course!" In a file cabinet to the side of her desk Stella kept an old day-planner she hadn't used since transferring almost all of her handwritten information to digital format. She went right to the Ks in the contacts section and looked up her ex-husband, Griffin Kelley. Stella placed the leather-bound scheduler on her desk and walked into the kitchen. Looking around, she saw the bottle of Black Label and decided she could use a drink.

She hadn't thought about Griffin in quite some time. Not since he was promoted to Brigadier General and moved over to the National Security Agency from Army Intelligence. She had read about it in the D.C. *Tribune.* She let the scotch chill for a couple of minutes, waiting to hear Robert turn on the shower. Once he did, she took a drink. It felt cool and velvety going down, and then the warmth slowly made its way from her stomach up to the back of her throat. It felt good. She looked up at the clock and added three hours for East Coast time. "Ten p.m. in D.C.," she said, walking back into her study to call her ex-husband. "I doubt if he's even home by now."

"General Kelley." He said picking up the phone after one ring. The quickness and sharpness of his answer didn't catch her off-guard as much as the fact that he was actually home. When she heard his voice, it reminded her of the stern scolding he had given her after she had caught a young doctor stealing narcotics at Walter Reed. She had hoped to get the answering machine. "Hello? This is Griff Kelley."

"Griffin?" Her voice was unmistakable. Even after all the years that had gone by since the last time they spoke.

"Stella!"

"Yeah, Griff, It's me. Is this a bad time? Sounds like you're expecting a call."

"I'm always expecting a call. But no, this is fine."

"Are you sure? I can call back in the morning."

"The calls come at all hours these days, but now that I'm with NSA, I have two secured lines into the house as well as a dedicated cell phone for *those* calls."

"Sounds like you have very little free time."

"No, I really don't. At least not since 9/11. It's been a long time. How are you?"

"Can't complain, and you?"

"Made Brigadier a few years ago."

"I know. I read about it in the Trib."

"You've been keeping tabs on me?"

"Well, I never did get out of the habit of keeping up on things inside the Beltway."

"It does get in your blood. Just like certain people. I suppose you're calling about your boyfriend?"

"My boyfriend? Whaddya mean?"

"Robert Long. He's your boyfriend, right?"

"Yes, but how do you know that?"

"NSA, Stella. You'd be surprised what we know."

"No, I guess I wouldn't. Even though that's not why I called, Griff, is there something that I should know about?"

"Well, to be honest, I was getting ready to call you. Not tonight, but soon enough."

"Sounds serious."

"You're not under any kind of active investigation, if that's what you're worried about."

"Well, I wasn't, but hearing the word 'active' causes me concern. Should I be?"

"You do know what he does for a living, don't you?"

"He does a lot of venture stuff. Start-ups and stuff like that. Here in the U.S. and in Europe, the Mideast."

"Yes, that's true, but what else does he share with you? About his activities?"

"What I just told you is all I know. Honest."

"He also buys and sells just about anything. And apparently to anyone. We actually began looking into him a number of months ago when one of our targets, um...I mean, a suspected Al Qaeda operative contacted him to purchase a shipload of fertilizer."

"Fertilizer?"

"Ammonium nitrate. Terrorists use it to make bombs."

"Are you saying that Robert was going to sell bomb-making material to a terror suspect?" Stella looked to make sure she was still alone.

"Yes, but we weren't sure if he was knowingly doing it or if he was under the impression that he was just selling fertilizer for crops. Given the other questionable transactions he's been involved in, there's serious doubt he's that naïve. Unfortunately, the geniuses at State squashed his most recent deal and got in the way of a joint investigation. Your boyfriend is a real piece of work though."

"Meaning what, exactly?"

"After State told him his buyer was an Al Qaeda suspect, he didn't care that he could have sold a ton of bomb-making material to our enemies. He was totally pissed about the lost sale. Unless it was all an act, to come off looking clueless. Personally I find it hard to believe he didn't make the connection. Since the Oklahoma City thing in `95, this stuff has been a red-flag item on the watchdog list of every intelligence and law enforcement agency throughout the country."

"I'm sorry. I had no way of knowing. Like I said, he really doesn't tell me much."

"Just the same, we've got eyes on him. You're gonna wanna be careful, ok?

"Like how careful?"

"Let's put it this way, and keep in mind that I could get in trouble for this. I don't know how deep you're invested into this guy, emotionally speaking, that is. But you may want to think about getting away from him."

If it were anyone but Griff telling her this, she would have thought it was some sort of bad joke. Her mind began to think of the options she had.

"Stel? Are you still there?"

"Yeah, Griff. Still here."

"Look, if I call to tell you to get out of there, like pack up and leave get out of there, are you able to do it?"

"Yes, I can, but I'll need some time to get all the pieces into place."

"Good. Now you don't need to run out of there tonight. But please start putting things in order. Keep in mind that it's not just NSA on this. It's also the FBI and Homeland Security. So there's still a good deal of territorial issues that's slowing things down for us."

"Griff, why are you telling me this, why are you taking a risk like this?"

"Because I know you, I know the kind of person you are. Like I said, you're not under any active investigation, but because of his activities these agencies do have a profile on you. Not my doing, but I was questioned about our relationship...and that actually got me thinking about how I screwed things up for us." It was quiet for a moment. "Hey, while I got you on the phone, something else came across my desk a few weeks ago and it made me think of you."

"I'm afraid to ask."

"I know the VMC is a big place and you have a large staff, but does the name Raymond Silver sound familiar to you?"

"Hold on a sec." Stella once again looked out of the door from her study to make sure that Robert was still in the shower. She heard the water running, but decided to step out onto the terrace anyway. "Yes, I know him. He's a chiropractor and he works out of the same department as me. What's this about?"

"I really can't say too much on this one. I just know that his name came across my desk, and it had something to do with the fact that his brother was with a SEAL team unit and then worked with the CIA some years back."

"What? No way. Listen, Ray told me his brother was killed on a training mission in the Philippines. 1980? Or `81, I think he said."

"Yes, that's what he and his family believe because that's what they were told. Look, I've said too much. I was just wondering if you knew who this guy was."

"Griff, he's a straight-up guy. Honest. His family has a long military history. All Navy, going back to his grandfather and even now with both of his kids."

"Yeah, Stella, we already know. We have no problem with him. I was just asking if you knew him. Do me a favor, it's important that you don't tell him anything. In fact, I'm also gonna ask you to keep quiet on your boyfriend. Are we together on this?"

"Yeah, sure thing, Griff."

So, what makes you call after all this time? You miss me?"

"Yes...sometimes."

"Same here."

"Griff? This is really hard for me, but I have a favor to ask. I know this is not NSA territory, but I was hoping that with all the different agencies you deal with, if you had any connections, perhaps maybe you can help me get some information on one of our docs at the VMC."

"Stella, I think this is where we left off."

"Yes, it is, isn't it? But this is different this time. My actions now are not going to impact you in any way."

"Stella, you do know that the guy you wanted to barbecue back at Reed was related to a High-ranking Congressman, right?" It was quiet for a few seconds. She had never known why people had gone running from her as though she were contagious. It all made sense to her now.

"I had no idea. Nobody told me. Why didn't you say anything to me?"

"I should've. We had our issues back then. Mostly...well, all my doing, and I didn't treat you or handle our relationship the right way. Like I said, I'm the one that screwed it up."

"Why, Griffin Kelley! Is that an apology?"

"Yeah. I guess it is. So what's going on, another drug thief?"

"Griff, this is more serious. I think this guy's on Visor's payroll to perform medical experiments on veterans without their knowledge. Many of them are dying, Griff."

There was a long silence on the phone, and then she heard telephones ringing in the background. "Stella, I'm sorry, but that's work calling me. Give me his name and I'll see what I can find out for you."

"Dr. William Harrison. And Griff, thank you. Really, I mean it."

"If I'm ever out your way maybe we can have dinner."

"You know where to find me."

3 0

Seduction
by
Leigh Anne McMillen

Sunset
silhouette invites
wisteria teases
intoxication

A slow caress
shallow breaths
her camisole ignites
his desire

Lips to ear
a whisper
quickened pulse betrays
his anticipation

Velvet thigh
a lustful eye weakens
hesitation
abandoned

Sunset
silhouette incites
invitation
accepted.

Ray looked up at Leigh after reading the poem she had written for him. "This is nice." She smiled as he gently folded the page.

"Really, do you like it?" She reached out and touched his hand. He nodded and smiled back.

"Ya know, this is the first of your poems that you've let me read."

"It's new. I wrote it while thinking of you. That's why I wanted you to have it."

"It's beautiful. Really. Thank you. Maybe when you get back you'll let me see some more of your work."

"Maybe. We'll see. It's not that I don't want you to see them. It's just that most of them are personal. It's how I... well, let's just say that writing is my way to express what's in my heart. It's my outlet." She looked over her shoulder to survey the line of passengers waiting to go through the security checkpoint and then looked at the time on her cell phone. "I better get going. My flight starts boarding in about fifteen minutes."

"Are you nervous?"

"Ya know, I was during the first interview, and maybe after the phone call asking me to come back out for this second one. But not now."

"Good. Then it's a lock. I'll bet any amount it's yours for the asking."

"I hope you're right. But either way...right?"

"Right," he said, knowing what she meant. He quickly scanned the growing line then returned his focus to Leigh Anne. "Ok then, I've got your return flight info and I'll see you in a few days." Ray leaned forward and they kissed. He waited for her to turn and head for the end of the security line, but she didn't move. He saw the slight trepidation in her face and gave her another hug. "You'll do great. Honest."

She squeezed him tight, brought her lips up to his ear, and whispered. "I love you, Raymond Silver." Then, to the looks of passersby, she gave him a long, deep kiss reminiscent of that night in Kelsey's.

"I love you too, Leigh. I really do." His heart rate doubled at the sound of those words. Not because he knew them to be true, but because it surprised him to hear them out loud. Leigh Anne was off to Hawaii for her second interview at the university, and although this would be a short trip, he knew that the next one would not be far off. That was the one he was going to have a hard time with.

Ray waited and watched as the line slowly inched forward until Leigh Anne was at the first checkpoint having her identification and boarding pass scrutinized by a Homeland Security Agent. It was very Nazi-esque, in a Monty Python sort of way. To him, the whole "Homeland" phraseology was akin to "The Fatherland". That, coupled with the mass deployment of hastily-trained uniformed "agents" who now freely intimidated little children and eighty-year-old grandmothers—while unchecked tarmac workers loaded unscreened parcels into the cargo holds of every passenger jet—was the epitome of government knee-jerk reaction, careless implementation and non-existent oversight. "It's amazing that, in spite of the government's best efforts to discourage patriotism, people still love their country" he said to himself.

Before Leigh Anne moved forward to the next station, where she would no longer be in view, she turned one last time to see Ray looking down at the poem she had given him. When he finished reading, he once again carefully folded the page and placed it in his pocket. He glanced up and she was gone.

* * *

Driving back from the airport, he didn't want to go directly home. It was close to the dinner hour and he knew he wouldn't feel like cooking for himself. He decided to head for Kelsey's for a bowl of his favorite chili and cornbread. And perhaps he and Kelsey could commiserate over a few ice-cold Pipelines. As he drove up the freeway, his cell began to buzz.

"Jimmy, how are ya kiddo?"

"Great, Dad. Is this an ok time?"

"Yeah, everything ok?"

"Couldn't be better. Got some great news, Dad...I found him. I mean, I found it. The log book to the 606, I found it!"

"You're kidding, where? how?"

"Dad, after you asked me, I went to my C.O. and told him what you told me. He got me in touch with an agent at our investigative unit. It wasn't easy because Robert Lee Johnson died a few years ago, but he had...I mean, has a daughter. She lives not too far from here. Over in Fairfax."

"Hold on a minute," Ray said excitedly. He put the phone down, quickly swerved from the center lane over to the right shoulder of the freeway, and came to a stop. "Were you able to contact her? Did you speak to her? What did she tell you?" He blurted out in rapid succession.

"Dad, calm down. One question at a time, ok? Yes, I called her. I introduced myself and explained why I was calling. She was very kind, and said that she had the log book as well as other personal notes that her father had written. She invited me out to her house to take a look."

"So when are you going?"

"I was there just two days ago. Dad, it was all there. Everything that happened. He even made revisions in later years to reflect his treatment of Grandpa as well as Abner Lewis. The daughter also added that over the years as her father got older, he changed a great deal. He became very repentant for his attitudes and his actions."

"God, I wish I could have been there. Is there any way I can get a look at the log book?"

"Probably not for awhile. My C.O. said we had to turn it in for further investigation. There's a good chance that Grandpa could still get proper recognition for his actions at Peleliu. You wanna tell him?"

Ray not only thought about what had been recorded in the 606 log book about his dad, but what might have been said about Abner's actions that day. "No, Jimmy, not just yet.

Perhaps next month. I'm hoping he'll be well enough to come out here for Thanksgiving. You're still coming out, right?"

"Yeah, Dad. Still planning on it."

"Keep me up to date on where the Navy is going with this, ok?"

"Yeah, sure thing."

"Hey kiddo, you did a great job with this. I'm really appreciative."

"Grandpa's a hero. He deserves to be recognized. Talk to ya soon."

31

Ray almost lost his footing as he raced up the dew-covered ramp of the 776. Puget Sound mornings in October were deceiving. Since the rains were another month away and days were still filled with sunshine and warm autumn temperatures, It was easy to forget that in the early morning the surface areas around the waterfront would be quite moist before the sun had a chance to dry everything off.

There was an energy onboard that morning. All the volunteers who had worked so hard restoring and modifying the 776 were ready to take her out onto the Sound for her first voyage. Abner had arrived a few hours before anyone else and cooked up a load of his special griddle cakes and brewed several pots of coffee. His little CD player was turned up loud as he kept time to Glenn Miller's *"American Patrol."* People moved up and down the passageway, smiling at each other as if they were actually getting ready to head out on a real patrol. Ray had not seen or felt this kind of energy aboard the 776 before and it didn't take him long to feel the same excitement.

He was hungry after his walk at five that morning. Having put on a couple of pounds as a result of a gradual return to his old nervous grazing habit, he had purchased a pair of five-pound ankle weights and increased his standard three-mile morning walk to four. After a quick shower, change of clothes, and a brief detour to the local market, he headed for the ship—making the galley his first stop once he was onboard.

Abner smiled when Ray came up behind him, reached over his shoulder, and tickled his ear as he retrieved his coffee mug from the shelf above the sink. He placed two cartons of eggs on the counter. "Fresh pot, Doc. Jes made. An' grab yoself somma mah griddle cakes. Ah bet ah make 'em betta than ya daddy."

"Thank you, sir. Don't mind if I do." Ray said as he also grabbed a plate and a fork. "Would it be ok if I made myself a fried egg to go with that?"

"Ah don't spose ya want that sunnah side up?" Abner said as he drizzled a little oil onto the griddle.

"Yes sir, I do."

"Ah don't spose ya gonna slide that egg 'tween two a mah griddle cakes an' then squish it down so the yolk come oozin' out all ovah, are ya?"

"Yes, I am."

Abner began to laugh and shake his head. "Man o' man, the apple don't fall far from the tree! Jes like ya daddy used ta do."

"Still does." Ray smiled as he poured a cup of coffee and watched Abner cook the egg for him. When it was cooked so that it was still a little runny on top, he slid a spatula under it and gently laid it on top of a griddle cake. Then topped it with another one and handed the plate to Ray.

"Man o' man," Abner repeated, "the apple don't fall far from the tree." Ray made his way over to the tables in the crew's mess and found himself watching the goings-on while eating his breakfast. The griddle cakes definitely reminded him of his dad's.

Chuck Shimkin came by and stood at the head of the table. Flipping up a cigarette from his pack of Tareytons, he looked at Ray with a grin from ear to ear. "Hey pallie, you ready to help me get those puppies barkin'?"

"Can't wait. I'm anxious to see what they can do."

"I'll go get everything ready. Finish your breakfast, then go topside and see Walters. Then come join me." Chuck flipped open his zippo and lit his cigarette. He took a big first drag and exhaled. Laughing as he walked aft Ray heard him call out, "This is gonna be a real trip, man."

"Sure thing, Chuck." Ray said. He took a sip of coffee and closed his eyes. The sounds of rushing footsteps along the steel deck plating, the faint smell of coffee mixed with a tinge of diesel fuel coming down the main passageway, and Cab Calloway's *"Jumpin Jive"* filtering out of the galley made him wish his dad could be there to share the experience. After he finished breakfast, he walked back into the small kitchen. "Got any Bassie on that box?" he said to Abner as he placed his plate and cup into the sink.

"Ya know ah do. Ah not only got the Count, ah got the Duke' an a little Dizzie too. Got any requess?"

"Nah, I'll let you spin `em the way you want." Ray leaned back against the small countertop opposite the sink. "I heard you almost got caught going through Harrison's desk."

"Ya did, didja?"

"Heard it was pretty close."

"Well, *close* only counts in horse shoes." Abner said, wiping his hands on a dish cloth. "An' besides, ah wasn't goin' through his desk. Ah was jes lookin' at the stuff on top a his desk."

"I know you're helping Stella, but just the same, I really wish you'd be more careful."

"Ah'm careful. An' if ah get caught, what they gonna do, fire me?"

"I don't know, let's see." Ray looked at Abner. "Breaking and entering, unauthorized access to government correspondence, stealing private medical records, and that's just for starters."

"Breakin' an' ennerin' mah ass! Do' was unlocked an' a man mah age ain't worried `bout that stuff. Ah wanna help nail that bastard an' ah don't mind the risk."

"I just want you to be careful is all. I don't want to see anything bad happen to you."

"Ah'm a big boy, an' ah know what ah'm doin'. Ah `preciate ya concern. Ah do."

"Ok. I'll leave it at that, then. I also wanted to ask you if you had any plans for Thanksgiving, because if you don't, I'm gonna have a bunch of people over my house."

"Thas very nice a ya, Doc, but ah don't like bein' wit' a bunch a strangers on the holadays."

"They won't be strangers, just people I consider family. Both my kids will be there, Leigh Anne and Stella too."

Abner's eyes widened. "It'd be nice ta meetcha kids. What aboutcha daddy?"

"I wanted him to come. It would've been great for you and him to get together after all these years. I had also promised to bring him back out to see the 776. He'd have loved it, but with his health being what it is, he's just not up to doing that kind of traveling anymore."

"Thas too bad. Ah'da loved ta see him again," Abner said as he turned away and then continued without turning back "Thanksgivin' atcha house would be real nice, Doc. But one condition."

"Sure, name it."

"Ah do the bird an' the stuffin'." He turned back and smiled. "Aaannd, ah get ta sit next ta Nurse Stella."

"Are you sure it's not Nurse Stella you wanna be stuffin'?" Ray said as Abner let out a howl.

"Does ya daddy know ya think that way?"

"Never you mind. You can do the bird and sit next to Stella." They shook on it.

Ray headed up the ladder to the bridge looking for Walters. Steve Scott was setting up one of two GPS units, the other being up in the conning station. "Walters?" Ray asked him.

"Up above." Scott replied without looking up from his work. Ray continued out of the bulkhead hatch to the gun deck and up the ladder to the conning station.

Walters turned to acknowledge his presence. He lifted the brass cover plate over the voice tube and called down to the engine room, "How's it all looking down there, Mr. Shimkin?"

The tin-can sounding reply came back, "All good down here."

"Then go ahead and fire `em up."

Walters could have easily controlled all operations from the newly installed helm controls, but preferred to involve his volunteer crew as a way to provide them with the needed experience—as well as to establish his authority as the ship's ocean-going commander. As the engines roared to life and a cloud of black and then white smoke came out of the exhaust pipes at the ship's stern, a steady vibration could be felt throughout the ship. Ray felt butterflies building inside of his stomach as Walters looked at him.

"I wanted you to see this from this vantage point since you won't be joining us in January." He picked up the heavy bakelite phone receiver from its cradle and pressed the small button to signal the bridge. "Mr. Scott? You all set down there?"

"Ready to go," he replied, standing at the bridge helm controls. Walters leaned over the port side of the conning station, looking forward to the bow and then aft to the stern. Again he picked up the receiver. "Mr. Scott, rudder amidships."

"Rudder amidships." Scott replied.

"Cast off all lines," he yelled out to the men on the dock below. As the lines were released from both fore and aft, they were drawn up by Danny McKay and Tom Gilmartin at the bow and by Sam Lipton and Tex Warren on the stern. "Retract the portside ramp." Walters called out and looked aft to see Gordie taking down the ensign from the stern. Walking back over to the voice tube, he called down to the engine room once again. "Mr. Shimkin, how's our oil and manifold pressures?"

"All good, John."

Walters flipped a switch on a small aluminum box mounted to the quarter-inch-thick steel that made up the perimeter wall of the conning station. "Gentlemen," he said into the small box, his voice echoing through the ship's public address system, "I thought I'd first take us over to Bremerton today. We'll sail past the USS Turner Joy and then head over to the Bremerton Navy Yard so those boys can get a look at a real ship. While there, we'll pay our respects to the decommissioned carriers that are sadly rusting away. Then, we'll head north to Whidbey Island before coming back home. All in all, we're looking at about five hours back and forth, counting wait time at the Ballard Locks. So, without further delay, Mr. Scott...all back slow."

"All back slow, Mr. Walters," came the reply.

The engines engaged in reverse and the 776 easily slid away from her moorings. As she did, she belched more smoke as the loud, deep-throated chugging noise of her eight General Motors diesel engines woke up the residents living along the eastern slope of Queen Anne Hill. Once the bow cleared the end of the dock, Walters again called down to the bridge. "Left fifteen degrees rudder."

"Left fifteen degrees rudder," came the reply as the stern of the 776 swung to the east.

Ray watched as Walters effortlessly issued commands back and forth to the bridge and the engine room. "All stop. Ease the rudder."

"All stop." From the engine room.

"Easing the rudder." From the bridge.

"Rudder amidships." The 776 straightened and continued to slowly move in reverse. Once there was ample room to negotiate a turn to starboard, Walters again called out his commands. "All ahead slow. Right fifteen degrees rudder." The 776 began her turn to starboard, and as the bow came about he called, "Ease the rudder."

"Easing the rudder."

"Rudder amidships, nothing to the left, Mr. Scott."

"Rudder amidships, nothing to the left. Aye, Mr. Walters."

As she began her forward progression through the mirror-like waters of a still-sleeping Lake Union the entire volunteer crew came topside and watched as Gordie hoisted the ensign up the main mast.

3 2

The 776 performed well, effortlessly plying the fairly smooth waters of Puget Sound. Which is more than John Walters could say for most of his crew. Between the hot afternoon sun, fresh salt air, and a few "emergency" drills he had them perform, by the time they got back to their home at the abandoned naval reserve center on Lake Union, his "crew" was exhausted. Gordie Smithfield had laid down on one of the bunks in the commanding officer's cabin and was fast asleep. The swing music from Abner's CD player had long since stopped, and Ray had spent the last half-hour of the short cruise cleaning up most of the galley for him. Since Gordie and Abner weren't making the trip, Walters hadn't been worried about them. But Chuck Shimkin wasn't used to being in a steel-encased room with continuous loud noise, exhaust fumes, and excessive heat from eight diesel engines. He drank so much water during those five hours that the combination of the heat along with frequently climbing the ladder to take breaks or hit the head simply wore him down. Several others who would also be making the trip were tuckered out as well. After successfully tying up at the dock and going through the checklist of shutdown procedures, they each bid an early farewell and headed home to a variety of pain relievers.

Walters, Jeffries, and Peters stayed behind to discuss the latest developments coming out of the Philippines along with Walters' concern that it might not be a good idea to have the volunteers come along.

"No, absolutely not!" He said, coming out of the officers' head and stepping into the wardroom. "We had a pleasure cruise today. That's all this was, a pleasure cruise, and these guys were just completely worn out from it. We can't have them come along with us. They're not only gonna get hurt, they'll jeopardize the whole mission."

Jeffries and Peters disagreed with his assessment and actually saw this situation to their advantage. "Look, John, when we get there they'll be expecting to see a bunch of rank amateurs who've come looking to purchase an old war relic. When they get a look at your boys, outta shape and green to the gills, they'll be convinced that we're who we say we are."

"Green to the gills? You bet they'll be green to the gills. The Sound out there today was smooth. Nothing like we'll experience once we get out onto the open sea. Plus, we're guaranteed to hit some rough weather come January. Just think about this flat-bottom boat slapping up and down against twenty to thirty-foot seas. Your guys might be ok, which I doubt, but my guys will be spending most of the voyage in the head. They'll be useless to us in a storm. It's not worth the risk."

"Look, it's not like we're gonna be out there in the Bering Sea. You're not gonna be needin' these guys to be haulin' in those big steel crab pots," said Peters. "Plus, we made some modifications to the hull."

"Whaddya mean you made some modifications to the hull? What kind of modifications?" Walters now focused on Jeffries.

"We used a poly-carbon material with an added 'V' shape. She's lighter and faster. But seriously, John," Jeffries continued as he stood up and squeezed between Peters and the bulkhead to get out into the passageway, "who cares if they get sick during the voyage? We won't really need them until we get to Lamon Bay. Window dressing, John. That's all they are, and that's all we really need them for, window dressing. They stay on the ship the whole time we're there. Excuse me, I gotta go take a leak." He went in to the officers' head.

Walters lit a cigarette and looked at Peters. He shook his head and unfolded his map of the Philippines to study the Island of Luzon—specifically, Lamon Bay. As his finger traced down to the coastal village of Capalonga, he asked Peters, "This is where they got her?"

"We heard from Rat Pack. There's a small dive bar on the outskirts of Capalonga. It's their hangout. It's just about a mile from where they dock their LCI. It's called Felipe's. It's classic. Like it's outta some old Bogart film or something like that. A dark, smoke- filled bar with cheap booze, drunks, thieves, and bar girls. A lot of bar girls. From what I hear, it's the best fuck for five dollars you'll ever have. That's where we're gonna meet Enrique, their leader."

"You can keep your five dollar fuck. I once had one of those, in `Nam. Believe me, once is enough." Walters said as he unconsciously began rubbing his crotch. "So this Enrique thinks that we think he owns a commercial fishing company?"

"Absolutely," Jeffries called out from the head. "He has no clue who we are, and as far as he knows, Francis is a deserter from the U.S. Navy who's been living in the hill country and operates as a smuggler and trader."

"He must be very convincing if he's got those guys fooled. I hear they don't trust any outsider," said Walters.

"Very true, they don't trust outsiders," Jeffries agreed. "But for all intents and purposes, Francis *is* a local. He's lived up in the hill country for a number of years. Has a wife, even a couple of grown kids."

"In fact," Peters continued, "he's the one who thought up most of the cover story for this operation after he got wind of their plan to set off dirty bombs at Clarke Air Base and one at Subic Bay. They've been masquerading their LCI as a fishing vessel for a couple of years working those waters, so that it's become commonplace for everyone to see it out there."

"Meanwhile," Jeffries added as he came out of the head, "they put everyone to sleep while sailing back and forth fishing those waters as they survey everything from security to ship movements, troop movements, you name it. They were even able to figure out the best places to send people ashore, which they did a number of times on dry runs. I mean, they took their time on this one."

"Yeah, I know all that," Walters said. "But I still don't get why they wanna sell it now. Especially since it's become a part of the scenery, so to speak. If you were the head of that group, would you wanna risk bringing attention to yourself by doing something out of the norm? It just doesn't make any sense to me. It just doesn't feel right."

"I think it makes perfect sense." said Jeffries. "Now that they're ready to go, they no longer need her. By selling her, they keep up the charade until the last minute. Meanwhile, we've learned they have an old swift boat and several Zodiacs, which gives them the speed they'll be needing. That LCI is no good to them anymore. Let's be happy they took our bait."

"Yeah, I guess so," Walters said, unconvinced.

"So as of right now, this is what we know and what we're gonna do." Jeffries pulled the map closer for a better view. "As of three days ago, Francis confirmed they're still keeping two high-impact attaché cases, you know the kind that have that brushed aluminum on the outside? Each one of those has a dirty bomb rigged to a timing device. That works in our favor, since they can't set `em off by a remote device like a cell phone. They're keeping them...where's that schematic of the ship?" he asked, looking around the table. Walters walked over to the small radio shack, grabbed a binder from the rack above the radio sets, and came back to the wardroom. Jeffries took it from him and began flipping through the pages until he came to a schematic of the LCI. "Let's see, we got storage, troop compartment one, troop two. Right here, troop compartment three. That's where they've been keeping them. When we get a half day out of Luzon, we contact Frank..."

"You mean, Rat Pack," Peters jumped in.

"Yeah, that's what I said."

"No, you said Frank." Walters confirmed the slip up.

"Shit! Ok, bad mistake. Just goes to show you that we all need to be careful." Jeffries looked at both men. "A half-day out, we contact Francis—Rat Pack—to give him enough time to meet us down the road from Felipe's. But first we're gonna go to this small inlet just to the east of Capalonga." Jeffries pointed to the little cove on the map. "That's where Peters and four more of our guys will go ashore. From there, they'll proceed on foot through the jungle until they get to Enrique's LCI. Meanwhile, after we drop them off, we'll take the 776 to this abandoned dock over here. Me and Walters will meet up with Francis, and the three of us will then meet with Enrique." He looked at Walters as he tried and failed to liberate his pack of cigarettes. "Are you with me so far?"

Remembering the last time Jeffries had stolen his smokes, Walters fished one out of his top pocket and flipped it to him. "Yeah, I'm with you."

"While we're meeting with him at Felipe's, we'll need to keep him there long enough so that Peters and his guys can gain access to their ship, neutralize or steal the two cases, and make their way back to the where our ship will be docked." Jeffries turned to Peters as he pulled a grainy color photo from a folder. "Here, you haven't seen this one yet. Over the last couple of weeks Enrique has had these two on the docks at night keeping guard."

"Girls? He's got two girls guarding that vessel?" Peters asked.

"Don't let that fool you. Remember who we're dealing with. Yes, they're trying to get Al Qaeda's attention, but they're also Filipinos. They have a long, proud history of guerilla warfare, and they've always trained and used women. They'll kill you without hesitation and I guarantee they've killed before. Look at the AK-47s they're holding. They know how to use them. So I'm just telling you that you're gonna have to dispose of them right away."

"So how are we gonna keep Enrique occupied long enough for Peters to do his thing?"

"I'm still working on that one, John. Over the next two months as we get new information, some things might have to change. That's when we'll finalize all of the details. One thing's for sure, though, we can't let him take us for a tour of their vessel that night. We'll have to convince him that we're exhausted and try to arrange it for the next day. Which we won't show up for, because we'll be long gone."

* * *

Gordie Smithfield lay as silent and as still as he could in the lower bunk of the darkened officer's cabin. With just a thin black curtain covering the doorway, he had heard almost every word of the conversation between Walters, Jeffries, and Peters. He was groggy when he woke from his unexpected nap. Having grown fatigued during the 776's cruise on Puget Sound, the eighty-seven-year-old needed to lay down to rest. The commanding officer's bunk was the closest and the most private, and as it turned out, very comfortable. The next thing he knew, it was several hours later, they were back at the dock, and almost everyone had gone. The conversation between the three men seemed surreal. After realizing he wasn't having a dream—and a bad one at that—his heart began to pound in his chest. His breathing became fast and shallow as he feared being discovered, and it surprised him that while laying there he recalled being in a similar situation in July 1943. A couple of weeks after the invasion of Sicily, he had found himself hiding in the bedroom closet of a young Sicilian girl. His heart pounding away, he was sure the girl's angry father had found him when he heard the breach of a shotgun click as it closed. He was lucky then, but wasn't so sure he would be as lucky now. He was confident they had no reason to look in to the small cabin as long as he remained quiet. He just wasn't sure that his heart would hold up—this time.

After the three men concluded their meeting, Jeffries and Peters disembarked the 776 as Walters headed up to the conning station to double-check that all had been secured. Gordie continued to lay in the bunk in order to give Jeffries and Peters enough time to leave, as well as to allow time for his heart rate to settle down. When it looked like it wasn't going to, he decided to get home as quickly as he could—to get to his medication. He carefully got up and tip-toed down the main passageway out to the quarter deck and then down the portside ramp to the dock.

Jeffries and Peters were sitting in Peters' van discussing their ongoing concerns about Walters when they noticed Gordie sneaking off the ship. At the same time, Walters glanced up from tightening the GPS unit to its mounting bracket, and he too saw the old vet sneaking away as if it was the dark of night rather than the afternoon. Immediately, Walters felt a heaviness in the pit of his stomach. He knew Gordie had to have heard everything the three men had been discussing. He also knew that he was going to catch a bunch of shit from Jeffries for not knowing that they hadn't been alone.

"You see what I see?" Jeffries said to Peters.

"What the fuck? Where the hell did he come from?"

"The old man had gone to lay down during the tail end of the trip. I forgot all about him."

"Yeah, I think we all did. You suppose he heard us?"

"We gotta assume he did."

"That sucks. That fuckin' sucks."

"Yeah, you're right. Too bad, he's a nice guy." Jeffries looked at Peters. "You got this?"

"Yeah. I'll take care of it."

33

While waiting for a report from his lieutenants, Enrique Aquino sat in a back booth of the dimly lit, smoke-filled bar known as Felipe's. Addressing his hunger with a bowl of kare-kare—his favorite stew made from oxtails and peanut sauce—the thirty-year-old, Western-educated leader of a growing regional terrorist group slowly worked up another appetite. This one for the newest girl working at the roach-infested hangout.

"Hey dalagita," he called out to the young bar girl as he put another spoonful of stew into his mouth. She sat at the bar, not turning to acknowledge his call. "Hey dalagita, I'm talking to you, girl."

The bartender noticed she was nervous and walked over to caution her. "Do you know who that is?" he said, wiping down the bar with a dirty rag. She half-turned to look as Enrique smiled at her. Turning back to her Pepsi, she stared at her reflection in the broken mirror on the wall behind the bar.

"I know who that is…He's Enrique Aquino. Everybody knows who he is."

"Well, he's calling you. Did you not hear him?"

"I heard him call 'dalagita'. I'm not a little girl."

"Oh, I see. A little makeup, some stockings, and a short, tight skirt and now you are a woman, huh? You're a dalaga?

Well, your first customer is calling you. When he is finished with you…maybe then he will call you dalaga."

"Hey, dalagita," Enrique called out again. "Come here and sit down."

She got up from her barstool, and with one hand on her hip, slowly walked over to the booth at the back of the room. He watched her approach and was impressed with her attitude.

"Dalaga," she said when she got up to the table.

"Yeah, sure. What are you, thirteen?"

"Sixteen!"

"Excuse me. In this poor light and all this smoke," he said, making a sweeping motion toward the ceiling with his hand, "you looked so much younger. But now that you are close, I can see you are a dalaga. You most certainly are a woman." He watched her as she shifted her weight to her other leg and snapped her chewing gum. "Do you know who I am?"

"Yes, I know you."

"Good, then sit. I won't ask you again." His brow lowered, and she heard the tone in his voice change. She slid into the booth. "This is your first night here, you must be nervous."

"I'm ok."

"Uh-huh. You *are* nervous. You can't fool me. But you got attitude. This is good. It'll serve you well… dalaga. You're also very beautiful and men will pay a good price for you."

"I know. I will make a lot of money."

"Maybe…maybe not."

"But you just said so yourself. You just said I'm very beautiful and men will pay…"

"Yes, men will pay a good price for you. But how much of that do you think you'll see? Huh? Your pimp will take all your money. You will have a dozen or so dirty, filthy, smelly men crawling all over you every night. Some will be so drunk they will throw up all over you. Some will even urinate all over you, and some will even beat you out of frustration when they can't get a fuckin' hard-on." He looked at her eyes and saw she was scared.

This wasn't the glamorous picture that her pimp had promised when he came to her village with several of his most beautiful girls to recruit new material. With promises of easy work, adoring customers, and lots of money, she had envisioned an escape from her life of hunger and poverty. "Well, I will just refuse to go with the filthy ones. I will not do business with the men who are so drunk they cannot stand up."

"And what do you think your pimp will do to you for turning away business, huh? He will beat you, that's what. He'll beat you so bad that you won't be able to show yourself for days, if not weeks, until you heal. Is that what you want?"

She didn't answer him. She had heard a few stories from other girls who had been used up and tossed aside, but didn't want to believe them.

"I know why you are doing this. I know that you come from a poor village not too far from here. Am I right?" She nodded. "You want to make some easy money, buy yourself some nice things, and help your mother and father, right?"

She nodded again. "I like you...dalaga. I can help you. You know who I am. You know what I do, yes?"

"Yes, I know what you do."

"Then you know I mean what I say. What's your name?
"Daisy"

"No, not your working name, your real name."

"Dalisay."

"Dalisay? That's Tagalog, meaning pure."

"I know what you are thinking." She hung her head.

"No, *you* do not know what *I'm* thinking. But I will tell you. *I* am thinking *you* do not want to be here and that you don't want to be doing this. I'm also thinking that you can make more money working for me."

"But you kill people."

"Yes, I do. I'm not going to lie. But me and my men, we are freedom fighters. We fight against the people that make us... who make you and your family live in filth and poverty. Just like the man who owns this place and put you to work as a whore. It's only when they come to silence our struggle that we have no choice but to fight back. Sometimes… people, bad people, get killed. Do you understand?" She nodded. "You're young, Dalisay, but you are very smart, and I could use a smart and beautiful dalaga like you who wants to be, and who should be with one man each night, not dozens, yes?" He looked at her eyes and knew that he had found the replacement "wife" he had been looking for.

"Yes," she said, "but what about the man I work for? He gave my parents a lot of money for me."

"Not a problem. I'll have a talk with him. He'll understand and he won't bother you. This I promise."

At that moment, several of his men came into the bar and immediately made their way to Enrique's booth. "Starting tonight, you will stay with me at my place." He turned to one of his men "Juan, take Dalisay to gather her things at…" He looked at her and shrugged his shoulders.

"I'm staying where all the other girls stay. At the hotel just two streets from here. By the river." She looked at both men. They nodded to each other as she slid out of the booth.

"Juan, take the truck and help her gather up her things from the hotel, and bring her over to my place. Then you come right back here. You understand?"

"Yes, Enrique." He and Dalisay turned to leave.

"Juan?"

"Yes, Enrique," he said without turning around.

"I'm timing you."

"Yes, Enrique."

Enrique looked at his other two lieutenants—the twenty-year-old Alissandro twins, Hector and Jonny. At first he let them stand there while he took a few more spoonfuls of his stew. "Jonny, what the fuck is wrong with you walking around with everybody seeing your gun exposed like that?" Jonny looked down at the handle of his 9 mm sticking out of his belt. "Do you think that makes you look tough?

"No, I'm sorry, Enrique. I just like to keep it ready when we're up in the hills. I forgot about it."

"And how *is* the pot harvest going, boys? Have you had any more trouble?"

"Just a little now and then, but much better since Francis tipped us off that Datu and his guys were gonna hit us," said Hector.

"That's right," added Jonny. "We were ready for them that day. Remember?"

"Yeah, I remember." Enrique said motioning to a waitress for another beer. "It's amazing how helpful Francis has been to us these past few months. Don't you think?"

"Seems ok to me." Jonny too signaled for a drink. "Just a local guy doing business. We've dealt with him from time to time. He's been straight with us, right?'

"Yes, Jonny, he's been straight with us and he's been quite helpful. Wouldn't you say so, Hector?"

"I'd say the past few months he's been more than just a little helpful to us, boss."

"Good, Hector. Good observation. Now both of you sit down, I have good news. We are all set to make our move in February. The word is, America is going to go into Iraq in March. When we make our strike, they will have to postpone that attack, giving our Al Qaeda brothers more than enough time to get all those chemical weapons away from Saddam. Now, our friend Francis tells me that he's been contacted by a group of amateur war buffs that have a ship just like ours. He also tells me that they are very interested in buying our old Navy vessel."

"But our ship is not for sale," said Jonny.

"But they think it is. Because I told Francis to tell them it is. And they are coming here with two hundred and fifty thousand American dollars to make the purchase."

"Why would they want to buy our old Navy ship? And for two-fifty American?" A suspicious Hector asked. "It's a piece of junk."

"Because, Hector, Francis says they are middle-aged naval enthusiast nuts who want a sister ship for some sort of stupid floating memorial. So I told our smuggler friend to tell them to come and visit. But here is the beauty of this whole thing. When they get here, we are not only going to take their money, we are going to take their ship as well."

"And what about them?" asked Jonny as he noticed the waitress coming to their table with three bottles of beer.

Enrique watched as she bent forward to show off her cleavage when she placed the bottles down on the table. She winked and smiled at him before she walked away. Once she was gone, he continued. "From what Francis tells me, there's only going to be about six of them, maybe seven. My guess is these guys are in their fifties, maybe a little older. Greatly overweight and out of shape. You know the type…typical lazy, fat Americans who gorge themselves on fast food and watch football games. It's no wonder their wives are fucking their gardeners." The others laughed. "They'll be no trouble for us. You two will see to it that they are turned into chum. And this time, make sure you mix them into the rest of the fish bait so that no one can tell the difference."

"Ok, that shouldn't be a problem, but what are we going to do with another piece of shit boat?" Jonny said as he looked back and forth between the two men.

Enrique took one last big spoonful of stew and chewed a hunk of oxtail as he smiled. "There is, my trusted companions, a slight change to our plan. We will still put a man ashore to the north of Subic Bay. He will go on foot to Clarke Air Base and set up his case there. The second case will stay on our old fishing vessel, and we will sail it straight up Subic, where it will go off right near the Navy base. Of course no one will be onboard. We'll just rig the controls to hold a steady course straight up the bay. And the third…"

"There's a third?" Hector asked in surprise.

"The third one will be planted on the American vessel—that is, once we get it and make it look more like ours. We will send her straight into the main harbor in Manila. Once we do that, Al Qaeda will surely take us seriously and they will send us more weapons, as well as money."

"And what about the other factions in these islands?" asked Hector.

"They will start to answer to us." He looked up to see Juan walk in through the front door and make his way to the table. Enrique slid out of the booth and took a long drink from his bottle of beer. "I also think," he said as he wiped his mouth with the back of his hand, "that perhaps it's time our friend Francis retires. Make sure nothing happens to him until our naval buffs arrive here in January. Then he can go into the grinder with them at the same time." He took another long drink, emptying his bottle, and looked around at his men. "And now if you'll excuse me, I have a young lady waiting for me."

3 4

Jack Peters calmly sipped on a lukewarm cup of coffee as he sat in his van across the street from the non descript two-family house in the Ballard neighborhood of North Seattle. Listening to his favorite syndicated radio talk show, he waited for the second floor bedroom light to go off. "Eleven thirty-five," he said to himself as he looked at the clock on the dashboard. "I'm surprised the old man isn't asleep by now." He took note of the police car that had just passed by and again noted the time on the clock. "First patrol car in three hours. Glad I don't live in this neighborhood."

Peters thought about the first time he had been asked to take care of a "loose end." In spite of his military and agency training, the first time he had to kill someone on his own—in cold blood—was very hard for him. He had always thought that the first one would be some ruthless terrorist, or perhaps a communist spy caught stealing vital information. Someone who was a threat to national security. Someone who deserved to die for being an enemy of the state. He had never counted on it being a young mother of two who had simply been in the wrong place at the wrong time and saw something she never should have seen. But it made perfect sense that this was the way to break in a "newbie". If he screwed up a hit on a high-value target, the potential fallout could run the spectrum from compromising a mission—along with the identities of field agents—to exposing highly placed political connections. Cutting one's teeth on someone who'd be given a twenty-second mention on the six o'clock news was the best way to gain experience without the risk of it being connected back to Langley if the agent screwed it up.

He had been told to make it look like a sexual assault and strangulation. The look of shock in her eyes, along with her fading pleas of *"my babies…please, not my babies"* just before she died, kept him awake for many nights during those first years. But he had been highly praised for his efficiency and thoroughness, and as such, he was given more "clean-up" jobs to perform. Eventually, the jobs and the faces blended together as it became easier for him to perform them without remorse. That is, except for that first job, which had stayed with him all these years.

* * *

Gordie's mind continued to race back and forth between what had he heard on the 776 and what, if any, action he should take—as well as the old war memories that kept flooding over him. He was becoming overwhelmed. He was confident that no one had seen him disembark from the ship, but no matter how he tried to calm himself, his heart rate would not settle down. As he paced his bedroom floor he continued to try to rub away the increasing pain in his left bicep muscle. Earlier in the evening he had taken a baby aspirin, a blood pressure pill, and a muscle relaxant. Now he was trying to calculate how much longer he needed to wait before he could take another dose of each on top of adding ten milligrams of Valium—which he was hoping would settle him down enough so he could get some rest. "This is crazy," he thought. "I can't believe this is happening. Who the hell are these guys? I need to call someone. I should call someone. No, I can't call. The other guys, oh my god. They're in danger too. But what if they're in on this? No, they can't be. What did Jeffries say…window dressing?

Yeah, that's right, window dressing. He said they were needed for window dressing. Oh my God. Oh my God. What time is it? I better take my medicine. This pain just won't stop. I should call someone. Who can I call, who can I call? Can't call Walters. No, not him. Lipton? No, no, not Lipton. Should I call Lipton? No, if anyone else was in on this, I'll bet it's him. Steve? Tex? Ray? Oh God, I don't know, I don't know."

He looked at his watch and walked into the bathroom. He was shocked that his complexion was now ashen gray. He was becoming nauseous. "I'll call Chuck," he said as he opened the medicine cabinet and took out several brown plastic vials of pills. His hands shook as he fought with the childproof caps, switching back and forth from one bottle to another. "Damn tops, how the hell are you supposed to open these things when you're sick?" He managed to force one off, as several pills spilled out from the sudden jerking motion of his hands. He tried to stop them from going down the drain, but even the reaction time of a man half his age wouldn't have been fast enough to go after several pills simultaneously rolling around a smooth porcelain bowl. He began to laugh and cry at the same time as the sight of the capsules rolling around in the sink reminded him of the time his daughter, then ten years old, had saved up thirty-five cents to send away for Mexican jumping beans that had been advertised on the back page of her comic book. And how she sang the Mexican Hat Dance over and over to them while the pill-shaped beans laid lifeless on the kitchen table—thinking that they needed motivation after the long trip from Mexico. Why he thought about that now he didn't know, but random memories like this had been flooding his thoughts all evening.

He placed the vials back on the shelf in the medicine cabinet and walked back to his bedroom. "Cell phone. I need my cell phone. I'll call A.J., no, I'll call Chuck. Yeah, that's who I'll call." Gordie walked over to his nightstand by the window and glanced out through the curtain onto the street. He spotted Peters' van. "I know that van. That's the same as...I've seen that van before. I know that van. Is there someone sitting in it?

I think there's someone sitting in it. Oh my God, what if they're watching me? They must have seen me leave the ship this afternoon. No, no, calm down, Gordie, calm down. Nobody saw me leave the ship. But what if they did?" He hurried over to the opposite side of the room and flipped off the light switch. His room was completely dark. Then he tiptoed back to the window and watched the black van across the street as he made his phone call.

When Peters noticed that the bedroom light had gone out, he realized that it had been a good fifteen minutes since he had last looked across the street at the house that Gordie Smithfield shared with his daughter and her husband. For all he knew, the old man could have gone to sleep right after he last checked or the light could have gone out just a few minutes earlier. Either way, he felt he had waited long enough, and now it was time for him to take care of business. He turned off his radio and removed the keys from the ignition, placing them into the side pocket of his jacket. A quick look into the rear and side view mirrors, then he got out of the van and slowly walked across the street.

In the darkness, Gordie stood to the side of the window and recognized Peters as he crossed the two-way street. He dialed Chuck Shimkin's number but got his voicemail. He didn't leave a message. As Peters made his way around to the back of the house, Gordie frantically searched through his contact list for Ray's number but quickly realized he didn't have it. "I'll call A.J. Better call A.J. He'll be..." At that moment, a sharp stabbing pain shot across his chest and it felt as if his heart was suddenly being squeezed in a vise. The pain radiated from front to back. It travelled from the center of his chest up to the left side of his neck and down his shoulder into his arm. His left arm became so heavy he couldn't lift it. His knees buckled, and Gordie fell onto the bed. As quick as the jolt of pain had struck him, it let up just as fast. He began gasping for air. "Oh thank God. It stopped, it stopped. A.J., got to call A.J. Medicine. I need..."

He dialed Abner and slowly got up from the bed, stumbling as he went for the medicine cabinet in the bathroom. He placed the phone down on the sink, as he fumbled for his medications. When the mirrored door of the medicine cabinet swung closed, Gordie saw Peters' reflection standing directly behind him. He turned to face him and a second jolt of pain—this time a crushing sensation more intense then the first—filled his entire chest and he went down to his knees. He felt as if he couldn't breathe and began to get light-headed as the flow of blood to his brain was choked off by the intense spasm of his heart muscle. He looked up at Peters, who stood over him without emotion.

"Help me, please," Gordie said out of desperation. But he knew Peters hadn't been there to help. Gordie grew weaker as the pain grew to a crescendo. He collapsed onto the floor, his right hand reaching out, grabbing Peters' pant leg.

Peters stood over Gordie and watched as another sharp jolt contorted the old man's body. Once he had lost consciousness, Peters eased his leg to free himself from Gordie's frail grip. "Sorry, old man" he said. He hadn't looked forward to eliminating the old veteran. And although his method would have been more merciful than the heart attack, he was glad he didn't have to do this one. From the little he knew of Gordie, Peters felt he was harmless. He didn't think he would have gone to the authorities with tales of black ops or Filipino guerillas. The cops would have probably thought he was delusional. Peters and Jeffries were concerned, however, that he would have gone blabbing to the others, and that would have created big problems.

He turned to leave, stopping abruptly when he heard a faint ringing coming from the cell phone resting on the edge of the bathroom sink.

"Hello, hello, enahbody there?" came the tinny voice from the cell phone speaker. "Hello, Gordie, is that ya tryin' ta call me? Hello? Come on man, iss almos' midnight, stop playin' games, hello?"

With his latex glove-covered hand, Peters pressed the button to disconnect the call and saw that Gordie had been trying to reach Abner. "Well, obviously he didn't get through to him in time. But was he calling him because of his heart attack or because of what he heard today? I wonder who else he would have or could have called. Peters put the phone in his jacket pocket and turned to leave by way of the back staircase. "I'll just have to keep a close eye on people over the next few weeks and see who starts behaving differently."

From the bottom landing of the main stairs, Gordie's daughter flipped on the light switch and tied her terrycloth robe. "Dad? Are you ok up there?"

Standing in the shadow of his van, Peters' fingers quickly searched the deep jacket pocket for his keys. They had become tangled on the antenna stub of Gordie's cell phone. Jerking on the key chain he quickly spun around to the loud cry of the old man's daughter and didn't feel the phone as it fell from his pocket. He briefly watched her shadow moving back and forth in the second floor window before climbing into his van. He waited and watched a moment longer before driving off.

3 5

From his position at the head of the dining room table, Ray was content to be a casual observer as his guests—stuffed with Abner's slow-roasted Thanksgiving turkey, stuffing, and secret recipe gravy—engaged in conversation. He divided his focus equally between Jimmy and Abner as they talked about the 776, the Navy, the war in Afghanistan, and Seattle basketball; and Casey, Stella, and Leigh Anne's conversation about nursing, the latest fashions, and men. Magic, too, was content to lay curled up by the fireplace, safe from the cold November rains and wind that seemed more blustery than in previous years. She occasionally opened her eyes to check on Ray, as his voice was the only one she did not hear. As he watched and listened to the women talk, he caught alternating glances from Leigh Anne and Stella, smiling back at both. Once again, Stella's boyfriend was off on an extended business trip and she had been only too happy to accept Ray's invitation to spend the day with him and his family.

"This new team ownah knows nuthin' 'bout basketball," Abner told Jimmy. "He don't even no nuthin' 'bout makin' a good cup a coffee. What the hell's wrong wit' people anyways, payin' three ta fo' dollahs fo' a cup a that stuff. An' ya know 'stuff' ain't the word ah really wanna use. Peoples is jes crazy, ah tell ya."

Long a bachelor, Abner had not only been happy to be included as a "family" member, he was also thrilled to be sitting next to Stella. It seemed to be the perfect combination to lift his spirits. He had been extremely low after learning of Gordie's death, and that he had been the person Gordie chose to call while experiencing a massive coronary. That's all he talked about in the weeks following the memorial service, whether he was at the hospital or at the 776 on Saturdays. He was preoccupied to the point of distraction and began making mistakes at work—especially when Gordie's daughter had mentioned that they found her father's cell phone in the street.

"That jes don't make no sense," he said over and over. "He called me on his phone jes befo' he died. How could it end up `cross the street from his house?" He talked about it so much it got to the point that Jeffries became angry at Peters for having taken it.

Listening to Casey talk about Navy men made Ray think about her high school years, when topics of discussion with her best friends had been boys, football games, and homecoming dances. And then there were the past Thanksgivings that Jo insisted on hosting every year. She would then spend days baking desserts, preparing the many side dishes, and of course, brining the turkey for forty-eight hours before roasting it on Thanksgiving Day. With a large extended family on Jo's side, the holidays had always been an important time of the year for her. With Ray's help, it had been a labor of love to carry on her family tradition. Their house had always been full of family, friends, and the wonderful smells of homemade food and treats expected of the holidays. The smells that filled Ray's house this Thanksgiving easily brought back those memories and he was happy to have his children sharing his table once again.

He watched Leigh Anne as she talked with Casey and Stella. She was feeling good, and had more energy and better color in her face relative to the week before. Ray also noticed that she had her appetite back, which he was also glad to see. It had been about six weeks since her second interview with the University of Hawaii and she had yet to hear of their decision. With each passing day it weighed more heavily on her, as the spring semester would be starting in mid-January. As time began to grow short for her to give notice at the aquarium, sometimes so too did her patience. And as her increased stress had been obvious, Ray became concerned about her week-long fatigue and general disinterest in food. A few days prior, when Ray—in a kidding manner—suggested that she was acting like she was pregnant, she became very emotional and had asked him to leave. It hadn't mattered to her that they were in his house at the time. He had wisely spent the rest of the afternoon in the safety of his workshop. She had a great deal on her mind, and apparently the best course of action for him was no action at all—especially no wisecracks. Except for insisting that she allow him to give her a few spinal adjustments, he let her have her space. Ray was pleased with her lighter mood and increased appetite. "She probably had some sort of bug," he thought to himself. "I should adjust her more often."

Earlier in the day, with Abner, Leigh Anne and Stella taking over the kitchen, Ray and the kids had taken a ride out to the cemetery and paid their respects to Jo. He was hoping for a short visit due to the bad weather, but because it was their first time back to the cemetery since the funeral, the kids insisted on spending a little more time. He gave no argument. It was a good opportunity for the three of them to be alone. Standing around Jo's grave, they couldn't help but feel her presence as Casey discussed her duties at the Navy Medical Center in Portsmouth, New Hampshire. After the doubts that his father had placed into him all those months ago, Ray was relieved that she had not drawn an overseas assignment. Jimmy announced that he had an early departure back to Bethesda and would be heading back in two days. He had just been assigned to be second counsel on his first "real" law case and he needed to get going on it right away. He anticipated that it could take anywhere from two to four weeks before they wrapped it all up, and was anxious to get it done so he would be free to sail with the Enterprise—scheduled to leave Norfolk right after New Years.

"The Big E?" Ray asked.

"Yup, can you believe it?"

"Persian Gulf?"

"Yup. She's gonna rejoin the 5th fleet. I think the first time I was on her, I must have been all of seven years old," said Jimmy.

"You were five, and the Enterprise was the very first ship I ever took you to. I don't suppose you remember what happened that day?"

"What, did something happen?" asked Casey, looking at her brother. "How come you guys never said anything?"

"I don't remember anything happening. You're fooling around, right?" Jimmy said as he looked at his dad, expecting a subtle hint that he was joking.

"Oh, something happened alright. It was fleet week of course, and your brother kept running back and forth on the flight deck with his arms stretched out like he was a Tomcat flying off to battle." They both looked at Jimmy as the three of them laughed.

"Then top gun over here did a face-plant right into a puddle of water and was soaked from head to toe."

"Oh yeah, I remember that," Jimmy admitted.

"Fortunately I had a change of clothing for you in my backpack."

"Probably thanks to mom's planning," Casey added.

"Yes, thanks to your mother's foresight, I had drinks, snacks, and a change of clothing in the backpack. So with you crying like you had been shot out of the sky, I approached a seaman and had to plead with him to let us into the operations' island so I could get you changed."

"Yeah, so," said Casey, "what's the big deal with that?"

"Oh, it was no big deal, until he brought over a Chief, who went and spoke to a Lieutenant who was the O.D. After explaining the situation for a third time, he brought over a two-man security detail and we were escorted in to the flight sickbay.

That's where they searched my backpack and temporarily confiscated my camera before they allowed me to get your brother changed. Then we were escorted back out onto the flight deck where they returned my stuff. And now here it is all these years later, and your brother's first sea duty is on that very same ship."

"I guess it was just my destiny," Jimmy said with pride.

Ray didn't answer at first. He looked over at Jo's headstone and then back at Jimmy and Casey.

"What is it, Dad?" Casey asked when she noticed the serious look on her father's face.

"There's something that's been on my mind for awhile now. I've been meaning to talk to you guys about this and there just never seemed to be a right moment." The kids looked at each other and then back at Ray.

"Is everything ok, Dad? Are you sick?" asked Jimmy.

"What? Sick? No, no, I'm feelin' fine. Really, I am."

"Is it Leigh Anne? Are you guys thinking about getting married?" Casey asked as Jimmy looked at his dad, surprised at the question—but not disapproving of the idea.

"What? Geez, no... Although...that's worth thinking about" Ray said as the kids' eyes grew wide. "Nooo, I'm just kidding. You know she's waiting to hear about this professorship at UH right? Besides, our relationship isn't...hey, you guys got me off-track here. That's not what I wanted to talk about." Ray started walking away. "I'm freezing my butt off out here. You guys take another minute or two to be with your mom. I'll wait for you in the car."

Casey turned to her brother as Ray walked off. "He's definitely got something serious on his mind. I don't remember the last time he was like this."

"That's for sure. At least he's not sick. Or at least he says he's not."

"No, he's not sick. I've never seen him look healthier. He's exercising more, his sex life is probably really good," she whispered. "He and Leigh may not be getting married, but he's most certainly in love with her."

"How can you tell?"

"Trust me, I can tell."

"No, seriously, how do you know?" Jimmy insisted.

Casey looked down at her mother's grave and then took Jimmy by the arm walking several feet away as if whispering wasn't quiet enough and Jo could somehow hear what she was going to say. "Have you ever taken a good look at dad's face whenever you mention her name, or when she walks into a room?"

"No, not really. Well, not at all."

"Typical guy! When we were kids, grade school days and even middle school, he used to be the same way with mom. Trust me. I know these things." They walked back to their mother's grave, spent a few more moments in reflection, and then headed back to the car.

On the drive back to Seattle, Jimmy mentioned that there had been no further news on the log book of the 606 since Lieutenant Johnson's daughter had been interviewed by the Naval Investigative Service. The account she gave of her father's deathbed confessions tied with the amendments that the former 606 skipper had made in the log. All Jimmy really knew at this point was that reports had been written and recommendations had been made and forwarded up the chain of command. He had no idea what those recommendations were or how long it would take for the Navy to act on them. All they could do at this point was to wait and see.

"So what was it that you wanted to talk to us about?" Casey leaned forward from the back seat of the Jeep.

"When your grandfather was last here," Ray said as he turned down the volume on the radio, "when we buried your mother, that night we were sittin' around in the living room, by the fireplace. Just talkin'. Naturally the conversation turned to the two of you, and your grandfather suggested…" he grew silent as he searched for the right words.

"What?" Jimmy asked.

"Are you two happy with what you're doing? I mean, are you not only happy with your choice of profession, but also that you're doing it in the Navy? And don't just say yes because that's what you think I wanna hear. I mean, deep down in your heart, is this what you wanna be doing with your lives?"

RICHARD I LEVINE

"Well," Jimmy rushed to answer first, "it's been part of me since I did my face-plant on the flight deck of the Enterprise."

"But that's what I'm getting at. Your grandfather seems to think that because of my obsession, you two were conditioned, brainwashed to the point that you probably never gave civilian life a second thought."

"I can't speak for Jimmy, Dad. But as far as I'm concerned, this is what I want to be doing and this is where, I mean the Navy is where I want to be doing it. For right now, that is. We both know you were somewhat obsessive about it. Mom pointed that out to us plenty of times. She also tried her best to steer us away from a military life, always talking about all the wonderful things we could have with high-paying private sector careers. Trust me, between the two of you I think we got a fair look at both sides of the equation. For what it's worth, Daddy, you introduced us to the military, to the Navy, but I chose it of my own free will. Do I want to do this my entire life? No. But for right now, and for the next few years, yeah... this is where I wanna be." She looked over at her brother, and he concurred. She patted her father's shoulder. "You weren't feeling guilty that maybe you talked us into doing something we didn't wanna do, were ya?"

"No, not really. Well, maybe a little. Like almost everyday for about the last nine months."

"Man!" Jimmy said as he turned in his seat to look at his sister. "Grandpa really did a number on him."

* * *

There were plenty of leftovers to go around and Ray made sure that Abner and Stella went home with enough to not only have a midnight snack, but to also have sandwiches for lunch the following day. The kids borrowed the Jeep and went off to visit friends in Eastridge Heights, and Casey had also expressed a desire to take a ride past the old house. Ray looked at the mess in the kitchen as he wrapped an apron around his waist and rolled up his sleeves.

"If you're too tired," he said to Leigh Anne, "I've got this. In fact, I do have it. I know you've been zapped of energy this past week, so why don't you turn in? I promise I won't attack you tonight." He gave her a slight smile.

"I am a little tired, but I don't mind helping. We're alone, so it's a good time to talk."

"Oh? Is this a 'we need ta talk' kind of talk?" He joked as she picked up a dish towel and walked over to the sink.

"Your kids are pretty amazing."

"Thanks. They're a lot smarter than me. Better looking, too."

"Don't sell yourself short. But they are smart. Jimmy's a handsome young man, and Casey? I'll bet she's gotta beat the guys away."

"I'll bet people said that about you when you were her age," Ray said in a failed effort to be funny. "Wait, you're only about ten years older than she is. They're probably still saying that now. I wonder about that all the time, ya know. Well, not exactly all the time, but I see the looks you get from the guys when we're down at Kelsey's." Ray took note that Leigh Anne didn't respond to the age remark. He did wonder sometimes if their age difference bothered her at all.

"Stella's very nice. I like her."

"Yeah, she is. She's been a major help to me at the medical center. My biggest advocate, ya know?"

"I know. You've told me before, and quite honestly I can see it. That she'd be an advocate for you."

"How so?"

"I see the way she looks at you."

"She was just happy to be here tonight."

"No, it's more than that. I think she's in love with you, Ray."

"Aw, go on. That's silly!"

"No, it's not. She's in love with you. A woman can tell these things."

"I'm telling you, she was just happy to be here tonight is all. She's got this absentee boyfriend that she lives with. He's always away on business, she's all alone, it's Thanksgiving, and…"

"And you probably give her the attention that she doesn't get at home."

"I don't think I give her that much attention. I mean we have a cup of coffee now and again, discuss a case here and there, but that's all."

"It doesn't take much sometimes, Ray. She's grown fond of you. Very fond of you. That's all I'm saying. I'm not trying to make anything of it. It's just what I see in the way she looks at you," Leigh Anne said insistently.

"Growing fond of someone is not the same as being in love with someone. And even if that's true, I've done nothing to encourage it. I mean, sure, I like her, but as a peer, as a coworker. She's been a big help to me when no one else except Abner stepped forward. I'll bet you didn't watch him when he looked at me," Ray added in another failed attempt to ease the growing tension. Leigh didn't answer as she opened the dishwasher and began placing drinking glasses onto one of the racks. It was silent for a minute before Ray spoke again. "Seriously, it's been a long day. I can see that you're really tired. I don't mind cleaning up. Honest."

"You two probably have a lot in common." She said without looking away from the dishwasher.

"No, not really" he responded wishing she would drop the subject.

"You're the same age," she pressed on.

"So?"

"You grew up during the same time."

"Yes, we did. She in Boston, me in New York."

"You have similar political leanings."

"Leigh, you're fishing. We're coworkers, and I invited her to share a meal with the other people that I care about."

"Well, there you go," Leigh Anne put the dish towel down on the counter and walked out of the kitchen.

Ray rolled his eyes up to the ceiling and let out a sigh. "Whaddya mean 'well, there ya go'? There ya go, what?" He followed her into the bedroom. Leigh began putting some of her clothes into a small duffle bag that she had taken from the closet. Ray reached out and placed his hand on top of it to prevent her from adding more of her things "Leigh, what are you doing, what's this all about?"

She took a deep breath and let it out as she turned to face him. "I'm sorry, Ray," she said as her eyes slowly began to well up. "I thought I'd be able to handle all of this but I don't think I can."

"Handle all of what? Leigh, I don't understand. Help me out here, ok?"

"Handle all of *this*," she said with outstretched arms. "You, me, us. Waiting to hear from the university. You being older than me. All of this, ok? I know that the way I'm feeling isn't making any sense to you, and it might even drive you nuts, because lately I can't figure out what it is that I'm feeling and I know it's driving *me* nuts, as if you couldn't tell."

Ray began to recall a similar conversation they had had during the summer and which he had thought, at least in his mind, that they had resolved back then. "I'm sure if I brought that up," he thought, "I'll be told that I misunderstood or that we never discussed it. And this time, she's so much more emotional. Hormones. Gotta be fuckin' hormones!"

"Alright, you've got a lot on your mind. I get that. Stella has nothing to do with this. She has nothing to do with us. I can't help the way she feels or the way you think she feels. I don't feel the same way. I don't love her. I do, however, love you."

"And I love you too. I do. but…"

"But what, my age? You going back to Hawaii? I can't do anything about my age. And forty-five is not that old. We're only fifteen years apart. For the life of me, I don't understand why people think I'm old. I think, no, I know we've been able to connect on many things and on many issues. And I know that ever since we met there's been a chemistry between us that goes beyond explanation. And I know you've felt it just like I have."

"And what about kids?" She looked right at him. In the back of his mind, Ray had known that the longer they were together, this subject was going to surface. He hadn't wanted to think about it out of fear that it could be the deal-breaker.

"What *about* kids?" He asked innocently. "We never discussed kids before."

"We're discussing it now. You have two grown kids, and they're wonderful. They really are. It takes a lot of work to get kids like yours to turn out the way they did. Do you want any more at forty-five? Because I'm only thirty and I want to have a family." She looked at Ray.

He couldn't answer her. He knew that if he told her that he didn't, she would be out the door and that would be the end of it—the deal breaker. His mind was racing but couldn't get focused. He never could stay focused under pressure. "Perhaps that's why she brought up Stella," he thought. "No, that doesn't make sense. What does Stella have to do with kids? Maybe she was looking for a reason to pick a fight. No, no she wouldn't do that. Hormones!"

"Your silence, Ray Silver, just answered my question." Leigh Anne pulled the bag away from him and resumed packing the things that had slowly accumulated at Ray's place over the past several months. "I think we need to take a break for a little while, Ray."

"A break?"

"Yes, a break."

"From each other?"

"Yes, Raymond, from each other."

"Leigh, please, not so fast. This is coming out of left field. I don't know if I wanna start a family again. How can you ask me that and expect an honest answer when I haven't had the time to consider everything, or anything, for that matter?" Ray looked at her appealing to her sensibility.

"Ok, fair enough. But I need to have some time to myself, though, and you need to have some time to think about this. And like I said, I think we need to take a little break from each other. So I'm going to ask you to do me a favor. During this time, I would like for you to think, to seriously think, about whether or not you want to have a family again and if you want to have that family with me. And if you do, are you willing to come live on Oahu? Now I know that's a lot for one person to ask another, but that's what I'm asking you. And please don't say yes just because you think that's what I want to hear. And don't say yes just because you want to be with me, because I already know you want to be with me. Ray, I just don't want to have a baby with you if you're not gonna be there full out for that child. Physically, mentally and spiritually. If you're unable to give me that, then I'd rather be a single parent."

"I promise, I'm gonna think about this. Seriously. I'm not gonna take this lightly. You're too special to me. You're way too important to me. You do know that, right?"

"Yes, I know that."

"But...what If I decide that I'm not up for going through all that again?" Ray continued as she zipped up her bag. She walked over to him and gave him a light kiss on the cheek as a tear rolled down hers.

"Let me know what you decide, when you decide it, Ray. I know this probably seems like I'm holding a gun to your head, and maybe that's not fair for me to do, but it's because having both you and a family are that important to me."

"Exactly how long is 'a little break'?"

As she made her way to leave, she stopped and looked at Ray one more time. "I'm sorry to leave you with all the dinner mess."

3 6

A week after Thanksgiving, Ray found himself in the midst of another sleepless night. The third in a row since Monday. He looked at the clock over the fireplace as Cary Grant guided the USS Copperfin through an underwater minefield at the entrance of Tokyo Bay. Three o'clock in the morning, and it seemed that every time he was about to doze off he fought to stay awake. He hadn't even been able to concentrate on the movie, but that didn't matter to him. It wasn't because he had already seen it two dozen times, but rather because he felt as if he himself had been sailing through a minefield the past year with all the nonsense he was putting up with at work—and now with Leigh Anne's emotional upheaval. But unlike the Copperfin, which safely negotiated the minefield, he had steered right into a bunch of them and the fires were far from extinguished.

The Monday after Thanksgiving was slated to be a big day at the medical center. With glowing reports about him from Drs. Thayer, Araghi, and others—along with increasing demands from the veterans for his services—the heads of orthopedics and physical therapy had lobbied Peter McCain to move the chiropractic office out of the basement and incorporate Ray into the physical therapy wing on the second floor. In spite of the personal problems McCain had with him, he had reluctantly agreed—but only after a telephone call from Senator Murphy's office.

Apparently, the Senator felt the need to have more visibility in her home state. Since her re-election campaign would be gearing up in twelve months, it was never too early to start planting the seeds. She was already home for the holiday, so her staff began lining up media events and photo ops. This would be the perfect follow-up to a successful program that she had "spearheaded" the year before. Ray couldn't help but think that it was more than coincidence that in early November—nine full months after he had begun working at the VMC—all of the supplies and equipment that he had requested finally arrived. And with the addition of two chiropractic treatment rooms in the physical therapy ward, Senator Murphy was thrilled to have the opportunity to show off to the media at the Monday morning "christening".

When Ray arrived that morning, he was greeted at the second floor nurse's station by a visibly upset Stella. "Hey, was my Thanksgiving dinner that bad? Better not let Abner see you like this. He'll think you didn't like his turkey."

"They let him go, Ray."

"They let who go?"

"Abner. They fired him."

"Whaddya mean they fired him? Who fired him? Why?"

"I don't know exactly. I just found out about it thirty minutes ago."

"Did he come in at all this morning? Is he here?"

"He was." She looked around. Seeing other staff walking in and out of rooms and hanging around the nurse's station, she grabbed Ray by the arm and led him down the hall. "He came in about an hour earlier than normal and let himself into Harrison's office. Supposedly he was doing regular maintenance stuff. Changing some lightbulbs, emptying trash. That kind of stuff. The next thing he knows, Harrison, Brian Davis, and a security guard show up and Abner's being escorted out of the building."

"Damn it! I told him he needed to be careful. Did you get to talk to him?"

"No, I couldn't get near him."

"Did you get a look at him? Was he alright, was he upset?"

"He looked stunned."

"Ok, I'm gonna take a run over to his apartment to check on him and see what happened."

"You can't, not now. Senator Murphy's already here. She's down the hall with Davis, McCain, Kit Hiller from PT, and... Murphy brought a load of press."

"Shit, what else is new with that woman?" He asked rhetorically. "Alright, can you do me a favor and try to get Abner on the phone? See how he is and tell him that as soon as I'm done with the dog and pony show I'll be over."

As most of the staff made their way down the hall to physical therapy to get a glimpse at the senator, a forty-seven-year-old retired Marine gunnery sergeant in room 288—recovering from a second redo knee replacement—went into a full-blown asthma attack. He struggled for air as he strained to turn to his left in an attempt to reach for his inhaler on the nightstand. He was able to get a couple of fingertips on it but ended up knocking it to the floor. Once it hit the hard linoleum tile, it bounced and came to rest under the bed. He twisted to his right and frantically searched for the emergency call button—pressing it hard as soon as he found it. Ray saw the red light flash over the doorway to 288 as he walked down the hall toward his new office. At the same time, while trying to reach Abner, Stella saw the emergency signal from 288 flash on the computer monitor at the nurse's station. With no one else immediately in sight, she dropped the phone and began to run down the hall.

Ray was the first one into the room and saw the gunny turning blue around the lips—his eyes as wide as Ray had ever seen on anyone. He ran to the patient and watched him motion with his hand toward his mouth that he needed an inhaler. Ray quickly looked around the room but couldn't find one. The patient lost consciousness. He briefly attempted CPR and quickly realized that it wasn't going to solve the problem. He pulled a small switchblade from his pocket and cut the rope that held the retired Marine's knee in the air—yanking him out of the bed and onto the floor. Just then Stella made it into the room, followed by Harrison and two attendants. Harrison instantly began screaming, "Get your fuckin' hands off of my patient, you quack!"

Ray ignored him and proceeded to flip the man onto his stomach, running his hand down the middle of his back until he felt several thoracic vertebrae that lacked any motion and were out of alignment. Harrison charged at Ray and tried to pull him off of the unconscious man but was met with a fist to his groin. He fell back against the far wall. Without hesitation, and through Harrison's incessant screaming, Ray delivered a thrust as accurately as he could and a loud crunch silenced the room. Within seconds, color came back to the sergeant's face. He took in a full, deep breath and then exhaled. Ray carefully turned him onto his back, and they looked at each other as the Marine managed a smile and whispered, "Thank you".

Ray motioned for the two attendants to assist the patient back into bed. As he got up from the floor, he saw Harrison slowly getting up from his knees with Peter McCain and Brian Davis standing in the doorway— and behind them, Senator Murphy. Again Harrison began screaming. "You fuckin quack! What the hell are you doing with my patient? How dare you take it upon yourself to perform an unauthorized procedure on *my* patient!"

"Your patient was about to die, doctor, and I was the only one in here. I made a judgment call," Ray fired back, as he had had all that he could take from Bill Harrison.

"You clearly stepped out of bounds here, mister, and in front of all these witnesses. I'm finished putting up with you parading around this hospital pretending to be a real doctor."

Dr. Davis grabbed hold of Harrison's arm and pulled him back from Ray. "That's enough Bill, you're out of line."

"Out of line? Out of line? I'll tell you who's out of line. This fuckin' quack is way out of line and I think it's about time we did something about this bullshit voodoo experiment."

Red in the face, Harrison looked right at Senator Murphy as bright lights from a news crew video camera came on. Harrison turned back to Ray. "You did it this time. I'm gonna do everything I can to get your ass canned just like I did to your bumbling Stepin Fetchit janitor friend."

With that, every bit of frustration and anger that had been building up inside of Ray finally exploded. He didn't hear Stella scream out, "No Ray, don't do it!" as his right fist crushed Harrison's nose and his left came in just behind with an uppercut that sent the man down to the floor. Both McCain and Davis had to grab Ray and push him away, as he was setting up for a third strike—even though Harrison was already out cold.

* * *

The ticking from the clock on the wall of Peter McCain's outer office was loud. It also had a continuous low hum that was driving Ray crazy. From his chair, he glanced over at McCain's assistant. Her stare was expressionless as she watched him watching her. "Doesn't this noise drive you nuts?

"No," came the one-word reply. She sat stone-faced and Ray figured that she must have been at her position for quite a few years. She reminded him of McCain. Same deadpan face, same monotone voice.

The door to the administrator's private office finally opened and he was summoned in to learn his fate. He would have preferred that they got right to the point, but somehow government bureaucrats and politicians always seemed to drag on forever. He listened to Senator Murphy go on and on about how he had let her down after she had championed his cause. McCain, in his droll diatribe, seemed to take delight in reading complaint after complaint that had been filed by Harrison over the preceding nine months. Ray wasn't even familiar with half of the claims the doctor had made against him. Dr. Davis sat silently. He was happy that Harrison had had his clock cleaned by someone, but couldn't tell Ray or anyone else how happy he truly was.

For the second time in less than a year VMC staff members had been treated to a Harrison take-down courtesy of the person the man despised the most—a fete that forever elevated Ray to the status of VMC legend. In the end, and with Senator Murphy's support, McCain said he had no choice but to suspend Ray indefinitely, and that he was going to recommend to Bill Harrison that he file a formal complaint with the Veterans Administration. It would be Harrison's decision whether or not he'd also file one with the Seattle police.

"I assure you, Dr. Silver," McCain said, "this is an extremely serious situation that you have gotten yourself into. Not only may you lose your job, but Dr. Harrison, when he wakes up, may be inclined to file assault charges against you. A board of inquiry will naturally be convened."

"Naturally," Ray responded, to the furrowed brows of McCain and Murphy.

"Until that time, sir, consider yourself on indefinite suspension. You will be escorted off of the property by security and you are not to return to this facility without my written authorization. Do I make myself clear?"

Ray stood up to leave, then turned around. "You know, I sat outside this office for forty-five minutes while you people sat here and discussed my fate. Then, I sat here in your office and listened to you, Senator Murphy and then you, Mr. McCain, take turns lecturing me as if I were some schoolboy. For the past nine months I've put up with Bill Harrison's constant disparaging remarks, not only to me, but about me. I've watched him verbally abuse the janitorial staff as well as many on the nursing staff. He personally went after Abner Lewis, a kindhearted, elderly gentlemen, a World War II veteran who worked here part-time to supplement his income. And do ya know why Harrison went after him? Huh? Because he befriended me. Yeah, that's right. Abner saw to it that I got the help I needed in spite of Dr. Harrison's prejudice. I saved a man's life today, and while I was doing it, a pompous, arrogant, sanctimonious, self-serving sonofabitch jackass tried to stop me from doing so. And why? Because I'm a chiropractor.

That retired Gunnery Sergeant could have died today if that bastard had been successful in stopping me. I didn't hear one question from anyone about what I was doing or why I was doing it during your lecture of me just now. Not one question. If you people wanna fire me because of that, you go right ahead." He turned to leave. He was escorted to his car by two security guards, who both thanked him for decking Harrison.

* * *

As Ray lay on his couch, John Forsythe and John Garfield were completing their secret mission. Sitting on the rocky cliffs above Tokyo Bay, they radioed information back to the Copperfin that would eventually help Doolittle's raiders conduct the first U.S. air raid on Tokyo. He kept trying to remind himself that a lot of good things had happened since January and that he should focus on all the positives, like Leigh Anne. There was no doubt in his mind that he wanted their relationship to continue; however, he needed to focus on whether or not he wanted to start a new family.

"Ok, I'm forty-five," he thought. "I'm not too old to have another kid. If I had a baby, I mean, if we had a baby...say nine months from now, I'll be forty-six. Diapers, teething, two in the morning feedings? Shit, it's three o'clock now, I can handle a two a.m. feeding...I hope she wants to breastfeed, though. That would be so much better. For everyone... Am I gonna have to be diving into those ball pits when I'm fifty? I'll be sixty-one, no, sixty-two when he or she is learning to drive. Maybe there won't be cars by then. Maybe I'll be dead by then. Maybe that's what's gonna kill me. Maybe Leigh should take her out for driving lessons. I don't think I wanna go through driving lessons again. Teaching two kids to drive is more than anyone can ask of a man. A baseball catch would be a nice thing to do again. I miss that. First dates, break-ups, hell, I haven't even married off my first batch yet."

His thoughts kept swirling around, and again he found himself dozing off. He began dreaming and found himself back at Kimo's in Lanikai.

He glanced across the open air dining room, and there was Leigh Anne, sitting at the bar. He got up from his table and started walking over to her. She seemed more beautiful to him. As he tried to get closer, it seemed his legs became heavier, and he had a hard time getting over there. The harder he tried, the harder it became. She glanced over toward him and seemed to become impatient at his lack of progress. He worked harder and began to lose ground. And then he noticed him. A younger, more muscular man walked up to her with two little kids. Her husband? She got up and kissed him, the kids squealing, "Mommy, Mommy". She glanced over at Ray one more time before walking off with her family.

Ray woke up in a flop sweat to the ringing of his telephone. It was four in the morning. He jumped up and made his way into the kitchen. A phone call at this time of the morning could only be from or about four people: his dad, the kids, or Leigh Anne. "Hello, this is Ray."

"Ray Silver?"

"Yes, this is Ray. Who's this?"

"Hello, is this Ray Silver?" came the question again, from a voice sounding like an older woman.

"Yes, this is Ray Silver, who is this please?"

"Is this Ray Silver, Ronnie's boy?" Ray immediately felt his heartbeat increase and the pulse in his carotid arteries began to pound. "Yes, this Ronnie's boy, what's happened to my dad?"

3 7

Kelsey pulled back the bottle of Pipeline she had just opened before Leigh Anne could get her hands on it and stared at her in disbelief. "Wow, so this is why you wanted to talk after hours, you're pregnant?" she said scanning the darkened tavern that saw its last patrons an hour earlier.

"Yes! That's what I just said."

"And you're grabbing for a beer?"

"Reflex, sorry."

"You're sure about this? Being pregnant, I mean."

"Yes, I'm sure."

"You went to the doctor?"

"Home test kit. Three times."

"And you haven't told Ray? Is it his?"

"Yes, he's the father, and no, I haven't told him yet!"

"You're sure?" Kelsey said with a wink and a grin, trying to lighten Leigh Anne's mood.

"He's the only one I've been with since I met him. Hell, he's the only one I've been with since I've been living here, smart ass!"

"Well, first off, no more beer or any alcohol for you. Have you had any since you found out?

"No! Don't make it sound like I'm a lush, ok?"

"Yeah, sorry. The second thing is, how far along are you?"

"I think I'm about three weeks, could be four, but I'm thinking more like three. I don't know, I'm not sure."

Kelsey came out from behind the bar and sat down on the stool next to Leigh Anne. "Why haven't you told him?"

"I was going to. I mean, at least I tried to. On Thanksgiving at his house. During dinner I couldn't, he had guests. His kids and a couple of coworkers. But all through dinner I kept playing it out in my head, ya know? What I'd say, what he'd say. And I just kept imagining it being this warm, fuzzy, romantic thing. I was feeling pretty good about it. Then after everybody left and it was just the two of us, I couldn't think straight. I didn't know how to bring it up and I started thinking about all sorts of stuff, and then…I totally panicked and just blew it."

"What? Like you just decided not to say anything?"

"No, I said plenty, just not what I should've said. I got all freaked out, became this big bag of hormones. I got all emotional. That must've looked real pretty. I think I suggested he had more in common with Stella Leone."

"Who's Stella Leone?"

"A nurse he works with at the medical center. She was there, at dinner."

"He invited another woman to dinner?"

"It's not like that. She lives with a guy who's always away on business. It was a last- minute thing. I told you, I just kinda panicked. I had no business bringing her into the discussion. But I did, and before I knew it, I pretty much backed him into a corner and gave him an ultimatum."

"You didn't tell him you're pregnant, you bring up another woman, and then you give him an ultimatum?"

"Yup, exactly. Ray must be wondering what kind of lunatic he's gotten involved with."

"Those hormones are pretty powerful. Remind me never to get pregnant. Girl, exactly what did you say to him?"

"I told him that I wanted to have a family. I told him if he wanted to continue to be with me that he needed to want to have a family too. And then to top it all off, I told him I was still moving back to Oahu." She looked at Kelsey and then stared off into the vacant dining room.

Kelsey sat quietly for a moment, then reached over the bar to grab the open bottle of porter and took a drink. "What is that?" She asked, wrinkling her nose and looked at the bottle. "You and Ray like this stuff?"

"It's an acquired taste. For a more refined palate."

"Uh huh." She put the bottle down. "I can't believe you told him that. What are you, out of your mind?"

"I know, I know, it was stupid. The words came out of my mouth before I even knew what I was saying. That wasn't the way I had imagined the conversation, ok?"

"So what were you going to say?"

"I was going to say..." Tears began to well up in her eyes. "I was going to say something like, well...first I was going to be sitting down next to him...on his bed, just the two of us..."

"Of course, just the two of you."

"We're sitting on his bed, I pick up his hand and kiss it, then I place it gently on my stomach. I hold it there, ya know? Kinda like this." She picked up Kelsey's hand and placed it on her abdomen to demonstrate. "And then I was going to say 'Ray, we're going to have a baby'."

"Hmm. That's nice. I can picture it. It is kinda romantic," Kelsey said as she slid her hand out from Leigh Anne's. "So how did you get from that to 'you're gonna father my children and you're moving with me to Oahu'? What the hell happened?"

"Like I said, I got hormonal, I got nervous, I began thinking about how my dad abandoned me and my mom when I was young. I thought about Kenny and how Father Dominick suggested that maybe I got pregnant when we were still in school to trap him into a relationship. I thought about his cheating and his admission that he never want... that he never wanted to be with me long-term and he never wanted Mahina." Leigh Anne began to cry. "I got scared. I didn't want to go through that again, not with Ray. After I found out that I was pregnant, I began to wonder if I wasn't...Oh, I don't know, Kelsey. I don't know, I'm confused, alright? So, instead of telling him what I should have, I ended up backing him into a corner and didn't tell him I was pregnant. I told him…I just told you what I told him."

Kelsey got off of her barstool and took Leigh Anne into her arms. "There, there sweet pea," she said, pulling her head into her shoulder.

"The thing is," Leigh Anne continued, "I honestly don't know if I had wanted to get pregnant when I was with Kenny. I wrestle with that one a lot. Maybe I did and that's why I got careless. But I definitely wanted to get pregnant now."

"Leigh," Kelsey said as she pushed her back to look into her eyes. "What are you saying?"

"I'm saying that I've wanted another child for some time now. I know what you're probably thinking, and I'm not trying to replace Mahina. Nothing will ever replace my baby. And…I know how it looks, but I'm not trying to trap Ray.

"And the yearly trips to Molokai? Are you telling me that it's a coincidence that they correspond with the anniversary of Mahina's death?"

"I don't deny that I go on retreat to St. Philomena's at the same time. Maybe part of it is guilt-driven. But I find great comfort in being there, and if it weren't for Father Dominick's counsel…anyway." She slid off her stool and walked over to the window. "After being with Ray this past year, I realized that I wanted him to be the father of this baby whether we stayed together or not. But I really don't wanna lose him. I guess I was afraid that once I go back to Hawaii, we'll end up drifting apart. Look, I know this sounds stupid, illogical, crazy…"

"You forgot to mention selfish, thoughtless, and did I mention selfish?" Kelsey said and then paused. "I'm sorry, that was mean of me. You're in love with the guy. I understand that. I also understand the fear and insecurity you have, based on what's happened to you in the past. But sweetie, if you really love the man as much as you say you do then you need to be straight with him. Seriously. Now listen to me. In my line of work, I get to see a lot of shit that guys pull with women, and let's be honest, women aren't all angels either. Are they?"

"No, I guess we're not."

"That's right we're not. I think I've become a very good judge of men, and not only can I tell that Ray is an honest, straight-forward kind of guy, I know he's in love with you. And you already know that. If you're straight with him and tell him you're having his baby, I know he's the kind of guy who would do the right thing, and not just because it's the right thing to do, but because he loves you. And I'll bet this bar and everything in it that he wouldn't be resentful at all. Not even for a second. I'll also bet he'll love you even more."

"Maybe you're right."

"I know I'm right. And another thing, As bad as you wanna go back home, if you love him as much as you say you do, you better be willing to compromise. You've got a good job here in Seattle that pays damn well. Ray's got a great little house, and hell, where else are you gonna find a sports bar as good as mine? Now," She said as she took some bar napkins and wiped away the tears on Leigh Anne's face, "why don't you drive on up to his house, apologize for that jackass ultimatum you gave him, and tell him the truth?"

"I can't."

"Whaddya mean, you can't?"

"He's not home, he flew back east. His dad had a bad fall, broke his hip, and now he's developed pneumonia."

"I'm sorry to hear that. So he called you?"

"No, I went up there earlier tonight after I got off work…to apologize for that jackass ultimatum and to tell him the truth. He had left a note for me. He didn't call, because I had also told him that we needed to take a break from each other."

"Hormones, right?" Kelsey said as they both nodded in agreement. "Just as well, now you've got some time to calm down and get your mind straight. As soon as he gets back, though, you better go talk to him."

3 8

The hallways, nurses' stations and rooms at the Tampa Bay Veterans Hospital looked and smelled the same as the Veterans' Medical Center in Seattle. The same sterile whitewashed walls, the same constant low-grade buzzing from flickering fluorescent bulbs in their final death throes, and the same hollow echo that rang through the long corridors with each step taken as Ray looked for room 312. He stopped at the small rectangular sign glued to the wall just outside the men's room. "Let's see, 300 to 310 is back the way I came," he whispered to himself. "311 to 320 is down this way." He spotted room 312 a few feet farther down the hallway and quietly walked in.

Ron Silver lay in bed in a semi–upright position. A green-tinted oxygen tube lay across his upper lip with two very small nozzles extending out of the tube into each nostril. An I V line of saline was sticking out of his left hand, and a small sensor clipped to his index finger was attached to the monitor displaying his heart rate. He was in a cast from his waist down to mid thigh. He slowly turned his head and smiled when he saw his son walk into the room. Ray grabbed a chair from the corner, and slid it over to the side of the bed, and sat down next to his dad. He took hold of his right hand and gently rubbed it. He smiled back at his father.

"Hey, Pop," he said softly. "I talked to the doctor, and he said you're coming along fine."

"What the hell do they know?" Ron said in a barely audible whisper. "They can't feel the pain that I have."

Ray got up to look for a chart and found one in the Plexiglas pocket on the door. He flipped through the pages as he sat back down. "Well, your numbers are looking good." He lied.

"It hurts to take a deep breath and my hip is killing me."

"According to the chart, a nurse should be coming by to give you…" Just then, a young nurse came into the room with a couple of small plastic cups. One with pills, the other with water. Ron smiled and winked at her. Ray thought she was gorgeous. "It's time for your medicine, Admiral Silver," she said with a sly smile.

Ray looked at his dad and mouthed "Admiral?"

"I'm Christine Cappolano," she said to Ray as she gave Ron his pills and the cup of water. "The Admiral had one heck of a fall, but the doctors say he's doing ok. It's just a hairline fracture and he should be out of his cast in two to three weeks." She waited until he swallowed each one.

"What the heck do they know?" Ron countered. "They can't feel my pain."

Nurse Cappolano looked at Ray and held out her hand for the chart, smiling as she took it from him. She recorded the time and the types of medicines she had administered. Then slid the diaphragm of a stethoscope under Ron's gown and listened to his heart and lungs.

"Chrissy," Ron whispered, "why are your hands always so cold?"

"You know what they say, cold hands, warm heart. Now be a good shipmate and take a deeeep breath, then exhale. Good, again. Innnn and out. Good." She recorded that too. While she took Ron's pulse, Ray stared at the outline of her ass, as her panty line was clearly visible through her scrubs. Without turning around, she said, "Like father, like son. Wouldn't you say, Dr. Silver?"

"Excuse me? You know who I am?"

"Your father told me all about you."

"Oh, I see. Obviously none of it good."

"Nope." She smiled again before she left. Ray looked at his dad, who now had a guilty look on his face. Ray excused himself and followed the nurse out into the hallway.

"Excuse me, Nurse Cappo…"

"Lano. Christine Cappolano."

"Nurse, I already talked with my dad's doctor. Before I say anything to my pop, do you know if he's been told everything?"

"Did you speak with his attending or with the oncologist?"

"The attending. I guess the results came back from the lab just a little while ago."

"We like to coordinate with the staff and have a counselor in the room at the same time the doctor gives this kind of news. I'm sure he went ahead and told you out of professional courtesy."

"Ok, thanks." He turned to go back into the room.

"Dr. Silver, I'd like to suggest that you wait for his doctor and the counselor before you say anything. As close as your relationship may be, you can never predict how someone will react once they're told."

"Agreed. Thanks, Nurse." Ray stood by the door for a moment before going back in. "So, Admiral Silver, you told her all about me, huh?"

"Just a little bit, what are ya worried about?"

"Admiral?"

"She calls everyone 'Admiral', I guess she's trying to distract us from staring at her body and getting all worked up."

"Does it work?"

"What do *you* think?"

"I think she doesn't call you 'Admiral'. I think you told her you'd been one."

"What? That's nuts."

"Really? I suppose you forgot that when you first moved into that retirement community, you introduced yourself to all the widows as a retired gynecologist?"

"I got a lot of dates." Ron tried to laugh but it was too painful.

"You're feeling like shit, huh?"

"Yeah, Raymond. I'm not doing too good."

"You'll be ok. It's gonna take you a long time to heal. Just do what the doctors and the nurses tell you and you'll get better."

"I don't need to look at a chart to know that what I'm feelin' isn't normal."

"You always were a smart man, Pop."

"So how bad is it?"

"I think you already know."

"How are the kids?"

"They're fine, Pop. They were home for Thanksgiving. They looked great."

"How 'bout that girlfriend of yours?"

"You know about her?"

"Your daughter told me all about her. She's that cute redhead who ran into you that time at that sports bar you go to. If it wasn't for Casey, I'd never know anything about you, if ya know what I mean."

"Yeah, I know what you mean. Leigh's just fine, Pop. She really is." Ray thought back to that second time he and Leigh Anne had run into each other. He remembered walking up to the back booth at Kelsey's to join his dad and the kids for lunch before turning to find Leigh Anne on his heels. Her shoulder-length hair, the freckles on her face, and her brown eyes were all so clear to him.

"Oh, um, excuse me, I didn't mean to sneak up on you like that."

"No... not at all. I wasn't... I mean I didn't...."

"I recognized you from Kimo's...In Hawaii...Well, I just recognized you, and I wanted to say hello."

"I'm in love with her, Pop. I'm thinking about asking her to marry me," Ray said as he looked over at his dad and noticed he had fallen asleep. Ray was exhausted. It had been days since he had a decent night's sleep. He leaned back in the chair, put his feet up on the end of the bed, closed his eyes, and thought about Leigh Anne. His hand came up to rub the spot on his nose and forehead where she had crashed into him that day, as if somehow he could still feel it.

"Oh, jeez!"

"Oh, man...damn, that hurt. You have a hard head, Doc."

"Hey, I'm sorry, I didn't expect you to whip around like that."

"Seems to be a common theme here this afternoon."

"You ok.?"

"Yeah, I'm just gonna have a bit of a headache, but I'll manage. You?"

"Yeah, I'll survive."

"Hey, I'm sorry about..."

"No, not a problem. It was an accident...well, I recognized you, and I... I thought it would be a nice thing to say hey, remember me? That's all."

"Yeah, I see. Well, uh... I do remember our meeting at that place by the beach...Kiki's? Kono's?"

"Kimo's"

"Kimo's, yeah. You already said that. Great place, really good food, and what a great location."

"Yeah, it is a great place. I'll tell my cousin that you liked it."

"So, uh...listen, does it have to be just a passing hello, remember me? Nice to see ya, goodbye? I mean, if it's ok with you...would you like to meet here for a Pipeline? Well, that is if you want. I promise I won't butt into your head or knock your beer over...You don't have t..."

"Sure, that would be nice...this week, ok?"

"Yeah, sure, this week."

3 9

"This is silly" Ron insisted. "I'll be alright here at home."

"With a full-time nurse!" Ray insisted for the third time.

"I told you, I don't want a stranger living in my house. They'll go through my stuff and steal things."

"Pop, that's nonsense. You've made good progress these past two weeks, but I've gotta get back home. I can't stay here any longer. I need to take care of some things. I really need to talk to Leigh face to face. And after a couple of weeks, I'll come back and spend more time with you. Now, the choices are simple. Option one, you can come back to Seattle with me and we'll work with the VMC over there. Two, you can get a live-in nurse who will take you to your sessions, make sure you take your meds, prepare your meals, help you bathe……"

"Nope, not an option. Unless, of course, you can get Nurse Cappolano to do it."

"Or, option three, you can go to the veterans assisted-living and rehab facility that's a block away from the hospital."

There was a long silence from Ron. His hip was healing albeit slowly, but the pneumonia he had developed on top of his emphysema was taking a toll on him. He was weak. Weaker than he'd ever been before, and it was hard for him to accept.

But until he got a little stronger, he couldn't start his chemo. "Maybe I'll stay here with a live-in, but under one condition."

"What's that?"

"Get that Nurse Chrissy to come visit me while I'm here," Ron laughed.

"Now I'm convinced you're gonna be ok. I'm glad you're gonna stay here. You'll be more comfortable in your own place."

"I'm gonna be making so many trips for rehab, I hope this is the right choice."

"If it's not, you can always switch. I'll make the phone calls in the morning and we'll get it all set up. And I'll leave a note for Nurse Cappolano to ask her if she wouldn't mind stopping by to check in on you. Ok?"

"Yeah," Ron said with a smile. "I appreciate you takin' the last two weeks to be with me."

"Not a problem. That's what family is all about, Pop. That's what you and mom always taught us as kids."

"Well, at least something took. I'm surprised you were able to get off work for this long."

"I've been meaning to talk to you about that. I've been there almost a year now, so I had all my sick days saved up, and I also have vacation time that they make you use. You know the government, use it or lose it, right?"

"Yeah, I guess."

"Anyway, I've got a few more weeks off, and since we'll have you all squared away I was thinking of taking a little trip," Ray said. Once the doctors had informed him of the nature of his father's cancer, he decided he wanted to help bring home the 606, if it was in fact his father's ship, and in spite of Abner's suspicions that Walters, Jeffries, and Peters might be CIA. "Unless, of course, you feel you need me to stay."

"No, you don't need to stay. I'm doing a lot better and I'll be ok with a live-in nurse."

"You sure? Because if you want me to stay two more weeks, I'll stay."

"Where you gonna be going on this trip of yours?"

"Midway"

"Midway? Midway Island? What for?"

"You know I've been volunteering on this LCI restoration. Well, some of those guys located an LCI in the Philippines. It's owned by a small fishing company and it's been part of their fleet for many years. Anyway, the story is they wanna upgrade and get a newer boat, so they need to sell the thing. They agreed to sail her to Midway, and Walters is gonna take the 776 out there. Kinda funny, huh? Meeting 'em halfway at Midway?"

"That's insane, Ray."

"Yeah, I thought so too. But I've got the time. It'll be a quick two weeks. You'll be in good hands, but if I need to get back here for any reason, I can easily fly back from Hawaii.

"Ray, I think it's insane, but I don't have the energy to fight with you." He let out a big sigh. "Ray, Ray, Ray. God gave you a head, son. Please use it."

"They're going anyway. I think it'll be a once in a lifetime experience to sail and live aboard an LCI." Ray looked at his dad who was quickly growing tired.

"Oh, it'll be a once in a lifetime experience alright."

"They think it might be the 606." Ray waited for a reaction.

"The 606 went to Argentina at the end of the war."

"That's what the official records say, but that's not where she ended up."

"How do you know it's the 606?"

"We don't know for sure, but we have pictures of the Filipino ship and even though the bow numbers are almost completely faded, the last two look like a zero and a six. She's got a round pilot house and side ramps."

"It could be the 506 or the 706."

"Yes, I know. But the guys wanna bring her back and restore her, or use her for parts if she's in too bad of shape. I'm just sayin' that it could be the 606."

"Ok, if that's what you want to do. I think you guys are nuts." Ron began to fade off to sleep. "Socks."

"You want a pair of socks? Are your feet cold?"

"No, my feet are fine. White socks with palm trees sewn on them. That's how you'll be able to tell if she's the 606."

"What are you talking about?"

"I left a pair of white socks onboard. Not on purpose. They hid them on me."

"Now *that's* nuts. What makes you think they'll be there after all these years?"

"I was always complaining that we could never get socks. We'd get tons of stuff from the supply ships during the war, but we never got any socks. So my cousin Ellen bought a few pair of white socks, knitted a palm tree on each one, and she mailed them to me. It took three months before I got `em. Anyway, some of the crew took a pair out of my locker when I was on duty in the engine room. Never saw them again."

"What makes you think they'd still be onboard?"

"After I was detached in November `45, one of the crew who was with me on the ship back to the States told me that he and a couple of other guys had hid `em in the ballast of troop three. As a joke."

"What's the ballast?"

"It's like a crawl space that you'd find underneath a house. There's an oval-shaped hatch cover in the deck plate with about, oh I don't remember, eighteen or twenty big nuts and bolts. You gotta get that cover off to have access to the ballast. They hid my socks there. If she's the 606, I'll bet my socks will be there."

"I'll check it out."

"I'm tired, I'm gonna get a little sleep."

"I've got one more thing I need to tell you, Pop. Please don't get mad at me."

"Raymond," Ron said as he closed his eyes, "the last time you said 'don't get mad at me' you smashed my new `70 Impala."

"That wasn't me, Pop. That was Frank. I didn't get my license until `74."

"Oh, yeah, that's right. All these years I thought it was you."

"The last time I asked you not to get mad at me was when I was in fifth grade and Lisa Marcus showed me her vagina."

Ron laughed so hard he began coughing up phlegm. Ray quickly scanned his father's bedroom and found a box of tissues. He pulled out a bunch and handed them to his dad. "You ok?"

"Oh God, it hurts to laugh. I'd forgotten all about that. That's pretty funny. Oh man, my chest is so sore now. Maybe you should stay a few more days." He looked at Ray.

"Ok, I'll stay four, five more days. Is that good?"

"Yeah, that's good."

"So you thought that was funny, huh? Too bad, you didn't think so back then."

"Yeah, well, I had to put on a show for your mother. She would've been upset with me if I didn't get upset with you."

"Pop, Jimmy helped me locate the family of Lieutenant Robert Lee Johnson. The skipper from…"

"The 606, yeah I know. That's a name I'll never forget."

"He had a daughter and she lives in Virginia. In Fairfax. Jimmy took a ride down there to talk to her."

"Raymond, for God's sake, whaddya up to?"

"Pop, I know what happened on the 606. I know what happened at Peleliu and what you did."

"Raymond, what are doing sticking your nose where it don't belong?"

"Pop, you did some pretty amazing things that day. You did some pretty amazing things when Johnson left you stranded on that island. He kept the log book when he was reassigned to another duty station. That's why no one ever knew what you did. Johnson made a deathbed confession to his daughter several years ago. He told her the whole story. Jimmy got the log book from her and turned it over to the Navy. They investigated, spoke to sailors and Marines who witnessed what you did, both on the ship and on Peleliu with the 5th Marines. I even heard it straight from Abner."

"You know A.J.?"

"Yeah, Pop. I know all about your special griddlecakes. He even made some for me. They were good , but not as good as yours." Ray looked at his father and noticed the tears filling up in his eyes. "Pop, I spoke to Jimmy a few days ago to update him on your condition, and he told me that the Navy is going to award you the Bronze Star for your actions on the battlefield." Ron covered his eyes as the tears flowed. "Please don't be mad at me, Pop. You may not want any recognition, but you're a hero, and what's more, you know it. You deserve this honor." Ray placed his hand on top of his fathers'. Ron slowly pulled his hand free and placed it on top of his son's.

4 0

Ray stopped at a food concession stand as he made his way down the long corridor to the gate. He had a good fifteen minutes before his flight started boarding and he was thirsty. Even in December, the humidity in Florida was more than he was used to. Scanning the refrigerated case, he knew the chances were very slim that he would find a Pipeline or even a Longboard lager, but he was hoping to at least find a microbrew from the Pacific Northwest. No such luck. He did see an assortment of Colonial Boston's that made him think of Stella.

"It's been three weeks. I better call her. I'll bet she's pissed at me" Ray thought as he reluctantly selected a pale ale.

"That'll be eight dollars please," said the cashier.

"Eight dollars? What, for one beer?" Ray said in surprise.

"You're buying a handcrafted microbrew in an airport, pal, whadja expect?"

"Yeah, right, handcrafted?"

"Eight dollars, please."

Digging through his wallet for a five and three singles, he saw the cashier fiddling with the plastic tip cup next to the register. "Dream on," he muttered as he laid out the exact amount and walked off without waiting for a receipt. "Fuckin' eight dollars for a beer." He mumbled and reminded himself to call

Stella. He stopped at the end of the corridor as it opened up to the large circular area that housed a half-dozen gates and fished out his boarding pass from the side pocket of his sport jacket. Looking up and finding gate seven, he headed over to the waiting area and settled into a seat. He took a long drink and was reminded of Chuck downing a pint of Pepsi. *"Ahh, that's good stuff, pallie!"*

He thought for a minute, looking at the picture of Boston's Old North Church on the label, and made his call.

"Hey, I was wondering when I was gonna hear from you."

"Sorry. I had to leave in a hurry."

"You were only suspended indefinitely. That doesn't make you a fugitive, Ray."

"Ha ha, very funny."

"You ok? By the way, where are you?"

"Tampa. I've been taking care of my dad. It's a long story."

"Is he alright?"

"No. He's not. At best he's got a few months."

"I'm so sorry Ray."

"Thanks…So, what's going on there?"

"Well, you're still on suspension. A good number of the staff want to throw a party for you. Off the grounds, that is. Our friend Bill Harrison wants to have you charged with assault when you get back, but nobody who was in 288 that day, except maybe McCain, will say they saw you knock him out. But even he's having second thoughts."

"Something going on that I should know about?"

"Anybody ever tell you that you've got one hellofa combination right cross, left upper cut?"

"I had no idea until I hit our boy Bill. I didn't get into many fights when I was a kid. And when I did, people said my arms looked like one of those paddlewheel boats. Hey look, I'll be boarding my plane in a few minutes and I just wanted to touch base. I wanna apologize to you for decking Harrison."

"Apologize? What, are you kidding me? Ray, knocking him out was a blessing in disguise. You not only busted his nose, you also gave him a concussion."

"That's one heck of a blessing."

"No, really, check this out. Harrison was off his feet for almost two weeks. The hospital had to split up his active cases among three other docs. They began to see a pattern of impropriety almost immediately. So, just this past week the head of ortho, Brian Davis, called a meeting with the docs handling his cases, the nurses that were assigned to Harrison's patients, the head of pharmacy and the head ortho nurses."

"So you were there."

"Yup. I was there, and the timing couldn't have been more perfect. I had to speak up or lose the opportunity. After Thayer and Araghi made their presentations, I told them everything and handed over what I had. I told them how he first brought you those 'dead' files and about you bringing your observations to me. I told them how I became suspicious after what I was seeing in his notes so I began gathering information."

"That was risky."

"Trust me, there wasn't going to be a better opportunity to do this. Besides, you know I made copies of everything. And that's in addition to the disks I left with you. Ray, you should've seen it. Their jaws dropped to the floor."

"So what happens now?"

"Well, 'Wild Bill' is on administrative leave. The VMC is launching an investigation into him as well as the Visor rep. Depending on what they find, it's possible that this thing could get to a congressional sub-committee hearing and possibly go all the way to the DOJ."

"Don't count on it. I'll bet most, if not all of Congress is getting big campaign contributions from the pharmaceutical lobby."

"Maybe so, but enough people are looking into this now. I'll be surprised if it just dies."

"And what about you?"

"Whaddya mean? Credit? I don't want any credit."

"Backlash. I'm talking about backlash. How's this gonna affect you?"

"I don't think it will. Should it?'

"Don't get me wrong, I think all this is wonderful. You're right, the timing couldn't have been better. But once the investigation gets underway, they're gonna be asking you a ton of questions, like why did you wait so long to say anything to anyone? Were there any patient deaths that could have been avoided while you took your time gathering information? And let's not forget about how you got the information in the first place."

"Relax, I've got it covered. The first rule of being a government employee is CYA. Cover your ass. Which is probably why there's so much redundancy, or why it takes years to get anything done, for that matter. I'll just tell them that I didn't say anything until now because all I had were suspicions. I didn't want to risk damaging a doctor's reputation because of a suspicion. Second, as head nurse, and because of those suspicions, I chose to review his patient charts, past and present, in order to monitor my nurses and to make sure they were performing up to and above standard. Third, because I was reviewing records *after* hours, on *my time*, whenever I suspected improper prescribing practices, I brought my concerns to the on-call doctor and asked him or her to review, correct, or change any prescription that seemed excessive or conflicting with other meds the patient was taking."

"Damn, girl. You're good! "

"If you only knew," she sighed."Look, I've been burned before. Like I said, CYA."

"But one thing. When Harrison reviewed his charts, wouldn't he have seen that his treatment protocols had been changed?"

"By all appearances, every one of his patients had been given the same treatment protocol. It looks like it became so automatic for him that once his chart entry was made, he must've felt there was no need to review his notes. Or perhaps he did review them, but didn't question any changes that others' had made out of fear he would then have to explain what he was doing."

"And the docs making these changes, wouldn't they have been concerned enough to approach him?"

"Looking at one file as an isolated incident, you don't see a pattern of abuse or incompetence. Also, you have to understand that mistakes are commonplace in this profession. They're not intentional. They just happen. Humans make mistakes. Thankfully, we catch them most of the time before someone gets hurt or killed."

"Yeah, and sometimes the mistakes don't get caught and someone does die. But that's another story altogether, isn't it?

"Yes, it is."

"Stel, you've done a great job. You're very smart. You've done your homework. But they're gonna be asking you a bunch of questions as part of a formal investigation. I'm sure I'll be getting called as well. Do me a favor, will ya?"

"Sure, what?"

"I don't want you to take this on alone when it gets to that next level. I know you're the one who's been doing all the work and really sticking your neck out on this. I'm not looking to piggyback for any credit, but I don't want you to go any further into this without backup."

"Ray, I know you support me, you don't have to..."

"No, I want to. I think there are still gonna be some people who may try to take you down."

"I appreciate it Ray, but like I said, I've been there before. I know what I'll be up against."

"Even so, Stel. I wanna stand with you on this. Back you up and all that."

"I don't know. You're already in hot water as it is. Let me think about it, ok?"

"Fair enough. You hear from Abner?"

"Yes, just the other day, as a matter of fact. He's doing fine. He was upset for a little while, but he decided that he was going to go on that trip with that old ship you guys have been working on."

"What? He's going?"

"He said he had nothing else to do and they needed someone to cook for them. They'll be leaving in a couple of days."

"Ok, thanks." He let out a sigh. "I'll be back late tonight. We'll talk more in the next day or two."

"You know you're not allowed on VMC property, right?"

"Yeah, McCain made that perfectly clear."

"Hey listen, I'm glad you called. If you don't mind, I'd like to stop by your place sometime tomorrow. I've been wanting to talk to you about something."

"Face to face, huh?

"Yeah. Face to face. If that's alright?"

"How 'bout noon?"

"Sounds good. See ya then."

"Yeah, see ya soon." Ray ended the call and looked down at the brown bottle in his hand. He took a long drink of his Colonial and thought that it was a decent tasting beer, but he was definitely hooked on Pipeline. Then he thought about Leigh Anne and hit number three on the speed dial. *"Hey, this is Leigh. I'm not available right now so leave a message at the beep. Mahalo."*

"Hey Leigh…I know we're taking a break from each other…which is kinda why I haven't been leaving any voicemails. I just wanted to hear your voice message. I wanted to let you know that, just in case you were wondering why you saw my number on your caller I D. Um… I saw that you tried to call a few times as well, and I'm thinking that it was in response to that. Sorry I missed them. The hospital staff kept making me shut off my phone during visiting hours. Silly rules. Anyway, thought you'd like to know that I got my dad squared away. I'm actually at the airport in Tampa. My flight's boarding any minute now. I was curious how you've been and if you'd heard from the university,"

"Trans Western flight 1241 with non-stop service to Seattle is now boarding at gate seven. At this time we will begin seating all first class, premier VIP gold members, and families with small children. Please have your boarding pass ready for the gate agent…"

"Uh Leigh, you probably heard that. We're boarding, so I gotta go. These past three weeks away have seemed like it's been forever. I'm hoping we can talk when I get back. Love ya, and…I miss you."

41

The electronic voice on the answering machine indicated only one new message, although the caller ID showed four phone calls from the same number—Leigh Anne's. Nine calls in total, when he counted the ones made to his cell phone.

"Hey. Got your message. Sorry that we're playing phone tag. I've been calling you as well, as you already know. I wanted to talk to you and not to a mailbox. Ray, I'm real sorry about your dad. Take whatever time you need. I was looking forward to getting together as soon as you got back, but believe it or not, I've gotta head down to Coos Bay, Oregon. Actually, I was bored, so I volunteered. I don't know if you heard about that oil spill off the coast. Happened two days ago. Not a big one, but looks like it will have an effect on the wildlife. Anyway, I'm heading up a team to do an impact study and to see where else we can help. It'll be at least a week. No word yet from UH. It's frustrating. I can't wait to see you. Love ya."

"Can't wait to see you too," Ray said as he looked at his calendar and circled the day Leigh Anne would return—if she was indeed gone the full seven days.

"The 776 is leaving the day after tomorrow," he thought. "Should be a two-week trip, give or take a day or two. If I go, I'll be back in mid-January. She'll definitely be here. The university hasn't called her, there's no way she's gonna be going. Well, not right away at least. But of course they could call her last minute. What are the chances of that happening? It would've been nice to spend New Years with her. Hmm, I can still do that. What is it, a six, seven-hour drive down to Coos Bay? Yeah, but I'll just end up getting in her way. Don't wanna distract her from her work. Not with what I want to tell her. But if I do go, I'll miss the opportunity to sail with the 776. But what if Abner's right about Walters and Jeffries? We'll just have to see, won't we?"

He picked up his cell to call Leigh Anne, but noticed the late hour on the time display. "I can call and leave a message, but it'd be better to talk to her. If I call now, I might wake her up. Call!" He hit the number three on the speed dial but before it rang, he ended the call. Ray walked over to the bookcase and browsed his collection of DVDs. *"Run Silent Run Deep?* Nope. *Destination Tokyo?* No. *Operation Pacific?* Hmmm… John Wayne, Patricia Neal. Yup, this'll do." Ray put on the movie and laid down on the couch, continuing his debate between driving seven hours to see Leigh Anne or packing a duffle bag for his first ocean voyage.

He never made it past the opening credits. It was midnight. He couldn't quiet his mind. He couldn't sleep, couldn't watch television. "Too much to do," he thought. He went into the workshop and sent out an email to his kids, updating them on their grandfather and informing them of his intentions as well as his immediate plans. "That'll raise some eyebrows!" He clicked the "send" button. He then wrote out a note to the neighbor girl who had been feeding Magic. He stuffed it, along with some cash, into an envelope and taped it to the front door of her house. On his way back, Magic was sitting on the front step waiting for him. "You're home early," he said as he picked her up. She buried her head into the side of his neck. "What, no action tonight? Don't be mad at me, but this is just a one-day rest stop. I'm gonna be off again." As they entered the house she jumped from his arms and headed for the fireplace. "Sorry, Madge. No fire tonight. Let's see what we have in the fridge." She followed him into the kitchen. "Sorry again,

Kitty, I've been away too long. There's really nothing in here."
He opened a box of dry cat food and poured a small amount
into a dish. Magic pounced on it and began crunching away.
She was either starving, although she looked well-fed, or not
used to receiving a midnight snack. Either way, she was going
to devour every last morsel before Ray could change his mind.
Her chewing almost drowned out the ringing of his cell phone.
He immediately thought about his dad as he quickly felt his
pockets. They were empty. "Phone, phone, where's the freakin'
phone? Living room couch!" He ran to answer it before it went
to voicemail.

"Hello, this is Ray."

"Dad? Casey."

"Oh, hey Kiddo. It's pretty late. What is it three-forty-five
over there? You ok?"

"Yeah, oh-three-forty-five hours. I'm ok. Just saw your,
ahem...email."

"Whaddya doing up this late? This early, I mean."

"Midnight shift. Dad, you're going through some sort of
midlife thing, right?"

"No! At least I don't think so."

"Have you thought about this? I'm serious, have you taken
the time to think this out?"

"Are you referring to the first thing or the second thing?"

"Both actually."

"Yes, I thought this out. Can I count on your support?"

"Yeah, sure you can. As crazy as I think this is, you know
you've got my support and my love."

"Thanks, kiddo. You've got all the information on your
grandfather in that email I just sent. Just in case."

"Got it. When do you leave?"

"Day after tomorrow. No, wait, it's already past midnight,
so, tomorrow morning around Six o'clock, I mean, oh-six-hun-
dred. So, oh-nine-hundred your time."

"Ya know the Enterprise is also leaving tomorrow."

"Yeah, I know. You get a chance to speak to your brother?"

"Yeah, we spoke last night. You?"

"Yes, of course. Yesterday afternoon."

"Daddy?"

"What?"

"You're crazy, you know that?"

"Yeah…I know."

4 2

Ray couldn't sleep. There was too much to do before he left. He spent the rest of the morning going through his mail, paying bills, doing laundry, and sorting through his suitcase—repacking the essentials into a canvas duffle bag. He tried calling Leigh Anne around eight and twice again at nine, but couldn't get through. "Most probably in a dead zone," he thought after a third try.

Stella showed up at the front door at ten with suitcases in hand. "I hope you don't mind that I came early. I know we agreed on noon. Is this an ok time?"

"Yeah, this works."

"I've got some boxes in the back seat of my car," she said.

Ray took the bags from her and showed her in. "Is this what you meant by face to face?"

"Yeah. I'm hoping this is ok. If not, I could go to a hotel."

"Don't be silly. Did you have breakfast yet?"

"No, but don't do anything on my account."

"I haven't eaten yet and I'm starved, but I've got nothing here. I'll get those boxes out of your car and then we'll take a ride down to Kelsey's. She's got a great weekend breakfast menu. We can talk there."

* * *

Kelsey was surprised to see Ray after his three-week absence. "Hey stranger, what's up?"

"You got a few hours?" He grinned as he led Stella over to the bar, careful to make sure she didn't sit on Leigh Anne's usual stool. He took that one for himself.

"That bad?"

"No, just an endless saga, ya know? Kelse, this is my friend and coworker, Stella Leone."

Kelsey raised an eyebrow. "Whoa," she thought. "So that's Stella Leone!" The two women shook hands. "Have you spoken to Leigh?" she said as she continued to look at Stella.

"I just got in last night but we've been playing phone tag. I know she left yesterday morning for Coos Bay."

"So she hasn't told you?"

"Told me what?"

Kelsey realized she shouldn't have asked that question.

"Ah...when she's coming back? She hasn't said when she's coming back?"

"She said she'd be away for about a week."

"Oh, good, good. Very good...menus?" She held up one in each hand.

"That'll be great, and coffee please. Stel?"

"Yes, coffee sounds wonderful, thank you." Kelsey grabbed three mugs and filled them. Stella watched her pour without so much as a drop missing its target. "You come here a lot?" she asked Ray.

"Yeah, quite a bit, I guess. I told you how I first met Leigh Anne in Hawaii, but this is where we literally bumped into each other for the second time. Leigh knows Kelse from when they were little kids."

"That's right," Kelsey agreed as she took a sip from her mug. "Whoa, that's bad. Don't drink that." She took the mugs and waved a waitress over. "Please dump this and get me a fresh pot." She turned back to Ray and Stella and apologized. "I'm sorry. The staff knows better than to leave old stuff lying around." The waitress placed a fresh pot of coffee on the bar and Kelsey filled three clean mugs. "Here ya go. Now where were we? Oh yeah, we moved to Hawaii from Kansas when I was eight. My dad was stationed at the Marine base not too far from Kaneohe, and on my first day of second grade, Leigh was the first one to sit with me at lunch. We've been friends ever since. You could say we're kinda like sisters. So, what are you in the mood for?"

"I'll have my usual, I guess."

"Oatmeal and whole-wheat toast, no butter. Very imaginative, Ray. And you?"

"The Eggs Benedict with sausage sounds good," Stella handed back the menu.

"Good for you, hon." Kelsey stuck out her hand for Ray's menu. She looked at him and smiled. "I like her already. As long as you don't eat like this guy you're welcome here anytime."

After breakfast, Ray and Stella both nursed a third cup of coffee and talked. "The eggs were really good. I didn't realize how hungry I was. She seems like good people."

"Who, Kelsey? Yeah, she is. She really busts her butt in this place too."

"That's understandable. Her name's on the door."

"So how did you find out that Robert had a wife and daughter in London?"

"My ex, Griffin Kelley. He's with the NSA, and as coincidence would have it they, along with the FBI, had been investigating Bob's international business dealings when some red flags came up."

"So he called you, just like that?"

"I called him, actually. Some months back I ran into a dead end trying to get info on Harrison's connection with Visor, so I called Griff and asked for a favor. That's when he told me Bob was being investigated. Then, a few days ago Griff showed up at the VMC to tell me about Bob's business dealings as well as his family in London."

"Wow, he flew out here just to tell you that? I'm impressed."

She looked at Ray and smiled "After that initial phone call, which included his taking responsibility for our marriage failing, we began to talk more. A phone call here, a phone call there. Things have started to rekindle, a little. We'll see where that goes. Regardless, and to be perfectly honest, I had been thinking of leaving Bob for quite some time. There just wasn't anything there for me, emotionally speaking. So when Griff came across this info, I wasn't shocked or surprised, or even hurt. Actually, I was kinda glad. It suddenly became that much easier to pack up and get out. Plus, Griff saw it as a good excuse to come out here to see me." She paused and studied the features on Ray's face. "I wish it could have been us," she thought as she watched him take another sip of coffee. "So anyway," she continued aloud, "I was wondering if I could use your guest room for a few weeks or, until I find a nice place."

"Of course, not a problem," he said as Kelsey came by to warm the coffee.

"You do have two bathrooms in your place, don't ya, Ray?" she said, looking at both of them.

"Yes, I do. But I won't be there for awhile so it's not an issue."

"No, no, Ray," Stella said, placing her hand on top of his. "I don't want you to have to go somewhere else. If that's the case, I'll just find another place to stay."

"No, I'm not going somewhere else because of you. I've decided to take that trip with the 776. We leave at six tomorrow morning."

"Wait." Kelsey put the coffee pot down on the bar. "Where are you off to?"

"Midway Island, in the Pacific. With a bunch of my fellow naval buffs."

"Ray, that's nuts!" Both Stella and Kelsey exclaimed in unison.

"Ray," continued Kelsey, "Leigh is gonna be back in a few days and she's been wanting to talk to you. You should stay."

"She'll be back in a week, and I'll be gone for two. One week out and one week back."

"Ray, you two haven't seen each other in three weeks and the both of you have been playing phone tag. She really wants to talk to you. You should stay."

"I know it's been three weeks. Trust me, I've been thinking about her every day. I was hoping we were gonna be together today, but she had to go do this thing in Oregon and I understand that. I've got this opportunity that may never come again. I'll be back in two weeks."

"No, Ray," Kelsey insisted. "You don't understand."

"Kelse, I appreciate your concern. Trust me, Leigh knows I've been working on this project and she'll understand too. Look it," he said, pulling an envelope out of his jacket pocket. "Early this morning I wrote out this long letter addressing her concerns. I'm leaving it here with you. When she gets back next week, please see that she gets it. Once we sail tomorrow, I'll be trying to call her as long as we're within cell phone range. We should be heading south along the coast before we head west. I'm very confident that I'll finally get through to her."

Kelsey was biting her lip. She wanted to tell him that he was going to be a father, but Leigh Anne had sworn her to secrecy before she left for Coos Bay.

"A letter?" She picked it up from the bar. "A letter is not the same as you being here. You really should stay."

Ray got up from his stool and took another sip from his mug. "Kelsey, I see why Leigh feels you're like a sister. You're very protective of her, and that's one of the things I love about you. Now, if you ladies will excuse me, I gotta go give back some of this coffee." He smiled as he walked off to the men's room.

Stella took one look at Kelsey and waited until Ray was out of earshot, "Leigh's pregnant, isn't she."

"Yes. She's been wanting to tell him, so please don't say anything."

" 'Been wanting' to tell him? How far along is she?"

"By my calculations, I'd say six, maybe seven weeks."

"Almost two months? What the fu…"

"I know, I know, it sounds crazy. But in her defense, she didn't find out until a little over three weeks ago, and the two of them have been playing phone tag ever since."

"Well, he's about to leave tomorrow for another two-week trip. We should say something."

"I know, you're right, but she made me promise that I wouldn't say anything to him if he showed up before she got back." Before Stella could respond, Kelsey added, "You heard me try to get him to stick around."

"Yeah, I caught that. Let's call her, I mean, you call her."

"And say what?"

"Call her and tell her Ray's here, and then hand him the phone."

Kelsey smiled and nodded as she dug her cell out of the front pocket of her jeans. She quickly dialed and got nothing. "She must be in a bad cell area or something."

"Try again. Maybe if you get closer to the window," Stella said.

Kelsey agreed and came out from behind the bar—looking over her shoulder for Ray. She dialed again and heard ringing through the static.

"Leigh? It's Kelsey. Is this a good time?... I said is this a good time?...Is this a...damn, I lost her. I'll try again." She dialed and both women anxiously looked toward the bathroom door. "Leigh? Hey, it's Kelsey."

"Hey Ke...wha...p?"

"Leigh, you're breaking up. Can you hear me?"

"Yeah...bits and...ces"

"Look, Ray's here. You should talk to him. You need to tell him." She yelled into the phone, as if doing so would compensate for the bad reception.

"Tell me what?" Ray said, coming out of the bathroom.

"Oh, uh...Leigh called. I have her on the phone now, but the reception's bad. She said she misses you. So I'm telling her that you're here and she should tell you...that she misses you." She handed him her phone.

"Leigh, hey, it's Ray." He looked over at Kelsey and Stella "God, there's so much static."

"Ray...so...to...your voice...been...call...weeks."

"What? Baby, I'm getting every third word."

"I've...trying to...you...ry...got...thing to te..."

"Hey, this isn't working. I don't know if you can hear me, but I really can't hear you, so please just listen. I'm gonna sail with the 776 tomorrow. We'll be gone about two weeks. I left a long note for you with Kelsey, but when I get back we'll talk. There's a lot I've gotta tell you, and I know you'll be...Leigh? Hello? Leigh?...Damn, I've lost her." Ray handed the phone back to Kelsey. She turned to Stella with a look that said "I tried".

Later that evening, Ray made one more attempt to call Leigh Anne only to get her voicemail. He repeated what he had tried telling her earlier. Then he called his dad to check in on him. Their conversation was brief, and although Ron sounded a little better compared to the way Ray had left him less than two days before, he had already known there wasn't going to be much, if any change. Given his dad's situation, Ray was confident he was in excellent hands. Ron also expressed pleasure that Chrissy Cappolano had already come by to check up on him.

He looked through his duffle bag one more time to make sure he didn't forget anything, then stepped into his bathroom to get ready for bed. There was a knock on his bedroom door as Stella stuck her head in. "Is it ok if I come in?"

"Sure. I'm just getting ready for bed. I'll be out in a minute."

"Nine o'clock. It's kind of early, isn't it?"

"I haven't been getting much sleep lately and last night was no different. I wanna leave here around five, so I was hoping to get a few hours. Are you comfortable with where everything is?"

"Yeah, I made some notes and did a walk-through on my own."

"And you're sure you don't mind feeding the cat?"

"Oh, geez, no. It's the least I can do." She sat down on his bed. "Ya know, I feel kinda funny saying this, but I figure we're both adults, and, well, I like you, Ray. You've always been very respectful and thoughtful, not to mention kind." She brushed her hand across the top of his pillow.

He came out of the bathroom wiping his face with a towel and smiled at her. "Thank you, that's very kind. I like you too, Stel. A lot. I hope that doesn't make you feel uncomfortable. It's been very easy to be nice to you. In spite of the differences we have in our approach to healthcare, you were the first one at the VMC to give me the benefit of the doubt, and you went out of your way to help me transition there. I've always appreciated that. And over the past few months, I've really looked forward to your coming down to my dungeon for your coffee breaks."

"Why are you going on this trip? Really. And please don't tell me because it's a once in a lifetime opportunity."

"The other thing that I've always admired about you is that you always get straight to the point. You don't dance around an issue."

"That's my inner Boston. You still have a little bit of the northeastern 'goodness' in you as well. But I can see that your years out here have mellowed you some."

"Tell that to Bill Harrison's face," Ray said as he went back into the bathroom.

"Like I said, a little bit of that 'goodness' is still in you. It's good to see that you can bring it out when needed. So, why are you going?"

"For one thing, I'm antsy from not really doing anything these past few weeks."

"No, that's not the real reason. Come on Ray, just tell me, I'm not gonna pass judgment on you." She yawned and laid down, facing the bathroom door.

"There isn't just one reason. It is true that I'm bored. Ya know, my whole life I've always felt like there's gotta be something more than what there is. When I think of something that I want or when I feel I'm missing something, I go after it. I gotta have it, ya know what I mean? But when I get it, I don't feel the satisfaction to the level that I thought I would. I'm always asking myself 'Is that all there is? What's next?' I guess that's part of it. There's also this part of me, well, it's kind of hard for me talk about, but there's this part of me that feels guilty for not having done my part like my grandfather, my uncle, my pop and especially my brother Frank. Don't get me wrong, I'm not trying to be like my brother Frank. Although it has been suggested to me that's exactly what I'm trying to do. I just want to do my part is all. It's funny, I thought I would finally feel that sense of contributing when I got to the VMC. But that didn't do it. Perhaps bringing home the 606 will help. And perhaps I just need to have my head examined." He turned off the light and came out of the bathroom. Stella had fallen asleep in his bed.

4 3

At five a.m., John Walters was busy running down the final checklist prior to giving Chuck the order to start the engines. When he did give the order, the residents along the eastern rise of Queen Anne Hill were awakened one more time by the obnoxious chugging and plumes of exhaust from 776's eight turbo-charged diesel engines. And while they cursed Walters and his crew, he suspected it was going to be the last time they would be inconvenienced. He grabbed Chuck by the arm as they passed each other in front of a storage closet in the main passageway. "Come here, Chuck. I wanna show you something." Walters pulled back the black curtain covering the small closet and showed him ten cartons of Tareyton cigarettes neatly stockpiled along with a couple of cases of chocolate bars, chewing gum, playing cards, bars of soap, and toilet paper. "Your brand, right?"

"Yeah. You got those for me?"

"And anyone else who wants `em."

"Hey that's great, pallie. I brought a carton as well, but thanks."

"You check our fuel?"

"She's topped off at 130 tons with 200 gallons of lube oil. I'm set on my end."

"Good job. As soon as we're set to fire `em up I'll let you know." He continued to go through his checklist. On the bulletin board mounted in the main passageway just outside the galley door Walters posted a typed list that served as a roster with duty assignments. He also posted a separate sheet for bunk assignments. The five additional names on the list were the men Jeffries had said he would be bringing. They were much younger and in better physical condition than Walters' volunteers. They went only by their last names, and made bunk with their "supplies" in Troop compartment one—separate from everyone else.

TENTATIVE STATIONS/WATCH SCHEDULE (SUBJECT TO CHANGE)

Name	Station	Watch
Walters, J.	Helm/Lookout	0600 -0930/1200-1530
Scott, S.	Helm/Lookout	0900-1230/1500-1830
Thompson	Helm/Lookout	1800-2130/0000-0330 (lookout 2130-0030)
Jeffries, B.	Helm/Lookout	2100-0030/0300-0600 (lookout 0030-0245)
Shimkin, C.	Engine	0600-0845/1130-1345
Warren, D.	Engine	0830-1130/
Lipton, S.	Engine	1330-1600/1830-2115
Brewster	Engine	1600-1845 (lookout 1845-2130)
Martin	Engine	2100-2400/0300-0615
Gray	Engine	0000-0315 (lookout 0315-0600)
Peters, j.	Radio	0600-0930 (lookout 0930-1100)
Richards	Radio	0930-1300/0300-0600
Warren, D.	Radio	1300-1600/1900-2200
Walters, J.	Radio	1600-1900
Lipton, S	Radio	2200-0100 (lookout 1600-1700)
Brewster	Radio	0100-0330
Lewis, A.	Galley	0600-0900/1100-1300/1630-1830
Scott, S	Galley assist	0600-0830
Shimkin, C.	Galley assist	1600-1800

BUNK ASSIGNMENTS

CO's Quarters	Jeffries/Walters
Junior Officer's Qtrs.	Lipton/Peters
Troop Officers Qtrs.	Lewis/Scott/Shimkin/Warren
Troop1	Brewster/Gray/Martin/Richards/Thompson

Almost everyone had arrived early. For the first time since the original restoration began, the mood onboard was serious. Abner's CD player was silent as he went about his business, stowing all the extra foodstuffs that had been delivered the night before. Steve Scott was busy in the radio room finishing the installation of a backup GPS unit, and Tex Warren was double-checking the wiring on a backup radio he had added in the pilot house. With fully operational communications in the radio shack, the pilot house, and in the conning station, Walters had the option of keeping a radioman on station or leaving that decision to the on-duty helmsman. He would make that call based on weather conditions and crew fatigue. The extra radios would also allow Jeffries the privacy he would need when it came time to make contact with Rat Pack.

The five new men Jeffries brought were busy loading their own supplies into the storage compartment forward of Troop one. They kept the pleasantries to a minimum, and almost immediately Abner, Tex and Steve felt uncomfortable by their presence. Each man had a job to do though, and save for the occasional five-minute coffee break, they stayed on task as they readied the ship for departure.

* * *

Ray woke about ten minutes before his alarm was set to go off. He carefully leaned over to his nightstand to disengage the clock radio so it wouldn't wake Stella. He thought it would have been silly to wake her up the night before, just to tell her to go back to sleep in the guest room, but he did lay awake for a good fifteen minutes debating whether he should be the one to go to the other room or if he could get through the night sleeping on his side of the bed.

"This is nuts, nothing is going to happen. We're both adults. So what if she's wearing nothing but a nightgown? A very short nightgown. She's sound asleep. And I'm just gonna lie down on my side of the bed and do the same." Ray had quietly walked over to shut off the light and carefully lowered himself so that he was face-up on his side of the bed. Slowly placing his interlaced fingers to cradle the back of his head, he had looked to his left and watched Stella sleep before closing his eyes. "This isn't right," he thought. "I better go sleep in the guest room." Without warning, she had rolled over toward him. Her arm came across his chest and her leg interlocked with his. He had to admit he liked it as he lie there thinking of how he was going to get up in the morning without waking her. He didn't know how long she had remained in that position, but when his eyes opened the next morning she had rolled back over to the other side. He thought it best not to say anything.

Ray quietly dressed, checked his duffle bag one more time, and tiptoed into the kitchen to call for a cab. He saw Magic waiting outside and opened the front door to let her in. "Come here, you little fur ball," he whispered, picking her up and giving her a big hug and a kiss. "Come, I'll feed you before I go." They walked over to the garage, and Ray set out a fresh bowl of tuna for his cat. She was starved and gave the breakfast her full attention. He ran his hand over the plywood top of his "custom made" desk as he glanced at the pictures of his grandfather, Uncle Jim, his dad, Frank, and the kids. He smiled. "Well, guys, it's my turn to go to sea."

As he began to walk back through the garage to the house, Ray noticed the case of Pipeline Porter sitting on a storage shelf. He took out a six-pack and placed it into the small refrigerator under the work bench. "I'm gonna want a few cold ones when I get back." He patted the hood of his Wrangler as he walked out the door.

"Were you going to leave without saying goodbye?" Stella said from the top step at the front of the house.

"I was debating it. I was afraid to wake you."

"Because I fell asleep in your bed and you thought I'd be embarrassed?"

"Yeah, something like that."

"You know that wasn't my intention. To sleep with you, that is."

"Yeah, I know. You didn't have to say that."

"You amaze me, Ray Silver."

"Who, me? Hell, I'm just your average Joe."

"I'm not so sure about that. Your *average* Joe wouldn't have had such self-control. Hell, I would've jumped you if I didn't know you were gonna be a… a gentleman all the time," she said as the cool morning breeze played with her nightgown, highlighting her physical attributes.

"It's not like I haven't thought about it, Stel."

"But?" She watched him unable to find an answer. "Let me ask you something, and I'd like a straightforward, honest answer. This is between you and me, ok?"

"Ok, go for it?"

"If we had gotten to know each other before you met Leigh…"

"I would have been all over you like white on rice, like cheese on pizza, like lox on a ba…"

"Alright, I get it, I get it," She laughed. "Come here, I wanna give you a hug for luck." He walked over to her and they put their arms around each other. Her nightgown was shear and he could easily feel the heat coming off of her body. She squeezed him tight. He hugged her just as hard and gave her a soft kiss on her cheek, taking the time to feel the softness of her skin against his.

"Ray, don't do anything stupid out there, ok? We all want you to come back safe and in one piece."

"I promise," he said as his cab pulled up to the front of the house. "Is your ex still in town?"

"Yeah. He'll be leaving tomorrow. He's been looking into some possible private sector things."

"Sounds promising." He winked and then turned to leave. As an afterthought he turned back to Stella and said "Ya do know that it's ok with me if he stays here with you."

"Thanks. I appreciate that. I do. I'll let him know."

* * *

At the far end of the line of piers at Naval Station Norfolk, past guided missile destroyers, frigates, and amphibious assault ships, the USS Enterprise was idling her massive power plants as three huge harbor tugs positioned themselves to assist in her departure. Her flight deck carried several of the latest jet fighters as a token display for the family members who lined the docks to see their loved ones off on another six-month deployment. The remainder of the air squadrons would join the ship in a well-rehearsed but dangerous choreographed performance once she was well out to sea. Meanwhile, young children, some in dress Navy blues like their parents who proudly lined the perimeter of the mighty carrier's flight deck, stood and watched in awe as the aging grey mammoth underwent a sequence of activity that signaled she was getting underway. Flags and banners waved, a military band played, and young brides cried. A ritual repeated across the decades in times of war and peace from many naval bases around the country.

"Is this your first deployment, Lieutenant?" asked the Master Chief standing at the side of Jimmy Silver as they looked out at the throngs of well-wishers.

"Yes, sir. He responded and then turned his attention away from the pier. "I mean yes, Chief. It is. My first sea duty as well."

"If I may say so, sir, you seem a little nervous."

"No, not at all," Jimmy said to the unconvinced veteran. "Well, maybe just a little."

"Not a problem. Everybody's a little nervous the first time. It's easy to get caught up in the emotion of leaving a loved one, listening to the Navy band playing *Anchors Aweigh*, watching that great American flag flying against the sky. We all get those butterflies."

"That's exactly how I feel, Chief."

"The best part about it, Lieutenant, is that the feeling never goes away. At least for me it doesn't. If I may ask, sir, do you have someone special down on the dock?"

"Yes, I do. My girl's down there." He pointed into a crowd of people. "You probably can't see her, but she's wearing a black baseball cap that says USS Enterprise."

"No disrespect, Lieutenant, but there's a lot of those black caps down there today." The Chief said as he smiled at Jimmy. "But I know you can only see the one."

Jimmy looked at the Chief, smiled back, and they shook hands. "If you'll excuse me, Lieutenant, I've gotta take care of a few things. It's a pleasure to have you aboard."

"Thank you, Chief. You're very kind to say so, and the pleasure is definitely all mine." Jimmy watched the Master Chief walk off and then turned to look for Caroline once more among the waving crowd.

* * *

The taxi dropped off Ray by the side entrance of the abandoned naval reserve center on South Lake Union. It was ten minutes before six o'clock and he heard the engines of the 776 already chugging away. Rounding the corner of the building, he saw Walters perched in the conning station, pointing and waving his arms to his nervous crew like the conductor of a symphony leading his musicians through the prologue on opening night. Two slips over, on a small sailboat, an older man and his dog were the only ones on hand to watch as they prepped for departure. And even then it was only because the noise from the old ship had disturbed the morning peace. Seeing the portside lines cast off and the men starting to make their way up the ramp, Ray broke into a jog, fearing that he was going to literally miss his boat.

Above the noise and the vibration of the engines Jeffries heard Tex yell, "Hold up, It's Ray!" He looked up at Walters in the conning station and quickly made his way to get up there. Walters looked forward toward the shoreline and saw Ray pick up his pace as he pushed the throttle into reverse slow.

"Thompson, Gray," he shouted , "get that portside ramp retracted!"

Tex and Steve looked at each other and then up at Walters, surprised at the order.

Jeffries flew up the ladder from the gun deck and pushed the throttle into full reverse. "What are you, fuckin' nuts?" Walters yelled as he knocked his hand away and pushed the throttle back into slow before the engines could fully respond. "You wanna damage something before we even leave the dock?"

"We can't let him come along," Jeffries shot back.

"Don't you think I fuckin' know that?"

Just then, the tin-sounding voice of Chuck Shimkin came up out of the brass voice tube. "Hey, what the heck's goin' on up there?"

As the 776 started to slowly slip away from her moorings and the boarding ramp began to retract, Ray sprinted down the length of the dock to the cheers of Tex and Steve. He knew if he hesitated, even just a little, he would end up in the water. He leapt and landed at the very end of the retracting ramp, the jolt causing the muscles in his lower back to suddenly twinge.

Jeffries was not pleased, and his glaring look at Walters was met with protest. "What the fuck did you want me to do? I didn't know he was gonna show up."

"Well, let's put him off while we still can."

"And what reason are you gonna give to the others? Huh?" Walters argued. "Don't you think those guys are gonna start asking questions? He's onboard, and we'll just have to deal with it."

"He's your responsibility, John. He does not get off this ship. None of your boys do."

"Don't worry about it. I can take care of my shit, you just take care of yours."

Tex yelled up to the conning station, "Left rudder! Left rudder!" Walters and Jeffries broke eye contact. Walters looked aft, and saw they had been angling toward the western shoreline and a row of sailboats. He quickly spun the wheel to the left and the 776 swung back until she was perpendicular to the southern shore. He quickly brought the rudder amidships and put his engines in neutral. "Mr. Jeffries," Walters calmly said, "if you're through, please let me get us out of here in one piece." Jeffries turned and left the conning station.

Chuck moved his ear away from the brass bell-shaped end piece of the engine room voice tube. He wasn't quite sure what to make of the conversation he thought he had just heard between Walters and Jeffries. He only knew that he was going to keep it to himself—for now.

Ray made his way up to the quarter deck and was greeted by Tex and Steve. "This is a nice surprise. What changed?" Steve asked.

"I'm on an extended leave of absence," Ray said, rubbing his lower back.

"Nice. How'd you manage that?" asked Tex.

"I punched a guy." Ray looked up at Walters in the conning station and gave him a short wave.

Walters nodded as he put the throttle into ahead slow with a ten-degree right rudder, and the 776 turned north and headed up Lake Union on a path that would take them through the Ballard locks and out into Puget Sound. After a scenic cruise north through the San Juan Islands and west through the Strait of Juan De Fuca, they would enter the unforgiving north Pacific.

"Dr. Silver," Walters shouted down to Ray, "would you do us the honors and raise the ensign on the main mast?"

"With pleasure, Mr. Walters."

Along the banks of the western shoreline of Lake Union, a disgruntled condo owner stood on his balcony and saluted the departing vessel with his middle finger.

* * *

Leigh Anne and her team of three other marine biologists had set up home base operations in a bed and breakfast in the small fishing village of Charleston, just south of where the Coos River emptied into the Pacific. At 6 a.m. she woke to the sounds of hungry gulls and rhythmic surf. She felt nauseous and wondered briefly if it was from the fried fisherman's platter she had devoured the night before or if it was from the pregnancy. During the early weeks, she had experienced occasional bouts of morning sickness, which had been her motivation for purchasing the home test kits. Over the past week, though, her body seemed to be accepting the constant physiological changes. So she questioned the wisdom of giving in to her cravings for fried seafood. In the end it didn't matter, as she jumped out of bed and rushed for the toilet. When she was finished, she wiped her face with a cool, wet wash cloth and made one more attempt to call Ray.

Between the competing noise of the engines and the raised voices of people talking over them, he didn't hear or feel his cell phone ringing in his jacket pocket as he raised the American flag on the main mast of the 776. *"Hey, this is Ray. Leigh, if this is you calling I'm sorry you're getting my voicemail. Again. Please please please please leave a message. Love ya."*

"I'm beginning to think there's a force greater than the both of us that's keeping us apart. Anyway, Happy New Years, a day late. Love ya too. I'll try again later." After she hung up, she called her home machine to check for messages. *"YOU HAVE ONE NEW MESSAGE. TUESDAY, DECEMBER THIRTY-FIRST, SIX P.M.: Hello, this message is for Dr. McMillen. This is Aaron Tate, assistant to the dean of faculty at the University of Hawai'i. I just wanted to confirm with you that since you did not respond to our employment offer, that you are not accepting the position that was offered to you. If this is not correct, please call us no later than Thursday, January 2nd, as the semester begins in two and a half weeks. "*

"Thursday the 2nd. That's today!" she mumbled. In shock and disbelief, Leigh replayed the message, then called the university in spite of the time difference, knowing she'd be leaving a voicemail.

"Hello, this is Leigh McMillen," she said frantically. "Dr. McMillen. YES, I *do want* that job. You didn't hear from me becau…" The call was dropped. "Damn this shitty reception." She thought momentarily, then quickly got dressed, packed her things, and woke one of her colleagues in the next room. "Billy, get your pants on. I need you to take me to the airport."

"What the heck, Leigh. It's a little after six," he said, barely sticking his head out of the door—still half asleep.

"I'm sorry, but something's come up. I gotta get back to Seattle."

The commuter flight out of North Bend got Leigh Anne into Seattle by 9:30 that morning. Passing by Kelsey's on her way back to her place, she was tempted to have the cab driver drop her off, but during the week the place didn't open until noon. She hadn't eaten that morning, and throwing up three and a half hours earlier had left her feeling weak. It was important for her to get home to check her mailbox for anything from the university. She was disappointed to find nothing in the box except junk mail. She was also relieved that there was nothing there as she could honestly make a case to Aaron Tate that she had never received the offer package.

When she got into her apartment she checked the time. "Ten-thirty. That makes it eight-thirty on Oahu." Leigh Anne noticed the charge on her cell phone battery was down to one bar and decided to make the call on her house line. "I'm not getting cut off this time." She dialed and winced from the cramps she was now feeling in her stomach. "I better eat something before I faint."

"Aloha, this is Aaron."

"Mr. Tate? Hi, this is Leigh Anne McMillen."

"Yes, Dr. McMillen. I just finished listening to your message. It sounded like you got cut off mid-sentence."

"Yes, I did. I was in a bad cell area, and, well, you don't want to hear that. The thing is, I definitely want the job. I didn't respond because I never received anything from you, no letter, no offer, nothing."

"That's odd, doctor, because everyone here who interviewed you was absolutely thrilled with you. I'm surprised that no one called, plus we sent out a package over a month ago."

"Believe me, if I had received it, I would have completed everything and had it back to you immediately. Anyway, it's not too late, is it? Your message made it sound like it's not too late."

"No, we definitely want you, and it's not too late. You do need to be here for the start of spring classes. That's in two and a half weeks."

"No problem. That's plenty of time for me to give notice at the aquarium and get my things taken care of here."

"That's great, doctor. I'll inform the dean. Do you need a place to stay when you get in?"

She was quiet for a second before responding. "I think I might have a place for right now. But I'll call you to let you know for sure. And Mr. Tate, thank you."

Hanging up the phone, Leigh Anne walked into her seldom-used kitchen and scanned the almost empty refrigerator. If it hadn't been for her self-imposed hiatus from Ray, she wouldn't have even had the half-empty jar of applesauce and container of coconut milk that were nearing their expiration dates. She ate what was there and found that it quickly calmed her stomach. While eating, Leigh Anne took paper and pen and began to make a list of everything she needed to do prior to her departure. Furniture was going to charity and Kelsey would help her sell the car. She called the airline to book a one-way ticket, then telephoned her boss at the aquarium for an afternoon meeting to give notice. Exhausted from the hectic, morning she decided to put off going to Ray's place until the next day. "I need a nap before I go to this meeting," she thought. But before going to lie down she made one more call. "Hey Kimo, it's Leigh…"

* * *

When Stella got back from shopping, she noticed a black sedan sitting in front of Ray's place. "Definitely government issue," she thought as she removed the grocery bags from the trunk of her car. The door of the sedan opened as she made her way up the steps to the house. She heard Griff's voice. "What's for dinner, Stel?"

She turned around and smiled. "I picked up some fresh eggplant."

"You remembered, I'm impressed. I always did love your eggplant parmesan."

"Come here and help me with these bags, they're heavy."

Griff trotted up the front walk and grabbed them from Stella. "How did you know I was gonna be by?"

"I didn't. I just happened to be in the mood for this. Funny, huh?"

"Yeah, funny," he said as she opened the front door. They headed straight for the kitchen.

"How did things go around town?"

"Pretty good, actually. I made some contacts, spoke with some old friends, and it's looking pretty good." Griff leaned back against the counter and folded his arms across his chest.

"I want to thank you again for the heads up with Robert. Are you sure you're not gonna get in any trouble over this?" She said, while slowly unpacking the groceries.

"It'll be fine. Really. I had a whole bunch of favors owed to me."

"So how many did you have to cash in?"

"To get you outta there, no questions asked? All of them."

"Griff!"

"No, that's ok. I wanted to…I owed you."

"Is that why you're looking for work in the private sector?"

"That was part of the deal."

"Oh Griff, I'm sorry. I feel bad."

"Seriously Stel, I'm getting the better end of the bargain."

"How so?"

"I get to retire with full pension and benefits along with glowing references. And hopefully," he said as he looked at her, "I'll have a chance of making things right between us."

"Well," she said with a smile, "I'd say you're off to a good start."

"That's good, that's real good." He furrowed his brow.

"I've seen that look before, Griff. What's up."

"I need to talk to your chiropractor friend about that old Navy ship he's been helping out on."

"They sailed this morning. He went with them."

"Ahh, damn. I was afraid of that."

"Why, what's the matter? They're just going to Midway to buy another boat, aren't they? It's supposed to be like the one they have."

"There's stuff I can't tell you. The stuff that I can tell you, I can't tell you how I know what I know... although you're smart enough to figure it out." Griff walked over to the refrigerator and opened it. "Alright if I take a beer?"

"Sure. Grab one for me as well."

"Midway is not their final destination. It's also a 'closed' facility. Officially that is. It's being used as a black-ops staging area."

"You've got to be kidding me, Griff."

" No. I'm dead serious. There are eight guys on that ship who work for the agency, the CIA. Silver and the other civilians don't know that. At least they shouldn't know it. They've been mislead into thinking this trip was about buying some old ship from a Filipino fishing company." He looked at Stella and handed her a beer. She took it without saying anything, but didn't take her eyes off her ex-husband. He opened his bottle and took a drink. "Babe, I don't know how this all came about, but they're on a CIA-ordered mission, and they're not going for two weeks, it's more like four. Assuming they don't all get killed. Your friend and his buds are being used as decoys of some sort."

"This is just plain nuts, Griff. Since when does the CIA involve civilians?"

"From what I understand, the main guy running this op was given a free hand. I do know the boys back in Langley are not pleased with the direction he's taking."

"But not enough to reign him in? Is there something you can do?"

"There's nothing I can do. This is completely out of my league and out of my hands. Hell, I'm not even supposed to know any of this. I was hoping he'd still be here. What time did they leave?"

"Around six this morning."

"They should be through the Strait and on the ocean by now. All anybody can do at this point is pray for those guys." He helped her finish unloading the grocery bags. "I'm starved, how about you?"

"Sure," Stella said, worried about Ray and Abner. "I'll get things started."

* * *

By ten that night Ray had settled into his bunk in troop compartment two. Everyone had been assigned bunks by the time he came aboard, and since there was no room for him with anyone on the main deck—and since Jeffries didn't want him in troop one with his guys—troop two was the next available space. He had it all to himself and actually didn't mind being alone. He took out a blank hardbound book from his duffle bag and began a journal of the voyage.

Thursday 2 January 2003

Today is day one of the voyage of the 776 to Midway. Lots of activity onboard. Nervous energy. The five new guys are young and polite, but keep to themselves. Jeffries and Peters weren't happy to see me this morning when I arrived as we were shoving off. Can never figure those two out. I've concluded Abner's right about them. We'll see what they're up to. I doubt anything serious, otherwise they wouldn't have brought us (me, Steve, Tex, Chuck & Abner). Something to think about: maybe I'm the outsider in all of this (that's why they weren't too happy to see me this morning—ok, imagination getting away from me). I don't have any assigned duty as of yet, but Walters said he would make some changes in another day or two. Meanwhile, I think I'll help out Abner in the galley. Weather is typical for January. Thermometer mounted on the aft deck read 45 degrees.

Looks like clouds are rolling in from the southwest. Chugging through the San Juans and the Strait of Juan De Fuca was beautiful. Lying here in my bunk I noticed a small hole in the bulkhead that separates troop compartments 1 and 2. When I get up real close to it, I can see inside troop 1. It'll be interesting to hear what these guys talk about when they're alone. It's about 2200 hours (10pm), and I'm turning in for the night.

44

Stella reached over to stop the buzzing on the clock radio alarm. "Six-forty-five already? I've got...to go...to work." She rubbed her eyes while laboring through a long yawn. "Whew, I'm gonna need some coffee. Griff, you up?"

"Wha?"

"Wake up. You've got a flight back to D.C. this morning. You want coffee? I'm making some."

"Yeah," he said as he reached over and pulled her in tight. "I haven't been worked over like that in, oh geez, I don't remember ever getting worked over like that."

"It's been way too long for me as well. See what you missed all these years?"

"I've got no one to blame but myself. Seriously, I hope you can forgive me. I let my career ambitions get in the way of what's truly important."

"I think you've apologized enough, alright? Look, I've never harbored bad feelings," she said thinking about his statement. "Well, maybe I shouldn't say 'never'. I was pissed about the Walter Reed thing. But I will say, that incident made me a stronger, more determined person."

"Is that why you went after Harrison?" he asked. She pulled away and sat up to look at him. "You make it sound like I targeted him in order to make up for what I didn't get to do the first time."

"No, that's not what I meant."

"I didn't go after Harrison. I investigated an individual who was abusing his authority and responsibility to the extent that it was costing men their lives. Men, veterans, who put their faith and trust in his hands and he knowingly put their lives in danger."

"Stel, I didn't mean it the way it sounded, honest. I just meant that the incident at Reed, along with my lack of help, was what gave you the determination to see this thing through."

"What happened at Walter Reed, and the stone wall that was thrown up by everyone—not just you Griff, but by everyone—was something that really hurt me. I made a promise to myself that I would never let something like that happen to me again. Maybe it seems like I'm trying to make up for that. Perhaps I am. Because I allowed myself to be bullied into not pursuing something that I knew to be right, I swore I was not going to lie down like that again. I didn't go looking for Bill Harrison. He was dropped in my lap. And yes, this does even the score in my mind. Nailing him gives me closure. Is that bad?"

Griff looked at Stella and smiled. "No, that's not bad at all, just the opposite. You have more character and integrity then anyone I've ever known. It's the reason why I love you as much as I do, and it's why I respect you for who you are."

"I'm gonna go make us some coffee." She kissed him. "I got work and…"

"And I've gotta plane to catch."

"When do you think you'll make it back?"

"Sooner than you think. I'm gonna go jump in the shower. Where does Silver keep his towels?"

"They're in the hallway closet," she said as she quickly threw on Griff's shirt to cover her naked body. No sooner had Stella walked into the hallway than she saw Leigh Anne coming in through the front door.

She had woken up early and was anxious to see Ray after their four-week separation. Lying in her bed the night before, she thought about hugging him, kissing him, and lying beside him as she told him of her pregnancy. But now she stood in his front doorway, looking down the hall at Stella Leone dressed in nothing but a man's button-down shirt. Her heart sank and she felt like she had just been punched in the stomach. Leigh Anne turned to leave. She wanted to run, she wanted to scream.

"Leigh, don't go," Stella yelled out. "It's not the way it looks. Griff, get out here quick!"

Leigh Anne stopped and looked back to see a man in a towel standing behind Stella. Her mind was racing, trying to process everything. Her adrenaline rush was confusing her. She felt her heart pounding in her chest.

"Leigh, this is my ex-husband, Griffin. Ray's not here." Stella noticed the color draining from Leigh Anne's face and rushed to her side in case she fainted. "Come with me, hon, let's go sit so I can explain."

* * *

Leigh Anne was hungrier than she realized and ate everything Stella prepared for her. "So the two of you never told Ray anything?"

"Kelsey told me you swore her to secrecy. She honored that. I'd say she's a great friend. I wanted to tell Ray. I thought he should know, but it wasn't my place to say anything."

"Poor Ray, he doesn't know. We've been playing phone tag like no tomorrow. I didn't want to tell him about the baby unless we were actually talking to one another."

"That's completely understandable. No one can blame you for that. Before he left I know he went to talk to Kelsey, most probably about his trip. She'll tell you once you get down there. The only other change that I know about is that they're going to be gone at least four weeks, not two as originally planned." Stella cleared Leigh Anne's empty plate from the table. "You've got good color in your face, you should be feeling better now."

"Yes, I am. A lot better. The breakfast certainly helped. Thank you, Stella. You're a good friend to Ray, you really are and I appreciate that."

"Listen, I gotta get ready for work, and since it sounds like Griff is out of the shower, I better move my butt. Don't leave here until you're sure you're better."

45

Saturday 4 January 2003

3 full days out of Seattle and we're making good time. Chuck estimated we were doing a sustained cruise of 23 knots, which is unheard of for this kind of vessel. Talked about it over dinner and Walters confessed that the new bottom was made out of a poly-carbonate fiber that made the ship a few thousand pounds lighter. Should make Oahu in 24 hours. Hit stormy weather today. 12-foot seas for a while. Was a bit scary to see those waves washing up and over the bow. I felt queasy most of the morning, but three of Jeffries' guys were throwing up most of the day. Tex Warren is used to this, having been on a destroyer during Vietnam. He couldn't resist eating chunks of Polish sausage in front of those guys. Even Walters laughed as they ran for the head. The last time I saw anybody's face that green was at Kelsey's bar during a St. Patty's Day party.

Sunday 5 January 2003

A little concern amongst some of us in the crew (me, Tex, Steve, & Chuck). We should've made port in Oahu this afternoon, but Steve noticed that the coordinates entered into the GPS have us straight on target for Midway. Walters told us that we're bypassing Hawaii because of the excellent cruise speed and lower fuel consumption. That should put us there by Tuesday 1/7. Also took note that Lipton installed firing pins into the 20mm on the bow and the two 20 mils on the forward gun deck. Not going to say anything right now, but will mention it to the guys. Lipton is a gun nut. Maybe he wants to fire them off into the ocean. Steve mentioned on the down-low that he's blogging this voyage (never knew what a blog was before today). He set up a webpage (before we sailed) for his friends from his yacht club to follow along. Apparently word has spread to other boaters and WWII naval buffs who are now tracking our progress. He doesn't want Walters, Jeffries Peters, etc. to know. So far just me and Tex were told.

Monday 6 January 2003
Chuck and Brewster got into an argument in the engine room. Seems Brewster doesn't know much about diesels—or the modifications we made. Chuck was pissed. Never saw him angry until today. Walters asked me to take over Brewster's shift, 1600 to 1845 (4pm to 6:45pm). Thompson, another one of Jeffries' men, mouthed off to Abner about his being a "servant" during his Navy days. Thompson, like Abner, is African American. He seems like a respectable kid (25-26 y.o?) but definitely has issues with Abner. Don't know where that's coming from. Abner banned him from entering the galley. There is definitely tension between Jeffries' boys and us "old timers" (never thought I would call myself an old timer at 45). I am growing more concerned about this whole thing. I was awakened at 0200 (2am) to what sounded like intermittent firecracker noises coming from above (gunfire). Heard several of Jeffries' men through the small hole in bulkhead. A couple of them were cleaning sidearms. Looked like 9mms but not sure. Gonna compare notes with others. Seas are relatively calm. Outside temp at 81 degrees. Nice, but much hotter below decks.

Tuesday 7 January 2003
Midway! I had thought this was an active military base. Walters said it was shuttered a few years ago during a big round of base closures. There is activity here, though. Looks kind of creepy with armed guards all over the place (black ops?). Got refueled. Jeffries, Peters, and their guys took turns stretching their legs on shore. Some of us were also allowed to walk around on the dock for 5 minutes but had to stay by the ship. Walters said he didn't want us getting lost or hurt, plus he wanted us to stay onboard to make sure our stuff was safe (safe from who?). No sign of this other LCI. Walters called a full crew meeting. Raises more questions and concerns.

* * *

"Whaddya mean they're not coming?" Chuck asked Walters.

"We got a radio message saying they had engine trouble a day after they left Luzon. They said they were lucky to make it back to port."

"I don't like it," said Tex. "There's too many little things going on that make me feel uneasy."

"Such as?" asked Jeffries.

"Such as small arms practice in the middle of the night," Ray cut in.

"How about not stopping at Oahu as originally planned," added Chuck.

"Then there's Lipton here, who installed firing pins into some of the twenty mils and the Fifty-cal up on the gun deck." Steve said staring down at Lipton.

"Ah wanna know whas goin' on wit' this here island," said Abner. "Why's evrabody walkin' 'round wit' guns? An' whassup wit' them guard towahs?"

"Then there's this." Tex said as he took a Mac 10 automatic machine pistol from a bag and threw it onto the table in the crew's mess, startling everyone. "Jeffries' boys got a duffle bag with about a dozen of these things along with dozens of full clips."

Martin jumped up and grabbed the gun off the table as Jeffries began to yell. "You had no business going into troop one or the forward storage compartment."

"Calm down, calm down, Goddamit!" yelled Walters. "Everybody just sit the fuck down and relax."

As order was slowly restored, Abner leaned over to Ray and whispered, "Ya see? I told ya sumthin weren't right wit' these guys."

"Now everybody just relax for a minute and I'll tell you what's goin on. This is why I called this meeting. So I can update everyone." Walters looked around and waited for all the back chatter to stop. "Now, I told you guys," he said as he looked at "his" men, "there was a possibility we'd have to go all the way to Luzon, Lamon Bay, to be specific. And I told you guys that because of the possibility that this exact situation could happen. Ok? I had to plan for something like this. I didn't keep it a secret from anyone, and as it turns out, it's a good thing I did plan ahead."

"What's up with the weapons?" asked Steve Scott. "And like Abner said, what's goin' on with all the guards on the island?"

"Even though this base was officially closed, there's still a lot of expensive equipment on the island. The government is just protecting it until they get all of it moved off. We're allowed to stop because I asked permission to refuel. Trust me, they're glad to be able to sell it off instead of having to leave the stuff. And as far as the weapons go, once we sail outta here and travel further to the southwest, we lose our protection from air-sea rescue, the Coast Guard, and on and on. The Philippines are unpredictable. Modern day pirates are all over those waters. It's important to be able to protect ourselves. In fact, as soon as we found out they weren't coming, Peters suggested that you guys be trained on the 9 mils and the mac 10s and the M-16s, just in case. Isn't that right, Peters?" Walters raised his eyebrows, trying to get Peters to play along with his impromptu explanation.

"What?" he said, caught off guard. "Oh yeah. That's right. But uh, we uh, also discussed doing that months ago when we were discussing, uh, different scenarios. I actually forgot all about it. That is until earlier today." He hoped he sounded convincing.

"So that's what the hired muscle is all about?" asked Ray, noticing the sudden stares of Jeffries and his boys.

"They're not hired muscle, doc." Jeffries replied. "These guys work for me as trained security professionals. Don't refer to them as hired muscle. You know I do a good deal of international trade, especially in Southeast Asia. These guys will often accompany me or our shipments because of the high rates of piracy."

"That's right, doc. We've got a ship here that can be stolen. We have a good deal of cash onboard for the transaction, and we've got our safety and our lives to consider. That's why

Jeffries and Peters insisted on bringing some of their security people along," added Walters. "It's better to be safe than sorry. Wouldn't you all agree?" Walters looked around the crew's mess for a verbal or visual acknowledgment from everyone. "Now, we've fueled up and we're ready to continue the journey. If anyone is having second thoughts about continuing the trip, we'll have to put you off at Guam where you'll be able to grab a flight back to Oahu and from there back to Seattle. Please understand that given the increased speed and fuel economy from all the modifications, I was planning on heading straight to Luzon from here. If the weather conditions remain the same, we can be there in about seven days. But if anyone really wants off, I'll make the course correction. So what's it gonna be? Anybody want off?" One by one, each man replied that he wanted to continue on.

Jeffries looked at Walters, then headed up to the conning station. Martin made sure his rock-hard chest banged into Ray's shoulder when they passed by each other, coldly saying to him "Hired muscle my fuckin' ass!"

Ray winced, but tried not to show Martin or anyone else his shoulder hurt and waited until he was in the head before he allowed himself to rub it. "Damn, that guy's a walking brick wall." He thought.

The 776 weighed anchor and headed off to Luzon with full fuel, fresh water, an added cache of rocket propelled grenades, and several large cases of .50 caliber and 20mm ammo that had been stacked and waiting for them on the dock at Midway. When Walters came up to the conning station, he made sure the brass flap on the voice tube was secure and the public address system was off. He stuck his index and middle finger into Jeffries' top shirt pocket and pulled out his package of cigarettes. Jeffries watched him light one up and sit in the cushioned captain's chair.

"I knew this was going to happen," Walters said as he took a long drag from his cigarette and blew a thick white trail of smoke that was quickly dispersed by the breeze now blowing in from the southwest. He looked at Jeffries, who remained silent.

The handset buzzed. It was Steve Scott calling from below in the pilothouse.

"John, I'm gonna come up there. I need a better view to take us through the coral reef."

"Hang tight. The reef is kinda tricky, so I'll take her through." Walters slid off the seat and took the controls.

"John," Jeffries finally said, "that was pretty quick thinking down there, but I'm not so sure allowing these guys access to the weapons is a good idea."

"Ya know, Ben, you and Peters have been giving me a great deal of shit the past few months, accusing me of getting soft. Maybe after all these years I am, a little. But you guys forget that I did two tours in `Nam and commanded men in battle."

"That's all well and good, but your weekend volunteers are either untested or too old for battle, and they most certainly are in no shape should the shit hit the fan."

"Again, you're overlooking the obvious. You're the one who wanted them along as 'window dressing'. They're not stupid. They see the shit that's going on and they're slowly putting all the pieces together. It's to our advantage to do something to make them less suspicious. So your boys spend a few hours giving them hands-on training with some of the toys that you brought along. One, they stop feeling that they're being excluded. Two, they stop snooping around. Three, maybe they start getting along with your guys—and vice versa—and four, they don't all decide to jump ship in Guam, leaving us short-handed and overworked, not to mention leaving us short of window dressing."

"Ok, John. It makes sense to me."

"In that case, do me a favor and talk to Peters and your guys and get them onboard with this shit."

Jeffries noticed that Walters had pocketed his cigarettes. "Ya know, John, I've underestimated you. I still think you're getting soft, which can end up biting you in the ass, but you're a very smart guy."

* * *

Wednesday 8 January 2003
We're a day out of Midway. Tried to call Leigh but I guess the towers I saw on the island were not really cell phone towers. Walters also asked us to keep all phones off as the signals are messing with the GPS units. Steve Scott told me that's BS. I can't believe I was on Midway Island, even though I was only about 10 feet from the ship. Got my first "hands on" with a 9 mm handgun. Worked with the guy named Gray. Seems like a nice kid. His grand-father was with the 101st at Bastogne. Want to get as much gun practice as I can (just in case!). An oil leak developed in the #2 port diesel during Lipton's early afternoon shift. Between him and Chuck, they got it handled. I came on duty right after Lipton and got stuck cleaning the mess. I think the heat is getting to Abner. He seems to be moving much slower the past day or two. Will keep an eye on him. Make sure he's hydrated. Winds picking up out of the southwest. Got 5-6 foot seas late afternoon. Clouds thickening. Temps at 85 (storm brewing?).

Friday 10 January 2003
Didn't record yesterday. Too busy. #2 portside diesel had more trouble. We took it off- line and spent several hours working on it. Chuck thinks either Brewster or Lipton had something to do with it (not intentionally). Maybe that explains the oil leak 2 days ago. But Chuck is overprotective of his engines and even more suspicious. Can't blame him. Current sustained speed at 20 kts. Sets us back by a few hours. Still making good time. Older guys start-ing to experience aches and pains. Several of them asking me to work on them. I've been working on Tex the past few days. He's had chronic headaches for the past two years, which is why he's been on disability. 3 spinal adjustments and he says his headaches are gone. Should have brought a treatment table! Had rain and increased wind yesterday. Seas calm today. Blue skies temps at 87. Gonna sleep topside tonight. Too hot below.

Sunday 12, January 2003
A number of the guys haven't been showering as much as they should. Glad I have troop 2 to myself. Will ask Walters to say something to everyone.

Some are even getting fatigued and short-tempered.. Sustained heat and humidity not good. Nobody, except Tex and Walters, is used to being on a ship this long. Seems I've been designated the ship's doctor. People coming to me for cuts and bruises. Dehydration a factor. Handing out supplements of sodium, potassium, magnesium, and calcium. Making sure everybody drinks plenty of water. We have plenty of drinking water onboard, so supply won't be an issue. Got to find a way to replenish in Luzon. Didn't think of bringing sunscreen. Lipton and Peters spend too much time topside without shirts. As we get closer to the Philippines, Jeffries is having more eyes keeping watch (no sign of Blackbeard....arrgh! ha ha)

Monday 13, January 2003
Uneventful throughout the day. Guys still tired but better the past few days. Got Abner to cut back on the fat and grease in his cooking. That, plus the increased H2O and mineral supplements and everyone definitely has more energy. Should make Luzon tomorrow afternoon. Feel anxious to see this LCI. Hoping it's the 606 (hoping there's an LCI!).

Addendum to 13 January, written 0600 hrs Tuesday 14 January 2003 :
My suspicions were confirmed. Although there were enough red flags prior to this. Blinded by possibility of finding the 606, and I'll admit I was hoping for something more cloak n' dagger (be careful what you wish for). Couldn't sleep below last night. Again too hot. Found a little nook on gun deck between ammo storage box and forward portside gun station. Can't be seen there when lying down. @2300 hrs Jeffries, Peters, Brewster, Thompson, Gray, Martin, Richards, and Walters gathered just outside of pilothouse reviewing assignments and "contingency plans." Meeting some guys named Francis and Enrique in a dive bar outside Capalonga (sp?). Couldn't hear all of it. Just know that Brewster and Lipton are to stay behind to make sure "Walters' guys" don't get off the ship. Gotta find a way to talk to Chuck, Tex, & Steve without being heard or seen by anyone.

Tuesday 14 January 2003
A few miles off shore of Luzon. Walters insisting we wait until dark to avoid any contact with Philippine authorities because of the restored 20 mm AA guns and other weapons. Lots of activity, Jeffries' guys huddling throughout the day. Through hole in bulkhead of troop 1 & 2 compartments,

saw a number of duffle bags taken out of forward storage compartment. Automatic weapons, C4, etc. & Jeffries spending a lot of time in radio room. Can't get near to listen. Abner said he repeatedly heard him calling someone called packrat or something like that.

* * *

In spite of the nervous energy that permeated the ship, the morning and afternoon hours that the 776 lay off the Luzon coast were a welcomed respite for everyone onboard. Jeffries' guys either met in troop one for review sessions and weapons inventory or they congregated on the gun deck outside the pilothouse. Ray cautiously moved through the ship, quietly making contact with "his" guys. "Steve, wait for me in troop four. Important...shhh," he said real low. He found Tex by the galley and quietly took him by the arm to get farther away from the radio room. "Don't say anything. Go get Chuck. Meet me in troop four."

"Wha...."

"Shhh, important. Go." Ray had a serious look that immediately got Tex's attention.

Abner stepped out of the galley and watched Ray and Tex walk down the main passageway toward the engine room. "Hey Doc, you ok?"

Ray quickly turned around and put his index finger up to his lips. "Yeah buddy, doing good. You got any coffee brewin'?"

"Ah, yeah sure. Come grab ya mug."

With one ear free from his headset, Jeffries heard the noise in the passageway and stopped talking mid-sentence. He listened intently and leaned over to gently nudge the edge of the doorway curtain enough to see Ray enter the galley to get a cup of coffee. He watched for a few moments more until the voice in his headset redirected his focus.

"Don't say anything A.J., just listen," Ray said in a low voice as he turned on the CD player. "I'll tell you everything in a little while. Just know that you were right about these guys. I should've listened to you. It's not that I didn't hear what you

363

were sayin'. I guess…a part of me…I guess a part of me was hoping for some kind of bigger adventure. It's stupid. I'm sorry."

"Hey Doc, ah mean, Ray. If it's all the same ta ya, ah knew these guys wasn't right. Didja evah think ah might be lookin' fo' that bigga advencha too?"

"Ya know the old saying 'be careful what you wish for'? Well, our wish is gonna come true. I just hope we didn't wish for something more than we bargained for. Just hang tight, Ab…uh, A.J. I'm gonna go talk to Chuck and those guys. I'll get with you later and fill ya in. Meantime, just act normal."

Abner looked at him with concern. He felt the urgency in Ray's words and in the apologetic tone of his voice. "Ok, Doc," he said real loud. "There ya go. If ya wanna refill, ya jes come on back."

"Shhh, you're overdoing it. Just be yourself." Ray stepped out of the galley and walked forward to the small supply closet. He quickly looked through the shelves, grabbed a deck of playing cards, and headed aft to the ladder leading to troop four.

Peters was coming down from the pilothouse on his way to the head when he bumped into Ray. "Sorry about that, Doc."

"No worries," Ray said as he looked for a way around the much larger man. "Excuse me…uh…Jack, isn't it?" He smiled and side-stepped Peters to continue on his way.

"Hey, where is everyone?"

"What?"

"Where's everybody? It's too quiet down here."

"Well, a bunch of the guys are up where you just came from. And I'm about to fleece some guys in a game of poker down in troop four." Ray held up the deck of cards.

"Kinda hot down there, wouldn't you say?"

"Uh…yeah, it is, but uh, there's no sun. The guys have been trying to stay out of the sun. No sunscreen, if ya know what I mean."

"Yeah, sure." Peters said as he looked at his own burnt shoulders. "I haven't played poker in a long time. Maybe after I take a whiz I'll come and join you guys."

"Oh uh, yeah sure, sure thing. It's, uh, five-card straight nothing wild, and uh, it's a hundred-fifty to get in."

"A hundred-fifty? Fuck that," Peters said, walking into the officers' head.

Ray made his way down to the others waiting in troop four. In between gulps of water, Chuck opened up the questioning. "Hey, it's freakin' hot down here, pallie. What's up?"

Ray opened the pack of cards and knelt down onto the deck. "Get down, you guys, and make like we're playing poker. And be quiet." He started dealing around. Tex got down on his knees and began looking at his cards as Ray dug into his pocket, took out a number of bills, and tossed them into the middle of the circle.

"We're not here to buy an LCI, are we?" asked Tex.

"We've all had our suspicions about these guys. Well, I always say, trust your instincts. Now I don't know if there's an LCI or not."

"What the hell are you talking about?" asked Chuck.

"I'm not surprised," added Tex. "I knew those fucks were up to something."

"Hey, keep it down." Ray looked up at the ladder. "Peters is up there snooping around and I heard Jeffries in the radio room. Look it, we all see what's going on. The muscle that Jeffries brought along, the weapons, the unmarked boxes on the dock at Midway. There's a hole in the bulkhead that separates troops one and two. One night I was watching those guys doing an inventory check. They got blocks of C-4 explosives and a crate of RPGs."

"What the hell?" asked Steve. "You don't need C-4 to fight off pirates."

"Exactly," continued Ray. "Listen, I heard them talking last night. The photo that Walters had been showing all of us, I don't know if it's legit. There is a ship, but whether or not it's an LCI, I don't know. For right now, let's assume it is. But they're not here for the ship. They're here for something that's on it."

"Weapons? Drugs? Gold?" asked Chuck

"No, a bomb." said Tex. Everyone looked at him.

"That's fuckin' nuts, Tex" said Steve.

"Hey, I'm just sayin'. Who knows, it could be. Ya know, like one of them dirty bombs."

"Hey guys, settle down," Ray said as he looked up at the ladder once more. "It could be any one of those things. I couldn't hear everything. I just know that once we pull into Lamon Bay, several of those guys, like Peters, Martin, Richards, and two others, are being let off first before we tie up in a different location. Then Jeffries and Walters are going into town to meet up with two guys in some dive bar....Philip's, I think it's called."

"No, not Philip's," said Tex. "I heard Jeffries say Felipe's. I heard him mention it several times during the trip.

"Ok, they're meeting at a place called Felipe's. They're going to meet up with two guys...Francis and Enrique."

"What's going on with Peters that he's leading...what did you say? Four other guys? Separately?" asked Chuck. "What's up with that?"

"I'm not certain because I didn't get to hear everything," replied Ray. "But from what I can make out, Enrique is the owner of the ship. I think Walters and Jeffries are keeping him occupied while Peters and his crew go steal whatever it is they came here for."

"Oh my God." Steve shook his head back and forth. "So if I understand this, we were never going to meet them at Midway, and Walters planned on coming here the whole time—that no good lousy sonofabitch. When we dock, one of us is going to have to follow him to see what's going on."

"We should, but they're leaving Brewster and Lipton behind to make sure we don't go anywhere," Ray said. Suddenly they heard footsteps on the steel plating of the deck above. They all stopped to listen as the sound drew closer. "That's definitely Peters." Ray said as he motioned to everyone to pick up their playing cards. "I'll see your ten and raise you ten more." He looked at Chuck who caught on.

"Nah, not me. I'm out." He said, following Ray's lead. The footsteps reached the opening of the down ladder to troop four and then stopped.

"Come on Chuck. That's the third hand you've caved on. Whaddya, scared?'

"Shit, man," Chuck said. "You deal lousy cards."

"Well, I'm not scared y'all. I think you're bluffin'. I'll see your raise and bump you ten pounds of good ol' Texas barbecue" added Tex."

"Whoa, somebody's feeling lucky and it's not me. I'm out." Steve sighed completing the foursome.

"I call," said Ray. "Whaddya have, Sparks?"

"Sparks? Who me?" asked Tex. "That's funny. I haven't heard that nickname since I left the service. I got two pair. Jacks over..."

The sound of the steps resumed, but this time they trailed off toward the bow.

"Nines." Tex looked up at the ladder and listened to the fading sound.

"What makes you so sure those were Peters' footsteps?" asked chuck.

"It's something I picked up working at the veterans' hospital." Ray smiled at everyone. "Now listen, I've been thinking about this and I think I have an idea. Steve, you're still doing that web thing, whadja call it, a bog?"

"A blog. And yeah, I'm still doing it."

"You got people following you on that thing? People you can trust?

"I've got a ton of people who've started following us. My yacht club friends, retired Navy guys, history buffs, and on and on."

"Would any of them sound the alarm for us if needed? Ya know, like contacting media people or sending out mass emails to everyone they know. Maybe even calling out the Navy and stuff like that?"

"Yeah, I know a few. Some of my Navy guys have connections. Hell, I know a few guys at the yacht club who rub elbows with Senator Claremont. He keeps his yacht there as well."

"Senator Claremont has a yacht? Why am I not surprised?" said Tex.

"Ok Steve, keep doing it. Find some way to let people know what's going on. Well, hold up. Maybe that's not a good idea. Not just yet anyway. On second thought, keep a record of everything you can, and then if the shit hits the fan, then put it all out there, ok?"

"Absolutely, Ray. Not a problem."

"Hey, wait a minute," said Tex. "Do you have a wireless webcam?"

"Yeah, sure I do. I know what your thinkin'. Great idea." Steve smiled.

"Ok, that's good. But now comes the dangerous part," said Ray. "Someone's gonna have to follow Walters when he and Jeffries go to that bar. We gotta try to see what's up and who they're meeting. I know they'll also have some way to communicate with Peters and those guys." They looked around at each other and everyone realized it had to be Ray.

"Who, me?...Ok...If I can get off this ship I'll need to be able to listen to what's going on. Tex?" Ray looked up at the ladder and then back at the radioman.

"I know they brought some gear onboard. I can try and sneak one of the units to you. It's one of those little cigarette-sized boxes you keep in your pocket that has a little earbud and microphone," Tex said. "We'd be able to talk back and forth on a pre-designated channel. This way they won't be able to hear us."

"Good. Chuck, I'm gonna need you and Abner to distract Brewster and Lipton in some way." Ray began gathering up the playing cards and his cash.

"Lipton's no problem. Brewster? He's a big boy. Likes to eat," Chuck said. "I'll get with Abner and we'll make some of my dry rub. We'll keep both of them distracted long enough so you'll be able to sneak off the ship."

"Ok, then. If we're all set, let's get the hell topside. It's fuckin' hot in here."

"There's one other thing we should consider," Steve said before they headed up the ladder. "If these guys are CIA, we could be getting in the way of something we'd best be staying out of. What if we screw up something important?"

"I thought about that. I'm also wondering about the possibility these guys went rogue and they're freelancing. If they're legit, we let it unfold without interference. If they're rogue, we're gonna be toast when they no longer have any need for us, so we best find out soon. That'll give us our best chance to get off of this thing and get to the US embassy in Manila. Either way, we need to find out, right?"

Walters had come down off the gun deck and noticed no one around. "Jeffries? Peters? Where are you guys?"

Jeffries came out of the radio room and looked around while Peters stuck his head out of the galley chewing on a hunk of bread and made his way forward to the other two. "Jack!" Jeffries said to Peters. "Where the hell is everyone?"

"They're down in troop four playing poker."

"Jack, it's gotta be at least fifteen to twenty degrees hotter down below and there's no tables down there." Jeffries said as the three of them looked at the empty tables in the crew's mess area. With the forward and aft hatchway doors wide open, a breeze, albeit a warm one, blew fresh air through the compartments. Something that wouldn't be felt down below. "That doesn't make any sense." Jeffries quickly walked down the main passageway and got to the troop four ladder just as Ray and the others were coming up. "Sorry, Jeffries, game's over," said Ray. "Yeah," confirmed Tex. "The doc's cards were just as hot as the temperature."

"Speaking of hot, Tex, you owe me ten pounds of barbecue brisket." Chided Ray.

"As soon as we get back home, Doc."

"I wanna see those cards," yelled Chuck. "I think the deck's marked."

The chatter continued as they brushed by Jeffries. Ray headed into the galley for something to drink and the others headed outside for air. Walters walked over to the galley doorway and alternated looks with Peters, Jeffries, and finally Ray. As Abner handed him a large glass of water, he looked at Walters, saying "I swear the cards aren't marked. I just got lucky."

4 6

Alone on the forecastle deck, Ray leaned into the arc of the shoulder rests of the 20 mm anti-aircraft gun and looked out over the bow toward the barely visible Luzon coast. He stepped away and dug into his pocket for his phone. He tried to call Leigh Anne one more time, doubting any chance of making a connection to Seattle. "No signal damn it!" he thought. Again he leaned into the shoulder rests and swung the big gun to starboard. Looking up at the late afternoon sun, he squinted at the full-winged silhouette of a passing Egret as he heard the echo of Abner's voice.

"As that Zero made its pass, ya dad swung that twennah 'round and started firin'. Ah got up there but each step seemed ta take me foever. Ah was able ta reload a canista fo' him an' Ronnie was blastin' this guy an' took him out. Ah know he did. Ah saw the traceahs hittin' it as it blew."

He stepped away from the gun, walked over to the bow railing, and looked over the side. The sun danced and sparkled off the relatively calm water as it lapped against the hull. A few months ago, the gentle back and forth rocking motion would have surely made him seasick. Ray closed his eyes and tried to imagine the insanity of the battle.

"... the skippa started screamin' down the laddah outta the pilot house. He was screamin' fo' us ta get back ta the foward gun. Again

ya daddy went flyin' on up there. Ah hesitated but started ta go. Ah got outside in time ta get knocked backward on mah ass as the 606 jerked hard inta full reverse. Next thang I know, Ronnie went flyin' off the bow inta the surf an' the 606, well, she jes kept goin'. "He opened his eyes and briefly turned to see Abner come out onto the quarterdeck for some air then looked back out at the Philippine Sea. The old man looked toward the bow and thought his eyes were playing tricks on him when at first he saw a teenaged Ron Silver standing by the forward anti-aircraft gun. A warm breeze came across the deck when he heard a whisper— *"It's our time."* A chill ran down Abner's spine. "Ah been inside too long," he said out loud. "Either that or ah'm dehydratin'." He rubbed his eyes, then put his hands to his forehead to block out the sun. This time he saw Ray. Convinced he needed to drink more water, he decided to go back to the galley, where at least he could open a porthole for a breeze and use his small fan to help with the heat.

Ray heard the sound of hard boot soles coming across the deck and making contact with the metal ladder steps behind him. Without turning around, he nonchalantly greeted Jeffries.

"You either made a lucky guess or that's a very rare talent you have, Doc."

"It's nothing special," Ray said as he stepped away from the starboard railing. "Just one of those weird habits a person develops. Kinda like that word association thing that some people have. Like putting a face with a name. When I'm around certain people long enough, I get to recognize the sound they make when they walk."

"Maybe you can teach that to the recruits at the agency."

"The 'agency.' I'm surprised that you're willing to say that so freely."

"Yeah, well, you're a smart guy. We both know you've figured out who we are."

"It wasn't a very hard thing to figure out, with the way you guys went about everything.

And in my opinion, for professionals, you guys have been very sloppy." Jeffries ignored the critique. "By the way, it was A.J. who had you and Peters pegged months ago."

"You mean Gordie?"

"No, not Gord...." At that instant, Ray realized Gordie Smithfield's death had been more than just an old man having a heart attack. "Not Gordie. But that night A.J. and I came aboard with groceries. That's when we... when he made the connection. From then on it was easy to start putting the pieces together."

"Oh yeah. I remember that night. Anyway, you figured out who we were and you decided to come along anyway?"

"You make it sound like you guys have some sort of contagious disease." Ray gave a short laugh.

"Sometimes it seems like it by the way people react to us."

"Not all people."

"But more than enough."

"Can you blame `em? Your agency tends to trivialize the very people you risk your lives for. It's not as if you guys don't deserve it sometimes."

"What you don't understand is that we don't risk our lives for people, at least not for individuals."

"No? Then whom?"

"You mean for what. For something bigger than any individual, for the country. People like me will take that risk to insure its very existence."

"It's a noble cause."

"You disagree?"

"No, not at all...except when people's lives, innocent people, get caught in the crosshairs."

"It's very easy to criticize when you're on the outside looking in."

"No argument from me, but we are on the outside looking in, and it's very dark in there. And people are afraid of the dark. For the record, I appreciate the fact that you guys exist. I don't appreciate the fact that you can, and you do, cross the line now and again."

"Only when the situation requires it."

"Ya mean like when you cavalierly bring guys like A.J., Steve and Chuck along on an operation without being upfront with them."

"Would you guys have come if you had known what we're going to do?"

"Probably not. But take a look at these guys. A.J. a veteran of two wars. Tex, a Vietnam vet. Steve Scott, who sailed solo, and at times in the worst possible winter weather, from Alaska down to San Diego. Seems to me they're up for adventure, and they *are* patriots. I'm sure there are plenty of Americans who are willing to volunteer for God and country. All you need to do is ask. And, while we do know you're going to be doing *something* on that island tonight, we still don't know what or why."

"All we need to do is just ask. Huh?" Jeffries laughed sardonically.

"I'm sure there'd be a hell of a lot more people willing to step forward and do their part if there was more honesty coming out of Washington."

"You surprise me, Doc. You're either very naïve or you're living in a fantasy world."

"Naïve? No. Fantasy? Some might think so. I'm not stupid enough to think people would come running out of the woodwork if all of a sudden politicians and bureaucrats found their spines. But I do believe there'd be a lot more willing to step up."

"And what about you? What's your story, huh? Didja wanna be here because you're the only member of four generations of Silvers who hasn't served his country?" Ray shot a stare directly at him. "Yeah, I know all about you and your family. I had background checks done on every one of you guys. It's standard operating procedure in order to protect the integrity of the mission."

"Is it also SOP to kill off an old man like Gordie?"

"The old man had a massive heart attack before Peters could touch him. And he was only going to talk to him about stuff he heard. I wasn't aware you knew about that too."

"I didn't until just now," Ray said as Jeffries shook his head and laughed at his mistake. "And I don't believe it was just a heart attack. The old man was trying to call A.J. when it was supposedly happening. And when his daughter found him dead, they couldn't find his cell phone at first. Now I know how it ended up across the street from his house. That's all A.J. talked about for weeks after the funeral."

Jeffries turned and stepped over to the portside railing. Lighting a cigarette, he offered one to Ray before remembering he didn't smoke. Ray took one anyway.

"I've been around so much secondhand smoke over the past two weeks I might as well have one of my own." Jeffries cupped his hands around his Zippo and Ray leaned in to get a light. "I haven't smoked since I was twenty-two. It's amazing how after all these years I still have dreams in which I'm smoking." Ray turned and stared off into the ocean. "Each time it seemed so real. The feel, the smell. When I wake, I almost feel guilty for enjoying it so much." He took a drag and looked at Jeffries. "So, you know all about me and my family?"

"Yeah. In fact, you remind me a little of your brother."

"You knew my brother Frank?"

"We worked together on two occasions, but that was years ago."

"You mean before his accident in the Mediterranean in `83?" Ray said, trying to see if Jeffries would take the bait again. He didn't.

"Actually, last time I worked with him was when his chopper went down here in the Philippines in `81, but nice try."

Ray studied his eyes. "Anyone can read an official record and repeat the facts. You didn't know my brother. But to answer your question, it's true I knew you guys were gonna be up to something more than just coming for an old ship, which I now know you have no intention of buying. I chose to come along anyway, because, as crazy and as stupid as it sounds, I wanted to be part of something that was bigger than myself. I wanted to do something for my country. Even if it was just one time. Is that so wrong?"

"Even if you got killed doing it?" Jeffries asked. Ray didn't answer. He looked at his cigarette and flicked it over the side. "This is one of the reasons we don't get into the business of taking volunteers. This ain't no baseball fantasy camp for guys in their forties who wanna dress up and play catch with has-beens. I made a bad call on this one. I know I'll have to answer for that back in Langley."

"So what do we do in the meantime, huh? I'm here. We're here. We wanna help. Believe it or not, we care about the same country. Maybe not in the same way but we're on the same side. So, the way I see it, if you're not going to let us help, we'll just get off the ship in Luzon and head for the nearest embassy."

"Doc, we're dealing with terrorists. They're cold-blooded murderers who wouldn't think twice about cutting your throat or forcing you to get down on your knees to put a slug into the back of your skull before you had the chance to think about your mother as you wet your panties. These fucks kill at the drop of a hat. No hesitation, no afterthought. That's why you guys need to keep outta the way. That's why I don't want you taking one step off this boat when we tie up tonight…But I will say that you all have your shit together on these guns. I'm impressed at how good you've become in such a short time… Ok then, you guys wanna help? Once we dock, things are gonna happen pretty fast. We're only gonna have a few hours, and then we're gonna have to haul ass outta here. We're gonna need you guys to stand watch on the 776 and be prepared for a possible firefight. We're gonna need this thing to be ready to fly outta here. Do ya think you and your boys are up for that?"

"I'll talk to the guys. They'll be up for it. Just one thing."

"What's that?"

"Do they really have an LCI or was that all bullshit?"

"No, it's no bullshit. Why we came here, what we're after, is on that ship."

"One other thing" Ray said to Jeffries as he was about to leave. "Peters *is* gonna have to answer for Gordie."

"If that's the case," Jeffries said, making direct eye contact with Ray, "just know that I'm the one who gave the order."

47

Walters cut power a few hundred yards from shore and allowed the 776 to glide in through the dark water as quietly as possible. Once Peters and his group were well on their way through the heavily forested countryside, he would restart the engines and continue a few miles up the coastline to tie up at a small pier on the southern boundary of Lamon Bay—about two miles from where the other ship was docked.

Thirty minutes earlier, Jeffries had briefed the five-man group led by Jack Peters while they geared up in black, from shirts and pants to facepaint. Each man prepped his Machine pistol and 9 mm sidearm with silencers.

"Ok, one more time for review. By the time you guys get to their ship, Walters and I will already be sitting down with Francis and this guy Enrique. We're confident he'll have a few of his men hanging around inside and outside of the bar. They'll all be armed, but if they're openly carrying weapons then my guess is they're on to us and we'll be dead before we get a chance to sit down. There's no reason for them to be suspicious, but then again, these guys never need a reason. I'll have my 'hearing aid' in so I'll be able to listen to your guys' communications with each other and with Brewster, who'll be back here at the ship. You all understand that I won't have any voice. If things seem like they're going south on my end I can hit this button on my pocket transmitter, which will be the abort signal. Peters, likewise for you, press this button only if things fall apart. We all together on this so far?" He looked at each man for confirmation. "Richards, Thompson," Jeffries continued while pointing to the map. "Once you two get to this point over here you'll head off to the right and circle around to the west side. There's a good fifteen feet of open area between the edge of the jungle and the stern of the ship. Martin and Gray, at that same point where you guys split, you two head off to the left and follow this path so that you'll come out of the jungle closer to the bow. Peters, you'll have the backpack with the C-4, and you'll continue straight ahead through the jungle and come out at mid-ship. I spoke with Francis forty-five minutes ago and he says they now have three guards at night. One at the stern, one who walks from stern up to mid-ship, and a third who walks from mid-ship up toward the bow. Just the same, before you make any move into the open, scan the ship and scan the area. Make sure there's no movement topside. If you see anything that looks suspicious, make sure you talk to each other. Don't let the fact that the guards are women fool you. They're armed and they're not afraid to kill. The one walking from aft to mid-ship is their newest. She's young, about fifteen, sixteen. No experience. If there's a weak link in that chain, it's her. But you guys need to take 'em out simultaneously. We can't risk any of them getting off a shot. Once they're down, Peters, Richards, and Gray will go aboard and down below. Thompson, you and Martin will take up positions onboard where you can't be seen. Gun deck or conning station. If there's anything at all happening close to the ship, you use your headsets and communicate with the guys down below. Any questions so far?"

"Are you sure that no one is gonna come by to check on the girls or relieve them?" asked Richards.

"As sure as we can be. As you know, these situations aren't always static. Just know that anything can happen. No different from the last job you were on. Peters, once onboard give the backpack to Richards, and then you and Gray will head down into troop three and secure two, I repeat, two aluminum attaché cases. I don't know where in troop two they are, but as you know, the compartment is small. They should be easy to spot. They should have some weight to them. If you lift up a case and it feels like there's nothing in there, then it's probably empty and you'll have to make a quick search of the other compartments. Richards. You plant C-4 in troop one, two and the engine room. Set the charges for forty-five minutes. Once you guys are done, make your way back through this route over this way." Jeffries traced a path on the map with his finger. "Everybody get that?" They all nodded. "Peters, when you get to this point over here, say the phrase 'fourth down' into your microphone. Got that?" All five of them repeated in unison, "Fourth down."

"Got it." said Peters.

"While you're doing your thing, we'll be discussing the transaction and arranging a time with Enrique to tour his ship, sometime the following day. Once I hear 'fourth down,' I'll apologize and excuse ourselves, saying we're fatigued from the trip. Then we'll head on back and blow outta here before the C-four does."

"What about Francis?" asked Peters.

"Francis," Jeffries said, "is gonna excuse himself right after introductions in order to go home to care for his 'sick' wife. Enrique will definitely hold him responsible once this all goes down. He's already sent his wife up north to the Navy base at Subic Bay. He'll eventually join her there. His kids are grown and nowhere near here, so he'll be fine. And in case you don't already know, his call sign is 'Rat Pack.' So if you hear that over the radio, you know it's him or it's about him."

In spite of his earlier conversation with Jeffries, Ray still wanted to see if the Filipino LCI was in fact the 606. After coming all this way, he didn't want to go home not knowing. Except for getting together privately with Tex so he could take possession of the two-way radio that he would use to monitor the operation, he and the others—Chuck, Abner, Tex and

Steve—now met openly with Brewster and Lipton. They were each issued a weapon and extra ammo clips, and discussed stations for keeping watch.

The main cabin began to be filled with the smell of Chuck's dry rub on a large rack of ribs that Abner had put into the oven several hours earlier. Brewster already had the largest appetite onboard and the smell of slow roasting pork was driving him crazy. The last thing on Lipton's mind was food though. He had been constipated for several days and was now experiencing intermittent waves of abdominal cramps. Ray kept telling him to drink as much water as he could, but he refused to listen, and the combination of his high protein diet, constant sweating from the high humidity, and inadequate water intake was his digestive undoing. Because of that, his watch station was downwind on the stern and close to the crew's head.

4 8

Unlike the hot rainy and humid summers, January in the Philippines was practically rain-free, but still relatively hot and humid. The dense foliage of the undeveloped countryside was thick with the sound of crickets and the crunch of beetles, millipedes, and spiked ants under the boots of Peters and his men as they made their way as quickly and quietly as they possibly could. During a five-minute break, Martin made the mistake of leaning against the trunk of a dead tree only to find a centipede crawling over his shoulder. He jumped and wildly slapped at himself with fear and disgust. Remnants of the poisonous but non-lethal predator soaked into his shirt and covered the palms of his hands.

* * *

In a back room at Felipe's, Enrique sat with his lieutenants and reviewed their plans one last time. "I just got word from Eduardo. He spotted the American ship coming up the coast from the south. He says they look lost trying to find their way in the dark. They really are a bunch of amateurs."

"No kidding," said Jonny Alissandro. "They were supposed to be here yesterday."

"It don't matter. They're here now. We'll do this thing tonight. Francis tells me he's bringing two of their guys to meet with me and negotiate a price. We'll go back and forth a little bit and then I'll invite them to visit our ship in the morning. But they won't live to see the sunrise. Hector?"

"Yes, Enrique."

"Francis tells me there's a total of nine Americans. With their two guys coming to meet with me, that should leave seven aboard their ship. To be safe, let's assume they have a few more. There's only two places they can tie up, by our boat or one mile from here in the other direction. Take ten of your men, and head over to that other dock, and wait at the jungle's edge, but just outta sight. Be very careful you're not seen. I'll contact you when it's time to take them out."

"Yes, Enrique. But what if they're not there?"

"Then you'll make your way back up to where we're docked. Ok, now Juan" Enrique said turning to his younger cousin.

"Yes, Enrique."

"You did real good teaching Dalisay to shoot. She handles an AK-47 like a pro."

"She's just a natural, Enrique."

"Yes, she has a lot of natural talent." He smiled at his men. "Just the same, I want you to take your men and sweep southwest past the old pineapple plantation and then head over to the ship to relieve the girls. After I'm done with these tourists, I want Dalisay waiting for me."

"Why the plantation?" asked Juan.

"Just in case these guys are not who they say they are and their slow crawl up the coastline wasn't because they were lost in the dark. If they dropped anyone off, they will have to cross the plantation before they get to the ship. Also, I want you to get word to Miguel for him and his men to stay close to the swiftboat and the Zodiacs. I want those chase boats ready to fly at a moment's notice. Jonny?"

"Yes, Enrique."

"I don't wanna spook these guys when they come for our meeting. No weapons showing. Only two guys inside the bar, and I want you to keep an eye on this place from outside. You see anyone who looks out of place I want them taken care of. You understand me?"

"Yes, I understand."

"Jonny, I don't want a repeat of last time. Do you remember that?'

"Yes, I remember. I didn't mean to fall asleep. I was just tired."

"You got any coke on you?"

"Yes, Enrique. But just a little."

"Well, you take a hit of that. I want you awake and alert. And make sure it's just a little hit. I don't that stuff waking up the wrong head when Rosa is nearby."

"Yes, Enrique." Jonny replied, trying not to smile.

4 9

Just before Walters and Jeffries disembarked and headed for town, the men remaining on the 776 took up their watch positions around the ship—all except Abner, who was getting ready to serve up the ribs he had made to distract Brewster. A quick nod to everyone from Walters, and he and Jeffries were off. His waist wrapped in a white apron, Abner came out onto the small quarterdeck looking like the cook on a wagon train in an old cowboy movie.

"Ah got sum ribs if enabody wan' any. It's got Chuck's dry rub on `em and they're reeal good."

There were no takers. Even if they didn't know this was part of the plan, the nervous energy was so palpable that no one but Brewster was thinking of food. When he heard the call, he came down out of the conning station and looked at Abner.

"Well, whatcha lookin' at, boy? Nobody else wan' `em. Go hep yaself."

Brewster smiled and disappeared inside. Ray slowly stood up from his post on the starboard side retractable ramp and looked at Abner for his signal. They nodded at each other and Abner walked back into the main cabin.

"Don'tcha go takin' the whole pig now," he shouted. "Ya bes' leave sum fo' the others in case they change their mind."

Ray quietly stepped off the ramp onto the dock and quickly ditched into the overgrowth. There, he tested his radio and proceeded to make his way into town. Meanwhile, Steve told Brewster he'd take over the watch in the conning station and took the opportunity to secure a wireless webcam and began broadcasting the live feed over his blog. Within an instant, followers across the U.S. were being updated as Steve feverishly typed away on his laptop.

Walters and Jeffries met Francis about a hundred yards from the bar. "How was the journey?" he asked the men as they approached.

"Better than I anticipated." Walters shook Francis' outstretched hand.

"It's been a few years," Jeffries said to Francis. "Good to see ya again, Frank."

"Same here, Ben. So, where is he?" he asked Jeffries.

"Your brother? He's on the 776. Armed like the others and keeping watch."

"Does he know what he's doing?"

"Yeah. He's a quick learner. You'd be proud of him, Frank. He's a lot like you." said Jeffries.

"That's good to hear. Peters?"

Jeffries looked at his watch. "His team should be getting to Enrique's ship right about now."

"Ok then. If you guys are ready, follow me." Francis led them down the road toward the bar. Thirty yards behind them, Ray was just out of sight.

Except for the hunting knives that they openly displayed in sheathes attached to their waist belts, both Walters and Jeffries carried no other weapons as they walked the mile from the 776 to Felipe's bar. They didn't know if they would get searched by Enrique or any of his men, and they surely didn't want to run afoul of the local police should they be stopped and questioned. It wasn't every day two white guys casually walked the roads of this part of the island—let alone at night—and they felt the open display was a show of honesty. When they got to Felipe's, Walters laughed to himself realizing that Peters had been right—the bar did look like it was out of some Bogart movie.

Cigarette and cigar smoke filled the large main room while the one working ceiling fan did its best to circulate the cloud. Young prostitutes with faces covered in makeup, reeking of counterfeit perfume, wearing low-cut satin blouses and brightly colored skirts that barely came to mid-thigh lined the bar or worked the patrons in the darkened booths—all except Enrique's booth, that is. The only time a bar girl approached his booth was by special request. This night, there would be none. As long as he still had interest in young Dalisay, he would leave the other girls alone. It was not unusual for him to fancy one of the working girls for a week or two, but Dalisay was different, and she had already held his interest longer than any other.

* * *

Peters looked at his watch as he spoke softly into the microphone that swept down off of his ear bud and across his cheek. "We're in position now. Initial scan shows just the three female guards and nothing showing onboard. Gonna hold fast for a few minutes just to be sure." All five men knelt at their predetermined positions and studied the movement patterns of the guards. The one at the stern moved but a few feet in each direction across the width of the ship. The second girl slowly walked from the stern, reaching mid-ship at the same time the third girl made it to the tip of the bow. The youngest one was preoccupied with the music that filled her ears from the bootlegged MP3 player that had been given to her by Enrique as a token of his appreciation.

* * *

Enrique slid out of his booth when he saw his guests had arrived. He put on a wide smile as he called out loudly through the noise, "Francis! Over here, my friend. Bring our guests and sit with me." They walked past a dozen girls, who instantly noticed the new faces and buzzed with excitement.

"Enrique, I want you to meet the guys who wanna buy your rust bucket."

"Hey, you're gonna scare them off if you talk like that. Gentlemen, please sit down, and don't listen to my friend here. He's just foolin' around. Tell them, Francis."

"Yes of course, my friend. I'm just kidding. Please, forgive my bad manners," Francis apologized before introducing Walters and Jeffries.

Ray came up to the side of the building and crouched down at the window almost entirely hidden by the tall leaves of a thick fern. He slid between the large plant and the window, and except for his inadvertent rustling of the leaves, he couldn't be seen. He strained to see through the dim lighting, thick smoke, and constant movement of the bar girls intermittently obscuring his line of sight. He recognized Walters and Jeffries, sitting in a back booth facing his direction. The other two men were harder to make out—only the back of the head of one and just the left profile of the other guy whom he thought was "Rat Pack." He thought the face looked familiar, but then again from his vantage point, the guy looked like any of the worn-out veterans he had seen at the VMC. Ray studied the men as they talked. He wished he could hear what they were saying. With that thought, he remembered he had to check in with Tex. He pulled the small transmitter pack out of his pocket and switched to the predetermined channel.

"Ray here, checking in. you copy?"

"You're comin' in 5 by 5, Ray. This is Tex. Be advised Brewster knows you left."

"Understood. I'm outside of Felipe's. I can see through a side window. This is as close as I can get. They'll see me if I go inside. Gonna wait a bit and then head over to the LCI."

"No, Ray, I repeat, no. That wasn't the plan. If you can't get inside, then come back."

"Gotta go, someone's coming. Out." He switched back to Peters' channel in time to hear Brewster reporting that he left the ship. Ray saw the expression on Jeffries face and knew that he too heard the report.

"What's the matter, Mr. Jeffries?" asked Enrique. "You don't look so good."

"It's nothing, we're all just tired. It's been a long two weeks on the ocean and with a small crew, we got very little sleep."

Making his rounds along the perimeter of Felipe's, Jonny noticed the rustling leaves on the fern by the side window of the roadside tavern. He stopped and watched for a moment before slowly lifting his 9 mm semi-automatic out of its holster. As carefully and quietly as he could, he pulled back on the slide, advancing one round into the chamber, and eased his way forward toward his target.

"Jonny?" came a whisper from behind him. "Jonny!" came the call again.

He recognized Rosa's voice and smiled as he turned around. "Rosa, what are you doing here?"

"I didn't see you inside the bar and I missed you."

"So you came looking for me?"

"Yes. Are you not happy to see me, Jonny?"

"Yes, of course I am, but..."

"But what, you are busy hunting down kitty cats in the bushes? Is that the kind of pussy you crave?"

"You know what I crave, Rosa" He holstered his weapon and took the girl to his truck. Ray let out a sigh of relief and waited for them to turn the corner before he headed off in the direction of the other ship.

* * *

Just as Dalisay reached mid-ship and turned to walk back to the stern, the volume on her MP3 player suddenly spiked. She stopped to look down at the device and fiddled with the dial control in a vain attempt to fix it. She didn't see or hear her colleagues collapse to the wooden dock as Thompson at the stern and Martin at the bow fired the silenced shots that pierced each girl's heart. After slapping the small music player against the palm of her hand several times, she cursed, ripping the ear buds from her head and turned to whip the entire gadget into the woods. She instantly stopped when she saw the barrel of Peters' silencer not two feet from her forehead. Her heart rate never had the chance to speed up before everything went black.

As planned, all five men boarded the vessel, with Thompson taking a position in the forward gun turret on the bow and Martin taking the high ground with a position in the conning station. Peters tossed the backpack containing the blocks of C-4 to Richards, who made his way to troop one.

"We're onboard," Peters transmitted as he and Gray headed into the main cabin toward the ladder of troop compartment three. The men were immediately hit with the rotting stench of dead fish and other decaying material.

Gray began to feel waves of spasms in his stomach. He fought to suppress the building pressure rising up through his esophagus, but quickly surrendered to the inevitable. The main cabin was dark and all three had to switch on their miniature headlamps. Piles of garbage, fish carcasses, and other filth filled the passageway. Rats scurried away from the noise and the bright L E D headlamps. Peters grabbed Gray by his shirt and pulled him toward troop three. They headed down into the compartment, only to find more piles of food waste, soiled clothing, pornographic magazines, and semen-stained mattresses scattered across the deck. The heat of the compartment intensified the smell, and this time it was Peters who became sick. As fast as they could they dug through the piles, looking for the attaché cases.

* * *

Back at Felipe's, Francis apologized to Enrique and excused himself to go care for his "ailing" wife. "I'm sorry gentlemen," he said. "But Maria has been having a lot of difficulties lately.

Female issues, if you know what I mean. I hope you don't mind, but I need to tend to her."

"I'm sorry to hear this, my friend," said Enrique. "I'll have one of my men drive you back up the mountain. That should save you a good deal of time."

"That's very kind of you, my friend," Francis responded. "A ride is greatly appreciated."

As Enrique arranged for Francis' ride with one of the two guards he had positioned inside the bar, Jeffries heard Peters' frustrated transmission that they couldn't find the cases amongst the piles of garbage in troop three. He looked down at the table and briefly rubbed his head.

"Again you are not looking well," Enrique commented, returning to the booth. "Can I get you something, anything at all?"

"Thank you, I'll be fine. So, please tell me more about your ship."

* * *

Hector and his men had arrived at the 776 only moments before observing a number of armed guards carefully watching the jungle from key positions on the vessel. He knew then that this was no amateur excursion and decided quick action was necessary. Failing to reach anyone by radio, he summoned his fastest runner to carry a message back to Enrique. "Freddie, tell Enrique we're taking their ship. Also, tell him there's probably going to be a hit on ours. Tell him they are here for the cases. Now go as fast as you can."

If he took the main road, Freddie could have easily covered the one-mile distance in under five minutes; fifteen if he went through the jungle. After his young runner disappeared back into the heavy concentration of broad leafed plants, ferns, vines and bamboo, Hector passed word to his remaining nine men and within seconds they opened fire on the American vessel.

Sam Lipton had always heard that you never hear the bullet that takes you down. He didn't. But he definitely saw it. In fact, it was the very last thing he saw. It's debatable whether or not he felt the searing heat as the round fired from the AK-47 pierced his forehead and cooked his brain tissue sending thousands of electrical shock like jolts of pain through short circuiting neurons. There was no debate, however, that the shot turned his muscles into rubber, buckled his knees, and alleviated his constipation all before his head slammed against the steel deck he had carefully scrapped and painted just a few months earlier.

Chuck, Tex, and Steve immediately returned fire with an array from their M-16s and the .50 caliber machine gun. With his hands and face still covered in barbecue sauce, Brewster ran out of the officer's mess and headed to the stern to join in the fray.

* * *

Juan and his men were slowly making their way through the abandoned pineapple plantation when they heard the rapid firecracker-sounding pops coming from the south and knew that a gun battle was underway. From where they were, it was a mile in each direction to either ship. He chose to head south to support his comrades.

* * *

Richards too was sickened by the thick smell that lay heavy throughout the ship. He carefully made his way through the piles of debris and the rats, setting the explosives in the three compartments as he had been instructed to do. Gray went off to search troop one while Peters labored through troop two.

"There's nothing here!" he yelled frantically into his headset before hurrying to search the rest of the ship. "You guys got that? There are no cases!"

* * *

The gun battle going on at the 776 was far enough away that it couldn't be heard above the noise inside of Felipe's bar, but everyone did hear Jonny's weapon discharge as he crawled all over Rosa in the back of his truck. Having placed a round in the chamber not fifteen minutes earlier, the intoxicating combination of cocaine and Rosa's perfume made him forget about it. Now that bullet was lodged in his right thigh, clipping the femoral artery just above the knee.

For a brief moment, the entire bar went silent. Enrique was the first to react, jumping up from his booth.

"Take care of these two right now!" he yelled to his remaining bodyguard before running out the front door with guns drawn.

The guard approached the booth and pulled a .45 semi-automatic from his belt just as a knife thrown by Jeffries dissected his aorta when it sliced through the space between the fourth and fifth ribs just to the right of his sternum. He and Walters wasted no time running out of a side door and raced back to the 776.

* * *

Hearing Peters' frustration over the transmitter, Ray began to run toward their location as fast as he could. The jungle was thick and dark, and several times he fell after losing his footing on hidden rocks or tree stumps. One fall sent him rolling down into a small ditch and he felt a crunching shift in the defective lower vertebra that had only slightly bothered him through the years. Now there was a sudden burning in his lower back as his lumbar spinal muscles tightened. He lay there for a minute, afraid that any movement would trigger more intense symptoms. He listened to Brewster report the attack on the 776 while at the same time listening to Peters complaining of finding nothing in any of the compartments. As his pain intensified he thought of his father.

"White socks with palm trees sewn on them. That's how you'll be able to tell if she's the 606."

"What are you talking about?"

"I left a pair of white socks onboard. Not on purpose. They hid them on me."

"What makes you think they'd still be onboard?"

"After I was detached in November `45, one of the crew who was with me on the ship back to the States told me that he and a couple of other guys had hid `em in the ballast of troop three. As a joke."

"What's the ballast?"

"It's like a crawl space that you'd find underneath a house. There's an oval-shaped hatch cover in the deck plate with about, oh I don't remember, eighteen or twenty big nuts and bolts. You gotta get that cover off to have access to the ballast. They hid my socks there. If she's the 606, I'll bet my socks will be there."

Ray reached up to grab a thick vine and pulled himself to a standing position, wincing as a jolt of pain shot down into his left buttock. His pace slowed, but he continued to fight his way through the jungle, figuring he had another hundred yards or so before he got to the dock.

"It's in the ballast!" he screamed into his mic. "It's in the fuckin' ballast!"

"Silver? Is that you?" yelled Peters.

"Yes, damn it. The cases are in the ballast of troop three."

"Where's that?"

"In the floor, in the fuckin' floor. There's an oval cover bolted somewhere in the floor. It's got about twenty big bolts. The cases are under that!" Ray screamed as he continued to half-run, half-hobble toward the ship.

Peters looked around the mounds of oil-soaked rags covering the floor of the engine room. He found a tool box and grabbed a large socket wrench along with an assortment of sockets and made his way up the ladder yelling for Gray and Richards to join him in troop three.

* * *

The firefight continued at the 776. Abner huddled in the galley, once again fighting the same fear that had gripped him fifty-nine years earlier. "What the hell's wrong wit' ya, boy?" he asked himself out loud. "An' thas what ya are, a boy. Not a man if you's hidin' down heyah. This is what ya wanted, ain't it? This is why ya came? Ya damn right it is! Now less get our ass up there an' do what needs ta be done!"

He joined his crewmates on deck with an M-16 and began firing wildly toward the rapid flashes of gunfire coming out of the bush. Except for Lipton having been killed at the outset, the rest of the crew were holding their own, managing to kill three of Hectors' men.

* * *

Enrique quickly assembled seven more of his soldiers. They jumped into their aging SUVs and headed as fast as they could toward their own ship. When they arrived at the dock, they were met with gunfire from Thompson and Martin. Taking cover from behind his truck, Enrique was able to see Dalisay's body lying motionless, her MP3 player resting in her open hand. He became enraged and emptied his assault rifle toward the ship.

"Francis, you mutha fuckaaa," he yelled out. "I'm gonna fuckin' kill you!" He grabbed one man to go with him to the mountain home where Frank Silver had been living for almost twenty years—leaving the others behind to continue the assault.

* * *

As they approached the house, Enrique's bodyguard stopped his truck and looked at Francis when he thought he heard a distant gun battle. Before he could react, Francis slit his throat, pushed him out onto the roadside, and continued up the mountain to his home. He had little time to gather up and destroy any sensitive documents that still might be lying around.

* * *

Peters, Richards, and Gray kicked and shoved the mounds of debris until they found the oval shaped hatch cover secured with twenty 1-inch nuts and bolts. Peters fumbled through the sockets he had brought from the engine room until he found the correct size. He had just begun to loosen them when Thompson yelled into his radio, "We need help up here. Now! Damn it!"

"You guys get up there and I'll work on this hatch cover" Peters said to Richards and Gray, who were only too happy to get out into the fresh air. As soon as the two men exited the main cabin onto the outer deck, Gray took three hits to his torso and went down. Richards joined Thompson and Martin in the gunfight.

"Doc, where are you?" Peters called into his radio.

"I'm close. I see the LCI. I see the Filipinos."

"There's too many bolts on this thing and we're out of time. I need you to get onboard and fire up these engines."

"I'll never get onboard with all that gunfire. I'll get cut down for sure."

"You got a weapon on ya?"

"Yeah, but…"

"But my fuckin' ass. Circle around behind those guys and take `em out, goddammit!"

Ray swallowed hard. The only times he ever fired a weapon were onboard the 776 or at a gun range. As mad as he had ever been, he had never wanted to kill anyone—Harrison included.

"Hey Doc, you still there?"

"Yeah, I'm here."

"Time's running out. It's time to step up."

* * *

Walters and Jeffries made it back to the 776, watching as the battle continued. Walters was shocked and at the same time, full of pride that "his crew" were battling like old pros. Jeffries counted seven muzzle flashes coming from the thick bush that bordered the decaying pier. He slowly crawled toward Hectors' right flank until he came to one of the dead guerillas. He slid the weapon out from under the body and began firing, killing Hector and three more of his men. He and Walters made a run for the ship as Abner screamed out ,"Coverin' fire!"

A hail of bullets rained down into the brush. The last three of Hectors' men were easily torn to pieces. Abner checked his weapon. His heart and his mind were racing.

He paced back and forth with his chest out, his shoulders back, and he felt a sense of exhilaration. He felt a sense of vindication. In his mind, he finally made amends for his inaction all those years ago.

Walters wasted no time ordering everyone to their stations. Steve started the engines from the conning tower as the others released the lines.

The closer Juan and his men got to the 776, the faster they ran, getting to the dock just as the ship was pulling away. They unleashed a firestorm that sparked and ricocheted off of the superstructure as well as ladders, bulkhead doors, railings, and ammo storage lockers. Brewster danced and flailed like a marionette whose strings were jerked wildly as a dozen bullets chewed his muscular frame. Jeffries took a massive hit that blew his right shoulder apart and knocked him off his feet. Chunks of shredded muscle and bone splattered across the deck, his right arm and hand now rendered useless.

* * *

Ray knew he had no choice. He had to act. As his mind raced—debating if *this* was what he had wanted his whole life—recalling the words he had said to Abner several hours before. *"Ya know the old saying 'be careful what ya wish for'? Well, our wish is gonna come true. I just hope we didn't wish for something more than we bargained for."*

There wasn't any more time to analyze it. Peters was shouting in his ear. He double-checked his Mac-10 and ran, firing his weapon toward the half-dozen men hidden behind tall bushes and trees. He didn't know if they were startled more by the attack coming from their left flank or from his screaming like a wild man. But they were startled long enough to stop firing. He hit the first three before the others took aim at him. Before they could fire, Ray's bullets also tore them to pieces. Thompson, Richards, and Martin were impressed. Ray's adrenaline had him in overdrive and he stood there trying to process what he had just done.

"Silver!" Peters' voice echoed through his radio earpiece. "Engine room. Now!"

"On my way!" Ray hobbled up the ramp. He told the others to cast off the lines and headed into the main cabin. He was so pumped up he didn't even notice the heavy odor. "It's pitch black in here, I can't see!' he screamed. He ran back outside to see Gray lying dead on the deck. Only days before, the young man—no older than his son Jimmy—was telling him about his grandfather jumping into Normandy with the 101st. Ray grabbed his headlamp and rushed back through the debris, his left knee buckling from another lightening-like jolt of pain shooting from his lower back. Again he forced himself up, and sailed down the ladder as if he had been doing it his whole life.

Peters sent Thompson down to finish removing the nuts from the oval plate in the troop three compartment and headed up to the bridge. From what Chuck had taught him, it had only taken a matter of minutes for Ray to get five of the eight diesels running. The other three were in such disrepair he didn't even bother with them. Still, they had propulsion, and lights came on throughout the ship. Only then were they able to bear true witness to the extent of neglect and disgusting waste that filled every inch of the guerilla- owned vessel. At that point, Ray didn't want to know if she was the 606. He was saddened and disgusted with what he saw.

From the bridge Peters communicated with Walters, and they agreed on a rendezvous point. At full throttle and with only five engines working, they were lucky to be making ten knots, sailing away from the Camarines Norte section of Luzon, heading north by northeast cutting a path between the Polillo and Calaguas Islands.

In addition to the piles of oil-soaked rags that covered the deck in the engine room, the small auxiliary engine used to start the diesels was leaking gasoline. Between the fire hazard and the stench which soon began to overtake Ray, he needed to get topside for fresh air and to warn the others they may have to abandon ship.

* * *

Back on the 776, Chuck and Tex carried Jeffries into the commanding officer's cabin and set him down into the lower bunk. All color had drained from his face and his eyes began to glaze over. Jeffries was still losing blood and there was nothing they could do for him. Walters came in, took one look, and knew right away it would be a matter of minutes before he was gone.

"Come here, John. What's our status?" he asked Walters as he began to cough up blood.

"We've got three dead. Gray, Brewster, and Lipton."

"Four, with me."

"I'm not gonna bullshit ya. You're losing way too much blood."

"What about the cases?"

"Nothing yet. They searched the entire ship and couldn't find anything. Now they're trying to get into the ballast."

"They gotta get outta there."

"They're moving, don't worry. Ray's onboard. Got the engines goin' and they're on their way. We'll meet up with them when we get far enough away to stop and make the transfer."

Jeffries tried to laugh as he grew weaker. "Your boys did good. I never thought…"

"Ben?" Walters leaned over and felt for a pulse. He knew the answer before his fingers made contact with his neck.

* * *

Frank grabbed the last of the small stack of papers from his safe, threw them into the gasoline-soaked fireplace, and tossed in a lit match. He stuffed a wad of money and ID papers into the side pocket of his cargo pants but before heading out the back door he made the mistake of stopping to take one last look around. That's when he heard the whining engine of a truck coming up the long dirt road that led to his house. "I'm getting old," he thought. "I should have been outta here fifteen minutes ago." He pulled two 9mm semi-automatics from his desk draw, checked the clips, and walked over to the big leather club chair in the corner of his living room. He sat down and poured himself a brandy.

Enrique pulled his truck within thirty yards of the small mountain home that overlooked the village and the bay. "You wait here, Bennie," he ordered his man as they both got out of the SUV. "I'll take care of this one myself." He checked his weapons, then slowly walked up to the house.

Bennie leaned back against the truck, lit up a cigarette, and watched as his boss kicked in the front door, waiting a few seconds before entering. Except for the flickering light from the fireplace, the house was dark. It was quiet. The end of Bennie's cigarette glowed a bright orange as he inhaled. And then he jumped when a series of rapid explosions suddenly rang out as windows from both ends of the house lit up in an exchange of multiple bright flashes. Everything went dark, except for the flickering light of the fireplace, and all was quiet once more.

* * *

Through his binoculars, Steve saw the running lights of the other ship as she slowly made her way toward their rendezvous point. With the help of the full moon he was able to make out three small speed boats coming up fast from a few thousand yards behind. "Walters, I got a visual," he yelled into the public address system. "And they've got three assault craft coming up fast on their butt!"

Walters flew up to the conning station and took the binoculars from Steve. "We gotta get over there and help them."
Steve spun the wheel for a full right rudder and pushed the
throttle all the way for maximum power. Seven of the eight
turbo chargers kicked in. The 776 jerked hard and quickly
made twenty-three knots as they headed back to assist the others. "Peters," he called into his mic, "you've got company coming up on your ass."

Walters called into the public address system, "Somebody
get those RPGs on deck. Chuck, get on a twenty-mil!"

Peters stepped out onto the gun deck and looked aft, barely
making out the three Zodiacs coming up from their rear. He
alerted Martin, Richards, and Ray and they took up positions
in the two aft turrets on the gun deck. Martin grabbed a pry
bar and busted the lock off of an ammo storage bin and found
it to be empty. He jumped over to a second bin and pried off
that lock as well. "Pay dirt!" he shouted out when he found a
.30 caliber machine gun with a number of preloaded belts. He
quickly mounted the gun on the swivel ring of the port side
gun mount. "Locked and loaded." He called out and took aim
at the lead assault craft. Down below, Thompson had eighteen
of the twenty nuts removed and he had to come up for air.

As the the 776 raced back to help them, Steve saw a fast-
moving vessel off their starboard beam heading toward the
slower LCI. Walters immediately recognized the Vietnam-era
swift boat. "Chuck," he called down to the forward station on
the starboard side gun deck. "Swift boat off the starboard beam
five-hundred yards and closing. She's got two big fuel tanks
in the stern. Lead with your shots. Fire ahead of her bow and
watch the tracers to adjust your aim. Got it?"

"Yeah, got it!" he said as he swung the twenty around and
began tracking his target.

"Don't wait too long, looks like she's making thirty knots!"

The lead Zodiac carried four men and got within fifty yards
before opening fire, sending Ray and Richards diving for cover.
Martin returned fire with the .30 caliber, killing two before he
was mortally wounded. Ray crab-walked to the machine gun to

aid Martin. When he got to him, he was already gurgling blood from multiple chest wounds.

Luckily, he died within seconds.

"Doc," Richards called out. "Get on that gun!"

Ray jumped up, sighted in on the driver of the Zodiac, and depressed the trigger. Bullets riddled the small boat, with one lucky shot striking a fuel line. A ball of flame erupted and lit up the night sky. Ray and Richards immediately shifted their focus to starboard aft and simultaneously opened up on the second craft.

Two rocket-propelled grenades came off the second assault craft and struck the ship at the water line, putting a hole into the superstructure by the engine room. A third RPG hit close to the first two. The flames from the explosion ignited the leaking gasoline and diesel-soaked rags that covered the engine-room floor. A larger explosion soon rocked the ship, and she lost all power as water began to flood the aft compartments. Ray laid down a bead from the single-barreled machine gun and struck a box of explosives on the second attack vessel sending another fireball into the air.

"Here comes the 776," yelled Peters who had taken a position in the conning station.

At the sight of the second Zodiac going up in flames, the third attack boat and the swift boat veered off to regroup out of firing range. That gave the 776 time to pull alongside the heavily damaged LCI. Thompson had just a couple of more nuts to unscrew, but he refused to go back down.

"I'd rather take my chances in a gun fight than breathe anymore of that fuckin' shit," he protested. He jumped across to the 776, as did Richards.

Peters yelled to Ray, "I'm gonna keep watch up here, you go below and get that hatch cover off. We need to get those cases."

"Just tell me what the hell's in `em."

"Dirty bombs," Walters said calmly into his mic. Ray turned to look across at him in the conning station of the 776. "No shit, Doc. They're nuclear briefcase bombs."

"Ok, John," he responded without emotion.

"Hurry up, Doc. We're taking on water in the stern and we got C-4 that's gonna go," Peters reminded him.

Ray made his way down into troop three, unscrewed the last two big nuts, and removed the heavy hatch cover. "John, they're here. But there's three of 'em, not two but three. Can I move 'em or what?"

"Do you see any wires coming out of the cases?"

"No, I don't see any. Although the third case is just out of reach. I'll have to get into the ballast to get that one."

"Can you see if there are any timers?"

"No, I don't see anything like that at all."

"What are they sitting on? Does it look like there's any kind of triggering device that they could be sitting on?"

"I don't see anything but the three cases...and lots of rats. They safe to move?"

"Yeah, they're not active. Go ahead and lift them up."

Ray grabbed hold of the handle on the first case and lifted. "Should they have weight to 'em?" he asked.

"Yeah," Walters responded. "About fifteen pounds or so." He turned to Steve and noticed he was typing on his laptop. Then he saw the web camera. "What the fuck is this shit?"

"What shit?" yelled Ray. He stopped moving.

"Not you, Doc. You just go ahead and get those cases outta there. Steve, what the hell's with the camera?"

"I've been blogging this 'cause I thought we'd need help."

"You're shittin' me, right?"

"Nope. The Navy just detoured Amphibious group 3. Don't know when they'll get here but they're on the way."

"Who else is seeing this, Damn it?"

"More people than I care to mention."

"Fuck it, give me that thing." He reached for the web camera.

Steve pulled his 9 mm from his pants pocket and stuck it into Walters' right temple—his hand stopping within inches of the camera.

"I will pull this trigger, John."

The swiftboat regrouped with the third Zodiac as the fourth slowly came out of the darkness and eased up toward the stern of the 776. While Walters and his crew were pre-occupied, the attack boats began another run on the two aging ships. Looking off his port beam, the last thing Peters saw before his conning station and pilothouse disintegrated into a thousand pieces was the smoke stream of the surface-to-surface missile fired from the swift boat.

Ray felt the ship rock from the explosion as he lifted the third and final case out of the ballast. He carried each case up the ladder and out onto the deck in separate trips. Tex was waiting for him on the 776 to take the cases one by one. Steve followed his movements with the web camera and yelled at Ray when he stayed on the sinking vessel, navigating through the burning debris to get back up to the gun deck. There was nothing left of the pilothouse and Peters was nowhere to be found. The stern of the ship lurched and began to sink lower into the water. He walked over to Martin's body and hoisted him up across his shoulder. His lower back muscles twinged with pain from the extra weight. Gunfire erupted one more time from the 776 as their attackers made another pass. After Martin was passed on to Tex, Ray went back one last time for Gray. He knelt down beside him and looked into his lifeless eyes before gently sweeping them closed.

"Let's go, Ray!" yelled Steve.

Ray hoisted Gray over his shoulder and carried him back.

The crew pushed off from the sinking ship and watched her slowly begin to slip below the surface just as the C-4 in troop one exploded, sending everyone diving to the deck. "They're making another run on us," Walters yelled out. "Ray, get up to that forward twenty!"

Ray ran forward as bullets hit all around him, his lower back burning with pain. Abner stood at the bulkhead door and once again had to rub his eyes in disbelief as he watched what he thought was a young Ron Silver charging up the ladder to man the forward AA gun.

Walters slammed the throttle into reverse to get away from the suction created by the sinking ship, and Abner fell back off his feet and onto his rear end. Ray's forward momentum combined with the sudden backward lurch of the ship almost made him fly off the bow but he caught himself on the forward railing. He screamed as his back pain became even more intense. He climbed into the forward gun, took aim at the swift boat, and opened fire. All at once the remaining 776 crew opened fire on the third Zodiac. Within seconds they both blew. When he got to his feet, Abner looked forward relieved to see Ray still onboard.

Ray turned and looked for the other ship, but she was gone. An assortment of cheers erupted across the 776. Ray let out a big sigh of relief and slowly made his way aft. Richards patted him on the shoulder as he walked over to Abner.

"You ok, A.J.?"

"Yeah, Ray, ah'm doin' jeeees fine."

"You should have seen him," Tex said to Ray. "He came flyin' out of the hatchway and was blastin' away with that M16. The guy looked like a commando."

No one saw the fourth Zodiac. It had arrived on the scene from a different direction while everyone had been preoccupied with the swift boat and the other speed boats. Had someone taken up a position on the stern after Brewster was killed, they might have seen it coming up out of the darkness more than ten minutes before. Now, as two of Enrique's soldiers crouched quietly near the bodies of Lipton and Brewster, a third inched up the empty passageway of the 776's main cabin. Everyone onboard had been gradually mingling up toward the forward area or on the gun deck, taking stock of the insanity that had just unfolded in less than an hour.

Abner stood in front of the portside main cabin hatchway, talking and laughing with Ray and Tex. In the conning station, Steve had returned to his blogging, responding to questions that were now flooding in from concerned readers. He was amazed how word had spread, and his blog had been picked up by active duty naval personnel stationed at Pearl Harbor and other bases along both the east and west coasts of the United States.

Walters walked aft along the gun deck having a smoke and was thinking about the hours of debriefing they were all going to face when he spotted the two Filipinos on the stern below. "Boarders!" he screamed. "We've got Boarders on the stern!"

Before anyone could react, several shots from inside the main cabin slammed Abner square in the back, as if he had been hit with a sledgehammer. Ray heard the deep thud as the wind was knocked out of him, and he fell forward into Ray's arms. His knees buckled under the old man's weight and he fell back, making sure that Abner landed on top of him. The others responded, taking care of the three invaders within seconds. Richards dragged each of the bodies to the stern and dumped them off.

Ray repositioned himself into a sitting posture cradling Abner in his arms.

"Aw man," Abner said as he looked up at Ray. "This ain't no good, doc...this ain't...no good at all."

"Shhh, don't talk. Save your strength."

Abner laughed and then cringed in pain, coughing up a little blood. "Doc, you been watchin'...too many a them submarine movies."

"Yeah, ok." He looked at Abner and wiped his mouth for him. "Just the same, I know you're hurt real bad...but...I can tell you're gonna be alright." Ray studied Abner's face and his eyes began to well up with tears.

"Hey, cut that shit out. Ya...don't gotta worry. Ah'm free now, Doc. Ya shoulda seen me. Ah was really sumptin' out here tonight. Ah...Ah did...what ah had ta do...mah mind...mah conscious...is free. Ah'm at peace wit' that, Ray. Ya uner... stand?"

"Yeah, Abner. I understand."

"Ya do? `cause...ya earned...Ya earned it too. Ya know that, right?" He looked away and continued to speak. "Did ya see ya boy tonight? He earned it too, Ronnie. Ah hope ya saw that."

"Ronnie? It's Ray, I'm Ray," He said looking to where Abner was staring. Through the hatchway door, he saw what looked like his dad at the end of the passageway standing near the ladder to the engine room. It was then that Ray realized his dad had passed away.

"Do me a favah, Ray," Abner said as his voice began to trail off. Ray leaned into him, bringing his ear to Abner's lips to hear the old man's request. When he finished speaking, he gently kissed Ray on the cheek before letting out his last breath.

Again Ray looked down the passageway of the main cabin to see the image of an eighteen-year-old Ron Silver—dressed in dungarees, a powder blue work shirt, and white sailor cap—smile and wave at his son before heading down into the engine room.

5 0

Little did they know—thanks to Steve Scott's tech savvy—
that the events that had unfolded in the Philippine Sea
from the decks of an often overlooked World War II
relic would trigger a frenzy and a strange sense of underdog
triumph not seen since Doolittle's Raiders gave America hope
that they could successfully strike back against a fanatical
enemy. What had been an ill-conceived covert operation that
was now being passed off as an accidental encounter by amateur
sailors, was somehow being twisted by some in the government
and media alike into something to rally around in the new
global war on terror. But some argued that anyone who had
been following the live feed saw and heard John Walters tell
Ray that the attaché cases he needed to retrieve were nuclear
briefcase bombs. Those pro and con on the issue also witnessed
Ray emerge from the debris three separate times, carrying the
medium-sized aluminum cases and then calmly returning to
the burning and sinking vessel to carry back the bodies of two
crewmates. And as Steve kept adjusting the wireless webcam,
a myriad of people—from media and casual observers to NSA
officials, senators, and congressional representatives alike—
had seen Ray running through automatic weapons fire to take
up station on the forward 20mm AA gun, taking out a terrorist

vessel. Regardless of how it was being portrayed, Ray, Steve, Tex and Chuck wanted no part of it.

Over the next several days, the media had a field day with rumor and innuendo as they demanded answers from the White House, Congress, and the various security agencies. In spite of their refusal to talk publicly about the ordeal, the tattered surviving crew of the 776 were hailed as citizen heroes and true American patriots. The CIA denied any knowledge of a sanctioned operation, and the official story was the same one that Walters and Jeffries had originally given to the volunteers of the now damaged and "officially" seized LCI 776.

"A CIA spokesperson again stated today that crew members of that World War II naval vessel were part of a group of volunteers who had restored the ship and sailed to the Philippines with the intention of purchasing a similar craft. While there, they accidentally stumbled into an Al Qaeda operation that a combined team of U.S. Navy SEALS and elite Filipino commandos had been carefully tracking for many months. As excellent as the final outcome was, the President reminded us during his press conference this evening that the outcome could have been very different, resulting in catastrophic consequences. But many questions continue to go unanswered tonight as a number of Congressional members are demanding information from the CIA, and NSA as well as the White House. As always, as soon as anything new develops, you the viewing audience will be the first to know. For Coxx Cable News, I'm Jenna Grant."

Always on the lookout for political points, Senator Murphy was quick to telephone Peter McCain at the VMC to demand Ray's immediate reinstatement. Then she made the rounds on the Sunday morning news programs, making sure everyone was aware that she personally knew Ray Silver, and that it had been her who initiated the chiropractic program at the Seattle Veterans Medical Center. To her credit, however, she was genuinely proud of what Ray had done and didn't hold back talking up his family's history of service to the nation whenever she was with the press. Her persistence caught the attention of the Secretary of the Navy.

John Walters and the 776—along with the three attaché cases—were towed back to Midway under protection of Amphibious group 3 which had been on its way back to San Diego from Okinawa when the detour was ordered. Ray and the others were flown straight back to Seattle, where they spent several days debriefing with the NSA, CIA, FBI and Naval Intelligence.

5 1

Ray finished his Pipeline while watching the heavy raindrops hit the windowpanes and listening to the rhythmic sound of Magic's purring. He wanted to go to sleep for several days, and thought if he could just get through the next few, he would finally be able to lay down next to Leigh Anne and listen to the sounds of rustling palm fronds and the gentle waves washing up along the sands of Kailua. "*You*...little kitty, are gonna love your new home," he said as he looked at Magic. "I just gotta make one more trip. I promise this will be a short one."

"Hey Ray, you in here?" Stella's voice was unmistakable.

"In here, Stel." He slowly got up, nursing his lower back. She came around the Jeep with a big smile and wrapped herself around him in an embrace that was just as big. He took his time letting go.

"Do you know we saw the whole thing? Well, almost the whole thing. But we saw it. I mean people all over the place... all over the world were watching what you guys did."

"I heard. Crazy, huh?"

"Ray, my God! The whole country is talking about it."

"I know. It's gonna be quite some time before I can go out for a beer or coffee without being stared at."

"Can you blame them? I remember getting the call from Griff. They were watching you guys at the NSA! We were watching you right from this computer."

"Who's 'we' ?"

"Me and Magic. She was laying right here on the desk and we were watching the battle.

I just have one question for you. Are you outta your mind? You coulda been killed, ya big jerk!"

"Yeah...like Abner," he said very quietly.

"I'm sorry, Ray. I loved him too. What about the body?"

"His last request was that he be cremated, his ashes scattered in the Pacific. I'm gonna take care of that after I get back from Arlington. Speaking of which, I really need to get going on the flight arrangements."

"No need to. Senator Murphy called here twice wanting to talk to you. Not only is she having you reinstated at the VMC, but she also has a roundtrip ticket to D.C. waiting for you at the airport."

"Why am I not surprised? She probably saw political points all over this thing."

"You and those other guys just performed an amazing service to the country. You guys are being hailed as heroes. Maybe she wants to show her appreciation, and maybe you should cut her some slack."

"Yeah, maybe your right...But I'm no hero. I just did what needed to be done. I should've never been there in the first place. Stella, I killed a lot of people. In less than one hour I took the lives of at least ten men. I never counted on that, and now I gotta figure out how I'm gonna deal with it. I mean, I go out there trying to..."

"Hey, slow down. And understand this. You did what every man and woman who wears a uniform is called upon to do in the service of their country. You may not wear the uniform, but that's no fault of your own and it never has been. You participated in an event that saved tens, if not hundreds of thousands, of lives. The people you helped stop were gonna be the ones who committed that mass murder if you hadn't stepped up, and they would have killed you too. That's all you need to know, and that's how you justify it. You stepped up and served this country no different than any soldier, sailor, marine, or airmen, and you did it bravely and with honor. Isn't that the redemption you've been looking for all these years?"

"You know me pretty well."

"So I don't suppose you're coming back to work at the medical center?"

"I'm gonna have to talk to the Senator about the VMC thing. Anything new with Harrison?"

"Oh, you can put a fork in him. He's definitely done. But any further government investigation into his involvement with Visor has come to a dead end."

"There wasn't enough evidence to pursue anything?"

"Oh, there was enough evidence after their investigation, just not enough gonads at the congressional level for anyone to see it through."

"Didn't any of this get back to Senator Murphy, or even Claremont?"

"Neither. It seems they don't really know much or don't wanna know. I'm not sure which. I wouldn't be surprised if Visor makes big contributions to their campaigns."

"Are you ok with that? I mean, that it's not being pursued at a higher level?"

"No. Don't get me wrong, I'm glad Harrison's ass is fired and his license is suspended. I can live with that. So if this dies right here? Hey, I did what I had to do, so yeah, I'm at peace with it. But there should've been more."

"Well, since it seems I might have a little pull right now, I'll just have to talk to the Senator about that as well."

"Let it go, Ray."

"Are you sure?"

"Yeah, I'm sure. Let it go."

"So that's it then? You're just gonna let it die? Somehow I can't believe it." Ray looked at Stella and saw a sparkle in her eye that suggested otherwise. "You're not letting this go are you?"

"Well, I did send out copies of everything to the *Tribune* in D.C and to Coxx Cable News." She winked and they shared a laugh.

"Now that'll surely get some attention."

"I sure hope so."

"Hey, you hungry, Stel?"

"As a matter of fact, I am. Kelsey's?"

"I'll drive."

5 2

Kelsey let out a loud scream and cried like a baby when Ray unexpectedly walked in after his two and a half week absence. She came running out from behind the bar and nearly knocked him down with hugs and kisses. Then she punched him in the arm. "Goddamit, are you freakin' nuts? How could you do such a crazy thing?" She hugged him again. The usual crowd of patrons gave Ray a standing ovation and Stella saw his embarrassment. Kelsey rambled on.

"You guys come follow me," she said leading them to the back booth. "I'm so freakin' mad at you, Ray Silver. If you weren't going to be a father I'd kill you."

"What?" He looked up at Kelsey.

"Oops."

"Yeah," confirmed Stella. "Major oops."

Ray turned quickly to Stella. "You knew about this too?"

"Guilty."

"Leigh's pregnant?" he asked in disbelief.

Kelsey and Stella nodded simultaneously. Ray took out his cell phone and called her—again getting her voicemail. "I don't believe this. I can't believe no matter how many times I call her, I get voicemail. Leigh?" He shouted into the phone. "It's Ray, baby. Call me as soon as you get this message. I'm not taking any other calls or doing anything until you call me back." He looked at Kelsey and pointed to the booth for her to sit. "Fill me in."

The three of them talked and ate, and talked some more until Ray's phone finally rang. After seven weeks of not seeing or speaking to each other, they were almost speechless at first. Kelsey showed him back to her private office, where it was quiet and he could be alone. They talked until his cell battery began to die, hanging up only after arranging to meet at Kimo's in a few days.

When he came back out into the dinning room almost everyone had gone. Stella and Kelsey were up at the bar having a beer and fast becoming friends. Kelsey opened a Pipeline for Ray and put it on the bar.

"When you go off to Oahu, I'm gonna be left with a lot of this porter," Kelsey said as he pulled up a stool.

"I'm sure we'll be back for the holidays so the twins can visit their two aunties" he said as he took a long drink.

"Is that what she told you, twins?" Stella asked. Kelsey was too shocked to say anything.

"Twins! She just found out yesterday."

5 3

R ay tried to sleep on the red-eye from Seattle to Reagan
National in Washington D.C., but once again he was
preoccupied. He felt that he had too many things to
wrap up. He laughed at the irony of how things had changed
since the days when he and Jo were married. She had been the
one who sweated over every detail—staying up late planning
and executing projects. And she had often let him know how
easy he had it, as she did all the research and the groundwork
while he enjoyed the fruits of her labor. Over the past year, he
had found himself having many sleepless nights doing many
similar things. If he didn't appreciate all of Jo's efforts before,
he surely did now. He was reminded of something Abner had
once told him during one of their many conversations: *"Not
'til ya walk a mile in anotha man's shoes can ya fullah unerstand an'
'preciate what they do."* His voice was as clear as if he had been
sitting right next to Ray, who hadn't had a chance to think
about him in a sentimental way since his death several days
before. Exhaustion and his emotions were beginning to catch
up to him. He felt he needed to suppress those emotions just a
little while longer if he was going to get through the next few
hours. At least until he could be alone. Thankfully, the view
of the Capitol as the plane lowered its landing gear on final
approach refocused his attention.

The last time he flew into D.C. was for Jimmy's graduation at Georgetown. Throughout his son's time in law school Ray had made several trips to visit. The view of the city as they approached was always an emotional experience for him. He practically pressed his face up to the window like a little kid and smiled with satisfaction each time he recognized another landmark. The light dusting of snow that had fallen the evening before gave it an almost heavenly appearance as everything sparkled in the morning sun. "I wonder," he thought, "if the founding fathers were alive today, would they look at the majesty of this place with the same awe as I do, even if they knew all the fraud and waste that goes on inside of her walls?"

Senator Murphy—accompanied by several news crews— was waiting for him as he exited the terminal. She had been taking questions from several Capitol Hill reporters when she saw him come through the doors. "And speaking of Dr. Silver, here he is now."

The reporters turned as he stared at the senator, shaking his head as they descended upon him. "Dr. Silver, Scott Center from NCC news. Can you honestly say that you had no idea the people you were dealing with in the Philippines were part of an Al Qaeda terror cell?"

"Scott, we were on a trip to purchase an old World War II Navy landing craft. We wanted to bring it back to Seattle and restore it as part of a floating museum and as a memorial to a group of U.S. Navy veterans who played a major role during the war and whose efforts were largely forgotten by history. Honestly, if we even had an ounce of suspicion we would've never....we would've never gone."

"Doctor, Kelly O'Connell from American News Network. So you're telling us that you and all the guys who took part in this operation, guys like Charles Shimkin and Steven Scott, had no connection to any government agency? From what we saw on that video blog, you guys handled yourselves as if you had been professionally trained."

"First off, Kelly, this...wasn't an "operation," and as far as I know, I'm the only one...the only one on that excursion who's a government employee. That is, working as a staff chiropractor at the Veterans Medical Center in Seattle. As far as anyone else, I only know them from the volunteer work we all did on the LCI. But if you think about it, Ms. O'Connell, if this had been an "operation," as you call it, why would we broadcast it over the internet for all to see?"

"As a follow-up then, how do you feel about being reinstated at the Veterans Medical Center?"

"I've only been back for a couple of days now, so I haven't given it much thought."

"Dr. Silver, Jenna Grant from Coxx Cable News. We have information from our sources that the man who actually owned the ship you were volunteering on *is* a former CIA agent. Are you saying you weren't aware of this?" Ray stared at the Coxx news reporter, instantly recalling Leigh Anne's words: *"I had... have a younger sister. I haven't seen her since I was eight."*

"Dr. Silver?"

"I'm sorry. It was a long flight. Are you talking about John Walters?"

"Yes, exactly."

"To my knowledge... Jennifer?"

"Jenna."

"To my knowledge, Jenna, John Walters served two tours of duty in Vietnam as the skipper of a swift boat. He's also the recipient of two Purple Hearts. He's put a great deal of time, effort, and his own money into restoring the ship that we'd been working on. That's all I really know about him."

"If I can ask one more question, doctor..."

Cathy Murphy forced her five foot nothing frame between the reporters and Ray and was quick to cut off any more questions. "Dr. Silver is here in Washington on a very personal family matter. So I'm very sorry that he won't be able to answer any more of your questions at this time." With that, they made their way into the senator's limousine and headed for Arlington. "Sorry about that. Sometimes they're like sharks." Ray turned to catch one more glimpse of Jenna Grant as the car pulled away from the curb. He was stunned by how much she looked like Leigh Anne.

"Well, Senator, it's not as if you weren't laying out the bait."

"I had no idea they were going to be there. Honest. Someone from my office must have leaked my itinerary."

"Anyway, thanks for getting us out of there."

"I should've known they were going to hit you up with some pretty hard questions and I didn't know if you'd be prepared. You handled them quite well."

"We were very thoroughly debriefed, coached, and properly warned. Trust me...I'm not sayin' anything to anyone."

"Did you have a good flight?"

"Yes, I did. First class is a nice treat. Thanks."

"I must say you clean up pretty good. Suit, tie, wool overcoat. If not for the bruises, you almost look like a senator."

"It's amazing how you people keep avoiding the bruises."

"Well, we're lucky I guess. How's your back?"

"A lot better than it was. When I was home I stopped in to see *my* chiropractor. Makes a big difference, ya know."

"Yes, I do know. We have our own on the hill. I see him regularly. That's why I'm such a big advocate."

"That's funny."

"What? That I'm a big advocate?"

"No, that Capitol Hill has its own chiropractor, and yet except for me, the veterans don't have access and there still aren't any chiropractors as commissioned officers in the military. You guys give it to yourselves, but you won't give it to the people who defend our country."

"We're working on it. These things take time."

"So I'm told."

"I called McCain at the medical center and you're being reinstated."

"I heard when I was in Seattle and again from that reporter just now. If you can somehow make that work for Oahu, then I'll take it."

"Why would I want to do that?"

"Because that's where I'm gonna be."

"There's no position for you at the Oahu unit. Besides, chiropractic care in the veterans' medical system is *my* pet project. I got it started and that's where it's gonna stay for right now."

"Fair enough. I can recommend a few good people who could fill that role very nicely."

"No. It's you or nothing."

"A little over a month ago you endorsed my indefinite suspension, and now it's me or nothing? I must have some pretty big star power for you to insist on me. Are your poll numbers that low?"

"My poll numbers are just fine. Don't forget that I'm a liberal senator from a liberal state. We'd have to have a high unemployment rate and a major financial collapse before *I* get voted out of office. And yes, if you must know, you do have some star power right now. Don't tell me you don't know that you're a national hero?"

"And that surely helps you, doesn't it?"

"It helps me more in D.C. than it does back home. The way I see it, Ray, we both benefit."

He looked out across the Potomac at the Lincoln Memorial as the car turned off the George Washington Memorial Freeway into Arlington Cemetery. "Look it, I understand how me being considered a hero helps you. And I guess if I were in your position I would never turn down an opportunity to score political points, but I'm not a hero, I didn't ask to be a hero, and I do not want to use what happened out there in the Philippine Sea to help anyone's cause. Not even my own. Some very good people died out there in order to keep some terrorist wackos from detonating three nuclear devices. That shouldn't be trivialized." he looked at his watch. "We're early, can I ask the driver to take us somewhere?"

"Here in the Cemetery? Sure."

"Hey pal?" Ray called up to the driver. "Can you drive us over to President Kennedy?"

When the car pulled up in front of the Kennedy gravesite, Ray could tell they were the first ones there that morning from the lone tire tracks in the fresh-fallen snow. He came around to open the senator's door and helped her out. They walked up to the grave together.

"He's one of my heroes," said Cathy Murphy.

"Do you get up here much?"

"Sadly, I hardly ever get the time to come up here."

"My first and only trip here to Arlington, was in April of `64. I was six years old. Like most of the nation, my parents adored him. Little did anyone know how human he was. Perhaps that was because back in those days the press didn't have their own agenda like they do today." Ray squatted down and ran his hand over the textured stones. "None of this beautiful stone work had been done. This area was still basically dirt and sod, and it was cordoned off with a three-foot-high white picket fence. I couldn't figure out how the eternal flame stayed lit. My brother told me it was his spirit that kept it burning. I was old enough to know that the President had been murdered, but not old enough to understand why. In some ways I still don't understand why." He stood up and looked at the senator. "It's not because of all the conspiracy theories and nonsense like that. I just don't understand how and why people allow themselves to become so drunk and so corrupted by power and money that the wide-eyed optimism that makes them want to come to this town in the first place becomes distorted and perverted to the extent that they'll sell their souls to the highest bidder. And for what? Apparently, some people will go so far as to order someone's murder. I also don't understand how they could look themselves in the mirror at the end of the day."

"Do you think I like the game that's played in this town? I don't. But this has been going on in one way, shape, or form since the founding fathers. Just look at how Jefferson, when he was Vice-President, plotted to undermine President Adams every chance he got. Granted, the stuff that went on back then wasn't to the extent that it is today, but the basics haven't changed. I'm not justifying it, but understand this. There are things that I came here to do, and sadly, if I don't play that game then the people back home get the short end of the stick."

"So you *are* justifying it."

"But that's politics, and no matter how much people yell and scream, it's never going to change. They may vote for the next sweet-talking, innocent-faced, pie-in-the-sky dreamer who says he or she is going to clean up this place. They promise change. They provide a lot of hope with their polished teleprompter speeches, but once they get here, they get slapped around pretty hard. Reality sets in and then they fall in line. At the end of the day these people, myself included, can look in the mirror because inside this Beltway that's the morality that exists. Right or wrong, that's our norm."

"I guess when we're our own redeemer we can do whatever we want and find justification for it."

"Our own redeemer?"

"A friend of mine once told me that when it comes down to it, a man has to be able to look at himself in the mirror, and therefore it was in his eyes that he was his own redeemer. And that's the bottom line, isn't it?"

"We should go or we'll miss the procession. You should see it, it's really beautiful and your family would want you there." They began walking back to the limousine. "The fellow you punched out the day I was at the medical center to help open up your new office in the rehab wing..."

"Bill Harrison?"

"Yes, that's right. Harrison. He got fired because of negligence?"

"One of the head orthopedic nurses discovered he was on the Visor payroll, and was, for all intents and purposes, experimenting on the vets without their knowledge. From what I understand, the VMC did an investigation and came up with enough evidence to fire him. I heard there had been talk of a congressional sub-committee investigation, but I guess that went nowhere."

"So who is this person?" she asked, ignoring his comment.

"Now she's a hero. Served as an Army nurse during the first Gulf War. She was a Major, rode evac choppers into battle zones to recover wounded. She took a shrapnel hit herself while she was carrying a wounded soldier during a scud missile attack. She's a Bronze Star and Purple Heart recipient, and she's a head orthopedic nurse at the Seattle VMC. Her ex-husband's a Brigadier General with the NSA, and from what I understand they've recently gotten back together. There's your 'all-American' couple. Oh, and Senator, if you're looking for a new poster-child, Stella Leone will also turn you down flat."

"How can you be sure about that?"

"Because I know her and because she told me so."

"Well, it couldn't hurt to talk to her the next time I'm there."

5 4

Jimmy and Casey were waiting at the section marker for their dad to arrive. When he and the senator got out of her limousine, he took pause at the sight of his two children—United States Naval Officers in full dress blues—and was instantly filled with a pride that went beyond words.

"I wasn't sure you were going to make it," he said to his son as they shook hands and gave each other a quick hug.

"I didn't think I'd be able to come so soon after shipping out. But the Admiral, my boss at JAG, was well aware of Grandpa and then after what you did...Well, here I am."

"Good, I'm glad you could come. Your grandfather would have appreciated it...having us all together like this." He then turned to his daughter.

"Daddy, uh...I mean, Dad."

"Come here and give me a hug, Lieutenant." They laughed, hugged, and gave each other a kiss on the cheek.

"Dad?" Jimmy stretched out his arm to bring a young lady into view. "Dad, I want you to meet Caroline."

"So, a face to go with the voice." Ray said, to her quizzical look. "We spoke once, a few months back. I woke you up."

"It's nice to finally meet you, sir," she said, blushing.

Ray turned to Senator Murphy. "Senator, my apologies. I'd like to introduce you to my children. Lieutenants James Silver

and Casey Silver, and Caroline, this is Senator Cathy Murphy."
There was a chorus of "pleased to meet you" and handshakes
along with a further exchange of pleasantries.

"All I can say Dr. Silver, uh, Ray, is that I am truly honored
and impressed. Naval service really has been a tradition in your
family. I'll bet you're extremely proud of your children as you
two are equally as proud of your father."

"Thank you, Senator," said Ray. "You're kind to say so, and
yes, I am very proud of my children."

"We're just as proud of you, Dad," Casey said. "I only wish
Mom could be here."

Ray looked at his daughter. "So do I, Casey. I miss her too.
Ok, that's enough of all this sugary stuff." He turned toward
the sound of snow softly crunching under the tires of the
approaching hearse.

* * *

Twelve white-gloved hands held the American flag taut
above Ron Silver's casket as the Jewish Chaplin conducted the
service. Ray, Jimmy, Casey, and Caroline sat a few feet behind
three of the petty officer pallbearers holding one side of the
flag. Also attending were Senators Murphy and Claremont,
Congressman Reichman from the Washington 8ᵗʰ district and
the Assistant Secretary of the Navy.

The Chaplin opened his copy of the Navy Manual of
Committal Service and began to recite: "I will lift up mine eyes
unto the mountains from whence shall my help come? My help
cometh from the lord, who made heaven and earth. He will
not suffer thy foot to be moved; He that keepth Israel…" As he
spoke, Ray drifted back to earlier days, remembering several
events like snapshots in time.

"Do I look ok?"
"You're fine, Jo. Stop fussing."
"I'm not wearing too much perfume?"
"Jo, you smell fine, you look fine. Stop worrying."
"What about this outfit?"

"Jo, sweetheart, you look great."
"Why aren't they coming to the door?"
"I didn't ring the bell yet. Jo, you'll be fine. They're gonna like you."
"Ya think so? Did you tell them we're engaged?"
"We're telling them today, remember?"
"I'm so nervous."
"What's to be nervous about?"
"I'm Catholic, for one thing."
"Oh, yeah. Hmm... that may be a problem."
"Really? Do you think so?"
"Well, my mom's never had a heart attack before. Plenty of heartbreak, but no heart attack."

"O Lord, help us to find in these ancient yet ever new sentiments, the realization that through our tears we can reach the truth, through the darkness of our sorrow venture toward the light of hope..."

"What's that a picture of, Pop?"
"That's the ship that I was on, Raymond."
"She's kinda small, ain't she?"
"Isn't."
"Isn't what?"
"Don't say 'ain't,' it's not proper English."
"She's kinda small, isn't she?"
"Well, compared to the Arizona she's small, if ya know what I mean. But she was pretty somethin' for her size."

"O God, full of compassion, thou dwellest on high! Beneath the sheltering wings of Thy presence, among the holy and pure who shine as the brightness of the firmament, grant perfect peace unto the soul of Ronald Silver, who has gone unto eternity..."

"Oh man, Frankie. Mom is pissed at you."
"Don't worry about it, Ray. She'll calm down in a few days."
"Wait` til Pop finds out ya went and signed up. He didn't want ya to be an enlisted man."
"What I'm gonna do is better than officer stuff. Francis Albert Silver is takin' the family tradition to the next level. After boot camp, I'm signin' up for SEAL training."

"Whoa, Frankie. That's pretty intense!"

"Fuckin' right!"

"FRANK SILVER! DID I JUST HEAR YOU SWEAR?"

"NO, MA, I WASN'T CURSIN'. Ray, when I go off to boot camp I'm puttin' you in charge of all my stuff."

"Ya mean I get to use it all?"

"No. I'm puttin' you in charge of takin' care of it."

"All of it?"

"All of it!"

"Even your posters?"

"Especially this one here of the Rat Pack."

"The Lord bless thee and keep thee, the Lord make His face shine upon thee and be gracious unto thee, the Lord lift up the light of His countenance upon thee, and give thee peace. Amen."

Twelve white gloves, six pairs of hands snapped the flag taut and methodically began the first of several folds. White-gloved hands slowly reinforced each fold as it was made. Then came the first of thirteen triangular folds as the seven-man rifle squad fired a three- round volley—the crack of the first volley causing Ray to flinch. The bugler sounded Taps, and Jimmy had to nudge his father out of his deep thought to see that the officer in charge had knelt before him with the folded American flag.

"Chief, on behalf of the President of the United States and the Chief of Naval Operations, please accept this flag as a symbol of our appreciation for your loved one's service to this Country and a grateful Navy." He then passed the flag over to Ray and returned to his position by the pallbearers. With precision cadence, they turned and marched off. Ray turned to his kids and mouthed, "Chief?" They both shrugged and when he looked away, they winked at each other.

Ray thanked both senators and the congressman for attending and had begun to walk over to his father's casket when Jimmy took him by the arm. "Dad, there's somebody here I want you to meet."

The gentleman who had been seated in the second row of chairs with Murphy, Claremont, and Reichman was the Assistant Secretary of the Navy. "Dr. Silver, I'm very honored to make your acquaintance," he said as he extended his hand, which Ray shook without hesitation. "Lieutenants Silver, would you excuse us for a moment so I can have a word with your father?"

"Yes sir," they responded, watching the two men walk but a few steps away.

"I'm sorry to have to meet you under these circumstances. I wanted to give you this," he said as he took a small decorations box from his overcoat pocket. "The Secretary wanted me to convey his deepest sympathy for your loss and his regret that your father had been denied proper recognition for his actions while in the service of his country. We both hope that you will accept this long overdue honor."

Ray opened it. It was his father's Bronze Star. "Obviously I can't speak for my father, but if he were here I know he'd be humbled and he would tell you that he was just doing what needed to be done. However, I am only too happy to accept this on his behalf. Thank you."

"I also wanted to give you this. Do you recognize it?"

Ray took the letter from his hand and quickly glanced at it. "This is a copy of the denial letter that I got in `75 when I appealed the Navy's decision to reject my enlistment."

"You were rejected because of a slight defect in your spinal column. At the time, the Navy felt that any kind of physically demanding activity would incapacitate you, and as such, put other sailors at risk. Based on the actions you demonstrated this past week on that LCI, the Secretary feels that the Navy did you an injustice." He waved to the others to come back and join them, and Casey handed him a large leather bound folder.

"What's going on?" Ray looked at the others.

"What's going on is that the Secretary of the Navy has issued the following." He opened the folder and presented it to Ray. "The Secretary has seen fit to make you an honorary

Chief Petty Officer with all the rights and privileges afforded to this title. Congratulations, Chief. Welcome to the Navy."

"Thank you. I...I don't know what to say."

"You don't have to say anything, Chief. The operation you participated in has done all the talking for you. Now, if you'll excuse me, I'll let you get back to your family."

They shook hands and Ray turned to his kids. "Congratulations, Dad," said Casey.

"Yeah, congratulations," echoed Jimmy and Caroline.

"I just have one question. What *are* the rights and privileges that come with this?"

"With that I D card that's there in the folder, you can have access to any base PX." Jimmy took the card and handed it to his dad.

"That's it?"

"Yeah, but that's any U.S. Naval base around the world," added Casey.

"Well, ok then. Sounds like a good deal. But do me a favor and don't start calling me Chief...Hey listen, why don't you guys go wait for me in the car? I'd like to have a few moments alone with my dad."

"Sure, Dad." Casey smiled.

"And Caroline? During lunch, let's talk. There's a few things I wanna tell you about my son."

"Thanks, Pop." Jimmy shook his head.

"Don't mention it, kiddo."

Ray walked over to the coffin, placing his triangle-folded flag and the other items on one of chairs at the gravesite. He looked at the coffin and then down the hill that overlooked the Potomac. He closed his eyes.

"You're feeling like shit, huh?"

"Yeah, Raymond. I'm not doing too good."

"You'll be ok. It's gonna take you a long time to heal. Just do what the doctors and the nurses tell you and you'll get better."

"I don't need to look at a chart to know that what I'm feelin' isn't normal."

"You always were a smart man, Pop."

"So how bad is it?"

"I think you already know."

"How are the kids?"

"They're fine, Pop. They were home for Thanksgiving. They looked great."

"How 'bout that girlfriend of yours?"

"You know about her?"

"Your daughter told me all about her. She's that cute redhead who ran into you that time at that sports bar you go to. If it wasn't for Casey, I'd never know anything about you, if ya know what I mean."

"Yeah, I know what you mean. Leigh's just fine, Pop. She really is. I'm in love with her, Pop. I'm thinking about asking her to marry me."

Ray looked over at one of the attendants and asked if he would mind opening the casket for a brief moment. The attendant obliged him then walked off to allow Ray a private moment.

"So it looks like I'm gonna be a dad again. Can ya believe it? I didn't think I'd wanna go through this again, but I'm really excited about it. God, wait 'til I tell the kids. They're gonna think I've lost my mind for sure. Did ya get a look at Jimmy's girl? He's got that Silver charm, doesn't he? Hey, I'm a Chief. Just like that. Honorary, of course. All I had to do was steal three nuclear bombs and shoot some terrorists. That was still probably easier than basic training. Well, anyway, say hi to Mom and Jo. Oh, and uh… thanks for coming to get Abner."

Ray stepped back over to the chairs, picked up the case with his father's Bronze Star, and placed it into the coffin by his dad's left hand. Then he dug into the pocket of his overcoat and pulled out a small brown paper bag. He opened it up, removed a yellowed moth-eaten ball of socks with a hand-stitched palm tree on it and placed them into his dad's right hand. With a nod to the attendant, Ray made his way back to the car.

5 5

It wasn't until he got to the gate at Reagan National that Ray realized he was running on fumes. Given everything he'd been through, he was amazed that he hadn't already collapsed. He hoped he would be out like a light once he got onboard and settled into his first class seat. But he knew better. The events of the past year—especially over the last four weeks—would replay in his head the entire way back to Seattle. His cell phone rang, and he laughed when he saw Leigh's name on the caller ID.

"Hey there."

"Oh my God, Ray, is that really you and not your voicemail?"

"Amazing, isn't it? How ya feelin?"

"Everything's good. No, everything's great."

"The babies?"

"The babies are doing great in there. I'm gonna have to buy some stretch pants pretty soon." She laughed. "How you holding up?"

"I'm beginning to feel like a zombie."

"Poor baby. Come home and let me take care of you."

"Now that's the motivation I need," he said with a smile.

"How'd everything go?"

"Good. It was really nice. I wish you could've seen it. The kids say hi. Say, how's the job?"

"The job is great, Ray. I'm lovin' it! Annnnd, I found us a great little house in Kailua. Ray, it's a half mile away from Kimo's, just a block off of Kawailoa Road on Kaneapu."

"I'm not familiar with the streets over there," he said with a slight laugh.

"Not to worry. I'll show it to you when you get here. It's up on a little hill and it overlooks Kailua Beach Park. It's small, about sixteen-hundred square feet. It's really nice, Ray. I want to put an offer on it."

"It sounds nice. Expensive?"

"Ray, it's near the beach in Kailua."

"It's expensive. What about commute time to the University?"

"Easy. Kailua road leads right into the Pali highway. Fourteen miles door to door. And there's one more thing you might be interested in. There's an old stand-alone medical office between Kailua and Kaneohe. It's been vacant for a couple of years now. Just in case you're thinking about going back into private practice."

"Let's take a look at that too."

"Listen, I gotta get going. My next class starts in ten and I don't have a TA yet. See ya for lunch at Kimo's in two days?"

"See ya in two. Love ya."

Sitting there waiting for his flight to be called, he got the feeling he was being watched. He was. Ray looked up, glanced around the terminal, and noticed that people were looking at him. Some smiled and nodded when they made eye contact while others pointed him out to their traveling companions. He politely smiled back, but felt uncomfortable. There was a short queue at the coffee concession so he headed over for a cup to distract himself.

Even while waiting his turn he heard the whispers. "That's the guy, I'm tellin' you that's him. Look. No, don't look. Not while he's facing this way."

"Nah, that's not him."

"Sure it is. I recognize him from the news."

Ray wondered how long this would continue. He wondered if Steve, Tex and Chuck were dealing with the same thing back home. The smell of the coffee triggered a memory of Abner swiveling his hips to Glenn Miller while working in the galley of the 776. He also thought about him as he laid dying in his arms.

"*This ain't no good, Doc…this ain't…no good at all.*"

"*Shhh, don't talk. Save your strength.*"

"*Doc, you been watchin'…too many a them submarine movies.*"

"*Yeah, ok. Just the same, I know you're hurt real bad…but…I can tell you're gonna be alright.*"

"*Hey, cut that shit out. Ya…don't gotta worry. Ah'm free now, Doc. Ya shoulda seen me. Ah was really sumptin out here tonight. Ah…Ah did…what ah had ta do…mah mind…mah conscious…is free. Ah'm at peace wit' that, Ray. You uner…stand?*"

"*Yeah, Abner. I understand.*"

"*Ya do? `Cause… ya earned…ya earned it too. Ya know that, right?*"

He didn't hear the cashier when she called out, "next!" He didn't hear her the second time either.

"Can I HELP you?" she shouted a third time.

"What?" He saw he was holding up the line. "Just a regular cup of joe…uhh, I mean coffee. A tall please."

"Room for cream?"

"Can ya give me a shot of soy in that?"

"Sure thing," she said, and called out, "next!"

"You forgot to charge me."

"Oh that's ok, it's already taken care of."

"No, that's alright. I don't mind payin' for my coffee."

"That man over there took care of it." She handed him his cup. Ray turned around and recognized the professionally dressed man who had been standing a few people ahead of him in the line. "Thank you. That was very kind of you."

"Not at all. It's the least I could do, Dr. Silver."

With all the attention he'd been receiving, Ray wasn't startled that he knew his name. "Of course he would know my name" he thought. "why else would he buy me a cup of coffee?"

"You don't know me. We've never met." He extended his hand. "I'm Griffin Kelley."

Ray's eyes lit up. "Oh sure, General Kelley! It's a pleasure to finally meet you."

"The pleasure's all mine, Ray."

"Where're you off to?"

"Same place as you. Seattle."

"Business or pleasure?"

"Both, actually."

"Can I assume you'll be staying at my house with Stella?"

"As long as you have no objection."

"Hell no, of course not. If you don't mind me saying so, I think it's great you and Stella are getting back together...I'm not jumping the gun here, am I?"

"Not really. We're in the early stages on that. We're taking it one step at a time. And what about you? What's in your future?"

"Marriage, kids, small house near the beach."

"Ha, now that's funny," Kelley said as he looked at Ray and saw he was serious. "You're not joking, are you?"

"Nope. Gonna spend a day in Seattle wrapping up some things. Have to make sure Stella's got everything under control with the house. And by the way, she can stay there as long as she wants. You too, but that's up to her, of course. Having her stay there will save me the hassle of renting it out to a stranger."

"And then? Where ya off to?"

"Oahu. Hey, it looks like we're starting to board."

5 6

According to almost every resource on weather for Puget Sound, the rainy season runs between October and May—with February falling pretty much in the middle. Snow is a rare occurrence in the lower elevations, and the fifty-degree average temperatures sure beat the icy chill of the Northeast where Ray grew up. Still, he had long grown tired of the gray skies. It didn't faze him one way or the other that his last day there was overcast and raining. In his mind, it was what it was.

He had spent most of the day packing up personal belongings from his house and bringing them to the local parcel delivery service for shipping. Before it got dark, he drove over to the cemetery to pay his respects to Jo.

"Hey. Just wanted to stop by. You probably don't get too many visitors these days, but I guess that's not important as long as we carry you around in our hearts. I carry you around in mine. No kidding, I do. We had a lot of great times. Especially those early times, when Jimmy was born and we were still in school. Oh, sure, it didn't seem like fun then. It was pretty hard. But that's what made it special. That's what made you special. You had more patience and perseverance than anyone I had ever met. I'm sorry if I didn't tell you that as often as I should have. Listen to me, I sound like an Elvis Presley song.

I drove by the old house before coming up here. I hadn't been by there since your funeral. I just wanted to get one last look. It's gone. The new owners bulldozed it and now it's just an empty lot. My garden too. All gone. Can ya believe it? I guess that's typical of the Heights. People buy properties and just knock down the houses and put up new ones. I was shocked. Wait `til the kids find out. Casey will be sad. She loved that place. Do ya remember how she used to sit in the garden eating snap peas right off the vine? Or how about when Jimmy climbed up into the plum tree and got stuck on a branch? He was up there for forty-five minutes before anyone realized. I sat out there today for a half-hour thinking about all those Thanksgiving dinners and the times the four of us made calzones and stuff. Since we're talking about that, I thought you should know that I was the one who put too much concentrated soap in the dishwasher and caused the flood that warped the floor. Sorry. Speaking of the kids, you should have seen them, Jo. They're beautiful. Thank God they got your genes. They're so grown up now. Where did all those years go? Oh and ah, Jimmy's got a girl. They met during his last year at Georgetown. Her name's Caroline and she's a cutie. She seems nice, from what little time we were all together. But first impressions are usually correct, right? I think she'll be good for him. I can see it in both their eyes. Kinda like the way we were once upon a time. Sooo, I guess this is it, for a little while at least. I mean as far as visits go. I'll be back in a few months so I can have my Jeep shipped over. So I'll stop back. Ya know I will. In spite of your disappointment in me and the way we ended, I never stopped thinking about you...and you know I never will."

Final stop before he and Magic headed to the airport was Kelsey's. One more bowl of her homemade chili and cornbread along with an ice cold Pipeline was the perfect way to wrap things up. When he walked into the tavern, he went straight for his old stool at the bar. He couldn't help but to look over at what had been Leigh Anne's stool, imagining her sitting there laughing it up with Kelsey and her other friends.

"Thinking about your girl?" Kelsey said as she came out of the kitchen and saw Ray. She didn't even ask what he was drinking. She opened up a bottle of his usual beer and placed it on the bar. They looked at each other for a moment before she came around to his side. They hugged.

"I'm gonna miss you and I'm gonna miss this place," he said.

"You're gonna miss my food. Well, some of it anyway."

"Yeah, that too. So when are ya gonna come and visit?"

"As soon as you two set a date for the wedding."

"I still have to ask her, ya know. She just might turn me down."

"When pigs fly."

"Good ta know."

"I'm countin' on you to take care of that girl as well as those babies."

"Not to worry, Kelse."

"So what's it gonna be, sprouts on whole wheat?" She laughed at him.

"I have a better chance of winning the lottery then I do of finding sprouts in your kitchen. I'll just have the usual."

"Big bowl of chili, no cheese, extra onions and cornbread. Coming up."

Ray sat at the bar and took a good look around. He thought that if he concentrated real hard at the many pictures of Seattle sports legends lining the brick walls that he would be able to remember the sights, smells, and sounds of this place by merely closing his eyes. His beer was cold and it tasted good. It tasted even better when Kelsey returned with his dinner. As he ate, he heard Abner's voice.

"*Ya know ah makes a really good cornbread. Ah bet that one ya got is good but nuthin' beats the way us Southern boys makes it.*" Ray was startled. He didn't remember ever having that conversation with Abner. He looked over at the stool next to him. An elderly African-American man was sitting there. He hadn't noticed him before. "Excuse me sir, did you just say something? Were you talking to me?"

"I just said that your chili and cornbread looks really good. I was going to order one of the house burgers. I had heard that the burgers here were excellent, but now I think I'm going to order what you're having."

"Oh, I'm sorry. I'm a little tired and I misheard you at first."

"Not a problem, young man. Not a problem. You look familiar to me, do I know you?"

"No sir, I don't think so. Unless you've been to the Veterans Medical Center for any kind of care. You might have seen me there."

"Maybe that's it."

He finished his dinner, thanked the elderly gentleman for the forty-five minute conversation they had ended up having, and he and Kelsey said their tearful goodbyes. Ray stopped at the door and took one last long look around.

5 7

There were beautiful half-naked women running around all over the island of Oahu, but there was something about this one woman—sitting alone at the bar—that grabbed ahold of Ray and wouldn't let go. Perhaps it was the way her auburn hair lay across her shoulders, or how the bronze of her tan complimented her brown eyes and freckled nose and arms. It could have been the smell of passionflower as gentle warm breezes danced across the palm-thatched overhang of the open air dining room. Maybe it was the way a pregnant woman in her second trimester looked in a white linen dress. Perhaps it was the whole package. But it kept him stealing glances at her from his table at Kimo's in Lanikai.

The serenity of the moment was in stark contrast to the year that had passed since the last time he sat at this very same table. And yet here he was, back where it pretty much all began, looking at the same woman who had been at the starting line of one hell of a roller coaster ride. Since his constant staring didn't escape her, he figured, "what the heck?"

He got up and made his way over to strike up a conversation. "Excuse me," he said. "I'm Ray. Ray Silver from Seattle. I couldn't help but notice that you were sitting here all by yourself and I just was wondering if I could pull up a stool and join you."

443

"Gee, I don't know Ray Silver from…Seattle, did you say? I guess that all depends on what you had in mind." She smiled and took a sip of her ice water.

Ray stepped closer, gently rested his hand on her abdomen and whispered, "Well, I was thinking…marriage, perhaps at a small chapel over on Molokai, and maybe a small house with two kids and a cat just a few blocks from the beach in Kailua."

"I think that can be arranged."

"Really?"

"Sure. There are quite a number of local girls that I could introduce you to," Leigh Anne said.

"Hmm, I don't know. That could be a problem."

"How so?"

"Well, if you must know, there's only one local girl that this hoale is interested in."

"Really?"

"Really!"

"That's good to know Ray Silver from Seattle."

He leaned in to give Leigh Anne the deepest, wettest and longest kiss that anyone at Kimo's had ever witnessed.

* * *

If Ray had thought he was going to get any rest once he got to Oahu, he was sadly mistaken. During his first few days, Leigh Anne had him look at the house she had found on Kaneapu Place, the vacant medical office building that had once belonged to Dr. Tom Jackson, he had to get Magic out of quarantine, and he reluctantly took a phone call from Hawaii Senator Tommy Anoki. Once the senator learned from Cathy Murphy that Ray was moving to the islands, he had been anxious to have the now-famous chiropractor join the staff at the Honolulu VMC.

"Thank you, Senator. Your offer to help in this regard is very generous, but I think that after a short rest I just might go back into private practice."

"Things here will be a great deal different from Seattle. You'll really like working at this facility. The people here have a more laid-back and open-minded attitude toward other health-care disciplines."

"That's good to hear, Senator. But still, it's the VMC, which means layers of bureaucracy."

"Your exploits are well known, and you should realize that's going to work in your favor. And as long as you don't knock out any of the orthopedists, you can pretty much write your own ticket. Trust me," he said to a now experienced—and former—government employee.

To Ray, hearing the words "trust me" from a politician would always ring hollow. "You're very kind, sir, but I've gotta tell you I haven't had much time to myself in the past few weeks..."

"Then please, don't say no just yet. Take a few weeks, and when you're rested, I'd like to take you on a tour of the medical center and have you meet the staff, and then? Who knows?"

"Ok, fine. We'll talk in a few weeks. But please, don't be disappointed if I turn you down."

"Maybe you will, but I'm hoping you won't. I've already talked to the head administrator over there and she's enthusiastic at the possibility of you coming onboard."

"Again, Senator, you're very kind. I appreciate the telephone call and I appreciate your interest. We'll talk more in a few weeks."

* * *

The small building that was once the home of Dr. Jackson's family practice had been shut for several years. The neglect was obvious. It was a place Leigh Anne thought she would never return to.

"Well, whaddya think, Ray? Isn't this a great little place?" Leigh Anne tried not to smile too much. But the way her lips became pencil-thin as the corners of her mouth began to move up into her cheeks with her eyes growing wide easily revealed her excitement.

"It's actually not that bad, although I wouldn't call it a little place. It's a little big, which is not a problem. I've always considered having a multi-disciplinary office. There's room here for an acupuncturist, a naturopath, a massage therapist, and perhaps even a midwife."

"There's a great view of the ocean from that back room." She grabbed his hand and led him toward the back. "See, isn't this nice? This room could be your private office."

"Well, we'd definitely have to build a lanai off of that room so I could sit back here and chill during the lunch hour."

"A must have for sure" she said sensing his growing interest.

"The reception area needs a little work, though."

"Come." She led him back to the front. "I was thinking we could knock out the wall over there to open it up more. That far wall over there would look great with one of those big salt-water fish tanks and…"

"Hey, slow down. Sounds like you've been thinking about this for awhile."

"Years ago I was a patient here. So was Mahina," she said as she looked around the empty space and reflected upon her past experience. "There were many times I sat in this waiting room just thinking about how much nicer it would look with certain changes. Like over here in the front, if we put in big picture windows, like the ones you have in the living room of your Seattle house. Then just outside, we plant some bamboo and a couple of those big banana leaf plants?"

"Yeah, I can see it. It'll have a nice calming effect and there will still be plenty of natural light filtering in."

"So, you like this place?"

"Yeah, I do. I really do, Leigh." Ray got quite as he looked around.

"What?"

"Just thinking. I'll definitely need to put the Magnolia house on the market. But not a problem. I'll bet I already have a buyer."

* * *

The temporary living arrangements that Leigh Anne had been provided by the university were adequate for their current needs. Located on a quiet shady street, the house was close enough to the campus and local markets that one could forgo the use of a car. It was an older house, but had a simplicity to it that both appreciated. Except for their laptops and cell phones to remind one of a modern day existence, the wicker furniture, ceiling fans, and museum-quality kitchen appliances harkened back to a generation long forgotten by time.

"Ya know, if we do buy that house in Kailua, I wouldn't mind if we could somehow tweak some things inside to make it kinda like this place," Ray said as he lay in bed enjoying the wisteria scent drifting through the window on the evening breeze.

"I kinda like it too. I'm sure there are some simple things we could do to give it that same feel." Leigh Anne finished in the bathroom and shut off the light. She slipped into bed next to him and he gently cradled her belly as they spooned. He buried his face into her neck and softly kissed her. She closed her eyes and smiled. "Damn boy" she said without turning, "doesn't that thing ever get tired?"

As Leigh Anne slept, Ray lay wide awake. His mind once again restless with unanswered questions—bits and pieces of conversations replaying in his head.

"So, you know all about me and my family?"

"Yeah. In fact, you remind me a little of your brother."

"You knew my brother Frank?"

"We worked together on two occasions, but that was years ago."

"You mean before his accident in the Mediterranean in `83?"

"Actually, last time I worked with him was when his chopper went down here in the Philippines in `81, but nice try."

"So Jeffries knew Frank," Ray whispered to himself. "The guy they met outside of Felipe's, he kinda looked like Frank."

"...Jeffries and Walters are going into town to meet up with two guys in some dive bar...Philip's I think it's called."

"No, not Philip's. I heard Jeffries say Felipe's. I heard him mention it several times during the trip."

"Ok, they're meeting at a place called Felipe's. They're going to meet up with two guys...Francis and Enrique."

Ray's mind continued to race. "Frank's legal name is Francis. Francis Albert Silver. Both Mom and Pop loved Sinatra. They named him..."

"What's that babe?" Leigh Anne stirred.

"Nothing, sweetie. I didn't mean to wake you. Go back to sleep."

"Oh man, Frankie. Mom is pissed at you."

"Don't worry about it, Ray. She'll calm down in a few days."

"Wait`til pop finds out ya went and signed up. He didn't want ya to be an enlisted man."

"What I'm gonna do is better than officer stuff. Francis Albert Silver is takin' the family tradition to the next level. After boot camp, I'm signin' up for SEAL training."

"Whoa, Frankie. That's pretty intense!"

"Fuckin' right!"

"FRANK SILVER! DID I JUST HEAR YOU SWEAR?"

"NO, MA, I WASN'T CURSIN'. Ray, when I go off to boot camp I'm puttin' you in charge of all my stuff."

"Ya mean I get to use it all?"

"No. I'm puttin' you in charge of takin' care of it."

"All of it?"

"All of it!"

"Even your posters?"

"Especially this one here of the Rat Pack."

"Oh man," Ray said. "How could I have been so dense? Sometimes I'm so freakin' slow!" He slowly and quietly got out of bed, threw on a pair of pants, and tiptoed into the small dinning room. He turned on his laptop, his hands resting on the keyboard waiting for the system to boot. When it did, he typed into the browser **United States Navy Seal Team Eleven.**

ABOUT THE AUTHOR

Richard Levine is a native New Yorker who was born and raised in the shadows of Yankee Stadium. "Even after we legally crossed the border to settle in Westchester County, I fondly remembered and longed for the days of watching Maris and Mantle from the bleacher seats or playing street games such as Stickball and Johnny on the Pony as mom called out from our fourth floor apartment window to come home for dinner." After working in the auto parts business several years and a one year wanderlust trip that took him coast to coast and back again, this one time volunteer fireman, auxiliary police officer and bartender returned to school and eventually became a chiropractor. "I have been married to the same wonderful woman since 1987, I am blessed with two fantastic children who embody all the great qualities that I envy and somehow escaped me, and we have lived and I have been in practice in the beautiful Pacific Northwest for the last twenty years. That, save for the New York Yankees, has everything a person could ever want."